JOHN LAW
Money to Burn

OTHER BOOKS by Pat Silver-Lasky

2020 MALICE IN BLUNERLAND, Ouroborus Books
2019 UNDER THE MAGIC MOUNTAIN, Ouroborus Books
2017 HOLLYWOOD ROYALTY: A FAMILY IN FILMS,
    BearManor Media
2014 THE OFFER (updated), paperback/Ebook
2012 SCAMS SCHEMES SCUMBAGS (with Peter Betts),
    Ouroborus Books
2010 RIDE THE TIGER, paperback & Ebook
2005 SCREENWRITING FOR THE 21ST CENTURY,
    (Batsford, UK) 2006 (Republished by Ritchie Books, UK)

With Jesse L. Lasky Jr.
1981-1982 THE OFFER, Berkley-Jove, Doubleday
1980 LOVE SCENE, Sphere Books UK
1978 LOVE SCENE T.Y., Crowell/Angus & Robertson UK
1977 MEN OF MYSTERY Allen/Star U.K.
1977 DARK DIMENSIONS Everest House USA

For film and TV credits, see:
www.Pat Silver-Lasky.net, IMDB.com, Wikipedia

JOHN LAW
Money to Burn
A biographical novel

Pat Silver-Lasky

THESPRING

Washington, DC

Printed in the United States of America
Library of Congress Control Number: 2021951877
ISBN 978-1-9558350-0-8 (alk. paper)

THESPRING is an imprint of New Academia Publishing

New Academia Publishing
4401-A Connecticut Ave. NW #236, Washington DC 20008
info@newacademia.com - www.newacademia.com

CONTENTS

ILLUSTRATIONS

JOHN LAW

Attributed to Alexis Simon Belle,
circa 1715-1720
National Portrait Gallery, London

 PROLOGUE

This is the story of John Law, a pied piper who led rich and poor alike across the barriers of reason and plunged them into disaster. Was he a genius, wizard or charlatan? Was France victimized by a gigantic fraud perpetrated by a scheming Scotsman?

Sex, Money, and Power are the most powerful forces that drive mankind, and John Law was hell bent on having them all. This handsome Scottish adventurer stepped onto the stage of Europe at the dawn of the 18th century to alter forever the shape of international commerce. Born in Edinburgh in 1671, capable of hypnotizing women, monarchs, and whole populations, he escaped the hangman's noose in England to travel the capitals of Europe, received by kings and sovereigns.

Daredevil and genius, rake and economist, mathematical wizard, gambler par excellence, womanizer—and most of all: original thinker, the paper money in your pocket, stock market reports, banking credit, stocks, shares and investment systems are all the legacy of this charismatic adventurer.

John Law was a real person. His exciting story is proof that truth is stranger than fiction. He himself said of his spectacular life and fantastic achievements, *'I changed the world more than Columbus's discovery of the Americas.'*

ONE: LONDONTOWN—
AND KATHERINE

'There it is, Johnnie! Just waiting for you.'

John Law climbed out of the coach and strode to Highgate Hill's verge to gaze down at the vista below. In the slanting orange light of a sparkling autumn afternoon, the town of London lay spread out below him, a tapestry of distant rooftops and spires. The sky was clear, and the long four o'clock shadows dramatized the picture like the Italian paintings Law had marveled at in Rome.

His excitement was shared by his cousin Archibald Campbell, Earl of Argyll. The older man clambered out of the couch after him, shaking his legs to restore circulation and calling over to his coachman, 'Let the horses rest, Andrews.'

'Aye, Your Grace.' The coachman led the horses steaming from the long journey to graze on the plentiful grass. He ran his tongue between his lips, pulled a water bottle from his satchel, and drank. He could have used a tankard of ale. The journey had taken four and a half spine-crunching days from Edinburgh. Today, they had made nearly one hundred miles since early light. He glanced across at his master and Mr. Law. At twenty-six, the younger man cut an uncommonly tall figure. Unquestionably a man of striking appearance, with dark, intelligent eyes. Certainly, the gifts of nature had been plentifully heaped upon this young Scotsman.

John Law stood silent, taking in the scene, holding back the excitement about to burst inside him. His glance traveled the expanse from the east, across the city's heart to the green fields rippling down to the river in the west. Although it was not his first visit to London, it was always a breath-taking moment to behold the largest city in the world, threading its way along both banks of the River Thames. Small craft and barges loaded with supplies journeyed up and down the waterway. Law could distinguish bales and barrels being unloaded onto docks in the east—and in the tangle of streets running south to north, he could make out carriages worming their path along the roadways.

'Would you believe it is only thirty years since the Great Fire burned down nearly the whole of the city?' Archie Campbell observed with a touch of amazement.

'It helped to quell the plague,' his cousin replied dryly. ‹How angry God must have been with the English.›

Archie chortled, then pointed to a domed church still framed in scaffolding, looming above the city's center. 'See over there, Johnnie. That is where the old St. Paul's once stood. Completely gutted, it was, and rebuilt by Sir Christopher Wren.' Archie hunched his shoulders with the air of one imparting confidential information. 'Wren told me that he copied that dome from the Pantheon in Rome. But I'd say, Sir Christopher has bettered the Italians with that lofty spire.'

Law was not looking at the spire. His gaze had fallen on his illustrious cousin. In outward appearance Archibald Campbell, having reached his forties, was a good-natured, modest fellow. But Law knew his reputation was quite different. In the past, the Earl had been able to acquire great sums of money, but all of it had been squandered upon personal pleasures. He'd also heard reports that Archie was capable of dubious tactics to promote his business schemes in Edenborough.

'We shall make London take notice, eh, Johnnie!› Archie exclaimed, clapping his cousin on the back. 'This trip can reverse the fortunes of us both. I shall open doors for you, my boy! Yes, and I do not mind saying that I shall follow you through them.'

Law smiled. 'Then which of us would be using the other, I wonder?'

Archie gave him a sharp look, then burst into laughter. 'Well said, John Law! Who, indeed?'

ARCHIBALD, THIRD DUKE OF ARGYLL

'Do not belittle your own talents, Archie,' Law advised. 'When you set yourself to it, no man is more capable. I've heard you address the Scottish Parliament, and you could indeed be a great statesman.'

But Archie had heard praise from Law before and was well aware of his own shortcomings. He turned his attention to the horizon once more. 'Over there, John. You can just see St. Michael's, Cornhill. And over there!' Archie pointed further to the right. 'That is St. Bride's, Fleet Street. And that, St. Mary-le-Bow, Cheapside with its graceful spire and the most tuneful set of bells in London. All of them, Sir Christopher's churches. That is a great man for you, even though he's English!'

'Churches enough for some six hundred thousand people who call this center of commerce home,' Law replied, gazing across the rhythm of roofs, excitement welling up in him now that the city lay literally at his feet. He frowned. 'Truly, there is nothing of such magnificence in Scotland.'

'London is a place to visit, but not to live,' Archie said firmly. 'A man might easily get lost in such a city.'

'Or find himself,' Law mused softly, wondering where this visit might lead.

Archie sighed, 'Of course, your business here has nothing to do with churches or architecture, does it?' He turned from the view and stepped back to his coach. Archie's coachman held the door for the men, then came around and mounted the driver's bench.

The Duke had his old vehicle newly painted for this important journey. Bright gilding highlighted his coat of arms embellishing the doors. Blazonry marked the lines of division and heraldic animals of one of the oldest clans in Scotland. In former days, his ancestors would have had the coat of arms embroidered on their surcoats worn over chain mail.

'Well, cousin?› Archie asked, settling back into the seat, ‹The financial heart of this entire kingdom is about to open its doors to us when they hear what you have to say. A Scotsman the English will look up to. Are you ready?'

'I shall be a match for them, I assure you. And I know exactly where we must establish ourselves, Archie. Where one meets all the right people these days,' Law told his cousin as the coach started its descent into the city.

As Archie had predicted, people looked up to and *at* John Law almost every night from his position at a roulette table. It had not taken Law long to discover the most fashionable gaming houses and most luxurious rooms frequented by the aristocracy, high rollers, and lowlifes. Archie›s title and Law's remarkable looks, charm, and gaming skills had admitted them into the finest circles.

But the weeks had rolled by, and they had been waiting nearly four months for the appointment that they had traveled so far to keep. It seemed the man they wanted to see had more pressing matters on his mind, which was the reason Law had occupied himself at the tables as a means to support himself and Archie. Resplendent in a pink and green striped waistcoat and rose-colored silk coat, a light brown wig cascading about his shoulders, his father's gold ring shining on his finger, John Law looked every bit the young dandy as he and Archie entered Bartholomew's gaming house.

The Major Domo recognized them at once and bowed low. 'Good evening, Your Grace. Ah, Mr. Law. Are you going to teach us some of your amazing skills tonight?' His tone held awe, not sarcasm.

'It's all there for anyone who pays attention to the cards and the numbers, my friend,' Law said smoothly and moved toward the center table, already circled with players who favored the wheel to the pasteboards.

The room was richly furnished with mahogany chairs, claw-footed gaming tables in the earlier Queen Anne style, and draperies of a watery green damask. Matching silk paneling was adorned with Dutch flower paintings. Tapestry sofas offered privacy where two could hold an intimate conversation about love, politics, or money, between bouts of losing their savings.

The games of chance took place beneath the glow of crystal chandeliers, each holding at least two dozen tapers. It was altogether a setting more opulent than some of the elegant townhouses in Leicester Street, where Archie was staying with friends. Law had lost no time in finding himself extremely comfortable lodgings in St. Giles-in-the-Fields, at the newly built intersection called The Seven Dials.

In the indulgent glow of Bartholomew's candlelight, the ladies' faces took on a rosy velvet hue. Fans fluttered, eyes danced and glittered perhaps too often in Law's direction. He was already known among them as 'Beau Johnnie'.

Archie surveyed the ladies eyeing his younger cousin and paused as a footman came by with a tray of champagne. They took some wine and stood apart from the others for a quiet word as they sipped. 'I hope you're in a lucky mood tonight, Johnnie,' he whispered. 'I'm a bit short, actually.'

'Your hope is my greatest desire, Archie,' Law said flatly. 'My rent is due next week, and I have spent a great deal on flowers for two ladies.' He eyed his cousin with slight annoyance. 'I had not planned on so long a wait. When do you think the great Lord Godolphin will have time to see us? I am beginning to think he is a mythical character.'

'Real, I promise you!' Archie said. 'And he has assured me that we shall be personally seen by him! And having seen us, he will take us straight to the King.'

'If he approves,' Law pointed out with some logic.

Archie preened slightly. 'I still have some influence at the English Court.' He took a pinch of snuff and added, 'Do not forget, John, it was my grandfather who placed the crown on the head of Charles the First at Scone!'

'And got himself beheaded for his trouble,' Law reminded him, his eyes searching the room. The one he was looking for had not yet arrived.

Archie scowled. 'True, my boy. But old scandals are as much a credit to a family as new ones are an embarrassment. King William will forgive the Campbells many things when I bring you to him—and all because of your wonderful schemes!' They moved a step nearer the tables.

'May I remind you that the Scottish Parliament didn›t wish to listen,' John replied, a small seed of doubt taking root in his self-assurance.

'Politics!' Archie dismissed the thought.' Your ideas are truly extraordinary, and they shall revolutionize the financial state of England.'

'And the financial state of the Laws and the Campbells, I do hope,' Law whispered as they moved to the dice table to play. Dice was a popular game, and Law was able to work out the odds against a player throwing any given combination of numbers with the dice. As they approached the table, several players stepped to the side to make room for them. Murmurs went around the table and eyes fixed on Law.

Noting that the man across the table had made double sixes three times running, Law placed a ten-shilling bet against one shilling from the house, that he would not throw double sixes six times running.

The man threw the dice and rolled another pair of sixes. A gasp went around the table. And again, he threw a twelve! A silence fell as he rolled them out once more. A two and a four!

Archie watched Law scoop in his winnings. Since he rarely seemed to lose, these evenings had provided the Scotsman with a sizable income and many new friends.

They moved away from the table, taking another glass from the footman. Truly, fortune has not smiled on the historical choices of our clan,' Archie admitted. 'I am thinking of the sad case of dear great-grandfather Archibald.' They had reached the roulette wheel, and with not much forethought Archie placed a few coins on the number six.

'Your great grandfather,› Law said dryly, ‹was a hot-blooded fool who not only organized a massacre against the McDonalds of Glencoe but was stupid enough to brag about it. Best not to bring him up in certain circles, Archie.'

Archie scowled as the croupier took away his coins. 'True, great-grandfather Archibald made the Campbell clan many enemies—and himself, a victim of the chopping block.'

Law's eyes circled the room. Still, she was not there. Other ladies smiled at him and signaled suggestive messages through the language of the fans. But Law turned his attention back to the table long enough to place a bet on the number eleven, speaking softly into his cousin's ear. 'And your grandfather fared no better, Archie. Two Campbells beheaded seems a bit careless!'

Law knew the family history. Archie's father had tried to clear the family name by siding with King Charles II and had been forced to escape. Wisely, he'd formed an alliance with the son of William of Orange. A lucky choice for the Campbells in a century of ancestral blunders. Still, one would have imagined that cousin Archie was on the verge of greatness to hear him talk.

'Now that King William and Queen Mary have restored our

lands and titles,' Archie was saying slightly louder so all around could not miss it, 'you shall see, I shall yet be made a Duke!'

'Are not Third Marquis and Tenth Earl of Argyll titles enough for you?' Law chided in a whisper as he placed a coin on number four. 'God created man, Archie. It was men who created titles.'

'Aye,' said Archie. ‹But the new century is only six short years away. You shall yet see the Campbell clan restored to its former glory before the year 1700.'

'From your mouth to the King's mistress's ear,' Law said with a smile and left Archie, moving away to another table.

Many eyes were watching Law's every play. And although he had a reputation of being extremely fortunate not only with the cards but with the ladies, *Beau Johnny* or *Jessamy John*, as some of the ladies called him, was in no mood to seek a wife. Although it must be said, there were fortunes to be won down that road as well, his aspirations reached towards different stars of desire.

Among the new friends that Law and his cousin had made was another nightly player at Bartholomew's, Thomas Neale, Master of the Mint and Groom Porter to King William III. In his early forties, a slender fellow, highly energetic, and well-liked by all, Law knew that Neale could be an instrumental champion for his own cause with the English King, although he had not yet told him his purpose in seeing the First Lord of the Treasury. However, Law had demonstrated to Neale some of his theories about numbers, as he did now.

'Where seven is the main and four is the chance, the odds against the placer are two to two. And so on in proportion, Thomas,' he explained. 'But you must memorize the numbers as they come up.'

'I cannot do sums in my head so instantly, as you seem to do, John,' Thomas Neale said. 'Nevertheless, I am beginning to win more than I lose, and therefore, I am your friend for life, sir. But you have not told me what this business is, that has brought you to London.'

Archie, who had been listening to their conversation as they stood away from the tables, said, 'What is it you should like to know, Thomas?'

Neale looked from one to the other. 'You fellows have been jolly secretive, you know. What exactly is it that you are presenting to Lord Godolphin?'

'It is time we told you, Thomas,' Law said and drew Neale over to a long tapestry sofa in a more private position. Archie sat on the sofa, Neale beside him, and Law took an armchair facing them. He drew a pamphlet from the depths of his brocade pocket.

'Johnnie carries that pamphlet with him everywhere,' Archie said. 'It is exactly as he presented it to the Scottish Parliament.'

Law handed the pamphlet to Thomas Neale, who read the title: *A Council of Trade, in which should be vested the whole of the King's revenues.* He looked up. 'A Council of Trade? You are presenting this to Lord Godolphin?'

'Read on,' Law said.

Neale read the following quietly: '*including the bishops' lands and rents and all charities. One-tenth of all grain and malt, a twentieth of all funds sued at law, one-fortieth of all successions legacies and sales...*' He looked back at his new Scottish friends.

'Why, this is a serious business!' Neale said. 'And you are presenting this to England?'

Archie nodded. 'When John read that out in the Scottish chamber, the enthusiastic look on the faces all around was fine to see!' Archie replied proudly. 'Until that damned Paterson fellow stood up.' Archie's voice took on a simpering tone: '*Now then, Mister Law, how do you propose that this great income be employed?*'

'Who is this Paterson?' Neale asked.

'An old enemy of the Campbells,' Archie told him.

'Of course, I was ready with an answer.' Law said. 'That after deducting a suitable sum for his majesty's personal needs...' he smiled 'You know, Thomas, one must first put some honey in the King's mouth.'

'So true,' Neale chortled as Law went on.

'I told them we must make a clean sweep of the antiquated past, must regulate weights and measures and dispense with monopolies. Liberate honest debtors and punish fraudulent bankrupts!'

Neale looked at Law with amazement. 'Why, John, I had no idea your mind ran to more than a decent flutter at the tables.'

Archie cut in excitedly. 'At first, as you can imagine, Thomas, they were enthusiastic about John's project. But the Paterson faction was quick to silence my men in The Squadrone.'

'I tried to speak above their din,' Law said. 'But Paterson waved his arms and silenced the room. 'Gentlemen,' he shouted, 'if Mister Law's proposals were actually to take effect, it is clear that all estates would be dependent upon the government and what landowner would be safe?'

'Naturally, I came to John's defense,' Archie said. 'But that devil Paterson stopped me again, shouting, 'Are we to listen to the Earl of Argyll on such matters? A man who – who…' Archie broke off.

Neale waited expectantly. 'Who what?'

John Law half-smiled. 'Go on, Archie,' he said. 'Tell him.'

Archie's expression shifted from haughtiness to anger. '*Who is by any social standards, addicted to a lewd and profligate life!*' Imagine Paterson saying that about me. Me!' He caught the look in Law's eye. 'Well, perhaps I have not always attended to business. But that is all changed now.'

'But what happened to your plan?' Neale asked Law. 'It sounds quite sensible to me.'

'Rejected.' Law frowned. 'After that, it was clear that I could gain neither honor nor profit in Scotland, and I told Archie I must look elsewhere.' He smiled. 'So, as you see, here we are!'

'We hope the English will be more visionary,' Archie said. 'There. Now you know our business here, Thomas.'

Law rose, tucking the pamphlet back into his pocket. 'And now we must spend some time enjoying our luck at the tables!'

'Thank you for telling me,' Neale said and got up with them.

That evening at the tables was a woman with whom Law had been carrying on a casual liaison and was the recipient of some of his flowers. Some said of the aging Elizabeth Villiers, a favorite of William III's, that she used a powerful opiate brought from China to revive the King's lessening libido, and gossip whispered that Elizabeth was soon to become the Countess of Orkney. The marriage would be conveniently arranged by King William. He had done as much for other mistresses.

Taking Law to one side, Thomas Neale warned him, 'Take care, John. Villiers has a penchant for young men, and her eyes have not left you all evening.'

'Indeed, she has already invited me to her bedroom, and not to see the wall hangings,' Law replied with a sigh. 'I felt duty-bound to surrender to her desire.'

'She arouses a passion in you, then?' Neale asked, recalling that the lady was into her thirties. Yet she was sensuously attractive with smoky eyes the color of a hazelnut.

Law nodded. 'I have paid her several visits, Thomas, and find her extremely knowledgeable in the skills of Venus.' He did not add that it would not do to have the King's mistress speak against him to the King.

With the beautiful Lady Katherine Knollys, it was another matter. She had come into the room only a few moments earlier and positioned herself across the table from where he and Neale were. Law watched her roll the dice and lose. She pouted.

Katherine had just turned nineteen and was of such a slender, delicate build, and her waist so narrow, that Law could span it with his hands. And had. Soft blonde hair curled naturally about her face and exploded into a profusion of curls that danced across bare shoulders when she let it fall loose. Her heavy white lace under-gown peeping beneath the rich blue of her dress, heightening the burnished glow of delicate skin. As always, she remained distant from him in public. They might appear to be mere acquaintances, but their relationship had progressed so far over the past four months that she had visited Law's apartments at St Giles in the Field. They had become lovers in every sense of the word, except commitment.

'I may hazard a guess that your interest lies in the direction of the lady in the blue gown,' Neale buzzed in Law's ear.

'This is hardly the moment to lose my heart to anyone, Thomas, and besides, the lady has a husband.'

'Ah, yes,' Thomas Neale acknowledged. 'In his seventies, they say. A wealthy Frenchman named Signeur. But no one ever sees the gentleman in London society.' He lowered his voice as Katherine glanced their way. 'She is the second daughter of Nicolas Vaux, Third Earl of Banbury. Her father was a great-grandson of Mary Boleyn, sister to Ann, wife of Henry VIII.'

Law nodded, placing his bet. He had been told all that by Katherine herself. And that her dowry had been too small for anything but marriage to a country squire. Signeur, though hardly a husband made in heaven, provided her with a townhouse and total freedom.

'I should not care to dissuade the gentleman from his country pursuits,' Law said.

'It is *what* he pursues,' Neale remarked with a sly grin.

Archie Campbell came over to them with Katherine on his arm. 'I have told Lady Knollys that I shall introduce her to a real Scottish treasure—aside from yourself, John.' He signaled a footman. 'We shall all have a sip of usquebaugh.'

'What is usquebaugh, your Grace?' Katherine asked warily.

'The water of life, my dear Lady Knollys. You will find it quite drinkable,' Archie assured her.

The footman brought a decanter and glasses and poured a small amount of clear amber liquid.

'Revives the spirits, so long as you do not drink too much,› Archie said, taking a deep drink himself. 'They are calling it whiskie down here. But I prefer the Celtic *Uisqui-beatha*.' He sighed. 'At last, the Scots have something the English want!'

'I should say the English want too much of Scotland, Archie,' Law put in. He finished off his glass and held it out to the footman who had brought the decanter. 'I shall take another if you please. He glanced at Katherine. "Does it suit your taste?'

'Admirably, Mr. Law,' she said. 'I seem to have acquired a taste for all things Scottish.' Her eyes tipped up slightly like a gazelle's and could tell a far different story from the truth when she wished. At that moment, they were focused on Law, causing a tug at his heart.

According to Sir Thomas Neale, before Law arrived in London, Katherine was being courted by a dashing young dandy-about-town, Edward Wilson. Law had observed him playing regularly at the gaming tables. In his mid-twenties, Wilson was said to be wealthy and was a heavy loser. Worse, a bad loser.

'They say his money comes from Villiers,' Neale had told Law, and that the King's mistress had picked Wilson up in the park one day and taken him home with her. If true, Wilson was hardly a faithful lover.

Although they had never spoken face to face, Wilson had written to Law on several occasions demanding he must stop seeing 'the lady to whom I have given my heart.' Uncertain whether the lady Wilson referred to was Elizabeth Villiers or Katherine Knollys, since Law, too, was seeing them both—he had chosen to ignore the letters. If the unnamed lady preferred Law's company to Wilson's, bad luck for a bad loser

When they first began their liaison, Katherine denied that she had been seeing Wilson. But Law didn't believe her. He'd confided to Neale that Katherine had come to his rooms heavily masked on more than one occasion. 'But she never allows me to visit her,' Law complained.

Thomas Neale, who reveled in the minutia of scandal, warned Law to take care. 'The rumor is that Lady Katherine has replaced Villiers as the King's newest favorite. It's more likely he, who has given her the lavish townhouse and the sapphires, not her husband, and certainly not Wilson!'

Throughout the evening across the gaming table, Katherine had been watching her *Jessamy John*, and Edward Wilson had been watching them both. Law had lost only one stake, and Wilson had lost nearly all.

'More coins!' Wilson cried, holding a hand out to his servant, always standing behind, guarding his purse of gold.

'I am afraid your purse is empty, sir.'

Wilson's eyes focused on Law, who laid his entire winnings on an eight straight and eleven and twelve split. The croupier spun the wheel. A gasp went around the table. Once more, Law was the winner. The croupier raked in a sweep of gold coins and pushed them towards Law.

Edward Wilson glared at the Scotsman. Jealousy had a double edge. 'Curious, how a fellow can win so consistently and yet be an honest man!' Wilson remarked under his breath, just loud enough to cause a murmur of speculation.

Law chose to ignore it, finished his glass, and gathered up his winnings. He always knew the moment to quit. Just as he knew how to calculate the odds against a player throwing any combination of numbers. He had studied the mathematics closely enough to be right seventy-five percent of the time. Enough to keep his winnings ahead of his losses. As he moved away across the room, Katherine caught up with him again.

'How much did you win?' she asked, her voice low and throaty.

'Two thousand five hundred and forty-six guineas,' he replied, leading her towards a curtained alcove.

She was surprised at such an exact figure.

'Simple. I keep count,' he said. She looked at him questioningly. 'In my head,' he added.

She shook hers. The idea seemed inconceivable. And yet he had won. Kept winning.

He drew her further out of sight of prying eyes behind the heavy silk curtains and into his arms. She lifted her mouth to his. Her lips were filled with promise and soft as down, and he yearned for more.

'Do you love me, Kate?' he asked.

'More than I ought—and as much as I can. Be satisfied with the way things are, Johnny. For they are the only way they can be.'

'Will you come to me tonight?' he asked.

'I am expected…elsewhere.' She did not have to say more. Tonight, she would be with the King. He let her go reluctantly. If Katherine had other commitments, so did Law.

She smoothed her dress, and they moved out of the alcove. Edward Wilson stood blocking their way. 'I have had as much of you as I can take, Law!' he declared, his speech coarsened by wine. Heads turned to watch. 'We do not need a Scotsman coming to London to show civilized Englishmen how to gamble. Lady Knollys is my friend, and I will not have you soiling her reputation.'

'I don't believe, sir, that I have had the pleasure of being introd…' It was as much as Law could say before Wilson slapped him across the face with his open palm; he did not bother with a glove. He raised his voice in an angry shout for the entire room to hear.

'Tomorrow Law, I shall meet you! Bloomsbury Square at midday. Have your Seconds ready. The choice of weapons is yours, sir!'

A voice from behind Law intercepted the argument. 'Mister Wilson, this is not a matter for hotheads.' It was Archibald Campbell, who had come across the room and now stepped between them. 'In any event, sir, it is not for you to interfere with whomever the lady wishes to see. Lady Knollys has a husband.'

'No concern of yours, Argyll,' Wilson said angrily, cheeks flushing. He turned his attention to Law. 'Tomorrow, then, Law.' Wilson turned abruptly and swaggered out. A whisper followed him.

Law looked at his cousin. 'I thank you for interceding, Archie. But I fear there is nothing for it but to give that fellow what he demands—and that is satisfaction.'

He glanced over to where Katherine had been standing. She was gone.

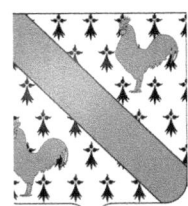

TWO:
WILSON AND THE DUEL

That night John Law lay awake listening to the thunder that clapped invisible clouds with giant fists and pummeled the earth with rain. The rain had stopped in the morning, but there was no warmth in the thin sunlight that seeped back into the leaden sky. He rose from his bed and crossed to the window that faced St. Giles-in-the-Field.

Law could look down upon the meeting point of seven roads. It was his new friend, Thomas Neale, who›d laid out the plans for this recently built section of London upon what had been open fields. Now, seven streets converged at an impressive obelisk that bore seven sundials, their faces turned towards each street and angled to tell the time whenever the sun chose to shine on a sundial. Neale had named the corner appropriately The Seven Dials, and the area around it was bustling with life.

While not the richest community in London, St. Giles consisted of some three thousand houses set apart from the Royal Borough of Westminster and the City by fields of wildflowers called Long Acre, where Law soon took to walking. He found Long Acre residents were a cross-section of society: Men of rank and ladies of fashion were established in the country houses around Great Queen Street, which linked it to Lincolns Inn Fields.

For these past months, Law had been happy to be in London, enjoying the richly colorful city life. He had much to look forward to if his meeting went well with Lord Godolphin. 'Patience', had been Archie's advice, but John Law was not a patient man, and it seemed he'd been waiting for ever. Instead of facing the First Lord of the Treasury, now he was to face a ridiculous duel!

The night before, he'd sat up late with Archie and Thomas Neale at a coffee house. The two men agreed to act as Law's Seconds in the duel, and Archie had brought along his fine boxed pair of Scottish flintlocks with curved steel butts and offered them to his cousin. But Law shook his head at the thought of pistols. 'A bullet is so final, Archie. I have no desire to do this headstrong idiot any serious damage!'

'Then I recommend swords,' his cousin advised. 'You are certainly adept with a blade, and being in control of your weapon, you're less likely to kill Wilson.'

'Swords, then.' Law nodded glumly. How, he wondered, had he got himself into a duel after so short a time in London? What on earth did Wilson intend, anyway? Surely it was clear that Katherine did not love him. Law was not certain that she loved *him*, for that matter, and now they were to fight over her!

A shout from the street below brought Law back to the present and his window. An old woman opened her window across the road and emptied a chamber pot into the street below, narrowly missing an elderly gentleman who seemed not to notice. The shadow on the sundial facing Law was almost vertical, and as Law peered down, Archie's head protruded from his coach, which had just drawn up by the obelisk.

His cousin waved and climbed out with Thomas Neale. They crossed the cobbles to his building and clattered up the wooden stairs. Law, bare to the waist, was still holding a pair of black leather shoes with large silver buckles and bright red heels when he opened the door.

Neale greeted him and looked around. 'Nice rooms, aren't they?'

'Yes, I've enjoyed it here – although the wait has been. . .' Law stopped, seeing Archie's expression.

'You have not wasted your time when it came to the ladies,' Archie said with a touch of rancor.

Neal eyed Law's small traveling trunk standing open in the corner. On the bed were lying two silk scarves and a pair of knitted stockings with gold-threaded clocks up the sides. They were the newest fashion. Law had purchased them from Nottinghamshire, especially for the trip. Beside them were two fresh lawn shirts, a pair of ruffled lace cuffs, a lace neckband, and a plain linen stock, which it must be admitted, looked a bit frayed. The concierge had brought all back, washed and ironed, that morning. Law chose a shirt and put it on.

Neale surveyed the traveling trunk and items on the bed. 'That is all you brought?'

'Didn't imagine that Archie and I would be kept waiting for so long,' Law said, eyeing Archie.

'You are not in Scotland now,' Neal advised. ‹One must ring the changes in London.' He glanced at Law›s red-heeled shoes admiringly. 'Those shoes–now those you can wear to the finest houses in London. Where ever did you find them? Red heels! 'They are all the rage in Paris, I hear.'

'Which is exactly where I purchased them. And I must say, they have been appreciated at Bartholomew's. For as much as the English say they hate the French, they secretly admire them.'

Neale eyed Law›s black broadcloth jacket lying next to his brocade jacket on the bed. ‹But that, John, I would say, is not suitable for social occasions.›

'It shall do perfectly to visit Lord Godolphin,' Archie put in, with a worried look. 'And I think today, Johnny, that you must put on the broadcloth.'

'For a duel?' Law raised an eyebrow. 'One definitely wears silk brocade when fighting a duel, Archie. I have observed that London society does not trust a man who cannot afford a fine silk coat.' His attempt at humor received no response from Archie. Law looked questioningly at his cousin. "Surely you're not worried about today?' Archie's expression revealed that he was holding something back. 'Well then, Archie, what is it?' Law asked with some annoyance.

Archie stared at him, almost afraid to say what he must tell his cousin. 'Today - would you believe - just today of all days, John! Lord Godolphin has agreed to see us!' He passed his cousin a note on official crested paper.

Law took it in his hands, staring at it. 'Today. . ?'

Archie nodded. His tone was stressed with anxiety. 'He will see us at one-thirty p.m. exactly! And *exact* is what we must be, in arriving at Whitehall Palace.'

Law sank on his bed, staring at the letter. 'Only five months ago, I stood before the Scottish House dressed in that same black jacket. But it seemed that I could obtain neither honor nor profit in Scotland, and I told you, Archie, that I must look elsewhere. So, here we are. And now. . . Today? This very day! A bloody duel! I cannot credit it, that after all these weeks of waiting, the First Lord of the Treasury picks this very day!'

They were silent for a moment, no one knowing what to say. Finally, Law rose and finished dressing, donned the black broadcloth coat, tucked his papers into the deep pocket, and threw on his dark grey cloak. 'Come, gentlemen, let us get this nonsense over and done with quickly. I have an important appointment to keep.' He smiled, throwing back his shoulders. 'Isn't it wonderful!'

The three men descended the stairs.

In the coach, Law sat between the others. For the first time, he felt nervous. The carriage jounced them over the cobbles towards Bloomsbury Square. The bells of Mary-le-Bow were chiming the hour. It was just midday.

'. . .Wonderful.?' Archie picked up Law's remark as though there had been no break in the conversation. 'What if you are killed? What shall I do then?' Archie cried.

Law smiled dryly. 'More to the point, what shall *I* do, cousin?'

'Well, I am glad you can make so light of it,' Archie said bleakly. 'Could you not have kept your small companion tucked inside your trousers until we had our business completed?'

'I have never noticed that such considerations deterred you, Archie,' Law replied. Nor can I help it if the lady prefers me and my companion.'

'Duels are never fought over a lady's preferences, dear boy,' Archie said. 'Points of honor are about a gentleman's pride. And that is a commodity more delicate than any gentlewoman's blush.'

Thomas Neale had been inspecting the swords. Now he turned to Archie. 'Where did you obtain these, your Grace? The pommels are of weighty iron, though I suppose the blades' steel is of sufficiently fine quality to do the job.'

'Five shillings each,' from that shop near The Royal Chocolate House in St. James's Street,' Archie replied. 'Not new, but the best they had at such short notice. I understand they have already killed two men.'

'Not my first choice for such an endeavor,' Thomas said, feeling the blade edge with the flat of his index finger.

'My kinsman is a fine swordsman, and they shall do nicely,' Archie said and turned his attention back to Law. 'But are you prepared with what you shall tell Lord Godolphin, Johnny?'

'Engraved in my soul, Archie.' Law tapped one of the deep pockets on his long jacket where he had put his papers. He glanced at the swords with distaste. 'Killed two men, you say?'

Thomas folded the swords back into the stiff leather case and returned his attention to Law. 'You realize, of course, that dueling has been outlawed in England for some time, John. Perhaps you would not be aware of it in Scotland?'

Law shook his head. 'We are not such a wild place as all that, Thomas. At home, killing somebody in a duel is considered murder and treated as such, no matter how illustrious and honorable the cause may be. But I do not intend to take the fool's life, I assure you.'

Thomas nodded. 'When the affair is finished, we must make haste to leave. Otherwise, we may all find ourselves detained by the sheriff for dueling. More than a few people overheard Wilson challenge you at Bartholomew's last night.'

Law nodded. He suddenly had an uneasy feeling he could not stifle. They rode on silently until they reached the square, Thomas mumbling a prayer. John, too, bowed his head, praying silently that all would come out well.

The square was empty as Archie's carriage approached, and the sky had darkened once more. 'Now all we need is rain,' Archie muttered.

From behind a thick stand of trees, they saw a black coach pull out. Wilson and his two Seconds descended from it, cloaked and wearing tricorn hats. Wilson swaggered towards them, called out loudly as the coach came to a halt, ‹Is that you, Law?›

Law climbed down and stepped forward to meet Wilson. Neale followed, carrying the sword case, which he opened. Archie came behind them.

'Ah, I see it is to be swords, then? No matter. I can dispatch you as easily with one of those,' Wilson said coolly, tossing his hat and cloak to one of his Seconds.

To Law, Wilson did not look like a man willing to see reason, but he decided to give him one more opportunity. 'See here, Wilson, I am quite ready to forget the insult you have paid me and offer you a drink at The Fountain Tavern,' he said, trying to keep his voice amiable.

Wilson's expression was grim. 'All I shall accept from you is your blood, Law.'

He stepped towards the cased swords Thomas Neale was holding. 'Let me have a look at 'em.'

'Your choice, sir,' Thomas Neale told him, opening the case. The dull steel had an ominous deadliness about it; these were no toys.

Law glanced across to the road ringing the edge of the field. He half expected Katherine to appear in a dramatic, even theatrical attempt to intercede and stop the duel. But perhaps, after all, that was a scene she would not think of playing. Thomas had warned him that there had been duels fought over Katherine Knollys before. A touch of anger clouded Law's brain. Perhaps he was no higher on Katherine's priorities than another notch on Cupid's bow. And he might even die for it.

Wilson picked up one of the swords, weighing it in his hand. The balance was good, though they were heavy weapons.

'Excellent,' he said. 'This will do nicely.'

Law sighed, taking up the other sword. 'I do not wish to kill you, Wilson, and since I cannot dissuade you of this folly, I wish you luck.'

'Go to hell, Law!' Wilson cried and wielded his weapon, ready to attack.

'Take hold of yourself, Wilson...!' Archie called firmly. 'Gentlemen's rules...!'

Wilson's Seconds drew him back, calming him with whispered words. It was clear to Law that he had been stiffening his resolve with liquid courage. One of Wilson's Seconds marked off the distance for the duelists.

The two men took their places. At the signal from Wilson's man, they moved towards each other at a measured pace, then stood on guard according to the rules, swords touching at fighting distance.

Wilson's Second called out, 'Are you ready, gentlemen?' Wilson and Law nodded. The Second signaled them to begin by dropping a white kerchief. '*Allez!*' he called.

Wilson raised his sword in *prime* and brought it down heavily, to be met by Law's *parry* with a resounding ring as the blades clashed. Wilson had the advantage of rage and alcohol to set his adrenaline flowing. Law had a sleepless night. Parrying against the stinging steel, Law disengaged Wilson›s blade again and again. And still, Wilson pressed his seeming advantage forward!

Steel clanged on steel, as Law found himself forced to defend Wilson's heated attack. He had not expected such violence and parried *quarte* to the shoulder, and then *sixte* to the neck. The man seemed determined to slice off his head!

The next attack caught Law across the arm and ripped his broadcloth coat sleeve, drawing blood. He had dressed that morning to meet a statesman, not a jilted lover.

Archie tried to interject to stop the duel and staunch Law's wound with a cloth, but Wilson, like a madman, pushed Archie out of the way.

Law got a grip on his sword once more in time to meet Wilson's next blow—aimed wildly at Law's belly. Wondering how he'd ever agreed to such a duel, Law countered, then struck once again! This time Wilson stumbled, and his fighting arm flew up, opening his guard.

Although he had not intended it, Law's blade caught Wilson sideways across his chest. Wilson dropped to his knees with a groan and then seemed to sink slowly onto his back. His Seconds were upon him instantly, to staunch the wound.

Law stared at the wounded man. He had meant merely to scare Wilson off. Hopefully, to acquit himself with no damage to either contestant. How had he been so stupid?

He hesitated. 'Is there anything I can do…?'

One of the Seconds looked up at him without rancor. 'Nothing, Mister Law. It has been a fair fight. We shall take care of him.'

Law stood there, paralyzed. Archie took the sword from Law's hand. Thomas retrieved the other blade, wiped them both, and returned them to the case. 'Hurry, Johnny,' Archie whispered, taking his arm. 'We must be on our way! Godolphin is waiting.'

Law glanced once more at the fallen man. 'He will be all right?' he asked Wilson's Second.

'That is not your concern now, sir,' the Second said tersely.

Law turned away and allowed Archie to bundle him into the waiting carriage.

Unseen by them, a sedan chair and two bearers stood just out of sight behind the trees at the far end of the field. Inside, Katherine Knollys tapped on the window. 'Take me to Great Queen Street,' she called to her bearers.

In Archie's carriage, Archie was fussing over Law's wound. 'What shall we say to Godolphin about your arm?'

'It's not too deep,' Law replied, removing his jacket to examine it. It was deep enough. Thomas had white linen ready. He tore off a strip and tied it around, binding Law's wound. Law put back his jacket. His face was pale, and his pupils dilated.

'Are you all right, Johnny?' Archie asked, giving him a shot of whiskie from a pocket flask.

'I could have killed him, Archie. It is not a feeling I relish,' Law said with some alarm.

'He'll go home and lick his wounds and think better of it before he gets himself in another duel,' Archie assured him. 'We did not need all this foolery at this precise moment! And—I did not tell you—a meeting with the King scarcely a week away!'

Law stared at his cousin as the coach crossed the Horse Guards Parade.

'John, I wish you the good luck you deserve,' Thomas said, as Archie's coach approached Whitehall Palace. It would take Neale home and return for Archie and Law.

Whitehall was still the center of Court activities, although King William III suffered from asthma and preferred Kensington palace's healthier air. As they entered the building, Archie whispered to Law, 'Your jacket is bloody! Pull your cloak over that sleeve!'

Law did so just as they were ushered into the sumptuous offices of the First Lord of the Treasury.

'Please take a seat, gentleman. Lord Godolphin will be with

you directly,' the secretary said with a slight bow and left them, just as the Finance Minister entered from another door with a sheaf of papers.

A tall man, dark-complexioned with a flat oval face, thick eyebrows above tired eyes, he seated himself behind an expanse of mahogany desk and finished fussing with the papers. He folded them away, fixing his shrewd glance upon John Law.

'So, Mister Law, you are a Jingling Geordie, are you?' he asked with a smile. It was the nickname for Scottish goldsmiths, and he meant it by way of jest. The First Lord of the Treasury was well aware that in Scotland, goldsmiths were by trade, lenders of money, and jewelers.

Law measured his words in reply. 'The Laws have traded as goldsmiths in Edinburgh since the 16th century, Lord Godolphin.'

Law knew money-lending was an occupation that only Jews were permitted by law to perform on the continent,. But since borrowers rarely cared to repay their loans or any interest on them, the money-lenders were looked upon with some contempt. Not so in Scotland, where lending money was considered a gentleman's profession for men of any faith.

'But that is not where I have developed my ideas on finance,' Law continued. 'Since I was a lad, I've traveled at my father's side across most of Europe. I speak French, Italian, and Dutch.'

'I did not think anyone could speak Dutch but the Dutch themselves,' Godolphin said with a smile, adding hastily, 'Although, of course, the Netherlands is dear to the heart of our Sovereign. King William, of course, coming from the Netherlands.' He smiled. 'What is it you propose, Mr. Law?'

'Sir, as you are aware, there are only two banks in the world, both private. One in Genoa and one in Amsterdam. Places where a person can put money on deposit and arrange loans. I have studied both banking systems and the judicial use of finance to promote business.'

Godolphin furrowed thick brows. 'My informants tell me that you win heavily at the tables at Bartholomew's and other gaming houses almost every night. Is that your idea of a judicial use of finance, Mister Law?'

Law was uncertain whether this was a commendation or a

criticism. He spoke with more confidence than he felt. 'Sir, I shall not go into my theories and practices at the gaming tables for the moment, but perhaps another time you will allow me to demonstrate them to you, personally. I have named the two private banks which now exist. What I should like to present to you is a plan to create the first *national* bank in the entire world. The National Bank of England.'

'A *national* bank. . .?"

'My proposal vastly improves on the two banking systems now being employed. This national bank would allow England to lead the rest of the world in commerce!'

'The National Bank of England. . .' Godolphin tasted the words, appraising the man across from him. What was he to make of John Law, the older man wondered? His tall figure and open, intelligent countenance were enough to draw admiration in any crowd. A man of ideas, who spoke English in a rich and vibrant voice, with barely a trace of a Scottish accent. The sort of man King William would take to. But he would have to hear much more before venturing to present such a novel *projection*. He framed his reply carefully. 'It is a daring idea, certainly, Mister Law. But is it practical?'

'It will bring gold pouring into the King's coffers, Sir. And there is also a further project.' Law was warming to his subject. He passed Godolphin several sheets of paper upon which were written figures.

As he did so, Godolphin noticed that Law was favoring his right arm, and though Law's cloak covered it, he had seen a flash of the torn sleeve. The Finance Minister leaned forward. 'Are you hurt, Mister Law?'

Instinctively, Law pulled his cloak tighter across his injured arm. 'It is no matter, sir. I should like you to have a glance at those projected accounts of how this bank would operate.'

As Godolphin studied Law's figures, the room was silent, his thoughtful expression growing intense as he absorbed percentages and totals. Finally, he looked back at Law with new respect in his eyes. 'I do believe you may have devised a noble plan, sir. And one that well might catch the interest of the King.' His eyes went to Archie. 'Indeed, your Grace, I shall be delighted to arrange the interview that we discussed.'

Law drew from his pocket a sheaf of small papers about seven inches long by three inches wide. 'Sir, I also wish to place before you a proposition that has never been tried anywhere in the world! One that will totally revolutionize and open world trade.' Law was just about to hand across the small slips of rectangular paper when a discreet knock preceded Godolphin's secretary, who re-entered. The man looked extremely agitated as he came over to whisper something in Godolphin's ear, his eyes on Law. With a look of alarm, Godolphin stood up, pushing Law's paper 'projections' away from him. 'What is this, Mister Law? What have we here? There are two sheriff's bailiffs in my outer office. They say they have a warrant to arrest you! On a charge of murder!' John Law rose to face Godolphin, the color draining from his cheeks. He felt suddenly chilled. His words came on a whispered breath. 'Edward Wilson is dead...?

LORD GODOLPHIN
FIRST LORD OF THE TREASURY (Circa 1698)

 THREE:
NEWGATE PRISON —
THE CHUMS

The bailiffs ushered into Lord Godolphin's office, manacled Law's wrists, and led him out through the waiting room, past a group of government ministers. The men turned to stare at the tall stranger and could not fail to see the gash in his sleeve and the darkened blood surrounding it. Had the blackguard attempted an attack on Lord Godolphin?

John Law averted his eyes. Only that morning, he'd been so full of hopes and plans, and within a few short hours, his entire future had become a jarring question mark.

The bailiffs led him down the stairs. A moment later, Archibald Campbell came rushing after them, out into the open courtyard in front of Whitehall, just in time to see his cousin being bustled like a common criminal into a closed carriage. Vainly he attempted to intercede but to no avail. The carriage sped its prisoner away, kicking up a spurt of gravel at Archie's feet.

Inside the carriage, Law sat hemmed between the two bailiffs. 'Where are you taking me?' he demanded.

'Newgate,' came the surly reply from the heavy-set fellow on his right.

In his few months in London, Law had come to know all the gaming houses and elegant streets but counted himself fortunate that he had never had a view of London's most fearsome prison, Newgate. He had been told that many of the men who gambled their fortunes away across the tables at Bartholomew's ended in a debtor's cell there. Murderers, too, were confined in Newgate until they met their freedom at the city's outskirts, hanging from that fatal tree at Tyburn crossroads.

NEWGATE.

'Rest assured, Newgate will hold you, sir. It 'as held the scum of Londontown since the year 1189,' the bailiff said with surly contempt. The older bailiff nodded agreement and added with some pride, as though it had been his ancestral abode. 'Full of history, Newgate is. Dates back to Roman times.'

This bailiff had the world-weary countenance of one to whom sending a man to the gallows was all in a day's work. 'Newgate were built and built again, you might say,' he said. 'For it were Dick Whittington hisself, the famous Lord Mayor of London, saw to its construction back in the 15th century. But then, it burnt down in the great fire, and 'ad to be rebuilt again.'

Law had been barely listening, his mind a jumble of thoughts all too terrible to countenance, until finally, the carriage drew to a sharp halt. His first sight of Newgate was formidable enough. The portcullis, a heavily spiked iron grating barred the entrance. It stood between two fortified Tuscan pilasters—square columns that projected from the building. In each were three barred windows that he took to be cells. If Newgate's exterior gave the impression of fearsome grandeur, it was merely a hint of the interior horrors that he knew awaited him and the other prisoners already locked inside. Still, Law had heard tales of people managing to escape with the help of plucky and undaunted friends.

Set in the most ancient part of the City and built at one of London's original gates, Newgate loomed five stories above the neighboring rooftops of shops along Newgate Street. On either side was the old Bailey and Sessions House Yard, with prison entrances into each. The back of the prison faced into old Warwick Square and Birdcage Walk. On the ride, Law had tried to picture the location clearly in his mind—just in case.

The burly bailiff pointed out three statues adorning alcoves above the portcullis. 'Peace, Security, and Liberty, them is called,' he said, pointing to the statues. 'Though I don't exactly recall which is which.' Above those, Law could see the coat of arms of the City.

'That one over on the right, that's Liberty,' the other bailiff put in. 'She used to have a cat at her feet in memory of Dick Whittington, though some say he never had no cat. I can still remember when it tumbled down and broke into pieces.' He pointed to a great arched window with heavy bars above the statues. 'That cell is called The Castle.' He threw his prisoner a piercing look. 'Don't you try to get out o' there! H'it's escape-proof! An' above that is the Red Room and the Chapel, and up at the top, there's the Leads, where prisoners is allowed to take a stroll.'

'That is if they've got the coin to pay for it,' the burly man chortled.' You see, Mister Law, nothing in a prison is free. Same's like us delivering you 'ere safe and sound, without your head broke in on the way, see? That'll be two shillings and fourpence for us each—and that's not counting the history lesson.'

He reached into Law's pocket, withdrawing the money purse, which was out of Law's own reach, with his hands manacled.

'Help yourself,' Law said wryly.

'No more, no less than is due,' the bailiff said, taking out the money and passing half to his fellow bailiff.

The abrasive grinding of heavy metal chain drew Law's attention, as the portcullis was finally raised to permit the carriage to enter through the ominous arch. He knew, without doubt, this might be his last glimpse of freedom.

Law was taken into a room called The Lodge, where the bailiffs bid him goodbye and placed him in the custody of a guard. With a touch of irony, they wished him a comfortable stay. Details of his arrest were written down. The guard sent for four Truncheon Officers and finally unlocked Law's manacles. Two of these strapping fellows lay hold of Law while the other two searched his pockets, claiming six shillings and eightpence each as privilege belonging to their office. One man took a silk handkerchief from Law's pocket.

'Won't do to have a thing like that in your possession, Mister Law. Too much of a temptation for the others,' he said and tucked it into his own pocket.

From the Lodge, the Truncheon Officers took John Law to the 'Condemned Hold', a gloomy chamber about twenty feet long, and left him with nothing but a thin straw pad.

'Take care of it,' one officer told him, 'and don't let none of the other *chums* get hold of it, for it›s all you'll ever get to sleep on ‹ere, and there is a good number of thieves about, for a fact.'

He chuckled at his little joke and locked the iron door after himself with a huge iron key.

Law's eyes had not adjusted to the dark before the foul, sweaty bodies, and stinking breaths that assailed his nostrils made him gag. The high, lone window admitted only a thin thread of light through thick iron bars. The stone walls and floors were sweaty with filth, and part of the cell had been boarded over to make a sleeping area. In one corner stood the shit tub. A handful of verminous beggars sat smoking *Mundungus* tobacco and playing skittles. Sighting a new arrival, they got up as one man and hurried to hover over him.

Quickly assuring him that they were all debtors and not murderers, and with palms outstretched, they cried out, 'Garnish, Garnish!', demanding two shillings each which they claimed from every new arrival. Law paid up, grateful that he had his winnings from last night in his purse.

Once locked up, the turnkey had told Law, prisoners were supposed to be asleep by ten o'clock. But since the lone window in the cell barely admitted any daylight, it was not easy to tell the difference between day and night. As the church-bell struck eleven, Law could see that such a rule was clearly impossible to enforce. The men argued, shouted, sang, and otherwise carried on as though it were day.

He tried to sleep, but his mind kept reliving the duel. If Wilson was actually dead, then he was a murderer! But the idea was too horrendous. He could not comprehend it fully.

The following morning John Law was taken before the magistrate in Sessions House to be formally identified and charged. When the magistrate was satisfied that they had arrested the right man, Law was returned to Newgate, this time to a cell in Wing Nine. The door was heavy, with spikes at the top protecting an aperture through which a prisoner could speak to the turnkey or a visitor. Here, the foul smells were far worse than a Southwark ditch or the Tanner's yard.

More intimidating than the last cell were the chains, hooks, and iron staples on the floor. Manacled ankles chained one prisoner who was seemingly ignored by the other human inhabitants as though he was contagious with 'jail fever'. By the look of the prisoners, some had been there for years. Many were enshrouded in no more than rags, heads covered with *bum* caps, or stuck into the tops of old stockings that were meant to keep the rats and lice out of their hair. The men scrambled over to inspect the new arrival like a tribe of cannibals about to devour him, and they cried out for their *garnish*!

'You must give them each two shillings, if you have it, sir, or they will take it from you by force,' the man in chains called out to

Law. 'It is an initiation fee, for now, no matter where you came from or what you have done, you are one of us. A *chum* amongst *chums*.'

Law reached into his purse and paid up quickly. The leader of the pack took the money and bowed low to Law. 'Welcome, good sir, to all the privileges and amnesties of prison life.' This little charade over, the sad-eyed men divided up the money and went back to their game of skittles.

'Could you fill my water cup, sir?' the man in chains called out to him. He seemed a friendly, gentle soul somewhere in his middle years, and although his clothing was nearly as filthy as the others, his were expensively cut and of fine cloth. Law took the man's cup over to where a bucket of water was set high on a three-legged stool which Law presumed was to keep out the other inhabitants of the room—a colony of rats. He brought it to the shackled man who thanked him gratefully and drank.

'They will take your bedding and your clothes if you do not keep your wits about you,' he said. 'My name is Brounley. And yours?'

'John Law,' the Scotsman replied. 'Why are you chained, sir? And why do the others ignore you?'

'Sit down, Mister Law, and I shall tell you how I came to be here. It was a case of murder,' he said with a smile. 'I am to be hung, and the men do not like to be reminded of their own fate. The day has not yet been chosen, for there are many condemned in prison, and they can only hang so many men a day, you see.'

Brounley seemed to need to talk and proceeded to relate in some detail why and how he had killed his wife. He said he had found her in bed with a neighbor and had stabbed her. But the neighbor had escaped and raised the alarm. 'And what is the crime that has brought you to this foul place?' he inquired.

'I killed a man in a duel. But it was unintentional,' Law told him unhappily. 'An accident.'

Brounley laughed. 'There are no accidents, sir.' Noticing the worried look on Law's face as he reached into his pocket to feel his slimming money purse, Brounley added, 'I see they have been bleeding you of your coin, sir. Unfortunate. It is not a good thing to be penniless in Newgate. '

'It is not a good thing anywhere, sir,' Law replied.

'Here, the prisoners have their own High Court of Justice,' Brounley told him. 'They will try a criminal for cracking his lice between his teeth and spitting out the bloody skins about the ward. As for our keepers, prisoners without money are put in the 'Tangier' cell where they are stripped, beaten, and abused for the guards' pleasure. If you have a friend on the outside, sir, entreat him please, to bring you money.' Brounley looked across at the others with some apprehension. 'But not sufficient gold for them to strip and kill you for it.'

'I shall soon be out of coin, that is certain,' Law replied. 'Nor have I been allowed to collect any of my personal belongings, such as a book or writing paper. And have had no word from my only relative here in London.' Law had no way of knowing that the authorities told Archie Campbell nothing. Archie was not even certain where his cousin was being held.

For most of the day, Law kept his distance from the others, leaning against the damp wall or sitting on the cold stone floor beside Brounley. A chill oozed into his bones until he was stiff from it. His mind, too, seemed numb, and he could not think clearly. He had scarcely noticed hunger in the greater concern for his desperate situation, but when at last he was brought a thin soup with rancid chunks of fatty meat in it, he wolfed it down, not caring how it tasted. Law eyed the other occupants of the cell, the rats, scurrying around the shit tub in the darkest corner. The creatures darted out at the smell of food, scavenging for any scrap a careless man might drop.

'Charity beef,' Brounley said angrily. 'Seven prisoners manage our allotment, one of whom, like me, is heading for the tree any day now; and although there are at least one hundred debtors here, not half their allotted beef is ever shared out between them.'

'What becomes of it?' Law asked, chewing on a piece of gristle. He tossed the inedible shred in the direction of the rats. There was a scurry of claws and squeals from the dark corner.

'The beef? Why sold, sir. For the benefit of the prison staff. There is charity money, too - given to the debtors. But when they receive it, it is demanded as 'garnish' by the others. Though you must have a ready coin, too much on your person is not safe, for the under-keeper will send in the pickpockets from other parts of the prison, and they will not leave empty-handed, I assure you.'

'If only money were printed on paper,' Law said. 'Nobody could steal it then, for you could line your shoe with it.'

Brounley laughed heartily. 'You do indeed have a sense of humor, Mister Law. Money on paper! Indeed, that is a novel idea!'

The next day when Law sat down beside Brounley once more, the chained man wiped tired eyes with a rag of dirty kerchief and told him in a hollow voice, 'When they take me away, you shall hear the great bell of St Sepulchre's ringing all through the night, Mister Law.'

Law remembered having walked past that church when he was inspecting the city. 'That is the large church at the eastern end of Holborn, is it not?'

'Indeed, the largest parish church in all of London. I used to attend regular services there,' Brounley sighed. 'For the last fifty years, St Sepulchre's bell has been rung all night before a hanging as a warning to all would-be transgressors. I never thought it would ring for me.' His face darkened, and his voice was filled with anger. 'I should not mind the ringing so much, but it is also telling the blood-thirsty that at first light they should get themselves over to Tyburn Tree, for it is there the condemned of London are hanged.' Unexpectedly, his face brightened into a devilish grin. 'Mark you, I expect I shall give them their money's worth, for I shall not go quietly. I shall struggle and cry out and make a fine show of it.'

Law shook his head sadly. 'I think you will feel differently when your dignity is at stake, sir.'

'Dignity? I do not give a toss for such things. You shall see how you feel when they come for you!' Brounley cried.

'My offense was quite different, 'Law said, trying to preserve the scrap of self-respect he still felt.

A harsh laugh escaped Brounley's lips. 'You do not think of yourself as a murderer, I see. But the law is the law, and the rope does not care how you come to it.' Brounley studied the Scotsman. 'Are you a religious man, Mister Law?'

No more than is natural,' Law said. 'Why do you ask?'

'Because on Sundays the prisoners are not allowed to use the chapel. Space is sold to sightseers curious to see those under sentence of death.' He leaned his head against the damp wall. 'We are no more than a show for the respectable rabble of London.'

John Law had spent ten nights in the cell, his cloak wrapped tightly around him, as much protection against theft as for warmth. But the other men did not bother him. He had paid two shillings for clean water to wash his wound. It was healing well enough. Then, one night when the men were bedding down, The Ordinary, a prison chaplain, appeared and offered scraps of consolation to Brounley, who understood full well what the chaplain's arrival meant. He always visited a man the night before he was to be hanged.

'You will not convert me to religion, my friend,' Brounley told him, 'for I lost my faith years ago and shall go to the gallows unrepentant.'

A few minutes later, the turnkey arrived to unlock Brounley's chains. The leg irons would have to be struck off elsewhere. This was the first time that Brounley had stood up for several weeks. He rose slowly and painfully, his legs trembling beneath him. He would spend his last night in another cell.

Law asked if he could accompany his new friend for part of the way. The Truncheon Officers extracted two shillings from him and allowed Law to go as far as the Press Room.

When they entered this chamber, they were confronted by the sight of two guards standing over a scarecrow of human flesh. The man was lying across a sharp block placed beneath his back. He wore nothing but a rag of cloth covering his genitals, hardly sufficient for decency. His head was covered, and each foot and each arm were drawn to the four quarters of the chamber by thick ropes. The man was barely breathing, his emaciated body weighted down by a heavy board beneath a crushing load of stone and lead.

'How long has he been there?' Law inquired, feeling his mouth gone suddenly dry.

One of the guards regarded the bound convict dispassionately. 'Three days only.'

The truncheon officer nodded to Law. 'Do not concern yourself, Mister Law. He has been treated exactly in accordance with the judge's ruling. All by the book.'

Law had heard from one of the others how the law dealt with such prisoners. Each day more lead blocks and stone would be added until the man was finally crushed.

'And he has had his rightful allowance of sustenance,' the guard added. 'All by the book.'

Law looked at this victim of judiciary kindness, his bones protruding from his arms. 'He has been allowed three morsels of barley bread but no water the first day. On the second, he was given three drinks of stale water but no bread.

'How long will he remain like this?' Law asked.

'It will not take too long to break him now. He will die by tomorrow, I shouldn't wonder,' the guard replied.

'And what was his crime?' Law asked.

'Ah, that! The villain has refused to plead,' the truncheon officer replied, turning his attention to Brounley.

He pushed the doomed man down to sit on the floor with his ankles across a metal plate. Then he picked up a hammer and began to strike off Brounley's leg irons, not caring too much if he missed the irons.

The other guards helped pull Brounley to his feet and pinned his elbows from behind, leaving him free to clasp Law's hand in the last goodbye.

'Think of me,' he said.

'I shall not forget you, sir,' Law told him truthfully.

Word had traveled through the jail that another convict was to meet his end in the dawn. But the howl of voices, the shouting of names by the turnkeys, the clank of chains, the cat-calls and laughter ringing through the corridors—all was as before. Despite what he had said, Brounley went with the guards without a struggle to the last cell he would ever see, and Law was led back to his former cell.

A short while later, Law heard the bell of St Sepulchre's beginning to ring. It clanged throughout the night until he thought it would drive him mad. One man mumbled prayers over and over. And as the first crack of dawn seeped through the one tiny window, the bell finally stopped ringing. The other prisoners bowed their heads, for indeed, its silence meant that the rope had broken Brounley's neck.

Sunk into a deep depression, Law sat alone for the rest of the day, his mind filled with thoughts of the life that might have been his, and of Katherine Knollys, the cause of the duel which had ended Wilson's life and was now to end his own. He did not expect ever to see her face again, and he was not certain how he felt about her. He did not realize that she had watched the duel.

It was late in the afternoon when the sound of footsteps brought the turnkey back again. This time he opened the door to admit the Earl of Argyll and bowed discreetly to the nobleman, tucking a clenched fist into his deep pocket where it deposited a substantial amount of Archie's gold.

'Thank God,' Archie breathed, seeing his cousin. 'It is as difficult to get in here as it is to get out!'

He clapped his arms around Law, who was so relieved to see Archie that tears welled in his eyes. Impressed by the regal bearing of Law's visitor, the other prisoners kept their distance from the display of emotion.

As the cousins moved into a more private corner of the dank stone cell, Archie tried to hide the shock he was feeling at the sight of his young relative. Without his wig, Law's sandy hair was matted around his face, his fair complexion grey with dirt.

‹You look well, Johnny,› Archie said, determined to be cheerful but feeling awkward and helpless. ‹. . . though perhaps not your usual self.'

'I assure you, Archie, your eyes are not deceiving you. Indeed, there is nothing usual about myself at this moment,' Law replied.

The sarcasm was wasted on Archie, who was carrying a wrapped bundle and now proceeded to open it. He had brought Law his striped waistcoat and rose-colored silk jacket.

'What on earth will I do with that in here?' Law cried, looking at his former finery as though it had arrived from the moon.

'Wear it,' Archie said.

'Kind of you, Archie, to think of it,' Law replied sourly, 'but hardly appropriate.'

'That is where you are wrong, John,' Archie explained, keeping his voice down. 'You are not a debtor. You're here on a charge of murder! If the jailers think of you as prosperous, you will fare much better, I assure you. That is the way of the world. And you shall make a far better impression in the Court if you are dressed like a gentleman.'

Law nodded. 'I am told I can negotiate with the jailer for a better cell for twenty guineas and a weekly rent of eleven shillings. That would be a cell with no *chums*, for that is what they call a cellmate here. But I am now down to my last few pence. They take coins from you for everything you do here.'

'Outrageous!' Archie replied.

'What is not, in this place?' Law asked. 'The keeper justifies his prices by saying that he bought his position for £5,000 and must earn it back from the inmates.'

'A temptation for a man of little principle,' Archie said and reached into one of his deep pockets and produced a flask of whiskie, handing it to his cousin.

Law took a hasty drink. He had eaten little since his arrival, and the liquor went straight to his head with a glow of warmth.

'Keep it,' Archie said. Law needed no more urging to slip the flask into his own pocket. 'You must prepare yourself for the trial, John. You will be asked to plead.'

I shall not plead guilty to murder,' Law said defiantly.

'Nevertheless, you must plead something, for if you refuse, you will be put to torture.

Law nodded grimly. 'That I have seen for myself. They call it *peine forte et dure*, Archie. But I do not understand why those unfortunates are prepared to risk this torture for not pleading, and if need be, die under it.'

'The law is quite specific on this point, John. A prisoner cannot be tried by a jury unless he pleads. If he is reasonably certain that the evidence against him will lead to a conviction, then his goods and property will be forfeit, and his family is left destitute. By refusing to plead, he is guaranteed that this will not happen, and since his death is certain anyway, he willingly undergoes the torture.'

'What shall I plead?' Law asked.

'Manslaughter. But I have no doubt they will free you, John. Of course, they will!

You and Wilson were not fighting like a pair of ruffians. Dueling is a gentleman's sport, after all. That is what you were doing; why you are here. Acting like gentlemen, nothing more.'

'*One* thing more, Archie,› Law pointed out. ‹Wilson is dead.›

'True, Johnny, but you did not set out to kill him. You must be certain that the judge sees this whole unfortunate accident from the proper social aspect,' he warned. His voice had risen into nasal tones resonating just enough to turn the other prisoners' heads towards them. 'You are not permitted a lawyer, so you must write out your statement, giving your side of the case. It will be read out in court by the Sergeant-at-Law, for you will not be allowed even to testify in your own defense.'

'I shall do my best to convince the judge that I am a gentleman by my demeanor, Archie if that is what it will take,' Law replied.

Archie nodded. 'Then you must look like one!' He insisted that Law remove his torn jacket then and there and put on his more flamboyant silk one. 'It would not do for the Court to see your sleeve torn in such a state.'

Law obliged him, exchanging his jacket, but hastily put his cloak over his silk coat. Archie slipped a fat pouch of coins into Law's pocket.

‹You can purchase some small civil treatment with this. And you must buy a cell of your own,› he told him, lowering his voice. ‹We must make a plan for your escape,› Archie whispered, his face screwed into a worried frown. 'Just in case you should not be acquitted.'

'But Archie! You said there would be no chance of a sentence!' Never in his imaginings had Law faced the thought that he might actually be hanged.

'In the hands of the Almighty, John.' Before Law could reply, the turnkey once more unlocked the cell door. Archie had been allowed only five minutes with Law. He kissed his cousin warmly on the cheek. 'I shall be back,' he said and turned sadly towards the door.

When he had gone, Law sat by himself away from the others, his head in his hands. Fleeting images filled his mind. The face of Lord Godolphin was etched in his memory. Godolphin's welcoming look of approval, which had changed so quickly to one of contempt. As he thought of himself once more in the duel, remembered Wilson's cock-sure expression of a man who thought himself invulnerable, Law found himself sinking deeper into depression. Something he had never before experienced. He pulled himself to his feet, pacing the cold stone floor. He must find a solution. But how? Where?

That night when the guard brought each prisoner his food, Law took him aside and counted twenty guineas into the man's hand. 'You shall have the rest when I have my own cell,' he said softly. 'No chums.'

Hastily pocketing the coins, the guard made no sign of even having heard. But that night, when the prisoners were asleep, he came quietly into the cell and roused Law and told him to bring his bedding. He led him down the corridor, and around through a series of barred doors, to another part of the prison where some of the cells had solid doors, some had only bars and appeared to be empty. The guard stopped at one of the barred cells.

'You are not the first gentleman we have had in here,' he assured him using his great key on the heavy lock. 'Several gentlemen, one with a title, have slept here on their way to Tyburn Cross. You'll find all the luxuries available to you. A cleaning woman costs one shilling a week...'

'I'll have her,' said Law.

'...And a whore for the night will cost twelve pence.'

'I think not,' Law said.

The guard shrugged. 'Suit yourself. Well then, a visit from a friend will be sixpence and furniture can be had for ten shillings rent every week.

Law gave the turnkey another guinea. 'There will be more where that came from. A steady stream to bring me candles, a desk, ink, and writing paper. And a good supply of wine and decent food.'

The following day Law sat down at the newly rented table and wrote out his sworn statement to present at his trial. It constituted a plea: guilty of manslaughter. He also wrote a letter to his family. After Archibald Campbell's next visit, he could dispatch it.

He knew that when he was first arrested, Archie had sent a letter to Law's mother, Janet, and younger brother Will. He had made it all sound of little consequence and told them he would look after things—no need for them to come to London unless or until he sent for them.

When he closed his eyes, Law could see Lauriston Castle and his mother and Will, the other children's eldest. He had left Scotland with such high hopes. Now, all he could do was wait and pray.

The Law family, unlike their illustrious cousin Archie, were not of the nobility. But thanks to John's father, William Law's prudent and judicious investments, they could call themselves landed gentry.

In 1683 John's father had purchased Lauriston Castle and the adjoining property of Randleston with its sweep of lands reaching down to the very edge of the Forth. Set in the Midlothian parish of Cramond. It was only a few hours' ride from Edinburgh. The house commanding an excellent view of the river, had been built to defend itself and had done so in the past, its thick walls equipped with apertures for defense.

Though small in size, Lauriston Castle stood five stories high. Oblong in shape, its dark grey stone blocks boasted a projecting circular tower centering the north side, surmounted by apartments above. Two angled turrets several stories high framed the south front. Dormer windows mounted with pediments in the Renaissance style, adorned with thistles and fleur-de-lis, reflected Scotland's on-going relationship with France. One bore the initials S.A.N., for Lauriston had been built in 1572 by Sir Archibald Napier. It provided the eldest son with a title of sorts. The new Laird of Lauriston could properly sign himself *John Law of Lauriston.*

FOUR: THE TRIAL

Lauriston Castle

John's letter to his mother took a week to reach Lauriston. In the long drawing-room, Janet Campbell Law smoothed back a sweep of red-gold hair and opened it with trembling fingers. She read it out to her younger son, Will. John's words were hopeful but realistic. He detailed exactly what had happened and said that now all he could do was await the trial.

Janet, a tall, slender woman with wise grey eyes, was in her mid-forties. She was in good health, and her skin was smooth and clear. Her gown of dark green wool was worn over a cream linen underskirt, which formed a bustle. She wore a tartan shawl of the Campbell colors across her shoulders. She'd prided herself that John took his looks from the Campbell side, although he had inherited his ready wit and engaging manner and abilities with financial matters, from his father. Her glance settled on the carved arms of Lauriston above the mantelpiece mirror.

ARMS OF LAURISTON
BLUE COCKERELS AND RED SASH

The shield was "Ermine, a band between two cocks Gules within a bordure invected gules; the crest, a unicorn's head Proper, and the motto: *Nec Obscura Nec Ima."* Neither Obscure nor Low.

How *low* could it be for her son to be tried for murder, she wondered? Janet's eyes drifted into the mirror. She touched the pearls at her throat, as fine as any in Edinburgh. Her husband had given them to her on their fifteenth wedding anniversary. She would gladly give them to anyone if they helped win her son's freedom.

Will, who had just turned twenty a few weeks earlier, tried to calm her fears and hopefully quell his own. 'Cousin Archie has great influence, Mother,' he told her. 'He will see that John is released. And home again soon.' 'Cousin Archie has the titles, yes, William, but he is profligate. Never could hold onto a penny, that man! The Laws, thanks to your father, have financial security. And money is what your brother requires now,' she said firmly.

'Cousin Archie has always been a good friend to John. . .' Will began, but his mother cut him off.

'You need to feel no deference to your cousin Archibald, William,' she told him firmly. 'Remember that *your* father was a respected man of great charm and style, while Archie›s father died in disgrace. Titles do not make the man.'

Although devastated by the news, Janet was not a woman to sit about weeping when something could be done. She rose from her chair. 'We must go to Edinburgh, Will. At once! And put together sufficient funds for you to take to your brother. There will be lawyers, and more than a few pockets to fill, if John is to be saved.' She hurried towards the hall. 'Tell McGregor to bring the carriage 'round. And then you must pack for London.'

'Yes. Mother,' he said, hurrying out. He was grateful for her ability to translate thoughts into action. Murder! How could John have done such a thing? He worshiped his older brother, but he had no idea of how to begin to set him free.

In their carriage ride into town, Janet returned to thoughts of her husband and all that the two of them had hoped for. Since his death nine years earlier, her one care had been to see her children well established in life. She had no desire to marry again, although there had been offers. Janet was a strong-willed woman who enjoyed her freedom.

'Your dear father›s family may have come from humbler beginnings than mine in his native Parish of Cramond, but he was greatly sought after to advise the businessmen and gentlemen of Edinburgh,' she reflected. 'And indeed, Will, to lend them money when they were in need.'

Will still carried the image of the elder Law dressed in his cocked hat and scarlet cloak walking to his offices in Goldsmith's Hall in Parliament Close and stopping to chat with people of the town along the Kirk Wall, past the many fine shops under the old Tolbooth Stair and then up Our Lady's Steps, jauntily swinging his gold-headed cane, the emblem of his trade.

The elder William Law had been a goldsmith, licensed to lend money in Scotland. Still, somehow when Will's mother spoke of it, she made it sound like his father distributed bounty from Heaven, and his aspirations demanded a higher place on the world stage for his sons. Though he had not lived to see it, their father had been certain that John, at least, would fulfill some great destiny. For himself, young Will had smaller ambitions.

'I do recall that Father would meet some of the common townsmen in the coffee shops and taverns,' Will said, adding, 'From time to time.'

Janet adjusted a stray wisp of hair with the expression of one who›d been caught in a slight untruth. ‹They did meet in taverns, that is true, Will. But it was to discuss investments. Your brother Johnny gets his excellent mind from your father.' Her hands suddenly flew up in anxiety. 'I thought how proud of John your father would be one day. And now this!'

'Try not to worry, Mother. Cousin Archie and I shall bring John home safely, I promise.' It was a promise he had no idea how to keep.

Having gathered up a sizable amount of money, Will packed hastily and left immediately for London. He did not arrive until the night before Law's trial. It took place before the King's and Queen's Commissioners at the Old Bailey and lasted for three days. Will had not been allowed to see John before it. He sat in the Court with Archie, his face pale and silent, and stared across the room to where his brother sat, guarded on either side by two armed Truncheon Officers.

The judge, Sir Salathiel Lovell, in the last doddering stages of a long career, had proudly boasted that he'd been more diligent in convictions than any judge in England. He seemed to relish his words as he read aloud the accusation against John Law for the benefit of the jury. 'John Law of Lauriston, you stand accused of having of your malice aforethought and assault premeditated, made an assault upon Edward Wilson with a certain sword made of iron and steel of the value of five shillings with which you inflicted one mortal wound of the depth of five inches, of which mortal wound the said Edward Wilson then and there instantly died. How do you plead?'

The only defense Law was allowed was the unsworn statement he had so carefully prepared. Unfortunately, despite what Archie may have thought, Sir Salathiel Lovell had no sentiment about the 'honor of gentlemen' when it came to dueling. He made it quite clear to the jury that this was a case of murder, not one of manslaughter.

And when the jury was sent from the Court to deliberate on the third day, they returned scarcely half an hour later. As they took their seats, Law tried to read in their faces what their decision might be, but most of them kept their faces averted from him. The decision was handed to Sir Salathiel Lovell by a Court attendant. He squinted through thin wire spectacles to make out the words, then picked up a black handkerchief and placed it on his head before reading aloud the sentence in a thin, high-pitched voice.

'John Law of Lauriston, you have been convicted of murder. You are hereby sentenced to hang by the neck from Tyburn Tree. May God have mercy on your soul.'

A cry, 'Johnny…!' escaped from William Law's lips. His brother returned his look before he was led away. They had not been allowed the chance to speak.

Archie put his arm around Will's shoulder. 'Do not fear, Will. Now we begin to fight! We shall appeal the case.' Having paid off John's landlady at Seven Dials and gathered up his brother's possessions and papers from his rooms, they took them all to Argyll's rented townhouse in Leicester Street, where Will had moved in with Archie.

The two brothers were nothing alike. William was cautious, quiet, uncomfortable in a social gathering. John was gregarious, always the center of any group. He was a good six inches shorter than John and not so fortunate in appearance, having a larger nose and smaller eyes of a much darker hue than Law's, which were a crystal blue and could pierce right through a person. Will turned a worried glance to Archie.

All that afternoon they'd been discussing the possibilities of arranging an appeal and who they might employ as a barrister when they were surprised by a visit from Lady Katherine Knollys. The butler had put her into a private reception room, where she was awaiting them.

She stood up as they entered. Will thought her the most beautiful woman he had ever seen and could well understand his brother getting into a duel over such a creature. She was dressed like no one in Scotland, in a pale blue moiré traveling suit with grey Persian lamb fur collar and hat. The profusion of violets pinned on her jacket matched the frill of lavender silk at wrists and throat. It seemed to Will that her eyes in the soft candlelight were the color of her violets. But angel though she might look, Katherine was certainly down to earth.

'I have come, your Lordship, to suggest that you launch an appeal on John Law's behalf,' she said in a firm, cool voice.

Archie was quick to assure her that was precisely what they intended to do.

'The jury may sentence how they like,' she told Archie firmly, 'but his Majesty still regards dueling as an honorable method of settling differences between gentlemen.' Her voice took on a note of confidentiality. 'Perhaps I shall be able to assist you in that direction?'

'We should be ever indebted, Madam,' Will said.

'I suggest you employ Sir Creswell Levins and Sir William Thompson. They are both Sergeants-at-Law. I am assured they are the ablest barristers in London, and the perfect choice to defend your kinsman,' she told them.

'I believe I have heard Sir Thompson's name,' Archie said.

'Indeed you might have done, for Sir William Thompson has acquired some little reputation lately for successfully defending Lord Mohun in a rather famous case.' She went on, confiding a recent scandal. 'His Lordship killed the actor, William Mountfort. But since Lord Mohun was allowed to be tried before his peers, that trial took place in the House of Lords.'

'Ahh! the House of Lords!' Archie said glumly.

True, his Lordship had friends on his side. Nevertheless', she said, 'Thompson is the best man to defend John Law.' With that, Katherine left them in a profusion of grateful thanks and the faint scent of violets.

The next day, following her advice, William and Archie employed the services of the two advocates who immediately set about presenting an appeal for Law's pardon. But another month passed before Law was taken to Westminster Hall to answer the appeal. His two lawyers put up a brilliant defense, based upon technical mishandling of the first trial, and Law was granted a reprieve. Elated, Archie and Will hurried to Newgate Prison with Thompson to hasten Law's release, only to discover that he was no longer being held at Newgate!

Thompson was handed a sheaf of documents, and the men were directed to an anteroom to study them. The barrister was a tall, stout man in his forties. He wore a dark grey wig and had a sharp-bridged nose upon which rested a small round pair of spectacles set in thin metal frames. Through these, he carefully perused the documents while Will and Archie sat waiting impatiently.

Thompson finally looked up, his expression grim. 'Your cousin has been moved from Newgate to the custody of the Marshal of Kings Bench Prison, to face a retrial!'

'A retrial?' A bewildered Archie cried. 'But surely, Sir William, he has just been reprieved!'

Thompson shook his head sadly and went on to explain. 'It would seem that Law's reprieve had been canceled!'

'But surely, that cannot be,' Will exclaimed.

'I fear that it can,' Thompson said and carefully folded the documents, slipping them into a voluminous pocket. 'You see, John Law is not the only one whose family is concerned. Wilson's brother, Robert, has stepped in. His new lawyer has dredged up an ancient, and certainly, archaic law called an 'Appeal for Murder.'

'What does it mean?' Will asked.

'It appears that a member of the dead man's family can block any reprieve, where the charge is of murder—and such an appeal is final!' His words resonated in the small room. 'You must both prepare yourself for the worst, for I warn you that the outcome to such an action is not in question. The reprieve, which I had argued so diligently to be granted, is now certain to remain blocked! Long enough, at least, for the noose to be tightened around your brother's neck.'

'Impossible!' Will cried. 'There must be something we can do!'

Thompson shook his head sadly. 'Robert Wilson's private action is entirely possible, Mister Law. It only took a good lawyer to dig it out. Wilson has employed Sir Bartholomew Shower, an excellent man and a former Recorder of London. And. . .' he pursed his lips before saying it, 'This sort of private action is irrevocable.'

They sat silent for a moment. Then Thompson's eyes brightened. 'However, your brother will not be sentenced until the New Year now, as it is near the end of the term for the Court. You shall be able to visit him.'

As the cousins walked out silently to their carriage, they looked at each other, the same thought running through both of their minds.

Now, there was only one thing left to do!

FIVE:
KINGS BENCH PRISON —
ESCAPE!

John Law was manacled and taken by carriage across the Southwark bridge to the borough of Southwark. His guards told him
nothing, but at the Newington Causeway, the carriage turned left
into Blackman Street, where he was to get his first glimpse of the
bleak red-brick fortress that was Kings Bench Prison. Law knew it
to be the second-largest prison in London, and that now, he would
remain there until the hour of his death.

KINGS BENCH PRISON

Imposing and menacing, the edifice made no pretense at architectural niceties. Law guessed the building stretched at least one hundred and twenty yards and the outer wall was at least thirty feet high, running level with the roof.

The guard followed Law's glance. 'If you're thinkin' of climbing' that wall, Mister Law, I shouldn't bother.' He pointed to the top. 'You see them iron spikes?'

Them spins if you touch 'em, they do.'

Law could see for himself that the spikes revolved on their axis. That would make it almost impossible to get a grip on it. And Archie had suggested escape?

'I'm not much at climbing,' he told the guards. 'Never had a head for heights.'

'Good, because escape from 'ere is impossible.' the guard said with a glance at his companion. 'Impossible!'

'Aye, but don't some of 'em just try it, though?' the other chuckled as they drove through the gate. 'Seems as though they're just crying out for a beating!'

'I'm sure I shall find Kings Bench very pleasant,' Law said, hoping that if given half a chance, he must somehow find his way over that wall. His eyes memorized the wide flagstone walk to a central courtyard where three small houses faced one of the squat, square wings. Houses that must back onto the side street!

Seeing where he was looking, the guard was quick to tell him, 'Them houses belongs to the Marshall, the Clerk of the Papers, and the Clerk of the Day Rules. And nobody gets through them, to be sure!'

'Indeed?' Law said. His eyes went to an ominous-looking chapel in the middle of the edifice. No doubt, like Newgate, it would be nothing more than a place for visitors to pay several shillings for the pleasure of a close look at condemned prisoners. In front of it, four elderly prisoners played rackets on a carefully laid out court in the courtyard. Seeing where he was looking, the guard added, 'Some prisoners is allowed to take exercise. For a fee,'

'And some of the debtors is allowed out of the prison by day, and if they can pay, even by night,' the other man said.

'I should enjoy that,' Law said, forcing a smile.

His partner laughed. 'Don't let it give you no ideas, Mister

Law. You're a murderer, sir, and you'll be under lock and key until you hang.'

'One must pay for one's crimes,' Law replied blandly. 'Exactly how many prisoners are here?'

'Seven hundred, by last count,' came the reply, 'Since we only have two hundred and twenty-five cells, it gets some' at crowded.'

Law had learned one lesson at Newgate: If a prisoner was rich enough, the penal system would bend. Hopefully, he could pay to live his last days in privacy. Will had provided him with plenty of money to purchase a 'cabin' to himself and buy proper food, soap and water, and writing paper.

Once inside, placing twenty shillings in the turnkey's hand bought him the cabin, but he was confined to it with no privileges, awaiting the new trial. If he climbed on his table, he could see through his tiny cell window, the thirty-foot wall surrounding the prison.

For the next month, by day, he occupied himself sitting at his table on a spindly wooden stool and formulating a lengthy proposal on his financial proposals. At night he thought about escape. Will and Archie managed to visit regularly, and Will always brought money. Archie brought whiskie.

Law had been pleasantly surprised to hear of Katherine's visit to Will and Archie, and half hoped she would personally send him some word. But he had heard nothing, and she had not contacted Archie a second time.

On Will's next visit, Law gave him a new draft of his financial proposals. 'I have called them, *Considerations on Currency and Commerce,* and I'd be grateful if you could have it printed as a pamphlet,' he told his brother.

Will read the proposal and was deeply impressed with the ideas, although now he believed his brother's schemes were a futile waste of time. But he tried to sound enthusiastic. 'I swear, Johnny, you are a genius! And you have put down your schemes in such a simple and exact way that even a dolt could see the value of them. I shall have them printed by the end of the week.'

'A politician is the one who must value them, and that is even more difficult,' Law said, hunched into his cloak. He had been incarcerated long enough for the chill to settle permanently into his bones. 'See that Archie gets a copy to Lord Godolphin, Will. He may yet present my ideas to King William,' Law suggested. 'Even though I shall not live to see these ideas put into practice, let alone present them to anyone who might promote them,' he sighed glumly.

It was the first time Will had heard the despair in his brother's voice. 'Do not give up hope, Johnny,' he assured him with much more confidence than he felt. 'They shall be printed—and read! And you shall yet see them put into practice. In fact, I shall send a copy to that man Paterson who has opposed you so strongly in the Scottish Parliament. When he reads this, he shall change his tune. I beg you, do not lose heart.'

Law shook his head. 'Paterson has already seen my projections, and I fear he has presented some of my ideas as his own,' he added unhappily.

On the twenty-second of June, 1695, John Law was taken to Westminster Hall to answer his appeal before Chief Justice Holt. There would be no doubt about the sentence; it was a foregone conclusion: death by hanging. Yet Law's counsel managed to slow the proceedings in a welter of legal details and arguments concerning the charge's wording, and other such trivia—anything to delay the noose! Since it was coming to the end of the Court's term, Sir William Thompson even managed to have Law's case put over. The weeks dragged on into three more months.

It was a useful time for John Law. He wrote a second essay on his theories, called *Money and Trade Considered;* but another more urgent project occupied his time. There was one small window just wide enough for a man to slip through. He was not certain where it would lead, but the drop was only one floor.

'One file is worth all the bribes in the world,› he told Will on his next visit. ‹I need tools.'

Will arrived the following day with several small files and the news that John's window faced into the courtyard. Even if he could get through it, he would still have to find his way across the courtyard and somehow scale the wall. And that would not be the end of his problem. The wall was still a thirty-foot drop to the other side!

Each night when the prison was quiet, Law would move his cot as quietly as he could to reach the window, then set to work filing the bars. He slept part of the day. Towards the middle of October, he had managed to loosen four bars.

'Your case is due back in court soon, John,' Will said on his next visit. 'You have very little time. How is it going?'

'I shall try to make it the night before the hearing because they might move me to another cell after that,' Law told Will.

'There will be a carriage waiting after midnight by Newington Causeway. Every night for the week before that, John.'

Yet, at two o'clock in the morning before his retrial, he had still not cut his way through the bars. When the prison was asleep, Law worked on the bars. Then he heard the guard coming down the corridor! A turnkey did not usually inspect the cells at that hour, so Law hastily climbed down, dragging his bed back to its normal position. He did not hear the file fall to the floor in his haste to feign sleep.

The latch on the peephole was slid back, and the guard peered in. Law lay still as a dead man in the dark cell. A moment later, the great key turned, and the heavy door was pulled open, allowing the turnkey's lantern to shine in.

The man followed it into the room, shafting the light around and coming over to Law. A burly, unkempt fellow as tall as Law, with one crooked arm, who looked strong enough to stop a bull full in its tracks. He peered down at Law, then shone the light around the room once more. Had he heard something?

His light caught the glint of metal on the floor! The turnkey walked over to it and scooped up the dropped file. His eyes went to the window. He set the lantern on the floor and reached up. A bar came away in his hand.

'Well, well, well,' he said.

John Law sat up. There would be no hope of escape by fighting the fellow. He gave the turnkey a wry smile and shrugged.

'You cannot blame a man for trying,' he told him sadly.

The guard burst into a roar of laughter and then slammed a heavy arm across Law's face sending him reeling to the floor.

'And you cannot blame me for seeing that this be your last try, Mister Law,' he said.

Law was beaten and placed in irons, and in the morning, he was dragged out of his cell, still in his wrist and leg irons, to face Chief Justice Holt once more.

Any hopes he may have had were dashed when Judge Holt overruled all the legal quibbles that Sergeant-at-Law Thompson had so cleverly produced. Although there would still be one more Appeal Hearing, it was merely a formality because Law would be sentenced with no more appeals. Then, Law would promptly be put to the rope at Tyburn gallows, as all condemned men had been since 1196.

Nor was Law returned to his comparatively comfortable quarters. Now he was placed in a bare cabin at the back of the prison. The rear of the building was so close to the wall that it shed an indescribable gloom over all the lower rooms. He knew he was somewhere near the kitchens because the sour, rancid odors of rotting meat, and the fetid, vile smell of the sewers permeated his cell walls. Fortunately, the Marshall had agreed to remove his irons since this cell was considered escape-proof.

'No chance of getting out of here, Mister Law,' the turnkey said. 'But since you've agreed to the fee, I shall fetch you a table and chair.' He took twenty more shillings for his trouble, bolted the heavy door, and peered through the peephole for a final look at his prisoner, calling back with a chuckle, 'That window there is too high to reach. And your bed is bolted to the floor.'

As evening drew on, Law could hear the sound of the great church bell of St Sepulchre's beginning its long vigil through the night. Some other man was to meet his fate in the morning. A man who would face a crowd of maybe thirty thousand people eager to watch him writhe on the noose. He knew he must think of a foolproof plan of escape and soon, or his gallows would be waiting where his last act would be to give a shilling to the hangman to see the job was done quickly.

But the weeks dragged on, and once again Law was taken for the last time before the judge, now to set a date for his hanging. It was to be on New Year's Day—and still, he had come up with no plan for escape! Then, the day before he was to be hung, Archie arrived with a dour expression and a large bottle of French brandy.

'I bring bad news,' he said.

Law broke into laughter—a sound he had not heard from his own lips for too long. 'Archie, I am to be hung in the morning, and you bring bad news? What can it be? That I shall be drawn and quartered first?'

'It is about your pamphlet and Lord Godolphin, Johnny. He was most impressed with it.'

Law's laughter grew bitter. 'That, I would take as good news, Archie. Although it is of little use to me now,' he added glumly.

'He was so impressed, Johnny, that he took it to the King himself.'

Law sat up. 'He actually presented my projections to King William?'

Archie nodded. 'But the Monarch told him that he would consider no proposals from a condemned murderer.'

A deep sigh escaped Law's lips. 'What does it matter now? After tomorrow no one will remember a few financial projections of a Scotsman, however original.'

Archie tried his best to look cheerful. 'Johnny, a plan is afoot. If all goes well, we shall get you out of here tonight! Will is taking charge of matters at this very moment.'

Although Archie's words held hope, his tone contained no conviction. The sound of the guard could be heard coming towards them. 'Do not drink that brandy!' Archie whispered mysteriously. 'You will have better use of it.' He pulled a single silver goblet from his pocket and set it on Law's table. 'Hide them for now. I can say nothing more!'

'You have said nothing yet, dear cousin,' Law replied, tucking both bottle and goblet away. 'But thank you for your efforts.'

They embraced warmly, and Archie left with a tear in his eye and a final enigmatic comment. 'Expect another visitor.'

Another hour had passed when Law heard the heavy step of the turnkey approach again. This time he was followed by the light click of a woman's heels. The turnkey opened the door wide enough for Law to see a woman with him, in a cheap black woolen cloak. In the dim light, the hood completely hid her hair and face. A bright yellow and black striped gown and white thread stockings flashed through the opening of her cloak. Law looked at her with some surprise. He had never been a man with a taste for the nymphs who plied their trade along the Strand for a shilling and perhaps a pint of wine.

'It's your *sister* here to see you, Mister Law,› the turnkey said with a wink. ‹As it is your last day before your hanging, I shall give you an hour together.›

'I do not require a whore,' Law said angrily.

'She says you are an old customer, Mister Law, and I would not doubt a lady's word. Particularly as she is paying.'

The turnkey held out his hand, and she dropped a gold sovereign into it. He allowed the woman into the cell.

When she spoke to the turnkey, it was in an accent of the streets, 'Don't feel you must hurry back on my account, love!'

She stood there by the door until he had relocked it and returned to his post. Then she removed her hood and mask. Even in her tawdry garments, she was beautiful.

'Have you changed your profession or just your lovers?' he asked ruefully.

'Lost your sense of humor, Johnny?' she asked. 'I thought my disguise rather fetching. Maybe one day, I shall wear it for his Majesty. It might amuse him. He likes a tawdry bit now and then.' She held her arms open to him. 'Now come kiss me,' she said. 'So that you will know it's really your Kate and not a figment of that calculating brain of yours.'

He folded her into his arms and kissed her deeply, aroused by the fragrant warmth of her skin. 'Katherine, I never believed I would see you again.'

'I have seen you though, my love. I am not a lady to miss a duel being fought over her. Poor Edward was such a foolish, headstrong boy.'

'I didn't mean to kill him, Katherine. I want you to know that.'

'I know,' she said sadly, then brightened. 'You smell like a brandy bottle and half the filth of this terrible place, but I still fancy you right here and now.' She threw her arms around him. Tears welled in her eyes. 'Oh Johnny, If I cannot save you, I shall die.'

He laughed. 'That makes two of us, Kate. But it is all of no use. Tonight is New Year's Eve. I am to hang tomorrow, and that's the end of it.' He paced the tiny cell like a caged animal.

'The law can only hang a man when they have him. Is that not true, my Jessamy John?' she asked with a mysterious smile.

He turned towards her and laughed, but it was not with humor. 'Have you seen the size of this prison, Kate? The height of the walls? I cannot even get out of this cell. No, escape is impossible.'

'There is an old proverb, John Law: "One hour's sleep before midnight is worth two after." But it will be your turnkey who sleeps and you who will get the worth of it.'

'What are you suggesting I do, Katherine? That I get the man drunk and tuck him in my bed?' he flared. 'That I knock him senseless before he shouts for help? Is that what you are thinking?'

She reached into her purse and drew out two tiny bottles. 'Here is enough opiate to put the entire jail into the deepest of sleep, Johnny.'

He stared at her with some surprise. She smiled back, sweetly.

'I suggest that in the spirit of the season, you invite your guard in and entertain him with a few of your famous card tricks. Offer him a brimming goblet of that brandy the Earl has brought you. Do it at exactly eleven o'clock tonight. And when he has drunk his fill, you will have no trouble taking his key.'

'Upon my soul, Kate, I knew you had a keen mind for intrigue!' he said, coming over to her.

She reached under her voluminous skirt and removed a butcher's hook tied to a length of rope, unwinding it from her hips and tucked them under his thin mattress, then placed a small map on his table. 'The plan I shall layout for you - after.'

'After what?' he asked, as though he didn't know.

She pulled him to her once more and kissed him passionately. 'It will take more than just a kiss to satisfy me, Johnny. Oh, how I have missed your body next to mine, and the touch of your skin.'

He drew her down onto the narrow bed and slipped his hand under her dress. 'Anything else hidden in here?' he asked, his fingers caressing her tenderly until he found the warm and secret source of his pleasure between her thighs.

'Come find out,' she said, allowing him entrance.

For the moment, Law was able to forget time and place. When all passion was spent, Katherine arose.

'Now Johnny,' she said, 'listen carefully, for here is the plan and you must carry it off without fail!' She outlined it quickly in a whisper.

A guard could be heard calling: ‹Strangers, women, and children! All out!' and the last warning, 'Past nine o'clock! All strangers out!'

'He will be back for you any minute,' Law said. 'After the third warning, the gates are locked.'

She kissed him goodbye. 'Midnight, Johnny,' she said as the turnkey came to unlock the door. 'The carriage will be waiting near the causeway.'

Between them, Archie, Will, and Katherine had devised a plan that seemed simple enough when she had told it to him. The doing of it might be another matter. But the odds were in favor of the attempt because he was holding the losing hand.

Somewhere in the night, the church bell of St. Sepulchre paused in its steady tolling to strike eleven o'clock. Then it continued in its monotonous dirge.

Through Law's window, the moonlight added a spectral glow to the snow clinging to the high walls. He was freezing, and a drink would warm him, but he knew he must remain clear-headed now if his escape were to take place without him being shot. And if he thought about it, he would prefer to be shot escaping than to be a willing accomplice at his own hanging. Perhaps Brounley had been right. Why go willingly?

To his surprise, he heard someone ringing a handbell outside his cell door. Whoever it was, rang the bell twelve times, and then opened the peephole calling through it: 'John Law! This is the church sexton of St Sepulchre. I have come to remind you of your fate!'

Without waiting for a reply, the sexton shouted a poem mournfully through the peephole:

'All you that in the condemned hold do lie,
Prepare you, for tomorrow you shall die;
Watch all, and pray, the hour is drawing near
That you before the Almighty must appear;
Examine well yourselves, in time repent,
That you may not to eternal flames be sent,
And when St Sepulchre's bell tomorrow tolls,
The Lord above have mercy on your souls.'

Brounley had told him of this curious practice, which had been carried out since the beginning of the 17th century. It seemed that a rich man of the parish had left money to the church for the poem he had written himself, to be read to the dying man.

Law heard the sexton's footsteps fading as he departed and the clink of a further door.

'Hardly Shakespeare,' Law muttered and banged on the door of his cell shouting, 'Turnkey! Hey Bill! Are you out there! Hey, I say, can you hear me?'

The commotion brought the dour-faced turnkey. It was a freezing night, and he would have preferred to be at home with his woman, tucked up into his truckle bed. But he was inclined to be benevolent when his charge was to hang in the morning.

'What is it you want, Mister Law? They shall not come to take you away for another hour yet.'

'It is New Year's Eve, my friend. And as tomorrow shall see the end of John Law, I invite you not to let a dying man drink alone. Come share a last drink of cheer with me,' Law said, holding up the brandy bottle. 'French stuff. The very best! Brought me by the Earl of Argyll himself.'

The guard hunched his shoulders against the chill, looking at the bottle. 'Aye, there's not much cheer out here tonight, 'tis true and bloody cold, too. My stove is near out of wood, and no one to fetch more 'til the dawn.'

'I shall be delighted to go outside and fetch some for you,' Law said with a grin. His remark brought a hearty laugh from the turnkey.

'And a swallow of brandy will soon put the fire back inside you!' Law said, pouring out a stiff drink into the silver goblet, holding it up temptingly.

The turnkey hesitated. His throat was dry, and he could almost feel the sharp burn of the brandy in his gullet.

'Come, my friend, and take a dram,' Law urged. 'It will do you a world of good, and I promise, you shall sleep like a babe tonight. You know, in Scotland, we say the taste is sweetest from another man's bottle.'

The turnkey hesitated, but Law was not to lose this round if he could help it. 'I shall give you a riddle, Bill. Why does salvation await you in this drink?'

'Sure, I'm no good at riddles, Mister Law,' Bill replied, scratching his head but somehow intrigued.

'I shall tell you the answer. Too much brandy puts you to sleep, does it not?

And sleep leaves a man no time for sin. Well then, since a man who avoids sin is a saved man, this drink offers salvation.' Law's voice sounded merry.

The turnkey scratched his head, figuring it out, then took up his large key. 'You do have a way with words, Mister Law.'

'Come in, my friend. We shall pass the lonely hour until they come for me, playing at cards. I shall show you a trick you will never have seen before.'

The flicker of Law's single candle sparkled on the soft curve of the silver goblet.

The guard unlocked the barred door, licking his tongue over his dry lips. 'Well, I reckon there's no harm in a little drop to see in the New Year, and you to swing at the dawn.'

'I only wish that infernal bell would stop ringing,' Law said, stepping back to the table.

'When it does, you shall be dead, and that is no joke, sir,' the turnkey said, locking the door after himself. The keys dangled from his belt. He stared at the silver goblet. 'Such a fine goblet. I cannot drink from that.'

'Nonsense, you are my guest tonight! And when I leave for the tree, the goblet shall be yours as a gift.' He filled the goblet, then raised the bottle to his lips. 'The bottle shall do me fine.'

The turnkey accepted the goblet from Law's hand and swallowed a mouthful.

'Now sit down, my friend.' Law indicated the bed. The turnkey sat down.

'You're a true gentleman, Mister Law,' he said 'I shall be sorry to see you go.'

'No more than I, and that is the truth,' Law said and took a tug on the bottle. He set it back on the table and pulled a deck of cards from his pocket, riffling them expertly. The turnkey took another deep drink, watching the cards, which seemed to flutter so fast that they were all of a blur. Law offered them to him, face down.

'Warm yourself with another sip, my friend, and pick one of these cards. But do not tell me what it is.'

The turnkey finished off the drink at a gulp and reached for the cards. Katherine's opiate acted quickly, for as he blinked groggily, the goblet fell from his hand. He followed it down, crashing head-first on the stone floor.

Law was instantly on his feet. They would be coming for him at midnight to put him in irons ready for the morning when they would place him on a hurdle and drag him to Tyburn tree. He hauled the bulky man onto the pallet, hastily removed his keys and dirty woolen jacket, exchanging it for his own silk coat. Now he would have no need for gentlemanly finery. He took the butcher's hook from beneath his mattress, tied the rope around his waist to make a secure belt, then rolled the drugged man over to face the wall, covering him with his cloak.

'Sweet dreams,' he said and hurried to the cell door, with the ring of keys.

He let himself out and closed the cell as quietly as he could, starting down the corridor. It was dimly lit by one small torchier stuck into a wrought iron ring on the wall. The light danced eerily, throwing sharply waving patches onto the floor. This corridor was reserved for men sentenced to hang, and for the moment, John Law alone had that honor.

From somewhere ahead, the movement of another guard brought him to a halt in a shadowy recess. Behind a second barred door, he could see a guard sitting at a small table. Law pulled Katherine's map from his pocket—a crude rendition made by an ex-prisoner, showing the jail's interior. It had a path marked for him to follow to the kitchens. He would have to pass that guard to reach it!

But how was he to accomplish that? Time was running out!

He waited in the shadows and carefully removed the key to his own cell from the ring. He crept silently to the bars and, taking careful aim, threw the key into a side passage to the guard's right. It clinked sharply on the stone floor. The guard turned towards the noise, pushed back his chair, and rose, going to investigate down the passage.

When his footsteps grew faint, Law hurried to the barred gate, searched out the right key, opened it stepping through. The guard's table stood just below another torchier. A movement turned him to face the man who was now pointing a large brass blunderbuss directly at him.

'I would advise you to raise your hands, Mister Law or I shall kill you 'ere and now.'

Law raised his arms much more swiftly than the guard had expected and caught hold of the torchier. Without a moment's hesitation, he jammed the burning stick straight into the wide bell-shaped muzzle of the blunderbuss just as the guard fired the gun. The blunderbuss exploded in the man's hands.

Law did not wait to discover the results of his act. He ran swiftly down the dark corridor until he saw a feeble light coming from what he guessed to be the scullery. He could hear the voices of the cook and his helpers preparing the breakfast gruel. There was an exit from the kitchens marked on the map, but there was no hope of escape there, with people inside. He moved on slowly. He heard the night patrol approaching the courtyard entrance just a few yards past the kitchens. They would catch him if he moved forward, and he could not go back!

He noticed two slops buckets standing between the kitchen door and the courtyard entrance. They smelled of foul, stinking bones. Law rubbed his hands on the sweaty, blackened wall and smeared his face with the soot. He took up a bucket in each hand and stooping like the old slops carrier he had seen carrying his buckets.

He started for the entrance just as the door swung open, and the Sergeant of the Watch entered, clapping his hands together against the freezing night. It had begun to snow again, and fine white dust powdered the man's shoulders. Law brushed past him, imitating the slops man's shuffling gate, and offered the Sergeant a grunted greeting.

The Sergeant eyed him, asking, 'Why are you taking out the slops at this hour, eh?'

Law cocked his head and made his voice into a croak. 'So's I'll be free to watch Beau Johnny Law swing on the rope in the mornin', Sergeant.'

The Sergeant of the Watch chuckled. 'Well, look out, you don't hang with him, old man!'

Law hurried out the door and into the narrow walkway between the building and the great stone wall—a wall surmounted by those revolving iron spikes! He could see a single watchman on duty in a sentry post at the top of the wall. The man had a long musket across his shoulder. Law knew he also carried an alarm bell.

He was outside the building but no closer to freedom. Somehow, he had to get to the top of that thirty-foot wall and over it! The narrow flight of steps up to the top of the wall was near the post box where the slops were regularly dumped over the other side. He moved purposefully to the steps, whistling as he had heard the old slops carrier do. The watchman looked down casually towards Law, but seeing that he was carrying the slops, paid him no particular attention.

As Law began to mount the steps, the guard came out of his post box, moving a few feet closer. Law reached the top and gave a sharp intake of breath as he looked down the other side at the thirty-foot drop. His glance lifted towards Newington Causeway. In the far distance, where it met Southwark Bridge Road, he could make out a coach etched in black silhouette against the ground's whiteness. It clung to the slender shadow of a bare-limbed tree, too far away to see who was inside.

The watchman had his back to Law, so he set the slops pails down on the top of the wall and removed the butcher's hook and rope from his belt. He quickly hooked it across an iron spike, jamming it, making it firm. Holding it tightly, he was about to jump when the watchman turned and glanced his way with rising curiosity.

The watchman started towards Law, calling out,' You...! What're you doin' 'ere at this hour...?'

Law caught the look of recognition as the watchman drew abreast of him on the narrow top of the wall. Law heaved a slops bucket into the man›s face, and the watchman reeled back, nearly tumbling off the wall. Law grabbed hold of his rope and jumped. But when he was but a few yards down the side, the hook slipped its anchor, and he plummeted to the earth below.

Above him, he could hear the guard cry out, 'Escaped prisoner…! Sergeant of the Guard!'

Law lay for a moment, stunned. A musket shot sent a flurry of snow and dirt into his face. He tried to get up, but his left leg gave way. The coach was moving towards him now, picking up speed. As it reached him, it paused, and the door swung open. Two men leaped out just as another shot was fired. The clanging of the alarm bell cut through the chill air!

As Law tried again to get to his feet, he felt strong arms lift him, and he was hoisted into the coach, which clattered out into the night, followed by a fusillade of shots from the wall.

Inside the coach, Law was given a drink of whiskie from a gentle hand. Katherine smiled at him.

'Surely you knew I could not let you make the journey to freedom without a proper send-off, Johnny. Now let me look at that leg.'

His leg had not been broken, but the ankle was badly sprained and already swelling.

'You are not the first man to leap from a prison wall, my love,' Katherine said, binding it with a strip of linen. 'The great artist, Benvenuto Cellini, leaped thirty feet to freedom from the castle of San Angelo in Rome, and he lived to tell the tale.'

'So will you,' Archie assured him. 'Now rest a bit, for you have a difficult way ahead.'

He had been sleeping fitfully in the coach, his head in Katherine's lap, for several hours when he woke with a start to a strong smell of sea air. He looked out the window, confused. 'This is not the road to Scotland,' he said.

'There is no place for you in Scotland now, John,' his brother told him. 'Since you've been in jail, England and Scotland have passed a treaty of Union. You are now a fugitive there, too!' He reached down and pulled up a valise. 'I have packed your papers and clothes. You must change.'

Law proceeded to take off his filthy garments.

'There is a fishing boat waiting at Dover to take you across the channel, Johnny,' Archie said.

Will handed him a money sack. 'It is as much gold as we could lay hands on.' He smiled. 'You will no doubt double it across some table very soon.'

'We will spend the night at an inn,' Katherine said. 'It is all arranged. She smiled. 'I fear I shall have to play the part of your wife.'

'Why don't you come with me and play the part forever?' Law asked.

'My road must take a different turning.' Katherine said sadly, forcing a bright smile. 'Where will you go, Johnny?'

He glanced out at the island that he never expected to see again. 'Wherever the boat shall take me.'

LADY KATHERINE KNOLLEYS

SIX: A SHIP TO WHERE?

In the small hours of the morning, Will and Archie Campbell saw the fugitive safely to a Norse herring boat sailing from Dover for the Netherlands; its destination, Rotterdam. It was raining heavily, and an icy wind slapped the limp sails of several ships preparing to embark as they stood on the dock for one last goodbye.

'Where will you make for, from Rotterdam?" Will asked his brother, his voice choked.

Law had made no such plans, but seeing the dismal expression on Will's face, he tried to sound positive. 'I shall stay in Holland for a while, Will. Go to the Hague. It's the center of diplomatic affairs.'

The men crossed the slippery wharf to the herring boat's gangplank. The Captain had been well paid to carry this passenger, asking no questions. Law set down the valise that Will had so hastily packed for him.

'The Hague. . .' Will repeated the word as though it were someplace on the moon.

'And then, I'll head for Amsterdam and their Bank,' Law continued. ‹It finances most of the Continent, and I should like to have another look at it. Then perhaps I shall make my way to Paris. France is a country whose finances always seem in turmoil. They could use a man like me.›

'But France and England are still at war, Johnny,᠈ Archie reminded him, pulling his hat down to shield himself from the rain.

'Don't worry yourself, Archie,' Law said. 'Fortunately, we Scots have always been friendly to France.'

Law was well aware that as a former Prince of Orange and Stadtholder of the Union, England's King William III, hoping to

maintain the balance of power in Europe, had united the Netherlands with England against Louis XIV of France. From Flanders,
William had led the English into annual campaigns, laying siege to
many of France's fortified towns.

Law squinted into the rain, feeling the ache in his leg. His
brother looked so worried he had to say something cheerful. 'And
thanks to you both, Will, I have not paid the hangman his shilling!'

Will forced a smile. 'No, Johnny. And France would not
send you back to England or Scotland.'

‹Still, it might be easier for me to travel through the Low
Countries first,› Law said, trying to sound optimistic. ‹Then I shall
take my chances at crossing the border into France.›

Archie nodded and was silent. He had supplied Law with
a paper giving him another identity. Law's name on the passenger
list was now John Gardener, Esq. The paper stated that Mr. Gardener was acting as an agent for the Earl of Argyll.

He and Katherine had said their farewells earlier at the Inn
where they had spent the night as John Gardener, Esq. and Mistress
Gardener. His leg hurt more than he cared to admit, but he did not
wish to leave Archie, and Will worried about his welfare. He knew
how difficult the moment was for the others. Will had given him all
the money that was left from the trial. It would be enough to buy
lodgings and a fine horse in Holland, and Archie had presented
him with his own two Scottish flintlocks. He would travel safely.

'Please write to Mother as soon as you are settled,' Will said.

When I can,' Law replied. 'Give her my love and remind
her I can look after myself, as she well knows. She is not to worry!'
He held Will close for a moment and then drew back. 'Nor are you,
Will!' He was not a man to whom tears came easily, and now he
was fighting them back.

Archie grabbed him and whispered, 'God bless you, John!'
The rain had stopped for the moment, and the wind had let up. It
was as though time itself had stopped. They looked at each other
for one last moment; then, Law turned and started up the gangplank.

Once on deck, he stood at the ship's railing and watched his
brother and Archie return to their waiting coach, wondering where
and when he would see them again. He knew they would dispose

of their affairs in London and return to Scotland as quickly as possible. He headed for his cabin and some rest.

But Law's plans were thwarted from the start. He had not counted on the strict security measures when the ship docked at Rotterdam. The Dutch were constantly on the lookout for Jacobite supporters, and just as Law was preparing to disembark, the Captain came to his cabin.

'Give me your papers and stay on your bed, Mr. Gardener. I shall deal with the authorities,' the Captain told him. He took Law's false papers, closed the cabin door, and walked leisurely back to the port guards as they came aboard.

Law could hear them questioning the Captain about his passenger. He was not the first man with a price on his head who had traveled on this ship, and the Captain gave away little in his replies. 'Mr. Gardener' is sick in his cabin,' he said and reminded the guards that unless a person left his ship without the proper papers, the port had no authority.

When they had gone, he came and told Law, 'I cannot put you ashore here in Rotterdam, Mr. Gardener, or I should never be able to land in this port again.'

Law rose from the bed, angry now. 'You were well paid to deliver me safely!'

'Be that as it may, you have had your safe passage, sir. This ship is to sail back to England, and by the book, you will have to be on it.' The Captain left Law in the cabin, locking the door behind him.

Law listened to the creak of the old boards as the ship swayed at anchor. He would, if he stayed aboard, be returned to prison and the hangman's rope! But he had come this far, and at any cost, he not to be taken back. Locked in the cabin, he waited. But time passed, and the Captain did not return. The ship still lay in anchor as darkness fell.

Finally, he heard the heavy steps of the Captain's returning, and a key was turned in his lock. But nobody entered—and the footsteps faded away. Law was on his feet in a bound, cautiously opening the door.

Nobody in sight. He picked up his valise, closed the door

quietly behind him, and hurried across the empty deck, taking shelter behind the lugsails waiting until the dock below was clear of workers. There were at least six ships in the port, and the dock lamps threw heavy shadows past stacked supplies waiting to be loaded aboard vessels, come the morning light. The sky was clear, and a crescent moon was tipped on its side. Tomorrow there would be rain.

Law made his way off the herring boat and was crossing the dock when the herring boat's alarm bell sounded. Taking cover in the shadows behind some bales, Law stood still, listening. The bell had alerted the port guards who came running onto the dock, pistols drawn, a short distance from Law.

Law could see no way past the guards and out of the port. He watched them troop up the gangplank to speak to the herring boat's Captain, who led the men into Law's cabin. Law smiled to himself. This Norwegian Captain was not such a bad sort after all. Still, he could have waited a few minutes longer!

Near him, a fully rigged three-masted schooner was preparing to set sail; he could not see what flag she was flying but was certain the ship was not British. He moved quickly to it as the crew was about to pull up the gangplank. He waved to them and called that was coming aboard. In the distance, Law could hear the port guards leaving the herring boat.

The schooner's Captain met him on the deck, demanding to know what he wanted aboard his ship. The man's accent was Dutch. Law hastily produced his bag of gold and his faked papers.

The Captain stared at him for a moment, then offered his hand. 'Your gold is as good as the next man's, Mr. Gardener.'

‹I must have a cabin to myself,› Law demanded.

The Captain nodded, leading him around the aft deck to a cabin. The ceiling was so low that Law had to stoop to crawl inside. 'This will do nicely,' he said, thinking it better than a cell. 'I have had a tiring journey and wish to rest now until you set sail,' He said and closed the door on the Captain, who went off jingling his gold.

It was not until the sails were hoisted, and they had captured the wind that Law stirred from his cabin and came out on the deck. He had not even thought to ask the Captain where the Dutch schooner was bound. Now he asked.

'To the Americas,' the Captain told him.

Law made an effort to absorb the news. The shock faded, and a smile lit his fine features, as the gambler in him took hold. 'The Americas, you say, Captain? He took in a chest full of sea air, reviving his flagging spirits. "Thank the good Lord! I just wanted to be certain I had taken the right ship."

For the first time since he had killed Edward Wilson, he felt a free man. Who knew what he might find in that far off continent? He had heard that escaped criminals could do very well in the Americas.

At Lauriston Castle, Archie and Will had returned to find Janet trying to hide worry but deeply distressed. She clung to her younger son, releasing the tears she had held back. Archie comforted her with the news that he had been able to put out a false description of Law that had been published in the London Gazette, along with an offer of a reward for his capture.

Janet donned wire-rimmed spectacles and held the newspaper up to the light to read: 'Captain John Law, a Scotchman, aged twenty-six. Tall, hair black, lean; well-shaped, about six feet high...' she broke off, looking up at Archie accusingly. 'But that is a very accurate description, Archie. Except that his hair is not black!'

'Read on, my dear Janet, 'Archie replied.

She returned her attention to the Gazette reading: 'With large pock-holes in his face; big-nosed, and speaking broad and loud.' The hint of a smile touched her lips. 'My Johnny is certainly one of the most handsome men in Scotland, and that is not just a mother's opinion,' she said firmly. 'And his voice is quite melodic, is it not William?'

'Yes, indeed it is,' Will said. 'So, you see, Mother, the reward will have to wait.'

'They shall never find him with that description,' Archie assured her.

She nodded, a smile softening her face. 'John is resourceful and of all men, most able to take care of himself. That is what his father said when John was merely a lad of twelve. He will be a great success one day. That was what you said, Archie! What all who knew him said of my eldest son!' Her eyes saddened again.

'And now he is fugitive with a reward offered for his apprehension, roaming the Continent, and perhaps starving!'

Tears blinded her eyes at the thought.

'Johnny will never starve, not as long as there is a gaming table in the world. He will be traveling in style, I warrant you,' Archie told her, and then his expression changed to one of self-importance. 'Now I must get down to Edinburgh, dear cousin. I have a meeting with my political allies of The Squadrone.'

Archibald, Earl of Argyll rose, kissed his cousins warmly, and vowed to see them soon. The first to hear from John would no doubt be Janet. She must let him know at once, he told her as he departed.

But several years were to pass without any word from, or of John Law, and 'traveling in style' was not what he'd found himself doing. After landing in the Gulf of the great Mississippi River, he traveled upriver from the French Louisiana Territories to the wilderness where trappers hunted for beaver skins to send back to Europe. Whenever his money ran out, he was generally able to find a game of cards. As usual, playing his odds, he won more than he lost.

In this wild land, nobody knew him nor could have cared less if they did. Nevertheless, he still traveled under the name of Gardener. The white men he had come across in these wilds were there to find a new life, however primitive. More likely, like himself, they had escaped from something in their past.

And so it was that on a Spring morning in 1700, John Law, alias John Gardener, was sitting on the flat bottom of a river barge floating down the Mississippi River. It had emptied its cargo of logs at Fort Maurepas and headed the last forty miles towards the river's mouth, in the Gulf. The air was heavy with the smell of the moist riverbank, the hum of bees, and the shrill calls of the strange large birds that Law had never seen in Europe.

Having finished unloading the logs, the bargeman and crew rested on the deck. They were rugged men all and used to the rough life. Law had paid the French bargeman named Antoine Desalt, his last few coins to ride back downriver, determined to reach its mouth. He had finally decided to take a ship, perhaps back to Holland.

Desalt was somewhere in his early forties. His chin had not been seen for years, screened behind a well-worn thatch of beard. He had accepted 'Mr. Gardener' aboard as a paying passenger and had taken a liking to him because he spoke French. He told Gardener his own story. He had arrived with the explorer la Salle, a man intent upon settling a colony in the territory. When la Salle failed, Desalt left him and took to running this barge.

When Law's money ran out, he taught the bargeman to play Hazard and, in exchange, learned the refinements of an American game called Craps. Desalt was a fast learner and had won a few hands at cards, but had great respect for his passenger's knowledge of numbers.

Desalt's wide-set eyes probed into Law, searching for the truth. 'I would have thought you were cheating, Mr. Gardener. But for the fact that the dice are my own,' Desault told him, pushing his hat brim back from thickly matted hair. But as fast as John Law won from Desalt and the logmen and the fur trappers they met along the way, he was forced to hand back most of his winnings in payment for his food and further travel.

At night they exchanged tales of the past. Although Law gave nothing away from his own background, it seemed that Desault was eager to talk. He had come from a small town in Normandy where he had been a school teacher.

'How I filled my students with tales of the New World, a place I had seen then, only in my imagination,' he told Law. ‹But I longed for a more adventurous life.' Desalt looked away, remembering what he had left behind. 'I am not proud of what I did, for I left a wife and two daughters and disappeared.' His voice took on a defensive tone. 'I venture that I am not the first man to have done so.' He looked up at Law. 'Sometimes, I think of going back, but I know I never shall.'

'I wonder if I ever will,' Law said, glancing across at the unfathomable forest that edged the upper banks of the Mississippi. He knew little enough of the place wherever he now found himself and was full of questions to Desault. In the evening when the work was done, the Frenchman spent long river hours spinning tales he'd learned of the territory's history.

'Spaniards were the first white men in these lands, and I

taught my students about the explorer de Pineda, who was said to have reached the Mississippi River in 1519.'

'Nobody seems to have done much with it since,' Law said with little enthusiasm.

Where the Mississippi crossed with the Red River, Desalt tied up the barge, telling Law about the Spaniard, Hernando de Soto, who had followed de Pineda's trail into the Territories. 'Come,' he said. 'De Soto's burial place is not far from here. You shall see it for yourself.'

Law had gone with him on a trail through a grove of trees and had stood over the grave. It was marked by a wooden cross with only the words 'de Soto' carved into it. Law wondered what made a man risk a lonely burial place for such wild explorations. 'I fear I much prefer the noise and chatter of a gaming house and the beautiful women who frequent such places,' Law remarked. 'The sight of hundreds of brightly lit candles softly glowing on pale skins. That is what excites me.'

'It is not a world I know, Mr. Gardener,' Desalt said wistfully.

Such thoughts made Law wonder where Katherine was now. She was the only person he had written to, and that, only once when he was staying for some time in the northernmost part of the river. Whether the letter had ever reached her, he could not know. There had been no answer, and he was certain that she had forgotten him with the passing years, no doubt with many lovers. When he closed his eyes, he could see her sly half-smile, so knowing, so sure of herself. And yet when he had held her in his arms so long ago, she was all giving and all desire for what he wanted most to give her.

Law's thoughts had been drifting. He focused once again on Desalt's tale. The Frenchman was speaking of the survivors of that ill-fated de Soto expedition. '. . . and they did not discover the mouth of the river until twenty years after de Soto's death.' Desalt shook his head sadly. 'That is Fate for you, Mr. Gardener. De Soto gave his life to the search, and someone else got the glory.' Desalt leaned back against a tree, lighting what the Indians called a *segar*, a practice he had picked up from them. Law had tried one of those segars, but it was a habit he did not like. Desalt puffed on the thick wad of tobacco tightly rolled into a leaf as they headed through the trees back to the barge.

'You know, Mr. Gardener, I have always thought it curious that Spain set no claim on this territory.' Law scooped up a handful of earth and smelled it - so rich! What crops could be introduced into such fertile soil, he wondered?

'I'd say there is a great deal here to claim,' Law said thought-fully.

Desalt nodded in agreement. 'Thank heaven they left it free for a Frenchman, or I should not be here. Robert Cavalier, Sieur de la Salle—that great man traveled down from the French posses-sions in the north when it was really all wilderness, as I can attest, He claimed the entire territory for France! And I was a member of that perilous expedition,' Desalt said with some pride.

Once again, the two men boarded the barge, untied the ropes, and pushing away from shore. The barge drifted out, and Desalt's crew used poles to steer it into the current.

'We shall reach a bend in the river by dawn tomorrow,' De-salt told Law. I shall drop my load of logs there, to be collected by one of the ships that come up-river.'

Law watched Desalt deftly controlling the barge downriver and wondered how a schoolteacher had ended up here.

'It was 1684 when we came,' Desalt continued with his tale. 'Robert la Salle named this place Louisiana in honor of King Lou-is XIV. But La Salle was not lucky. He missed the river's mouth. Landed further west. Where he was murdered three years later.' He paused. 'By one of his followers.'

His hand resting on his flintlock pistol, Desalt seemed re-luctant to discuss that part of the tale, which made Law wonder if he had been that murderous follower. Desalt related how, only a few years later in 1697, a second colony had been attempted under another Frenchman, Pierre Le Moyne d'Iberville.

'It was he who erected the fort we've just come from. Fort Maurepas,' the bargeman said. He told Law tales of the natives whom the white men called Indians—and of a beautiful princess he had encountered when trading beads for food.

On their many stops along the way, the Frenchman intro-duced Law to several friendly tribes. The Indians gave them strange golden stalks covered in coarse green leaves, which Desalt roasted over a fire. The leaves were thrown away, and the yellow kernels were sweet to the taste and quick to satisfy hunger.

It was plain to Law that this French-owned Louisiana Territory was a land without boundary and a land of plenty. For days on end, he had looked out at the vast emptiness, rich with timber, and who knew what else? Among the strange birds that he had seen along the shore were large creatures with a red crop that hung down at their throats like a scarlet lace stock. They made a gobbling sound unlike any he'd ever heard.

'What are these ugly birds?' Law asked.

'Those are called *Dindons*. If you frighten them, they do not fly away,' the Frenchman told him. He picked up his rifle. A fine marksman, he shot one of the birds, and later, they cooked it. 'The local Indians consider the meat a rare delicacy,' he told his passenger, and Law found the breast meat white and tasty. In the clear night sitting on the flat deck, the two men ate with their fingers and fell silent, listening to the birdcalls. Law's thoughts returned to the very different world of Lauriston and to his mother.

Dinner was always a special part of the day with Janet. She would lead the way into the dining room, its walls covered in dark tapestries to keep in the warmth spreading thinly from a large stone fireplace. Heavy silver sconces provided a soft glow of candlelight. Fat beeswax candles formed a neat row down the long oak board. The younger children would have eaten earlier, and John and Will ate with their parents. His mother was justly proud of her table. It was laid with a fine linen cloth and at each place was a silver-handled knife, fork, and spoon. At the head of the table in front of John was a large ornate silver saltbox. Few people except the nobility could afford such luxuries, but Law's father had made them all at his goldsmith's shop.

Lauriston was John's now. He had inherited it when he was twenty-one, and one day, he had hoped to see his own children running across Lauriston's park or playing by the hearth. A day that would never be… Never now.

As he lay on a pile of burlap sacking looking up at a night sky alive with millions of stars, John Law dreamed of an outrageous scheme to fertilize this uncharted new world he had come to. Who knew what treasures could be found in the hills, or deep in the ground in this wild land? Gold? Silver? Diamonds?

Why not? What would it take to develop such a territory, he wondered? Courage. Unique inventiveness, certainly. Men and ships to transport them, obviously. But most of all, money.

More than the wealth of one man.

It would take billions. The person who could develop such lands would have to be at least a king. And was there a crown head in all of Europe who would have the resources? Or the imagination?

This territory belonged to France, but Louis XIV concentrated all his attention on fighting pointless wars in Europe, and he did nothing with his foreign possessions. Now, like John Law, France was at its financial bottom. It was easy for Law to dream great schemes floating down this mighty river, like so many other of his great schemes in the past, schemes with no foreseeable future. But such odds never stopped a gambler or a dreamer.

He glanced over to where the bargeman had been sleeping. His place was empty. Desalt was standing, staring out at the river and listening to the distant cry of a lone wolf.

'Can't sleep, eh, Desalt?' Law called out.

Desalt turned to him, shaking his head. The moonlight was so bright his features were clearly etched. The long chin, the wide-set eyes, the long matted hair, the thick beard thatched with grey. 'That dindon - too rich. My stomach is not what it used to be.'

‹Fancy a game of cards?› Law asked, sitting up and drawing the well-thumbed pack from his pocket. Desalt came over with a smile and sat down beside him.

'You always win, Monsieur Gardener, but since you pay it back to me for food and transport, I am happy to pass the time losing to you. Voilá! We shall play one more hand before we reach the bend in the river. For there we must part company. It is as far as I go.'

Law passed the cards to Desalt to shuffle and cut. The older man dealt them slowly onto the top of a wooden storage box. They played until the horizon was filled with a golden light that touched their weary faces. Law collected his winnings and leaned back against a crate, closing his eyes. He had carefully tucked away from each game won, enough, he hoped, to purchase a ticket to somewhere.

When Law awoke, Desault and his men were maneuvering the barge to a landing at a narrow ledge of land on the east riverbank. Further on, cypress swamps lay between the river and a lake. The place was barren, save for a few shacks and a log cabin with a sign offering food and lodging for a price. Here, boats came up from the river's mouth to take the trappers' furs and the logs that men like Desault brought further down-river. It was a splendid landing point for small commerce. *What a place to build a city,* Law thought to himself.

But there were more pressing matters to concern this weary traveler. He had won enough of a stake from the bargeman, but a stake to where? France, maybe. Maybe now, the time was right. Maybe now in France, his ambitions could become realities. Maybe he could somehow get to the ear of Louis XIV.

'Nothing is impossible if one puts one's mind to it - and pulls the right strings,' he said out loud, climbing onto the river bank. Desalt looked over at him questioningly. It was an answer to no question. Standing on that lonely shore, Law felt as though he had been drifting not only down-river but through a long dream that had started the day he killed Edward Wilson. He looked at the sunrise highlighting the shoreline in a golden curve and breathed deeply of the fresh river air. Suddenly, and for no reason, he had hope. Maybe now was his moment in time. 'I said, sir,' he told Desalt. 'Nothing is impossible!'

SEVEN: SARDINIA
AND VICTOR AMADEUS

In Lauriston Castle, Janet Law looked up from her chair by the fire as Will burst into the room. She was knitting him a scarlet scarf to wear to Goldsmith's Hall with his cocked hat and a scarlet cloak, since he, not John, had taken up his father's profession.

'What is it?' she cried, seeing the intoxicated look on his face as he waved a letter in the air. 'It is from Johnny, isn't it?' she said, with a soft intake of breath.

'He has written, at last, Mother!' Will held the letter unopened, out to her.

'No, Will - you must read it first,' she told him, afraid of what it might say.

He tore open the red wax seal, coming over to the firelight, and slowly unfolded the sheet, reading it silently drinking in John's words. Finally, he waved it towards his mother. 'He is in Holland! In Amsterdam. Mother, he is alright!' Will returned his attention to the letter.

'But where has he been all these years, without a word?' she wondered.

Will stared at the letter, looking up puzzled. 'He does not say.'

Her lips pursed slightly. 'Well, I do not care where he has been! All that matters is that he is alive. And safe now.' Tears of relief dampened her cheeks. 'Read it to me! I cannot see clearly at the moment.'

'He has been traveling all this while and did not wish to write to us for fear the letter might be intercepted.' Will said and then read aloud: *'For the moment I am studying the mysterious Bank of*

Amsterdam and serving as Secretary to Matthew Prior, the British Resident in Holland. Prior is a man who writes poetry in his spare time.'

Will looks up with a grin. 'You know Johnny. It does not take him long to contact the finest people and find himself a place in any society. We must be happy for him, Mother.'

But Janet's eyes were sad. 'There were times when I thought he must be dead,' she sighed. 'I am sure he preferred us to think of him as dead until he had made some success of himself.'

'Oh, I do not think that is true, Mother,' Will told her. 'That would have been cruel, and John was never cruel. I am certain, as I have often told you that his letters were lost. That is why we have not heard until now.'

'He has written now because he is more confident about his future.' She brightened. 'What else does he say, Will?'

Will returned to the letter, reading aloud. *'I have been in Brussels where my gambling was highly successful, for they have no consideration for numbers in that place. In Genoa, where I went to inspect their bank, I won huge sums playing the English Hazard, a game the Italians have taken to. Aside from Italy, I have traveled to Germany and Hungary. However, I do not think I shall stay in Amsterdam much longer as the Resident has no more work for me.'*

'Where then shall he go?' she cried fearfully.

Will continued, *'Now that King William's war is over, perhaps I will be able to make my way to Paris. Do not worry about me. I am in good health. A vagabond, I hear you saying, dear Mother and brother Will, but I have traveled in style most of the time with my own coach and horses. Give my fond regards and heartfelt thanks to cousin Archibald, and of course, my love to you both.'*

Will folded the letter carefully and handed it to his mother. He knew she would read it over, many times when she was alone, and cherish it until the next missive arrived.

It was curious that his brother made no more mention of his long silence, and now a newsy letter of small successes. In his heart, Will agreed with his mother's appraisal. John would not have written until he was somehow settled. His circumstances surely must have improved, but Will, too, was puzzled as to where his brother had been. His mother looked up from reading the letter to herself.

'Traveling in style, he says. Living by gambling; that is what he has been reduced to!' She sighed. 'And as for all his marvelous projects and plans?' she asked, tears flooding her eyes again. 'What of them? Who would listen to his ideas now?'

Will shook his head. As much as he would like to, he could only believe half of what John wrote of his financial triumphs. Truly, there was no doubt that his great projects were lost.

'That fellow, William Paterson has had the luck that should have been John's, Mother,' Will said sadly, coming to sit by her chair. The firelight caught the glint on his soft brown hair. He wore it long and did not wear a wig at home. 'Cousin Archie tells me that Paterson has sold many of John's ideas as his own in the Scottish Parliament.'

I wonder,' she said, 'if the day will ever come when John can return to Scotland and take his rightful place here at Lauriston.'

Will knew this was not possible. If he were caught, he would be sent right back to England and to the gallows. But he did not care to tell his mother his true feelings. 'Paris, Mother! That is where he will go. I hear the Parisians are great gamblers,' he said. 'John should do very well there.'

John Law never spoke about his years in the American wilderness, sleeping rough in the open, hunting furs with the trappers, bartering with the Indians, hauling logs for Desalt when he ran out of money, and even gambling for pennies on the top of a barrel. Such exploits were not the image he wished to portray of a Financial Wizard presenting lofty schemes to the mighty Courts of Europe.

Having gambled his way across several countries since leaving Holland, Law had arrived in Sardinia in 1711. His outdoor life had left him lean and fit, and with his elegant manners and a newly purchased silk coat, he cut a fine figure when presenting himself to the ruler of the small principality of Savoy-Piedmont.

Victor Amadeus II was in his mid-thirties. Short of stature, with a sharp nose and crafty-eyes, he looked to Law like a man who would trust nobody. Yet he seemed to have taken a liking to this Scotsman who spoke perfect French and nearly perfect Italian, and he showed more than a little interest in Law's plan for a national bank. But Law had been in the Principality for some time before the Duke finally invited his visitor to come to his palace.

Victor Amadeus II

'There are many spies in my palace, Monsieur Law. Too many,' Victor Amadeus said, adding with a sardonic smile, 'In Sardinia, it can be truly said that here, the walls have ears.'

He rose. 'Come! We shall stroll in my gardens. The only place these days where I have a little privacy.

Victor Amadeus waved away his courtiers and led Law through a private door into a small garden where slender cypresses manicured to a flat top shaded a group of stone cupids cavorting in a splashing fountain. Flowerbeds, whose exotic blossoms peculiar to this hot Mediterranean climate, offered colors paler than in England and Scotland. Law wondered if the heat faded their intensity, just as it made the people more lethargic, for they all had the curious custom of sleeping in the afternoon.

Law had already presented his banking plans to several courts, but none had shown the least interest. Here, in this private garden attended by the soft hum of bees, the two men strolled past tall purple and red blooms lining the pink stone ramparts. Here, Victor Amadeus was about to offer a ray of hope.

'The King of France is old,' the ruler said finally and stopped to lift a bright pink rose between jeweled fingers, carelessly sniffing its fragrance. Law paused, waiting for the ruler to continue.

'Old, yes!' Victor Amadeus said finally, agreeing with himself and tossing the bloom to the ground. 'His health is failing, and his spendthrift ways have brought France to the brink of bankruptcy!'

Through the thick silk of Law's coat, he felt the sun hot on his back and stepped forward into a spot of shade. 'I have heard this in the German Court, My Lord. There, they believe that when Louis XIV dies, his great-grandson will inherit that throne,'

'Quite correct, Monsieur Law,' Victor Amadeus replied, eyeing his companion carefully. 'But alas, little Louis is hardly more than a babe. Until he becomes of age, someone must be appointed his guardian. Someone who will be created Regent of France until the child is old enough to rule for himself.'

Law was aware that Victor Amadeus had close ties with France since he was married to Princess Anne, a niece to Louis XIV. The numerous intrigues of statesmanship had seen the principality of Savoy-Piedmont shift sides more than once in the fighting of small wars and the drawing of lengthy treaties. It was clear to Law that this ruler leading him through his private garden was a survivor. But Law knew he needed to be on guard with Amadeus, and he chose his words carefully.

'Whoever is the new Regent will be a fortunate man, Sire. Certainly, he will be the most powerful man in France. Perhaps in all of Europe,' Law said.

'Ah, yes, Monsieur Law. But will little Louis be so fortunate?' Victor Amadeus' whole body seemed to tense at the thought of the next Regent of France. His voice thickened with anger. 'I know too much about living under a Regent as a child,' he said. 'My youth was spent under the Regency of my mother!'

'Then you were lucky, My Lord. A wise mother can be the best guide in the world.' Law replied tactfully.

'*Unlucky*, Monsieur Law!' came the sharp reply. 'My mother

was one of the world's true despots. In my case, she was *not* wise!›
Victor Amadeus›s face clouded over at the remembrance.

Traveling through the Courts of Europe as Law had done
since his return, he knew that most of the rulers were somehow related to each other, and he had carefully studied the relationships.
'Madamée Real was your mother, was she not, your Grace?'

'Indeed! And the Royal Madamée was as overbearing and
ambitious as any ruler since Genghis Khan. Far too ambitious for
a small principality like this.' A hint of a smile touched the ruler's
lips. 'Fortunately, Madamée's health could not keep pace with her
desires, so I was able at sixteen, to take control of my destiny and to
assume the reins of government of Savoy-Piedmont.'

'My Lord, across Europe, they speak of the progress you
have made in Sardinia and with what a fine hand you rule it.'

It was more than an idle compliment; it was the truth, and
Victor Amadeus accepted Law›s words as his due. He strode on
to another flowerbed. ‹Yes, I have done well—because I am wise
enough to know my limitations.› His eyes pierced Law›s. ‹The
proposals you offer are vast. Too vast for my small principality!
Only a powerful nation could carry out such schemes as you put
forward. But. . .› He paused with a mysterious smile. ‹Yes! I may
be of some use to you, nevertheless. I shall give you a letter of
introduction, Monsieur Law. To a person who might be the right
man to help you.'

Surprised, Law bowed slightly. 'For such an honor, I would
be most grateful, your Grace,'

Victor Amadeus looked sharply at Law. 'It is this Frenchman I speak of who needs the favor! You might be the right person
to provide it.' He paused. 'Ah. . . Look at that rose!' He moved to
pick the blossom and tucked it into the clasp of a portrait miniature
of Louis XIV that he wore pinned to a blue sash across his belly.

'A Frenchman, Sir?' Law prompted, to return him to the discussion.

Victor Amadeus nodded thoughtfully. 'My wife is sister to
the chief contender for the Regency of France. A man who hungers
after power as a cat after fish scraps.' He paused again to pick a fig
from the low branch of a tree and popped it into his mouth. 'But yet
it may elude him,' he said as he chewed.

'That man would seem ideally placed for the role,' Law said, not sure who this possible Regent might be.

The ruler shook his head. 'My brother-in-law is more known to the French Parliament for his self-indulgence and debauchery than for his statesmanship. Monsieur! You will understand when you meet him.'

Law frowned slightly, less sure of the *favor* Victor Amadeus was offering. 'From what you have said, your Grace, why should this man consider my project?'

'Because, Monsieur Law, he could march to power on the back of a man like you—a man of ideas! And while this Duke I speak of has brains enough, he has few ideas of his own, except where it concerns his mistresses and the fripperies that money can provide.' Amadeus gave Law a closer look and nodded to himself. 'Yes, he could use you, Monsieur Law. But while he is using you, you shall be able to use him and introduce your ideas!'

France...! Law's mind raced to another wild scheme that he had dreamed of but had voiced to no one. 'France is a country that especially interests me —for several reasons,' Law replied. His mind returned from the French territories of Louisiana lying fallow along the Mississippi to the Duke of Savoy. 'But you have not told me who this man is, sire?'

'But of course, it is *Philip*, Monsieur Law! Philip Duke of Chartres—and now of Orleans! Married to Mademoiselle de Blois,' Victor Amadeus snorted. 'Not that Orleans does more than his duty by her. But still, she is the legitimized daughter of Louis XIV, and her mother is the King's most powerful mistress, Madame de Montespan.'

Law paused, taking this in. 'They say in Hanover that it is de Montespan who rules France and Louis XIV,' Law told him. 'Is that the case?'

Being much shorter than Law, Victor Amadeus had to peer up into the sun to face his visitor. He squinted at Law with sudden disapproval. 'Well, everyone has mistresses, don't you know?' 'But Philip— I fear he is addicted to dissipation—as you yourself would seem to be!' His voice assumed a tone of accusation. 'You have been in my Court only a few short months, and I am told you have spent most of your time at the gaming tables removing money from the pockets of my courtiers.'

'I have been lucky because I understand the science of numbers, sire,' Law said.

'I would say. . . clever!' the Duke replied. His tone mingled admiration with the accusation. 'But my courtiers tell me that it is not trickery. Yes! That it is your mysterious knowledge of numbers that gives you the advantage over your opponents.'

Law had won a great deal at the gaming tables in Sardinia. He could not be certain where Victor Amadeus was leading him. 'Under the circumstances, I marvel that you should wish to help me,' he said, hoping his answer would provoke a direct reply. It did.

'The fact is, Monsieur Law, nothing for nothing is given, is it not so? I, myself have always been ready for the opportunities that life offers.' Victor Amadeus paused, facing the Scotsman, feet apart. 'To put it plainly, Monsieur Law, Savoy-Piedmont could use a friend at the French Court! A friend who will prove to be our ears and keep us informed of events. You comprehend, eh?'

'Indeed I do, My Lord,' Law said with a bow.

Victor Amadeus› tone became slightly arch. ‹And I suggest that this might be an excellent time for you to leave my Court for Paris. You will take with you a letter of recommendation from me to Philip, concerning your financial proposals.›

Stunned, Law bowed once more. 'I am grateful for your suggestion and shall prepare to leave at once, Sire.'

John Law gratefully accepted the ruler's letter of introduction to The Duke of Orleans, and the forceful hint to depart. Nevertheless, he did not go immediately to France since he was not granted a safe-conduct to enter France because he was still a wanted man in England.

Lady Luck had scattered her favors on John Law of late. But winning streaks are often followed by losing streaks, as every gambler knows. After leaving Sardinia with full pockets, he traveled for some time. First, he went to Switzerland and then to Genoa, where he doubled his winnings speculating in the Foreign Exchange and Securities market that existed in that principality. When the authorities thought he was winning too regularly, he was asked to move on.

He did and went to Venice, where he gambled the nights

away at lansquenet, écarte, and faro. Then, he moved on once again, aware that losers do not always like winners.

When Law learned that in England, Queen Anne had come to the throne, he wrote at once, begging the queen for a pardon so that he could return to England and present to her his banking ideas. But on the fifth of September, 1704, his plea was rejected.

Law drifted on, and the years seemed to be passing him by. Years wasted in wandering, waiting, gambling, drifting, always looking for the game-changing opportunity that never came. In a pocket close to his heart, Law always carried the letter from Victor Amadeus. But it was not until 1707 that he was finally granted a safe-conduct to enter France.

John Law found himself inside a stagecoach rattling along a cobbled Paris street, with the inevitable clutch of playing cards in his hand. A fat leather valise containing his few worldly goods was wedged between him and a smooth-eyed Frenchman with the nimble fingers of a professional gambler. Law's valise served them as a gaming table, and on it, Law set down a handful of aces. Looking for any ulterior movements, the stranger peered beneath the Scotsman's frayed lace cuffs at the hands of a fellow gambler.

'You defy the rules of chance, Monsieur Law,' he said. 'All the way to Paris, you have been winning.'

With a smile, Law scooped his winnings into his upturned hat. 'True, my friend, but these are *your* cards that we are playing with, remember?›

Law always tried to play with the other fellow's cards or dice, having no wish to be accused of cheating, which happened all too regularly. He watched the Frenchman's hand travel to the deep pocket of his jacket, his thin lips turning down with grim determination. He could see that the man's fingers clasped what Law could only assume was a pistol.

'I do not believe even with my deck you can be this lucky, Monsieur Law, and therefore I shall ask you to hand over your hat!' The man did not have the opportunity to draw his gun. At that moment, a rock crashed through the window of the stagecoach.

Outside, people were shouting and running, and the frightened horses whinnied! Before Law had time to see out, the entire coach was violently rocked back and forth, throwing its two occupants sideways. Angry voices were shouting and screaming savagely in defiance. The travelers had no time to right themselves when the coach was hurled over, to crash down in a tangle of broken wheel spokes and splinters of wood, down into the middle of a growing street riot.

John Law and the Frenchman crawled out of the shattered carriage and scrambled into the street. The first on his feet was Law's fellow traveler. Seeing Law's hat full of money fallen beside him, he swept it up, placed it tightly on his head, and hurried away into the angry crowd.

The coachman was trying to free the horses as Law pulled himself up, clutching his battered valise. Shaken and bruised, Law spotted the gambler's back disappearing into the crowd and shouted after him, 'Stop, thief…! Stop!' But the rioters were occupied with more important matters, and no one paid him the least attention. Law looked up at the street sign. He was in the Rue Quincampoix, a narrow street of small shops.

Three mounted gendarmes with drawn sabers discouraged any considerations of regaining his winnings. Law quickly switched to self-preservation as the shopkeepers and their wives and children ran for safety. Four of the shopkeepers were dragging away a man in a black coat who carried a large black satchel over his shoulder. The gendarmes rode in on their horses, shouting and laying about with the flat of their sabers, attempting to free the man in black at the center of the fray.

'Who is he? What has he done?' Law asked an old lady standing at the edge of the crowd.

'Tax collector,' she said. 'Collecting King Louis' salt taxes. And now they have sent in D'Argenson's butchers!'

Just in front of them, a small child fell beneath the scramble of legs. Dropping his valise, Law moved quickly to whisk her up into his arms, and with the child held tightly to him, was pushed into the thick of the melee. One of the horses trampled on Law's valise, spewing his clothes into the muddy street to be further trodden upon by dozens of feet.

The tradesmen who held the tax collector in tow were dragging him towards the open black-smithy. They disappeared from view behind a mass of jostling bodies. Then suddenly, the mounted gendarmes turned and rode off, no doubt, to return with more support.

A few doors further on, an old tailor came running out of his shop where he had been hiding. 'Bring him in here!' he cried. 'Bring the devil in here!'

The blacksmith and his friends obliged, dragging the tax collector across the cobbles into the tailor's shop, as the thunder of hooves receded in the street outside.

Still clutching the little girl, Law was swept along in the wave of bodies heading into the tailor's shop. Seeing the child clinging to him, a thin woman in a worn grey dress and tangled hair pushed her way to Law.

'Baba!' she cried. 'Thank the good Lord, and you are all right!'

The little girl let go of Law's neck and held her arms out to the woman crying, 'Mama! Mama!'

Her mother embraced her, taking her from Law. 'Bless you, Monsieur,' she said, tears in her eyes. 'You have saved my child.'

'Take good care of her, Madam,' he said as the woman pushed her way to the blacksmith's side. The blacksmith tore the large leather satchel from the tax collector's shoulder.

'They have left!' someone shouted from the doorway. 'Gone!'

'They will return! With more of D'Argenson's police,' another cried.

The blacksmith was still clutching the tax collector by the collar and shaking him like a rat in a terrier's mouth. 'We must settle this matter now,' he said, holding the satchel aloft. 'Here is our money, friends! The money this poxy collector has stolen for our salt.' He spilled a shower of coins from the satchel across the tailor's wooden table and glared at the cowering collector. 'Do you wish us to eat food with no salt?

We have little enough meat on our tables!'

'It is King Louis makes the taxes, not I!' the tax collector protested, not unreasonably. 'I only do my job! And you had better not harm me! Let me go before you all end up in the Bastille!'

'The gendarmes will return!' someone cried. 'We'd best let him go.'

The blacksmith put his huge hands around the collector's throat. 'You will not give evidence if I choke out your tongue!'

Law stepped quickly between them, staying the blacksmith's arm. 'Which is it you are after, blacksmith, eh? The money—or this man's life?' he asked in French.

All eyes turned to Law, for although the local people crowded the room, many had not noticed him until that moment.

'This is not your business, stranger!' The blacksmith scowled. There was a murmur of agreement from the crowd.' We need no foreigners to teach us how to deal with our pig officials!'

'Foreign or not, he saved our Baba!' the blacksmith's wife cried out, holding up her child for all to see.

'He cannot save us from taxes!' the blacksmith yelled back at his wife.

'So it's the taxes, is it?' Law said, speaking loud enough for all to hear. 'I suppose you think that in all the world, King Louis invented them. Why even in Scotland we have taxes!'

The men cried, 'We do not care what happens in Scotland!' 'We want our money!

'Then, my friends, why don't you use your heads instead of your fists? I can show you a way to settle this predicament.' Law turned back to the tax collector. 'Consider this, Monsieur Collector, these people wish to kill you, and there are more of them than you. I should be sorry to see them in the Bastille, and you die when you are only doing your job, as you rightly point out. Why not let chance decide the fate of your satchel? And of your hide?'

'Chance. .?' the tax collector asked.

'What has chance got to do with it, Monsieur?' the blacksmith asked, loosening his grip on the man.

Law took a pair of dice from his pocket. 'Since the money in the tax collector's possession does not rightly belong to him, nor any more to you good people, it should be of little matter to you— or to him, if I were to win it in a game of chance.'

'Wait a moment,' the tailor said, coming closer. 'Wait just a moment, Monsieur Scotsman. How will it help us if you win his satchel of money?'

'We want our money back!' the butcher shouted, and everyone began to yell again.

'The butcher is right. We want our money! Now !'

Law held up his hands for silence. 'Let me explain to you honest shopkeepers, for I think you will approve, once you have heard. If you take the money in that satchel, you will have stolen it, and the gendarmes will have you. But if I win it, the tax collector will have lost it fairly in a game of chance, and the gendarmes will have no charge against you. And then I shall use it to benefit you all.'

'How will you do that, if you have our money?' the black-smith asked, apprehensively. The others cried out in agreement.

'Ah, but then the money is no longer yours, or his, is it?' Law pointed out. 'And money is a curious thing, friends,' Law continued hastily, having got their attention. 'You cannot eat it, drink it, shelter beneath it or warm yourself with it—unless you destroy it by fire.'

There were shouts of disapproval from the room. 'Quiet!' the blacksmith's wife cried. 'Listen to what the stranger has to say.' Again they fell silent.

'I was speaking of the power of this gold,' Law said, holding up a single coin. 'One louis d' or. Useful for trade, is it not? But like the flow of blood in your veins, this money must circulate, or the Body Politic cannot survive.' He scooped up a handful of coins from the table. 'Friends, I propose to use these coins to stimulate the flow of trade.'

More voices were raised in protest. 'What do you mean?' 'How will you do that?'

Law turned to the tailor seeing that his shop was patheti-cally bare. Save for the tailor's table and the tools of his trade, only one bolt of brocade cloth hung on the rack alongside a brown velvet suit.' This is your shop, is it not, Monsieur?'

The tailor nodded. 'I can make as fine a suit of clothing as anyone in all of Paris,' he said, adding, 'when I can afford the cloth.'

'Then I shall order a suit from you if I win,' Law told him. He glanced over at a man in a long white apron and cap. 'By the look of you, sir, you are the baker?'

The man nodded. 'And I can bake as light a loaf as any in Paris.'

'Then I shall order bread for everyone in this room! And

from the wine merchant - where is he?' He glanced around, and a jolly round-faced man raised his hand. 'A flagon for each house in the street. You shall all have earned your money back, and none shall stand outside the law. There will be no theft. Only commerce.'

A cadaverous man stepped forward, in a rusty black outfit and croaked hopefully at Law. 'I am the coffin maker, Monsieur...'

'See me in thirty years,' Law told him with a grin, turning back to the tax collector. 'Now then, I shall not steal your money, my good fellow. I shall win it from you in a fair game of chance.'

The blacksmith glared a warning at Law. 'Just be sure that you win, Monsieur Gambler.'

Law pushed the dice across the table towards the tax collector. 'High roll, best out of three. The first throw shall be yours,' he said.

The tax collector looked around at the room full of angry faces. His choices were simple: be killed or play. Gingerly, he picked up the small carved bone squares and scrutinized them.

Sometime later, the street was once again quiet, and the tax collector was gone, his satchel empty, its contents now filling Law's pockets. The tailor flung his only bolt of cloth open across his worktable and fingered the colorful brocade.

'Exactly what is being worn in the French Court, Monsieur Law.' He eyed Law's hair tied back into a cord at the neck. 'But you must get yourself a wig to go with it.'

'Perhaps,' Law said and glanced over at the dark brown velvet suit hanging on a peg. 'Now that suit there, that is more my style, I'd say. Priests and gamblers should wear sober feathers.'

The tailor nodded towards the brown suit. 'That garment, I am afraid, was ordered by the Ambassador from the Netherlands. However, he lost a great deal of money at Madame Duclos's gaming house and has been unable to pay, so there it hangs. His loss and my loss.'

Ignoring the question of ownership, Law slipped on the jacket. 'I can afford to pay cash, Monsieur. At least today. Which reminds me,' Law said. 'Is there a woodcarver? There is a job I must have done.'

Three doors away, Monsieur, and I am sure he will be grateful for your trade. Is it a large object you desire?'

No larger than one of these gold louis d' or,' Law said, fingering some of the coins he had won from the tax collector. He hunched his arms forward in the brown velvet jacket. 'It is a bit snug through the shoulders.'

The tailor took up a long needle and white thread and moved towards him, starting to mark out where a new seam would be needed. 'It can be let out, Monsieur. I can have it ready in one hour.' He smiled. 'Before you lose all the money you have won.'

Law slipped out of the jacket. 'Or perhaps win more. Where is this gaming house, and who is the lady who owns it?

'Madame Duclos? A famous actress and a great beauty.' The tailor's hands formed the shape of a woman in the air. 'But the Duke of Orleans could give more intimate details, I think, for he loses money in her establishment almost every night, and it is well known that Vivien Duclos is one of his mistresses. Although some say, she has been replaced recently by an English lady, who'd been the mistress of the King of England.'

'Really? Law said, thinking the impossible. 'Have my suit ready, tailor,' Law said. 'Tonight, I shall visit Madame Duclos' gaming house and see these ladies for myself.'

'Oh, but Monsieur, I must warn you. No-one is admitted there without an introduction.'

'Have no fear, tailor. I have the oldest introduction in the world,' Law picked up the remaining bag of gold.

John Law walked the streets, delighted to see Paris, a city he had loved since his youth when he had come here with his father. Tomorrow, maybe, he would visit his father's grave in the Scots College Cemetery. When John was fourteen years old, his father had contracted what the doctors called a *stone*. The elder Law did not trust the Scottish doctors, so he decided to travel to Paris to see a famous surgeon there. His mother insisted that John accompany him, and he had gone only too willingly, not realizing the seriousness of the situation.

Once in Paris, the stone was so painful that John's father cried out all through the night. In the morning, the surgeon operated. His father never regained consciousness. It was John who saw to all the arrangements and had him buried in the Scots College Cemetery. Often, he had wanted to take his mother to Paris to visit the grave, but she was no traveler. He must have got his wander-lust from his father, for he was never happier than in a coach going somewhere he had never been.

He had learned much of Paris's history from his father. It was Henry IV who had hoisted the ancient town out of its medieval past and enriched it with circles and squares, fountains, and bridges. Henry built palaces and townhouses and the first multiple-dwelling buildings and paved and illuminated the streets. For a hundred and fifty years before John Law arrived, the amazing pumping station that Henry had built, called The Samaritaine, had pumped water to the city's right bank and continued to do so in the 1700s.

Since the late 16th century, Paris streets had been lighted by lanterns hung high from ropes stretched across the road from house to house. Thick candles burned in them from nightfall until midnight, and anyone caught tampering with them was sent to the gallows.

The Sun King had brought the city to a height of glory envied across Europe. Louis XIV's architect, Le Nôtre, had added the garden to the Tuileries, developed the Champs-Elysées as far as the Rond-Point, and built the Hôtel des Invalides as a home for the veterans of the King's many wars. King Louis's architect had turned a country town into one of the most beautiful cities in the world. Louis made Paris the capital and his Royal residence.

John Law felt he had arrived at precisely the right moment. But he had also glimpsed behind the marble palaces into the stinking alleys around the Cour de Miracles, where prostitutes and thieves kept police at bay. He had seen the people in the Rue Quincampoix, who were well off compared to some parts of this city, whose food was scarce to the point of starvation. Now, as he made his way through the streets, beggars were everywhere.

It was to a vast French baroque mansion situated in a torch-lit carriage-way framed by a high, well-manicured hedge that John Law was heading that night. At the entrance, a steady stream of fashionably dressed Parisians disgorged from sleek carriages. These were noblemen and their ladies who came nightly to throw their money across a table. Of that other Paris in the alleys behind the mansions, where the poor savored the joys of poverty, these people had no thought—except to avoid it.

# EIGHT:
MARIE-LOUISE
AND KATHERINE

Wearing a thick black cloak and a newly purchased black tricorn hat, John Law slipped out from behind the hedge and fell into step with a party of chattering, laughing aristocrats. The heavy scent of perfume was uncut by the crisp night air. It had been some time since he'd been with a woman, and though it was years since he had seen her, he could not help but remember Katherine Knollys and the soft scent of lavender that surrounded her delicate frame.

The footman greeting the arriving guests held a candelabra aloft. 'Welcome, Madame! Monsieur le Duc. Enter, please!' He paid no notice to Law, who had mingled with the crowd and had passed through the open door with them.

Madame Duclos' establishment was flamboyantly adorned in the baroque style made popular by the King. Law had not seen such luxury outside of palaces. Everywhere was the glint of ormolu and gilded bronze mounts in the shapes of fantastical animals, caryatids, and telamones supporting the legs of commodes, cabinets, and tables. A profusion of crystal, porcelain, extravagant silk draperies, and rich velvet cushions and beyond Law, a blaze of chandeliers played upon satin gowns as a turbaned blackamoor took charge of the ladies' wraps.

The years had added to Law›s appearance, giving his striking features new authority.

Law brought out two sacks from beneath his cloak. One was so heavy he could hardly get his hand around it, the other, smaller and much lighter in weight. He passed his cloak and hat to the blackamoor and stepped to the archway leading to the main salon. The gaming tables were coming to life with the flutter of cards and the click of dice.

Law glanced at the women. They were as flamboyant as their surroundings. Theirs was not the subdued natural looks of the ladies he remembered of the English Court. These women were swathed in bright taffetas, silken braids, feathers, flowers, pearls, and flashes of diamonds, emeralds, and rubies. Their faces glistened in a flaming manner, so monstrously unnatural that Law thought they had little resemblance to human faces at all. They wore no wigs. Their hair was cut short in front and curled around their faces and was so loaded with powder that it had the appearance of white wool.

A tall young nobleman in green velvet came up beside John Law in the archway eyed him, then paused to survey the room. 'Ah... the ladies!' he said.

'What is that they wear on their faces?' Law asked him.

'Obviously, you are new to Paris, Monsieur,' the gentleman replied. 'For here, it is all the rage for the ladies to cover their skin with shining red paint they call *japan*. They lay it on unmercifully, do you not think?'

Law nodded. 'They look like china,' he replied, taking in the elegance of the man who stood beside him. 'Allow me to introduce myself. John Law of Lauriston. A newcomer to Paris from Scotland.'

'Count Saint-Simon,' the gentleman said, eyeing the sacks of gold Law was holding. 'Bon chance,'

He said and moved on into the room.

Another blackamoor passed by Law carrying a tray with a bottle of champagne and a single glass. The footman came forward to stop the servant. 'What have you there?'

'It is champagne for Madame,' the blackamoor said, moving towards a beautiful brunette woman wearing a deep red satin gown beaded with pearls across the arched spheres of her breasts.

She was in her mid-thirties or possibly older, Law thought. And although nearly heavily made up like the others, she had exquisite features with large dark eyes above high cheekbones and a wide, sensuous mouth. Her movements were calculated and theatrical as she chatted with a guest. She held her head high with a regal flair that none of the ladies of the court who might have been born to such airs and graces could hope to attain.

AN 18th CENTURY PARIS GAMING HOUSE

'Who is she?' Law asked of the footman.

'Of course, that is Madame Duclos,' the footman said, moving away to greet a new arrival.

Carrying his sacks, John Law went purposefully over to her. Vivien Duclos turned, champagne in hand, to face Law as he bowed courteously. He spoke in a loud voice in French so that all could hear. 'Allow me to present myself,' he said. 'John Law of Lauriston. A visitor to your country from Scotland.'

'Enchanted,' Vivien Duclos said. Her eyes took in the handsome figure in the sober brown velvet suit, a fresh ruffle of lace protruding from the wide, silver-buttoned cuff. A striking man, she thought, and his French had little accent.

'I shall play at your tables tonight, if you will allow it, Madame. But first, I wish to place a deposit of one hundred thousand livres in gold coin. I should like you to count them, please.'

'Certainly, Monsieur Law,' she told him. 'I am not above counting money.'

'I am in your debt, Madame Duclos,' he said, bowing deeply.

She signaled one of the croupiers at the gaming table to come over to make the actual count. 'Come. Bring it to my desk.'

She noticed how gracefully he moved across the room to a long desk. It was beautifully made of inlaid brass and ebony worked into a tortoise-shell ground.

'A beautiful desk, Madame,' he said. 'I have never seen another like it.' He ran a finger over the surface, marveling at the intricate design and craftsmanship.

'A gift from a former patron. By the cabinet maker, André Charles Bouille, a favorite of the King's.'

And she was a favorite of the Duke of Orleans, Law remembered.

The croupier spilled Law's coins out across the desk and expertly piled them into stacks, counting, then looked up, whispering to Duclos. She turned to Law. 'As you say, Monsieur, there is exactly one hundred thousand gold Louis here. But why do you wish me to hold them? Do you not intend to play with them?'

'You have understood it exactly, Madame. I shall play, but not with those coins.' He opened the other sack and poured out a mound of thin wooden discs the exact size of the louis d' or. 'I have had them carved this very afternoon by an excellent woodcarver.'

'Wood?' Vivien asked incredulously. 'You wish to play with wood at my tables, Monsieur? Surely you are mad!"

'I call them *counters*, Madame. Each one is stamped to the value of eighteen louis d' or. You shall hold my gold, which is heavy and cumbersome, and I shall play with these lightweight counters, for they are much more convenient and easy to handle. If I win, I shall collect the equivalent value in gold from you, and if I lose, you shall keep that amount of my gold.'

He spoke loud enough for all to hear, his voice deeply resonant. All eyes were suddenly on Law's clean-cut features and finely arched eyebrows above eyes that sparked intelligence.

Vivien laughed heartily. 'I have never heard of such a thing before, but since I hold your gold, Monsieur Law, I can see no harm in it. Play away, and I wish you luck,' she said.

The room was hushed as John Law stepped up to the roulette table. The man in the green jacket came over with several ladies to see him play. 'Wood! He plays with wood, my dear,' was whispered around the circle.

Vivien looked on with some amusement. Here was a new kind of man to her. His poise and bearing could have suited him for a successful career as an actor, she thought. Or a statesman.

'*Counters*, he calls them? Worth the same as gold?' came hushed voices.

Across the room, a young girl who seemed to be the center of attention among a small circle of friends, a striking young army Captain at her elbow, turned for a look at John Law as he stepped to the roulette table. What she saw, she liked. She moved closer to see what was attracting the crowd to this new arrival.

'Come, Madame, which would you play, Bankafelet or Passage?' the Captain asked, trying to regain her attention.

'Neither,' she said and freed herself of his arm, moving towards Law's table. Her pale pink satin gown with a cross-work design of pearls covered a form so lean that she was no more than a wisp of flesh and bone beneath it.

Law looked up long enough to catch her glance and saw that her eyes were an odd shade of lavender in striking contrast to her hair, which, although framing her face in small à la mode curls, was not powdered in the style of the day. Instead, it glistened an exuberant copper-red.

'Bravo!' she cried as he scooped in a stack of gold to add to his wooden counters. Her cheeks were as highly painted as the ladies around her, but the girl's features were delicate and piquant with a small, retroussé nose. She had not a line on her face but the dark circles beneath her eyes attested to sleepless nights given to dissipation. For more than half an hour, the girl stood across the table watching Law place his counters on the baize tabletop, picking first one number and then another and constantly winning, the stack of wooden counters before him steadily adding mounds of gold. He had not looked at her again, for he was concentrated on his game.

The virile Captain, who was her escort, was getting quite annoyed that this stranger, far too handsome for his liking, was taking too much of the girl's attention. 'Come Marie-Louise,' he said. 'Have you not seen enough?'

'Leave me be, Henri. I must know why this fellow's numbers come up so often. Is it his wooden counters that make him the winner?' she asked loudly.

Her words caught Law's attention, and he looked once again into the depths of those lavender eyes. What he saw there fascinated and disturbed him. It was like looking into the eyes of a cobra that could both hypnotize and repel. From the jewels she wore, he could see that she was a person of some standing in the Court. 'It is not the counters, Madame,' he said. 'It is the odds.'

'Odds?' she asked in a challenging tone.

Law nodded. 'The laws of probability. How many times is it possible for the same number to come up, according to chance? That is the question.'

'I do not believe in these odds of yours, Monsieur. Come! I shall play against you with the cards, where skill is a necessity, and we shall see how your law of chance does for you then.'

'Very well, Mademoiselle,' he said, and scooped up his winnings, following her to a card table.

'Madame,' she corrected archly. 'And we shall play with gold, Monsieur if you possess it. I do not play with wood.'

'As you wish,' he said and went across to where Vivien Duclos had been listening to his conversation. She snapped her fingers, and a croupier brought two sacks, once more counting coins across the desk.

'Here, Monsieur Law, is your hundred thousand livres. And I see you have won forty thousand at my table.' As Law moved to take the money, Vivien took his arm and drew him closer. 'Tread carefully, Monsieur Law,' she whispered. 'That is a dangerous lady you will play against.'

'Dangerous? She cannot be more than twenty,' he said.

'Seventeen. Young though she may be, she is the most powerful lady in France.'

'Who is she?' he asked, intrigued now.

'Marie-Louise, Duchess de Berry. She sleeps with anyone she chooses, except her husband, who much prefers his officers.'

'A duchess? That is not so dangerous, I think. And the man with her?'

'Captain de Riom? Her latest lapdog. But Marie-Louise is not just a duchess, Monsieur Law.' She spoke behind her fan, lowering her voice. 'She is granddaughter to Louis XIV and daughter to Philip, Duke of Orleans. It is said she beds him, too.' Her voice dropped even lower. 'If she likes you, you are in trouble—and if she doesn't, you are dead.'

'I thank you for your advice, Madame Duclos,' Law said. 'And I shall see to it that the lady has no cause to be dissatisfied with my performance.' With a slight bow, he turned to join Marie-Louise. For the next hour, John Law did not move from the card table. Captain de Riom stood behind Marie-Louise's chair with several sycophantic friends. Law played for a one-thousand livre a point stake, and won nearly every hand. Marie-Louise was clever, and she was sharp, but she played by whim with no design.

Law memorized every card as it was played. Soon a mound of gold coins lay beside him. Marie-Louise had only a handful left.

'I am bored with the cards,' Marie-Louise said. 'Give me your dice box.' Law handed her his leather dice box. and she shook the dice, throwing a three and a two. 'Your point is five, Madame,' he said.'

'I'll raise the bid. Will you match me?' she asked, snapping her finger.

'Most certainly. But the odds are two to twenty you'll lose,' he told her.

'Odds again!' Marie-Louise picked up the dice-box and shook it angrily. She tossed the ivory cubes on the table. They came up with a three and a one.

'Unfortunate,' Law said. 'A four multiplies the odds against you, Madame.'

Biting down annoyance, she shoved another pile of gold coins on her bet. 'I told you I don't believe in odds. Another thousand!' She shook and rolled a six and a one. 'Seven!' she cried. 'Your dice obey you too well, Law!'

'They obey only the ruled of mathematics. Which I should be glad to teach you.' He paused. 'Some evening.' His smile held a tantalizing promise. Her eyes held something predatory. 'We shall see,' she said.

A rather effete nobleman, Count Saint-Simon, came over to observe the game with Vivien Duclos. He cast admiring glances at Law. 'Quite an entertainment, Madame Duclos. Where have you found this ravishing man?'

MARIE-LOUISE, DUCHESS DE BARRY

Before she could reply, a heavy-set man in a full curled wig and rich brocade suit came up beside the two of them. He paused, applying a pinch of snuff to each nostril. 'This Scotsman, what do you know of him, Madame Duclos?' he asked. 'Has he been properly introduced? And if so, by whom?'

'My!' she said. 'It seems everybody wants to know about my guest.' She favored the new arrival with a wide smile. 'I can tell you that he is an excellent player with the dice and cards, Count D'Argenson,' she said. 'I know nothing more. But should he remain in Paris, I shall expect to know him better. That is, if he does not break my bank.'

D'Argenson frowned and sneezed into a large silk handkerchief. 'I should be interested to know where the fellow obtained that brown velvet suit that he is wearing.'

Vivien regarded the Count with some curiosity. 'You admire his tailor?' she asked. 'I do not think you have the shoulders for it, Count.' She turned her attention back to Marie-Louise, who had thrown down the dice-box and now rose from the table angrily.

'I am tired of this game,' the girl cried. 'Champagne! Champagne for all!' As the waiters hurried to carry out the order, Marie-Louise walked over to a silvered glass mirror, Captain de Riom at her side. She glanced back at Law.

Law bowed to Marie-Louise. 'I thank you, Madame, for the game.' As he turned away, his heart caught in his throat. Facing him in a gold satin gown dripping with ivory lace stood Katherine Knollys. A mellowness of years had softened her sharply delicate features.

'Well played, John Law,' she said with a wide smile. 'I have never seen you play better.' Certainly, she had matured like a fine wine through the passing years, and she was more beautiful than ever.

As the waiter offered them champagne, Law drew her aside. 'I cannot believe my eyes. You, in Paris?' he exclaimed. 'What are you doing here, Katherine? I wrote to you but never had an answer.'

'Dear Johnny,' she whispered, freezing a casual smile on her face for prying eyes. It belied her feelings. 'However dashing a lady I may be, the scandal of the duel did me no good. And there was more than a niggling suspicion about your escape, my love.'

'I had no idea,' he said.

She nodded at a passing gentleman, dropping her voice to a half-whisper. 'I was forced to leave my husband and London several years ago. But do not worry for me, Johnny,' she said brightly. 'I have a new and powerful protector here in France.' She touched her throat encircled by an ornate diamond and pearl necklace, attesting to the validity of her statement.

Count D'Argenson approached them. He bowed slightly towards Katherine with a 'Good evening, Lady Knollys' and turned his full attention to Law. 'I believe you are new to Paris, sir,' he said. 'May I ask your business here?'

'If my business were *your* business, sir,› Law said, taking an instant dislike to the man. ‹Which I rather think it is not.›

Katherine stepped in quickly, with a warning look to Law. 'Monsieur Law, have you had the pleasure of meeting our Lieu-tenant-General of Police, Count D'Argenson?'

'Perhaps you *are* my business, Monsieur,› D'Argenson said, ignoring her. 'You are Scottish, I hear.'

'You hear correctly, Count. I come from Edinburgh.'

'Hmm,' he said glaring. 'We seem to have too many Scots-men in Paris these days; what with your ex-King James, whom I understand has fifty-seven heirs with a claim to that throne.' He took another pinch of snuff. 'But I digress. Just this morning in the Rue Quincampoix, a Scottish foreigner robbed a tax collector in a card game.'

'Really?' Katherine exclaimed. 'How very odd. I did not know your tax collectors had a taste for the pasteboards.'

Across the room, Marie-Louise turned from her mirror, which had reflected D'Argenson glowering at Law. The Lieu-tenant-General of Police's voice rose. 'And only this afternoon I ar-rested a tax-evading tailor who sold that same foreigner a brown velvet suit, Monsieur. A suit exactly like yours!'

'A popular color this season.' Vivien Duclos said as she came over to join the conversation along with the nobleman, Saint-Simon.

D'Argenson had assumed a bulldog stance ignoring any-one but Law. 'I have been watching your game with the Duchess de Berry,' he said. 'And from what I have seen, I do not doubt that there has been some sharp card-playing on your part. Indeed I am certain you have been palming your cards to win so consistently from such an able player as the Duchess.'

Hearing her name, Marie-Louise, too, joined them. Saint-Si-mon interrupted hastily. 'Allow me to say that I stood here during the entire play and watched Mister Law closely. I can bear witness to his honesty. There was no trickery. Only skill. This man's power of calculation is quite extraordinary!'

'Nevertheless,' D'Argenson said, turning a beady eye on Law, 'I shall have to ask you, sir, to accompany me to my office for questioning.'

Marie-Louise put an end to any further discussion. 'You

move too quickly, Count. I must say that I enjoyed my game with this Scotsman. And I would certainly know if he had been cheating.' She smiled. 'But since chance is what Monsieur Law seems to study, we can decide this issue here and now, with a game where *chance* is very real. Roet-Couteau!' Her tone brooked no disagreement. 'Monsieur Law shall play against you, Count D'Argenson!'

A hush fell over the room. What they had heard made them gasp, for Roet-Couteau was a dangerous game, played by the sailors in St Mâlo.

Noting the apprehension in D'Argenson's face, Law said, 'I am afraid I have never played this Roet-Couteau, Madame.'

'Then I shall explain the rules to you,' Marie-Louise said. 'For in this game, there is no science. No mathematics. Only luck, Monsieur. And courage!'

'As much as I should enjoy obliging you,' Count D'Argenson put in quickly, 'I must point out, dear Duchess, that Roet-Couteau has been outlawed in Paris for many years. As head of the Police, surely you can see that I must uphold the law.'

Marie-Louise threw him a vicious smile. 'Here in this room, my word is law, Count D'Argenson.' Her glittering eyes traveled to Law and lingered there. 'And Monsieur Law has my word on that.' She downed her champagne and snapped her fingers imperiously. 'Madame Duclos, have your croupier fix the daggers!'

Vivien signaled the croupier, who reached into a drawer of Vivien's desk, bringing out two double-edged hunting daggers with flat-ended handles, which he attached at opposite points on his wheel of fortune.

Marie-Louise picked up a lighted candle from a heavy silver sconce and spun the wheel. 'The rules are simple, Monsieur Law,' she said. 'One chance only. Each player must reach between the flashing blades - to retrieve a card. High card wins.'

'San Mâlo must be full of one-handed sailors,' Law said.

Ignoring the remark, Marie-Louise held out the candle. 'The stake shall be Monsieur Law's freedom or Count D'Argenson's interrogation, which I am told, is never very pleasant.' With a quick movement, she stuck the candle between the spinning blades. As she pulled it out, the flame end was chopped off and fell into the spinning circle, landing on the number thirteen. The onlookers gasped.

'Place the cards!' she ordered.

The croupier stopped the wheel, snuffed out the flame, and placed a handful of cards, face down into the trough. Law appraised his chances of getting his hand in between the blades and safely out again.

'Are you ready, gentlemen?' Marie-Louise asked.

'As ready as I shall ever be, Madame,' Law replied.

D'Argenson blanched. If it is your wish, I am at your service, dear Duchess de Berry.'

She smiled. 'Since he is Lieutenant General of Police, the Count shall have the first draw,' she said and spun the wheel again. The air was alive with tension as the Count prepared to reach for a card. He took a deep gasp of breath, and his pale eyes looked rheumy as he tried to concentrate on the spinning wheel, hoping it would lessen its speed slightly.

'Too slow! Too slow!' Marie-Louise cried and gave the wheel another vicious spin. 'Now, Count! Make your play!'

Wincing with fear, the Count reached in between the blades and pulled out a card. Blood spurted across his lace cuff. His hand was badly cut. Marie-Louise handed him a silk handkerchief.

'Well played, Count. Here, bind your wound, for we do not want blood on Madame Duclos' carpet.'

'The surgeon!' Vivien told her footman. 'Hurry!' The lad ran off at the double.

'And now, your card, Count?' Marie-Louise asked. D'Argenson placed his card face up on the table. It was a seven. Marie-Louise turned to Law.

'It is your turn, Monsieur. Perhaps you can show us French, what a Scot can do.'

Law tucked the lace cuff of his left hand into his sleeve. 'I shall save my right hand, Madame, in case I should need it to make my will.' A titter went around the table.

Once more, she spun the wheel. Calculating the spin, Law reached quickly between the blades. Katherine let out a small cry as he withdrew his card. His hand bore only a slight scratch. He placed his card face up beside D'Argenson's. It was an eight. There was a gasp from those watching.

COUNT D'ARGENSON

Marie-Louise smiled. 'My congratulations to you, Monsieur Law. We are delighted to have you as a visitor to our city.'

'But we know nothing of this man, Duchess!' D'Argenson complained, tending to his wound.

Law reached into his pocket. 'As it happens,' he said, 'I do have an introduction to this Court. It is from the Duke of Savoy-Piedmont of Sardinia. But as it is addressed to the Duke of Orleans, and is personal, I am afraid that I am not at liberty to show it to you, Count.'

'A letter to my father? From my uncle, Victor Amadeus?' Marie-Louise brightened. 'Well then, Monsieur Law, you must come tomorrow night to the fireworks in honor of my grandfather's birthday and present your letter in person. Eight o'clock then.' She turned to D'Argenson. 'And you must dine with us, too, dear Count—one day soon.' She smiled. 'When your hand is better. Come, Henri,' she called to Captain de Riom and turned away, exiting the Casino amid a cloud of whispers.

Law looked towards Katherine. He could see the relief in her eyes. 'When will I see you?' he demanded softly.

'Sooner than you think', she replied mysteriously, offering her hand. He brushed it with a kiss, and she turned away, following Marie-Louise out with the same graceful but jaunty air that he could never erase from his mind.

Across the room, D'Argenson, now being attended by the surgeon, glowered. He turned to his Agent of Police. 'I want a complete dossier on this Scotsman. Every wrong move he has ever made. Do you understand? Send one of your best men to London on the first available ship.'

Madame Duclos came over to Law, her sensuous lips in a wide smile, dark eyes washing him with a look of desire.

'You are quite a fellow, Monsieur Law, and you have made a conquest of the Duchess de Berry. I can see that you will do well in our Court. My rooms are open to you at any time.'

'Thank you, Madame Duclos. I shall take advantage of your hospitality.'

She held her hand out to him, and when he took it, a key dropped into his palm. 'My *private* rooms, Monsieur. Perhaps you would care to share a glass of champagne?›

He looked at her with some surprise. 'I should be honored, Madame.'

'Say in half an hour, then? At the top of the stairs.'

'I shall look forward to it.'

'And Monsieur Law, may I say that mistresses know how to please, not how to possess. Which is why men love them so much.' With a knowing smile, she turned away.

A short while later, he saw her mounting the stairs. He finished his play at the roulette wheel and casually followed her. The key fitted into the gilded lock of Vivien's door where more than a glass of champagne awaited John Law.

In Edinburgh, William Law made his way through Parliament Close to Goldsmiths' Hall under the old Tolbooth Stair. He wore the cocked hat and scarlet cloak of his office and carried his father's gold-mounted cane, signifying his trade. He paused here and there to be greeted by merchants of the town who showed him the marked respect as befitted his station; for goldsmiths could be depended upon to help a merchant when it came to buying merchandise and such, and charged small interest for lending money.

The men chatted amiably about the weather, which, as usual, was never good. The thing they did not mention was Will's brother. That was a name only whispered behind closed doors. John Law was still a wanted man. Were he to appear in Scotland, he would still be hunted down and sent to London for hanging.

At that moment, a bright new carriage drove up and came to a stop nearby. Archibald Campbell peered out. 'William. Hello there! Come, have a word.'

Will excused himself from the city's Apothecary and came over to Archie's carriage. The crest on the carriage had been elevated to accommodate Archibald's newly granted title. He had been raised from Earl to become the Third Duke of Argyll.

'Get in, get in!' Archie cried, opening the door. 'I have news. Some good, some not so much.'

'What is it, Archie? Have you heard from John?' Will asked, climbing in the coach.

'John is in France. But that you know. He has sent me some pamphlets. A brilliant treatise on the meaning of money. On his behalf, I have presented it and his principle work, *'Considerations on Currency and Commerce'*, to the Scottish Parliament.›

'He's written, of course, but has not sent me a copy, Archie,' Will said with some disappointment. 'What does it propose?'

'The formation of a territorial bank that would give the Scottish landlords a paper currency, to be worth a portion of the value of their estates. I tell you Will, the idea was well received and warmly supported by The Squadrone!' He was referring to his political coterie.

'Well received, you say?' Will brightened perceptibly. 'You mean that they have accepted his proposals?'

Archie shook his head sadly. 'Turned down. But almost to a man, they thought it was brilliant.'

'And still, they turned it down!' Will exclaimed.

'Parliament will have nothing to do with John Law as long as he is wanted for murder in England. Have you seen William Paterson's pamphlet?" Archie asked, handing a booklet to Will.

Of course, he had not seen it. He stared at the cover. It had no author's name on it. No name at all. He opened it and began to read. 'At least the man has had the good grace to print it anonymously,' he said, 'since he has taken all of John's ideas!'

'And it looks like Paterson may get his 'ideas' through Parliament this time! If so, Will, Scotland will be one of the few to have a private bank.'

Will nodded. 'But not a *national* bank, Archie. That was John's dream. And now there will never be a hope of his realizing it.'

# NINE:

MADMAN OR GENIUS?

A whirling explosion of fireworks rent the night sky in a blaze of colored diamonds above the Palais Royal gardens and sparkled in the fountain spray bathing a joyful stone Cupid riding an errant dolphin. The music of harpsichord and violins and the tinkle of laughter drifted from one of the grand galleries across the well-manicured lawns in a delicate texture of sounds that assailed the occupants of a small marble bench tucked into the alcove of a thick boxwood hedge.

Marie-Louise, Duchess de Berry wearing a candy-striped gown that defied gravity as it elevated two firm breasts to peek above the line of her dress. She turned to the man beside her with a sigh. 'How sad it is,' she said, 'that my grandfather is not well enough to attend his own birthday celebrations tonight.'

'Most unfortunate,' John Law agreed. 'After he has enjoyed such a long and glittering reign.'

'You may not know, Monsieur Law, being a foreigner, that he has been longest on the throne of any monarch in France,' she said proudly; then added, 'And the people—the simple French peasants love him so much they call him the Sun King.'

'Yes. A colorful title,' he acknowledged. 'But I doubt that King Louis has brought any ray of light to those simple peasants you speak of.'

If he had meant to provoke her, he had succeeded. She did not miss the note of cynicism in his voice and turned on him, a spot of color highlighting each unpainted cheek. 'Whatever do you mean, Monsieur? Grandfather is the greatest king in the long history of this country!'

He took her small hand gently. 'Dear Duchess, you lead a protected life and perhaps are not aware of the problems your country is facing. At this very moment, France is on the verge of financial ruin.'

'Who says such a thing?' she exclaimed angrily, extracting her hand.

'The whole of Europe, Marie-Louise,' he replied matter-of-factly.

'And what else does Europe gossip about, John Law?' she flared. 'Have they heard, for instance, that when Grandfather dies, my father will become Regent of France, to rule until the Dauphin is of age?'

‹That is certainly a possibility if your father does not find the seat already occupied. I hear that The Duke of Orleans has powerful enemies who think him unfit for the Regency. And there are several other contenders with more substantial credentials.›

'Who? Who...?' she demanded, her cheeks flushing. 'What other slanders have you brought us from your travels through the Courts of Europe?'

'Truth is not slander, dear Duchess. The King has another son with some claim to the throne, Louis-Auguste de Bourbon, the Duke du Maine. I understand he is also a strong contender.'

'My uncle? Why he is illegitimate!' she cried.' Her lavender eyes flashed as brightly as the sparkling fireworks. 'Du Maine is the son of the King's whore! Madame de Montespan.'

Law nodded. 'But in du Maine's case, I fear such indiscretions are of no consequence since your grandfather has acknowledged him. And I understand he is a sober man, with many friends in your Parliament. He does not frequent the gaming rooms as your father, and you and I do, and he contents himself with only his wife for company.'

'He is a boring old crow!' she cried.

He chuckled. 'Ah, to you, perhaps, my dear. And perhaps even to me. But du Maine has been making proposals to your Parliament about France's future—should they decide to elect him as Regent. What proposals has your father offered them?'

A frown clouded her pretty face. 'Do you intend to talk of politics all night? I thought we were going to have an enjoyable evening, Law.'

'Politics is power, Marie-Louise. I have seen you exert yours, and I do not think you would wish to lose it,' he said matter-of-factly. 'If your uncle becomes Regent, he proposes to declare France bankrupt! If that happens, this glittering world that you inhabit will never be the same.'

She glared, surprised at the foreigner's audacity. 'How dare you criticize our country? Besides,' she complained, 'men do not usually speak to me in this manner. Certainly never of serious things.'

He nodded. 'No doubt they flirt, kiss your hand, and if you allow it, your lips. In fact, they treat you like a child.' He paused. 'Is that all you really want, Marie-Louise?'

What he said was true. Some, like Captain de Riom, found their way to her bed by invitation. She had wanted to flirt with Law and had invited him here for that purpose. Men were supposed to understand the rules of the game! But this flirtation was not being played out the way she'd expected. There was much more to this handsome adventurer than surface good looks, gracious manners, and those 'laws of probability', that seemed to make him win too often, for luck. She glared at him. 'You seem to know too much about our politics. And you ask too many questions, Monsieur Law. For what purpose?'

'There are never too many questions, dear Duchess,' He threw her a maddeningly irresistible smile. 'Just not enough answers.'

She stood up, her hands on slender hips, a shower of sparks from the fireworks falling almost at their feet. 'I do not understand you, Monsieur Law! What is it you are really looking for in Paris? Love? Money? Adventure? Clearly more than winning pots of gold in the gaming rooms with those wooden counters of yours!'

'The answer to that is easy,' he said, rising to face her. 'I wish to be allowed to do a great service for your father,' he said quietly. 'I shall give him a project to present to the King that will save France from financial ruin and will absolutely guarantee the Duke of Orleans the Regency!'

Angry as she was, there was something about the man, something she could not quite understand or dismiss. John Law intrigued her and frustrated her because she sensed she could not control him. And there was truth in what he said about her father. Yes, Philip was a libertine, and who should know that better than she?

'Very well, John Law,' she said, 'Come with me. Father is in the Pavilion with his latest mistress. I shall introduce you.'

He followed her along the path lit by torchiers, past endless neatly manicured hedges and flower beds laid out in intricate designs. They turned a corner of the palace, and she paused under one flaming torchier, moving close enough to him to peer into his eyes. Her voice held the edge of danger. 'You are a strange man, John Law, with many sides to you. But I warn you: this plan of yours had better be foolproof because, in France, there are already too many fools in high places!'

'I shall heed the warning, Marie-Louise,' he said seriously, but a slight smile touched the corners of his lips.

She led him to a small pavilion illuminated by torchiers where two footmen in immaculate white satin uniforms and white wigs set a rocket into a launching trestle. A man of medium height in a long brown wig and pale blue velvet coat heavy with gilt embroidery waited impatiently for them to finish. He took a drink from a champagne glass, slightly unsteady on his feet. 'Get on with it, will you?' He exclaimed petulantly, stepping to the footmen,

As Marie-Louise and Law mounted the steps, the lady with Orleans had her back to them. 'Patience Philip,' she said gently, pronouncing the French words with a heavy English accent. 'They will have it ready in a moment.'

One of the footmen lit a taper and held it out to Philip. 'Now, your Grace,' he said. Philip took the taper like a spoiled child and touched it to the end of the rocket. The fireworks blazed skyward, trailing a path of sparks until it blossomed into a brilliant flower.

Katherine Knollys turned. She saw Law almost at the same instant he recognized her. She stood for a moment frozen in time, looking as she had ten years earlier when she had been mistress to the English King. Or so it was said; she had admitted nothing. Now, in the full bloom of womanhood, who else would she pick for a protector but Philip, Duke of Orleans, the man closest to power? That was the Kate that John Law remembered: a woman who selected her lovers carefully. Once, he had killed a man to win her favor. Now he was about to offer help to another who had her favors.

'Lady Knollys, I believe,' he said with a formal bow.

'Mister Law,' she replied in a tone that gave nothing away. 'How enchanting to meet again—so soon. I have been telling the Duke about your phenomenal winning streak at the casino.'

Philip, Duke of Orleans, turned from his fireworks to face the new arrivals, regarding Law with some displeasure. 'You are something of a magician with numbers, and with the daggers, from what I hear, Monsieur.'

'A game I should not wish to play too often, your Grace,' Law said with a slight bow.

Although he was scarcely forty, the ravages of dissipation marked Orleans' once handsome features. He scowled. 'Well, I see my daughter seems to have offered you our hospitality, Monsieur, but I understand you have made no friend of our Lieutenant of Police.' He frowned at Marie-Louise. 'Why have you brought this man to me, Marie-Louise?'

Marie-Louise went over and kissed her father on the lips. The gesture seemed unnatural and made Law think that what Vivien Duclos had told him about their relationship was true.

'Who cares what Count D'Argenson thinks, Papa? Monsieur Law has been filling me with fantastic tales of how he alone can save our country. He says he can guarantee you the Regency.' She looked back at Law, her laughter dancing in the soft night air. 'I have decided that this Scotsman is either a fool, a madman, or a genius. Perhaps all three! So I do believe you should listen to him, Papa.'

'I am in no mood for saviors at the moment, Monsieur Law,' Orleans grunted and turned back to his rockets. 'Did you know these damned things were invented by the Chinese?'

Law reached into his pocket and brought out the letter from the King of Sardinia. 'If you will pardon me, your Grace, I have a letter of introduction to you personally.'

Interested now, Orleans turned from the rocket and took the letter. He held it up to the light of a torchier, reading it quickly, then looked sharply back, studying Law with renewed interest.

'So! My brother-in-law thinks highly of you, does he? Well! This is another matter.' He smiled for the first time. 'Then, I am delighted to welcome you to the festivities. Champagne!'

He gestured to a footman who filled two more goblets standing on a thick silver tray. Orleans picked up another rocket and set it in the launcher. 'The most expensive fireworks in Europe for your grandfather's birthday, Marie-Louise.'

'A great deal of money up in smoke, for a sick country,' Law said bluntly.

Orleans turned sharply with a frown. 'Eh? Why is it foreigners always want to criticize the French? The Russian Tsar says we are too civilized. The Chinese Emperor calls us Barbarians. But they don't tell us how to collect our taxes without riots or how to keep our country from the jaws of poverty.'

'It has been said that the Scots know how to hold onto money, your Grace. I shall offer you a Scottish answer to a French dilemma—if you will allow me,' Law said seriously.

Orleans nodded. 'I take such promises with more than a grain of salt, Monsieur.'

'You must invite Monsieur Law to dine with us so that you can hear what he has to say. When you have not had too much wine, Papa,' Marie-Louise said pointedly.

'Very well, my dear,' Orleans said. 'I shall listen to his projections. Though I should not like Lady Knollys to think I give in to your every whim.' He sighed deeply. 'At least you do not propose to ruin my evening, for I intend to finish off another bottle of champagne with Lady Knollys.'

'When shall it be then, Papa?' Marie-Louise asked insistently.

Orleans bit his lip, considering. 'It is true I am somewhat out of favor at the moment with the old ram.' His features softened into a smile. 'Very well, Monsieur Law. Tomorrow I shall be all attention. We shall dine in my private apartments where not too many other ears can hear these projections of yours.'

'I shall look forward to it, your Grace,' Law said with a bow.

'May I come, Philip?' Katherine asked brightly. 'I should like to hear them, too.'

Orleans turned to Katherine, who until that moment had been standing silently listening, her eyes on Law. "Why not, my dear? Come, Katherine,' he said. 'I am tired of setting the sky on fire.' He bent closer to her, whispering in her ear, 'Let us make a few explosions of our own.'

Law bowed to the Duke again. But it was Katherine that his eyes lingered on for a long moment. Diamonds sparkling at her throat, and in her hair, she was irresistible in the moonlight.

'Enchanted to see you again, Lady Knollys,' he said. 'And I am grateful for your interest.'

'Good night, Monsieur Law,' Katherine replied. 'As an English woman, I shall look forward to hearing your plans for saving France from the French.'

She could not hold his gaze too long. As Katherine moved gracefully away on Philip's arm, his daughter watched her father's mistress with some envy. She had not missed Katherine's interest in Law, or his in her.

'Pretty, is she not?' Marie-Louise asked, adding hastily, 'In a pale English sort of way.'

'I suppose,' he replied. 'I hadn't noticed.'

Marie-Louise gave a throaty laugh. 'Only a dead man would not have noticed. But I like a man who can tell a graceful lie.' She took his arm and led him towards the music, stopping any protest. 'Come then, my man of numbers,' she said. 'Show me what sort of figures you can make on the dance floor.'

Music drifted from the ballroom in slow and staid cadence. Marie-Louise led him into the sumptuously painted gallery. Soft candlelight from huge crystal chandeliers created visual melodies across the color-wheel of silk and satin gowns moving sedately around the floor. To Law, the dancers were like actors, each playing a part, with a languishing eye and a smiling mouth as they curtsied and bowed and executed the dance's intricate steps.

'Most excellent musicians, don't you think?' Marie-Louise asked as she led him towards the far end of the room where the orchestra sat on a small platform dressed in pale green silk coats and powdered wigs. 'Grandfather has brought them from all over Europe,' she said proudly.'

'Indeed they play excellently well,' Law said, marveling at the quality of the music.

'A harpsichord, of course. And an organ to keep the bass continuo. The musicians must sit in a certain order, you see,' she said with some excitement. 'When I was a child, I was allowed up at night to sit by the orchestra until I fell asleep. My favorite was the string section.'

He viewed the front four First Violins, four Second Violins, and two double basses. His gaze followed her description of the other instruments.

'And in the center are always the woodwinds, the oboes, flutes, and bassoons. Behind them, the solo celli, two violas, and two contrabasses.'

His glance drifted above two trumpets, three trombones and a kettle-drum on the far left of the platform, to the painted wall panels behind them depicting a pageant of mounted French troops. There were various portraits of King Louis leading his army in triumphant battles. Law turned back to Marie-Louise, who was humming a small phrase of the melody. 'You are knowledgeable about music, I see.'

'Grandfather considers it one of God's finest gifts to man.'

'Quite different than our humble pipers and fiddlers in Scotland, I must admit,' Law smiled. 'Truly, I have never heard a finer orchestra.' He glanced around the room. Thin, mirrored stripes banded by gilded ormolu decorated the opposite wall where gilt chairs cushioned the bottoms of a ruffled row of ladies of all ages. Gentlemen in a bright array of colors clustered around them. A few of the older men, less nimble of foot, sat with the ladies. Footmen wearing the King's livery moved among them, passing trays of champagne and tidbits of food. The music started up once more.

'Ah, Law! It is the Courante!' Marie-Louise exclaimed. 'Grandfather Louis' favorite dance, and he was wonderfully adept at it.'

Law knew the French dances were more refined than those in London, with their hundreds of slow, calculated movements and each sedate pause meant to be filled by a neatly turned compliment to the lady on her beauty or gown. 'Very pretty indeed,' he said, not impressed.

'Pretty?' Marie-Louise exclaimed. 'You make it sound trivial. In fact, the King thought the dance of such importance that a nobleman's education could scarcely be said to have begun until he'd mastered it,' she said grandly. Her expression was that of a serious child. 'Dancing is not a frivolous matter to the King.'

'Of vast consequence,' he said with a touch of irony. 'I can see that.'

She brightened. 'Have you ever danced it?'

Law shook his head. 'I have danced the Minuet in England, which looks quite similar, and the Fling in Scotland. Which.' he added with a grin, 'does not.' He did not tell her how long ago were his dancing days.

'Ah, but Law, the Minuet is derived from the Courante!' Marie-Louise told him happily. 'The great composer, Lully set it to music, and I myself learned it from the King's own Beauchamp, the father of dancing masters! If you are to become a proper Frenchman, you must learn it, too. I shall teach you. Now, let us not talk of serious matters anymore. They are for the daytime. Come, let us dance.'

Reluctantly he allowed her to lead him onto the floor and into the flow of the other dancers. The movements were performed on tiptoe with slightly jumping steps and many bows and curtsies, and Law soon picked up the style of its graceful and courtly refinements. He could hear compliments being passed between the other dancers on the color of a lady's fan or the bravery of a gentleman's attire.

Many ladies smiled and curtsied to him as they moved around, and he could see whispering behind fans along the wall as to who the stranger might be that Marie-Louise had in tow.

That night they danced until the orchestra played the very last tune. Marie-Louise was light as a breeze on the dance floor, and her cheeks had no need of the 'japanned' rouge worn by other Court ladies; hers glowed with excitement. He found it easy to pay her the pretty compliments custom demanded.

The music over, people began to drift into the dining hall once more for refreshment.

'Not here,' she said. 'We shall have a private repast in my apartments.'

Exactly how far and on what merry dance she intended to take him, he was not sure. And although he was not immune to her charms, Law could foresee the dangers of becoming her lapdog, a position he was not willing to accept. He bowed low to her, aware of the many eyes on him. Two of them belonged to the Captain he had seen her with at Madame Duclos's gaming house.

'I should not wish to compromise your honor, Marie-

Louise,' he said. 'We shall meet tomorrow as you have arranged.' With that, he kissed her hand and bid her good night.

Marie-Louise stood for a long moment watching John Law cross the dance floor and then snapped her fingers for Count De Riom, who had been sulking at one side of the room all evening with Marie-Louise's lady-in-waiting, Mouchi. The two of them came hurrying to her. 'I want a bottle of champagne,' she said. 'Mouchi, have it brought to my apartments. She barely looked at De Riom as she spoke. 'Come, Henri.'

De Riom smiled. Whatever attachment she had developed for this Scotsman, she was back with him now. He took her arm and proudly led her up the grand staircase to her apartments.

That night Marie-Louise had little sleep in De Riom's arms, and when she did fall into slumber, she dreamed of John Law.

TEN: MONEY MATTERS

Law had taken rooms at the Place Louis le Grand in the new Vendome quarter of Paris, not too distant from the Palais Royal, and had bought a horse and a small carriage. The following evening he dressed carefully in his brown velvet suit, adding a new lace neckband and stock. He unwrapped his only tattered copy of the treatise of banking that he had formulated so many years before in his prison cell. He'd carried it with him down the Mississippi and halfway around the world but never found a government willing to try out his system.

John Law felt no allegiance to any kingdom. The world was his hunting ground ever since he fled England. He always knew that somewhere, somehow, he would find his place in it, somewhere that needed him. But here, now, there could be no mistakes. If France turned him down, for him, there were no more countries on the planet. No other possibilities. France was certainly a country in need, and for reasons that had nothing to do with politics, Marie-Louise had set his feet in the right direction. Certainly, a man ought to be grateful. But the old ache for Katherine had returned.

The dinner had been arranged and was being served in Philip's private chambers in the palace. The conversation was on horses and hunting and the extravagant flamboyance of Madame de Maintenon's gowns. Marie-Louise had been cool to Law when he arrived. Katherine sat beside Philip, but her attention remained on Law. Her eyes told him that somehow, they would have to meet alone.

But when he thought about the risks that it would entail, he could hear Archie's words to him on the way to that fatal duel when he'd killed Wilson and destroyed his own life. 'Could you not have kept your small companion tucked inside your trousers until we had our business completed?'

Then, he'd been too young, too eager for all the thrills that life offered, and sometimes his small companion had a mind of its own. Now, his survival depended on not being distracted from his goal: to make Philip, Duke of Orleans, want and need him so much that he would help his projects become realities. Now, he must think of his future. And that now depended upon the future Regent of France.

At the dinner table, John Law tried not to look at Katherine. He turned to Marie-Louise. 'I have not told you how attractive you look in that gown. The color is an inspiration with your hair.'

True, she did look quite beautiful. The royal blue silk of her dress set off her flaming hair, which she wore unpowdered. Although she received the compliment, he could see that she had not forgiven him for deserting her the night before. But as the dinner progressed, she softened once more towards him. When the dessert was served, she turned to Orleans.

'Now Papa,' she said. You have feasted well and have drunk a great deal of claret. Do you not think it is time to hear what Monsieur Law has to say?'

Orleans had certainly eaten well. In the new French manner, each food was served in a separate course: fish, duck, roast lamb, cheese, and sweet rolls, and he had put away nearly a bottle of claret. Still, Law considered him sober enough to pay attention.

The Duke pushed back an iced dessert as the footman refilled his wine glass. His look was challenging. 'Tell me, Monsieur Law, why you suggest that I would have difficulty gaining approval from the King to be granted the Regency. His daughter is my wife and my daughter, his legitimate grandchild.'

Marie-Louise interrupted before Law could reply. 'Really Papa, you know Grandfather thinks you are nothing but a libertine and a lecher, and anyway, you hardly ever see Mama! Grandfather is quite correct, too.' Her eyes went to Katherine. 'I am certain that even Lady Knollys would have to agree.' She gave Katherine a withering look and no chance to reply. 'Dear Mama often says you have wasted your youth in dissipation, Papa, but she still believes that there is more to you than that. You play the part of a witty, amusing bon vivant far too well. Yes, yes, but there's much, much more to you, Papa! I have heard you speak of serious things. Occasionally.' She paused with a slight frown. 'Not often, it is true.'

'Enough, Marie-Louise!' Philip cried. She was the only one who could speak to him in so critical a manner, and with Marie-Louise, he was never angry. He turned back to Law impatiently. 'You talk of schemes and a plan. A plan? What is this plan, Law? Let us hear it!'

Law leaned forward across the table, meeting Philip's eyes. 'It is simple, your Grace. I propose setting up a bank in France. A *national* bank. '

What is so original about a bank?' Philip snorted. 'I hear there is a bank in Holland already.'

'Indeed, there are several banks in the world, your Grace. But they are all *private* banks!›

Philip looked at him, incredulously. Then he began to laugh. 'A bank, Monsieur? In France?' The laughter rolled out of him. 'You expect a Frenchman to put his gold into such a place? If a Frenchman has money to put aside, he buries it in his shoe.'

'Exactly, sire. Where it is out of circulation, and doing the economy of France no good at all!' Law could see that he must somehow capture Orleans' imagination, to make him understand what he himself had so long dreamed of. He went on: 'This Bank of France would be unique. It would be the very first of its kind anywhere in the world! A *National* bank, owned by the state and under the protection of the King of France! It would be a secure place where merchants could put their gold and silver in return for French credit-notes that the King›s National Bank would print. With these French banknotes, the merchants could buy, sell, and trade with security throughout Europe. And all of the bank's profits would come into France's coffers, making the country rich.' He leaned forward. 'As I am sure you are aware, Sire, once the trade of a country is stimulated, the entire country begins to prosper.

'The profits in gold would all go to France...?' Philip mused.

'Indeed,' Law said. 'And we do value gold, do we not, by its weight!' He paused. "Yet, I must tell you that the other day, I picked up a handful of gold louis d' or and weighed them, Sire. They were all of different weights!'

Orleans looked confused. There was a moment of silence. Marie-Louise asked, 'But John, when the coins are minted, are they not all the same weight?'

'They are, Duchess, but many people shave the gold from their coins, and soon they have enough to mint another coin!' Law replied.

'Hmm. I have heard of that practice, but thought it of little consequence,' Philip mused.

'It is of great importance to the economy of your country, your Grace,' Law said. 'Your new National Bank of France will not accept gold louis d' or, or any foreign coin at face value! All gold coins coming into your bank will be accepted only by weight! Thus, the Bank of France will regulate international coinage!'

'But these credit-notes of yours—paper! What would happen to the gold?'

'The credit-notes are just what the name indicates. Sire. They will represent the true value in weight of all the gold being held by the bank, and recorded to each depositor's credit.'

'And what becomes of all this gold in the bank?' Katherine asked.

'The bank will use that money to lend! To all who show good reason. And to invest in various projects. The bank will charge, of course. France will profit by all transactions!'

'Are such credit-notes in use anywhere now?' Orleans asked, becoming slightly more interested.

Law took a Dutch credit-note from his pocket. 'Here is one from the Bank of Amsterdam. A *private* bank. I might add that the banker is a wealthy man!' He handed it to Orleans, continuing. 'Far more convenient to carry than gold.

'More convenient? Remarkable.'

Orleans felt the paper between his thumb and forefinger. 'And this is used instead of money?'

'It *is* money, your Grace. With this paper credit-note, knowing the gold it represents, Dutch merchants conduct their business, and everybody profits. 'It's so highly favored for trade that this private Dutch bank sells them for slightly more than the face value of the coin.'

'Remarkable!' Orleans exclaimed again and looked up from

the piece of paper in his hand. 'I have heard that the savages on certain islands use shells from the sea as money.' The thought made him laugh. 'Neptune's coin of the realm!'

Law took the note from him, reading. 'This note says that I have 20 gilders on deposit in the Bank of Amsterdam. Would you not agree that a man's gold is safer in a bank than under his floorboards, or in his shoe or his pocket?'

'Safer, perhaps, Law. But gold is what a man likes to carry in his pocket,' Philip said thoughtfully. 'Merely the feel of it gives a man confidence.' He laughed again. 'Maybe you should have tried selling seashells, Law. They are stronger than paper.'

'Seashells prove one thing, your Grace. That it is not the device, nor the symbolic worth of money that is important. It is the acceptance of it. Acceptance breeds confidence. and confidence in a country comes with its financial stability.'

'Just how will this bank of yours provide confidence, Monsieur Law?' Orleans asked with a flicker of interest.

'Business depends upon having the capital to invest, does it not, sir? If a man can borrow investment money from a bank by paying some interest on his loan, it will help his business grow. It will improve not only his but the entire nation's economy.'

'What a marvelous idea, Philip!' Katherine exclaimed as though she had never heard it before. It was the same old song John Law had sung ten years ago when no one would listen, and she knew it well, though she had never paid it much credence.

'Yes, Interesting. Interesting, Katherine,' Orleans said, looking at her sharply. He rose from the table. The others followed him into his private salon, where he made himself comfortable on a delicate giltwood sofa. 'But I am surprised you understand such matters, Katherine.'

'We women understand money matters, Philip,' Katherine said, sinking gracefully onto a pale blue silk chair. 'Enough to know what it can buy.'

'Let us hear some more, Monsieur Law,' Orleans said, helping himself to a sweetmeat from a bonbonnière.

Marie-Louise came and sat beside her father. Law strode around the room in thought for a moment. If he failed now, there would be no second chance. When he turned back to Orleans, his expression was confident, showing none of the concern he was feeling.

'Perhaps you are not aware, your Grace, but Holland enjoys commercial supremacy in Europe. It is entirely due to their private bank and its lending facilities.' His voice took on the urgency of the promoter. 'I tell you, were France to have its own bank, with this country's natural advantages, Holland would no doubt be uninhabited!'

Philip's eyes brightened. 'A government, lending money. Novel. Yes, quite an idea.' Then he sighed. 'But you see, it would never work in France.'

Marie-Louise rose to come beside Law, engrossed in what he was saying. 'But Law, here on the Continent, only the Jews are legally allowed to lend money. Is it not so, Papa?'

'Yes, and unfortunately, it has caused much ill will towards them in a Catholic country such as ours,' Orleans said.

'Holland holds no such religious stipulations,' Law pointed out. 'That is why the lending principal has been a great success there.' He came a step closer to Orleans, speaking earnestly. 'Your Grace, I feel certain that if a French bank were to lend money as a business enterprise, this country would prosper. Then Frenchmen could pay their taxes, and money would pour into the country's coffers!'

'What a clever man you are, John Law!' Marie-Louise exclaimed.

Orleans got to his feet. His figure was beginning to show signs of the excesses of the table. He paced about for a few moments, weighing what he had heard. Finally, he turned back to Law. 'A national bank of France. Well, certainly a fascinating idea, and I must say, highly original.'

'Thank you, your Grace. I ask that I be allowed to present it to the King, on your behalf,' Law said with a small bow.

'Mmm. We shall see. Any more dazzling ideas, Law?' Philip asked, looking at the Scotsman with growing admiration.

'One. The greatest and the most original of all. It is an idea that has never before been tried anywhere!'

They all waited expectantly. Law drew a deep breath. 'I propose that the government store all the gold in the land and do away with gold entirely as the actual currency. That France prints a new currency on paper, which is equal in value to the amount of gold it has in store.'

'Paper money?' Orleans stared at him, incredulously. 'You mean to say you would stop the people having gold?' Orleans asked, wondering if he was talking to a madman.

'Not immediately, your Grace,' Law replied with a half-smile, then earnestly added, 'If the face value of the paper money were honored and guaranteed by the King, then people would not need gold.'

'You are suggesting that this paper money would be specially printed by our government and be as official in value as gold?' Orleans frowned.

'Printed to the value of the gold on deposit in the bank.'

'You sound like the Pied Piper, Law. On what sort of a merry dance would you lead the French people?'

'Sir, they would soon accept the value stated on the paper as equal to the metal held by the King.' He took his pamphlet from his pocket. 'I have written a booklet on my principles which I would ask you to read.'

Law saw that he was losing Orleans' thin interest. The Duke's laughter cut him off. 'Enough, Law! For a moment there, you almost had me believing you,' he said. 'But no, Monsieur. You will never get a Frenchman to give up the hard clink of the gold in his pocket for a fistful of paper that he could not even trade back for the real thing.'

'Sir, a moment ago we were speaking of seashells,' Law said. 'What is the use of money if not merely a simple exchange voucher for the purchase of goods and services? So why use costly and inconvenient metals like gold or silver when paper would do just as well to carry around?'

He came a step closer and set his pamphlet on the table next to Orleans. Now was the time to play his trump card. 'I suggest, your Grace, that with the Duke du Maine as your opponent for the appointment of Regent, you have little to lose in presenting the King with my scheme—as a counter-proposal to his bankruptcy!'

Marie-Louise came over to her father. 'Goodness knows, Papa, it is going to take something sensational to impress

Grandfather and the Parliament with your abilities, you old darling,' she kissed his cheek affectionately.'

Orleans picked up the pamphlet and opened the dog-eared cover. His eyes traveled over the first page. It was written in English, but Philip could read it well enough. After a few moments, he looked up. 'We must have this translated into French immediately,' he said, then turned to his daughter. 'Perhaps I have underestimated you, my dear Marie-Louise. But I believe you are right about one thing: Monsieur Law is either a madman or a genius!'

Law smiled. 'Perhaps a bit of both, as all men of original thought might be.'

'Very well, Monsieur. Part of what you have told me might work. I shall present you to the King to tell him about the bank - the lending - the investment - and the banknotes. But I warn you, in the name of Saint Joan, do not mention the paper money!'

Marie-Louise clapped her hands like a child, then linked her arm through her father's. 'Don't you think, Papa, that with Monsieur Law newly arrived in France and with no townhouse of his own, that he should move into the Palais Royal for a while? With only Mama and Grandmama, and Lady Knollys, and Popo, of course, there are so many apartments not in use at the moment. And then you could have him by your side all the time to consult with.'

'Move him in here?' Orleans considered. Then he smiled. 'An excellent idea!'

'It is much more than I had hoped for, Monsieur.' Law managed a small bow.

'This was originally Cardinal Richelieu's townhouse, you know,' Orleans told Law. Then given by Louis XIV to my father, Charles. It became mine at his death.'

Law had heard about Philip's father, the Sun King's brother, lithe, effeminate, and everyone had flattered him by calling him Monsieur, and the courtiers were grateful that it was not he who was on the throne. But his family connection put Philip in a strong position. He was the King's nephew and also his son-in-law. Philip had married his first cousin, the plump Mlle de Blois, the King's legitimized daughter. Law had glimpsed her at the festivities, but Marie-Louise's mother kept to herself.

Philip popped another sweetmeat into his mouth, his tone edged with pomposity. 'Indeed, I am grateful to the old Cardinal. Yes, grateful to Richelieu,' he mused. 'As Prime Minister to Louis XIII, the man curbed the nobility's power and the Protestant opposition to the Royal family. It was he who made it possible to assert the unlimited power of the crown. Unlimited power...'

The thought brought a new light to his eyes. Orleans sat back on his chair, pursing his lips and rubbing his hands together at the idea of such power. It was a moment before he spoke again. 'It should have paved the way for an absolute state. But you know, Law, it is curious. This absolutist goal was not reached under the reign of my illustrious father-in-law, Louis XIV. For some extraordinary reason, he did not attempt it. But I intend to change all that when I am Regent.'

'I see, Your Grace,› Law said, worried slightly. ‹But as to my proposals, be assured that I would not ask you to approve anything that is not for the general good.'

'General good...?' Orleans looked puzzled. 'Oh, I see. Yes, indeed. The people. Well, we must take care of them, of course. But appearances...! We must keep them up, don't you see?'

'Appearances? Certainly, Your Grace,' Law said, wondering where this conversation was leading.

'What a fine idea to have Monsieur Law stay at the Palais,' Katherine exclaimed. There will be many things for you to discuss, Philip.' Her eyes went to Law's. He read in her glance things that had nothing to do with banking.

'Yes, yes. An excellent idea. *Your* idea, Marie-Louise.› Orleans studied the imposing figure of the man standing before him. 'Yes, as you say, an original thinker. People in high places need men like you close by.'

He turned to his daughter once more. 'If the King is receptive to Monsieur Law's plan, I shall have you to thank, my dear. You can name anything you desire, and it shall be yours.'

Marie-Louise kissed her father full on the lips with more than daughterly affection. 'I shall hold you to your promise, Papa - when the time is right.'

Philip II, Duke of Orléans

ELEVEN:
A LITTLE TOO LATE

Soft light filtered through the half-open curtains of a bedchamber in a palace wing, one corridor away from Orleans' apartments. Some days had gone by, and now the thin morning glow illuminated Katherine Knollys' delicate features. The man with her stripped back the silk sheets from her naked form to study its perfection and bent to kiss the tip of one upturned breast.

'You have a cool mind for a woman whose body causes such heat in a man,' John Law said. 'I thought you had forgotten me.'

She looked up at him through thick, unblinking lashes. She breathed a sigh. 'Forget my own Jessamy Johnny? How could I?'

'Too easily, it would seem.' Only a few hours earlier, he had drawn apart the heavy damask curtains to let the moonlight filter across the lady's bed. Absence had sharpened his desire. And having her had only served to stoke the flames even higher.

Her eyes read denial. 'Don't you know by now that I only come alive when I am in your arms?' she breathed.

He nodded. 'Mine and whose else's, dear heart? Not counting Orleans, of course. How many arms have been wrapped around you since you were last in mine?'

She sighed. 'A girl must take care of herself in these troubled times; surely you understand that, Johnny?'

'Naturally. I would expect no less of you, my dear Kate. But why is it the times, troubled or no, never seem right for us to be together?' he asked.

'You have never been out of my thoughts for a moment,' she said, enjoying the sensation of his lips on her bare breast. He proceeded to run his kisses down across her stomach.

'How dull for the Duke of Orleans.'

'That is unworthy of you, Johnny,' she complained. 'You were always the first to point out the difference between business and pleasure.'

'Pleasure, yes,' he murmured. 'And absence can be a pain so sharp a man can feel it! When I wrote to you, Katherine, I even dared to hope that you might be foolish enough to take a chance and join me.'

'Join you in the wilderness? Surely you did not really expect that, Johnny? You were halfway across the world. Someplace I had never heard of. It sounded like something to drink.'

'Mississippi,' he said.

'Precisely,' she told him, sitting up and stopping his lips from traveling further. 'Are you going to be cross with me just when we have found each other again?'

She rose quickly, throwing a voluminous robe of pale ivory satin around herself. 'I must hurry now. Philip will ask for me at breakfast. And he is expecting you there, too.'

He got up and came over to her. 'When will I see you alone again?' he asked, catching her arm lightly and turning her so that he could see her face.

'Don't be greedy, my darling Jessamy John. There will be sufficient opportunities now that you are actually living here in the palace.' She kissed him lightly, then drew away, moving on to her dressing table. 'Have they given you a nice apartment? I understand it belonged to the old Prince de Pauillac, who died six months ago.'

'It's nice enough. No ghosts,' he said, catching her hand. He drew it to his lips, kissing her palm. 'Love is a capricious creature. It desires everything and is never content,' he said.

She gave him a dry smile, pulling free. 'I do not ask you about the other women in between. We're birds of a feather, Johnny. How long would we last if we clipped each other's wings?'

'True, my dear,' he replied flatly, picking up a diamond necklace from where she had dropped it on the floor. 'and Orleans adorns his bird quite well, I see.'

'Don't be jealous, Johnny,' she said, taking it from him and tossing it casually into a large jewel coffer, which was already quite full. 'Philip could make you so rich that you could buy me ten like that.'

'Always thinking of yourself, my dear.'

'Johnny! I'm only thinking of you!' she exclaimed, seating herself at the dressing table and beginning to brush her hair. 'Philip is fascinated with your pamphlet. Although you might have given him a copy not quite so tattered.'

'It has traveled with me a long way from there to here,' he said.

'Well, trust me, Johnny. I shall do my part to convince him to help you. But couldn't you have given him something more practical than that same old scheme of yours? A National Bank! And paper money? Next, you'll be making paper diamonds.'

'If you will recall, dear Kate, I almost launched my bank in England until I killed Wilson,' he said, coming behind her.

She looked into the mirror, her china-blue eyes on him. 'Johnny! I know you blame me for the duel. I blame myself. Oh, I do! I do!' she said, and the emotion in her voice made him think perhaps she meant it.

'No, Kate, I blame myself for wanting you too much.' He looked over her shoulder at their reflection in the dressing table mirror and wondered how much *he* actually meant it. The crumbs of another man›s feast were all he might hope for. Those two people in the mirror suited each other—bodies and minds. And yet somehow, he could not imagine them descending into some idyllic old age together. ‹You are the only woman I have ever cared for,› he said.

She turned slightly and reached up to kiss him passionately. 'I promise you, Johnny, we will find other moments, perhaps hours. Now you must go quickly before anybody sees you!'

Law tied his cravat with immaculate precision, the lace cascading down his chest. A flowered silk waistcoat softened the severity of the brown velvet suit. He was wearing a new brown wig, his concession to Court protocol. She studied him with admiring eyes.

'The wilderness must have agreed with you, Johnny. You have not lost your golden touch with words. Let us hope they translate into real gold, not paper.'

'This may be the opportunity I have waited for all my life, Katherine!' he said with a burst of enthusiasm. 'At last, I have the ear of the one man who needs me enough to help me.' He turned back to her. 'And as for us, my own sweet dove, when Orleans tires of you, and men like him always do—I shall be there for you.'

Her laughter tinkled lightly through the room. "Do not hold your breath, Johnny, for I shall be mistress of the Regent of France, thanks to you. And do not think it conceit when I say that Marie-Louise's husband, Popo de Berry, will turn to women before Orleans tires of me.'

She led him to the door, and peering out to see that no one was about, he slipped into the corridor. As he headed towards Orleans' apartments, the scent of Katherine's soft skin still filled his nostrils, and it gave him a heady feeling. A noise turned him to see Marie-Louise coming out of the door of her apartments. She paused with some surprise.

'So early up and about, Law?'

'Your father wants to see me, Marie-Louise. He has asked me to breakfast with him.'

'Ah, well, then there is certainly no hurry. Papa is always late.'

She smoothed a hand across the white linen of her simple morning dress. Her hair was curled naturally about her face, and she wore no face lacquer. Law thought she looked no more than twelve years old.

'Come in,' she said with a wicked smile. 'I shall show you my apartment, which you would not enter the other night. We can have cakes and a pot of chocolate.'

'Thank you, my dear. But since the Duke has expressed the intention of taking me to the King this morning, I would not wish to keep him waiting.'

He drew a gold watch from his pocket and snapped the round lid open to read the time in its delicate gilt tracery. A timepiece he had won a few nights before. It was nearly ten o'clock.

Marie-Louise stared at the watch. The enameled lid depicted a gentleman with a young man reclining suggestively in his lap.

'Does that not belong to Saint-Simon?' she asked.

'It did,' Law acknowledged. 'Until the other night.'

'But it was his favorite possession!' she exclaimed. 'He never stopped talking of it and showing it off. It was made by a famous English watchmaker, Thomas Tampion, and worth a small fortune.'

'Well, well,' Law said. 'I had no idea. I shall have to allow the Count the opportunity to win it back.'

She frowned. 'Are you always the winner, Law?'

'Not always, Marie-Louise,' he said, then added with a grin, 'Only most of the time.'

'You will lose one day. Perhaps then, you will need my help again,' she said with a pout. 'Never forget, it was I who took you to Papa,'

He smiled. She really was no more than a child, and a petulant, demanding one. But what she said was true.

'Be patient, Marie-Louise,' he told her. 'The world is not coming to an end. We shall have ample time to get to know one another.' He kissed her hand. 'May I say you look particularly fetching this morning. But you must endeavor to help me remember that you are a married woman.'

'Must you bring that up, Law?' she cried impatiently. 'Popo de Berry has no more interest in me than I in him.' She took his arm and gave him a bewitching smile. 'One day, I think you shall want me.'

He laughed gently. 'I want you now, my dear. But one must choose the right moment, don't you see?'

'It had better be soon because I hate waiting for anything,' she said with a hint of anger.

'Then, this will be a worthy lesson, my dear Duchess.' He kissed her hand once more.

She smiled, her anger evaporating. 'Very well, if you are eating with Papa, then I shall go with you. He may need my encouragement.'

Indeed it could be true, he thought. Philip was as spoiled as she, and there was no telling when such people would change their minds at the least whim. Together they proceeded down the hall to Orleans' private apartments where two liveried lackeys stood guard at the large double door.

'No need to announce us. I shall tell Papa we are here,' she told the guards imperiously. They opened the doors, and Marie-Louise brushed past them, leading Law inside.

Orleans was standing at his window, his back to them. He turned as they entered, a serious expression on his face. It lightened at the sight of his daughter, who came running over to kiss him.

'Good morning, Papa,' Marie-Louise told him. 'I hope you slept well, and by now have read Monsieur Law's booklet.'

It had been three days since the night of the fireworks, and Law knew that Orleans had been unable to arrange his meeting with the King until this morning.

'The pamphlet? Yes, I have read it. Quite profound, Law.' The nobleman fondled Marie-Louise's cheek as he spoke then turned back to Law regarding him with a look of added respect. 'And congratulations are due you, I believe.'

'On my pamphlet?' Law asked, slightly mystified.

'No, no. I heard that last night, you were in the Rue Dauphin wagering against the Spanish Ambassador at Poisson's and gained one million eight hundred thousand livres,' Orleans said.

'A small victory,' Law demurred.

'Small? I should not call it that. And the night before, in the Rue des Poulies, you made another startling win at the Hôtel de Gesbres. Against Saint-Simon, I believe. Well done!'

'Thank you, Sir,' Law said. 'I have been acquainting myself with all your gaming houses, and my fortunes are indeed running high at the moment.'

Orleans nodded approval. 'It is the mark of a gentleman to play for high stakes. If one doesn't gamble in Paris, he is looked upon as either an innocent, stingy, or a beggar.' He took in Law's costume and the flowered waistcoat. 'And I see you have brightened your garb. Good! Good! Brown—too dull, yes. But the waistcoat, that is another matter.' The clock struck the quarter-hour. 'So late, already? We must waste no more time,' Philip said nervously.

'But I wish a glass of champagne, Papa,' Marie-Louise complained.

He tossed her an orange from a bowl. 'No time for breakfast, my dear. The doctors say that your grandfather is fading fast. We must present Law's plan to him immediately. Ready, Law?'

'At your disposal, Sire,' Law said.

'Excellent!' Orleans drew a deep sustaining breath and moved towards the door. 'Well, then, we are off.'

The door was opened for them, and Katherine stepped in. Orleans regarded her with admiration. 'Lady Knollys. You look positively glowing this morning. You must have slept exceeding well,' he said.

'Oh, I did, your Grace,' she replied with a curtsey. Her eyes went to Law. 'Mister Law. I did not think to see you so soon. Are you enjoying Paris?'

'Sufficiently, Lady Knollys.'

'Katherine, my dear,' Orleans interrupted. 'Marie-Louise shall entertain you. Monsieur Law and I have an appointment to see the King.'

'He will like your scheme, Law,' Marie-Louise said. 'And he will praise you for it, Papa.'

'Good luck, Philip.' Katherine threw Law a half-smile as he followed Orleans out.

Orleans led the way into an Ante Chamber of Louis XIV's bedchamber. Flanking the huge doorway bearing the Royal Arms of France stood two liveried footmen wearing the King's own uniforms resplendent with gold embroidery.

'Announce us,' Orleans commanded. 'We are in a hurry.'

'At once, your Grace.' The footman turned to comply just as the bedchamber doors were flung open from within.

An uneven footstep brought forth the slightly angular figure of the Duke du Maine. Orleans' cousin and arch-rival leaned heavily on a cane as he stepped out of the King's bedchamber. Law saw that one of his legs was shorter than the other. He wore a dark blue suit of velvet with a rich design, worked in gold thread. Du Maine's aristocratic features were a theatre for many emotions beneath a jet black wig. He took a step towards Philip and paused to face him. He could not hide the sardonic smile that touched the corners of his full lips.

'As usual, you are too late, Cousin,' du Maine said, his voice almost a snarl of pleasure. But a tear formed in the corner of his eye, and he daubed it with a lace handkerchief. 'Our gracious King, my father, is dead. Alas, the Sun King is dead.'

'Impossible...! I was to see him!' Orleans cried, stunned. 'When did he. . ?

'But a short ten minutes ago. A pity you were not here, for with his last breath, he has designated the new Regent.'

'He has...?' Philip's eyes brightened. Du Maine's words drowned all hope. 'The burden has fallen upon me, Cousin.'

'You. . ? But he cannot have. . !' Orleans said and stopped,

LOUIS-AUGUSTE DE BOURBON DUC DU MAINE
by Rosalba Carriara

seeing behind du Maine, a boy of no more than five years emerging from the King's bedchamber, accompanied by the elderly physician and the Abbé, a tall, heavy-set man. There were tears in the child's eyes. He came over to du Maine, who held out a hand to him, which the boy readily took.

'Great Grandpapa is gone, Uncle,' the boy said, rubbing his eyes.

'Yes, my dear boy. And now you will one day become the King of France—as Louis the XV! It is something to live up to.' Du Maine said and returned his attention to Orleans, with a smile of satisfaction. 'Yes, dear cousin, it is I who shall take upon my shoulders the heavy duties of Regent for this boy until he shall be of age. It is a task I did not seek but shall fulfill to the best of my abilities, poor crippled creature though I am.'

'*You*, as Regent! I shall oppose it!' Orleans cried. 'Parliament will never. . .'

Du Maine's words cut him off. 'Confirm my appointment? 'Oh, but you will see that they shall. And once they have, my first act will be to declare France bankrupt!' He turned to the child. 'It is the one hope of setting the economy right, you see. I shall instruct you in such matters, my dear child.'

'There will be no France if you do that!' Orleans cried. 'But I have the weapon to stop you, du Maine.' He turned to John Law standing beside him, who had been watching the byplay like a tennis game. 'My financial advisor, Monsieur Law has a project that will save France from ruin.'

Du Maine turned his attention to the stranger for the first time. 'So this is Monsieur Law! Indeed, I have had reports. But I fear he had best save himself first,' du Maine advised.

Behind him, Count D'Argenson now emerged from the bedchamber, his hand in a sling.

'As usual, you have been advised by the wrong people.' Du Maine's piercing gaze cut through Law. 'I see you are still in the company of brigands and gamblers, Philip. Monsieur Law wins too consistently at the green tables for an honest man. And as for the projects with which he has been filling your foolish head. . . Oh, yes, my spies keep me well informed about your associates, both male, and female.' He turned to the Prefect of Police. 'Perhaps,

Count D'Argenson, you would care to tell the Duke what you have discovered about our foreign intruder.'

D'Argenson stepped forward, glaring at Law with eyes full of hatred. His voice was shrill and loud enough to wake the dead King if such things were possible. 'Monsieur Law is a fugitive from both Scotland and England. And only a few days ago, he robbed a French Tax Collector!'

Orleans looked at Law in amazement. 'Is this true, Law?'

'Your Grace, if you will allow me to explain...' Law began.

Du Maine hobbled over to Orleans, chuckling softly. 'Poor, innocent Orleans. You thought to work your magic on the King, did you? Well, my dear cousin, it would seem that it is not only your timing that is at fault; I am afraid, Philip, that you have pulled the wrong rabbit out of your hat.'

TWELVE:
D'ARGENSON'S MEN

In the crisp light of dawn, a rabbit, short-eared and silver-grey, scampered across the Sannois road outside of Paris, narrowly missing the grinding wheels of a black coach lurching up the rocky hillside. The coach bore the gold and green insignia of Count D'Argenson's Office on its sides, and inside it, John Law could hear the two coachmen atop the box talking through the clatter of the horses. But he was not aware that their conversation was about their passengers and the orders they were duty-bound to carry out.

A spool of grey dust unraveling in the coach's wake as it wound its way up a tortuously narrow ascent towards the summit. It swayed heavily as it rounded a turn in the road, sending the passengers inside reeling across the seat. Law had been in the process of uncorking a flask of brandy, and some of it spilled on his jacket. He stuck his head out, calling up, 'Be careful there!' then drank from the flask before handing it to his companion. 'Afraid you forgot to pack the glasses, my love.'

'But the brandy is Philip's finest, I am happy to say,' said Katherine Knollys taking a healthy swig and handing it back. She unwrapped a serviette containing bread and cheese and broke off a piece, offering it to Law. 'Hungry?'

'No,' he said, taking it anyway and beginning to munch.

'Neither am I,' she told him and took a large mouthful. 'Poor Philip. He actually wept when he asked me to leave. But with the Duke du Maine in power, Philip will scarcely be able to afford his wife, much less a mistress.'

'You seem to have come out of it well enough,' Law observed, glancing at the diamonds glittering from the opening of her emerald green velvet jacket and the mound of her baggage. 'I have one bag only in this coach.'

'So near to glory and yet so far,' she sighed. 'Curious, how husbands return to their wives in times of crisis.'

'Things even out,' Law replied. 'In times of triumph, they stray from them. I am afraid, my love, that your former patron's only hope of victory could be to convince Parliament not to approve the Duke du Maine as Regent.'

'I do see that, Johnny.' She acknowledged. 'And since Philip is married to old Louis's favorite daughter, he must show Parliament that he has the fat and remarkably dim-witted Mlle de Blois. . .'

'. . .by his side.' They finished the sentence together, and Katherine burst into laughter. It burbled to a stop and then began again.

'What are you laughing about?' he asked.

'I was just thinking about how strange it is, Johnny. We are like a pair of loaded dice, you and I. We always seem to roll up side by side.'

Law smiled. 'That, my love, is because a dissipated life brings one into contact with the lowest brigands and the highest society. It has always furnished me with fertile ground and the opportunity of developing my theories.' He paused. 'If not practicing them.'

'Pity,' she sighed. 'I should have been fascinated to see your paper money.'

He nodded somewhat wistfully. 'Hmm. It's about time we rolled a seven.'

They rode on in silence for a few minutes, their private thoughts being shaken about with every bump in the road. The coach was nearing the crest of the hill when it jerked abruptly and swerved. Law tapped on the roof but got no response. His senses were suddenly alert. Something was wrong with the rhythm of the horses. He stuck his head out the window and saw to his shock that the coach was drifting dangerously near the sharp drop of the hillside. 'Say coachman!' he cried. He looked up in time to see one of the coachmen cutting the horses loose. 'Hey there, what are you...?' He got no further. The coachman jumped.

Quick as thought, Law grabbed Katherine and kicked open the door.

'Whaaa??' she gasped.

Law pushed her out, jumping down after her as the coach hurtled over the edge of the embankment. They tumbled and rolled and then slid down the hill. The coach crashed down, and they were swept along ahead of it—but it was gaining momentum! Law threw his body over Katherine's, rolling them away from its path. The heavy vehicle rolled on, narrowly missing them, and shattered into wooden pieces, spewing its contents of luggage down the craggy slope.

Katherine tumbled down, landing in a thick clump of bushes. Law plunged on past her, grabbing for anything to hang onto. His progress came to a halt at a tree. He lay there for a moment before managing to pull himself to his feet. His face was scratched, body bruised, clothes torn and dusty. He looked around for Katherine and saw her lying half-conscious in a tangle of brush. Glancing up, he spotted the fleeing coachmen making their way towards a pair of horses that had been conveniently tethered there, partially hidden by a clump of trees further up the steep hill.

'Bastards! Devils! Come back!' he shouted to no avail. He made his way up to Katherine. 'Are you all right?'

She stirred. Her hand traveled to her bare throat. 'My diamonds!' she cried, sitting up, dazed.

'To hell with your diamonds. Save your neck.' Law pulled her to her feet and, seeing she was not hurt, started up the slope after the coachman.

Both coachmen were attempting to mount the waiting horses, but the animals were highly agitated by the coach horses' whinnied cries and the crashing coach's racket. One reared and bolted. The younger coachman scrambled after the animal to bring him back.

The other coachman had his foot in the stirrup ready to mount when Law reached him. Law grabbed hold of his boot and brought him tumbling down. The burly fellow struggled to his feet and reached for the blunderbuss strapped to his hip. With only his wits for a weapon, Law grabbed the coachman's cloak, spinning him around and twisting it so tightly that the man could not reach his pistol. The coachman fell back, trying to free his arms, but Law grappled with him, in the rough-and-tumble struggle.

Scrambling painfully on hands and knees, Katherine spotted the glint of her necklace in the undergrowth. She scooped it up, lifted her skirt, and tucked the diamonds into her stocking top. From her garter, she drew out a tiny gold inlaid pistol. It had been given her by the Duke of Orleans as a going-away present together with a diamond bracelet and pearl earrings exactly like a pair he had also given his wife. She knew that Philip often ordered two of the same when gifting a favorite.

'For your protection, my dear,' Philip had said of the gun, but Katherine considered the jewels, security, too, against starvation. Her dress was torn, her hair falling about her as she pulled herself up the slope towards the struggling men.

The younger coachman had by now managed to catch the reins of his runaway horse. Hastily mounting, he turned the animal back to come abreast of the fight between his companion and Law. He pulled out a knife and hurled it at the Scotsman. But Law saw the flash of the blade and instinctively pushed his attacker into its path. The heavy weapon connected with the fellow's spine, and he fell forward, to trouble Law no more.

But now the mounted coachman rode at Law, drawing his pistol. As he aimed, a shot rang out, and the man fell from his horse. Law turned surprised.

Katherine stood some feet away with her small pistol smoking in her hand.

Law stared at her. 'I can always count on the unexpected from you, Katherine.' he cried happily.

'I have never fired a pistol before!' she said with some amazement.

'Thank Heaven!' he told her. 'Or no one would be safe.' The coachman groaned, holding his wounded leg. Law hastily appropriated his blunderbuss.

Katherine turned at the sound of approaching horses. 'Johnny! Look! Dragoons!' she cried, hurrying to his side.

Four mounted Dragoons were clattering towards them from the Paris road. The soldiers had not yet seen them, but the Lieutenant had spotted the plume of dust made by the crashed coach, although it was hidden from his view down the hillside. He reined in, pointing it out to the others.

Law aimed the flared brass barrel at the approaching cavalry. Seeing them, the Lieutenant of Dragoons halted his men and dismounted, coming towards them, calling out. 'Monsieur Law! It is you?'

'What if it is?' Law called back.

'I have orders to escort you back to Paris!'

Keeping the pistol aimed at him, Law asked, 'Whose orders, Lieutenant? Count D'Argenson's?'

The Lieutenant shook his head. 'No, no, Monsieur. It is from the new Regent of France himself.' He turned to his second in command. 'See to that wounded man, Sergeant.'

The Sergeant moved hurriedly with some men to take charge of the injured coachmen. The Lieutenant stepped to Katherine. 'Come Lady Knollys. You shall have one of our horses.' His eyes went to the tiny pistol in her hand, still aimed at him. 'And I suggest you will not be needing that on the return journey.'

He took the reins of the coachman's horse and offered his knee to her. She paused long enough to reach under her skirt, exchange the pistol for her diamonds and fasten them back at their rightful place around her throat. Then she moved grandly towards the Dragoon using his knee to mount the horse.

Tucking the blunderbuss into his belt, Law quickly mounted the other.

'I hope you will find the ride back more pleasant than the journey so far,' the Dragoon Lieutenant said, his eyes devouring Katherine's delicately chiseled features. Indeed, she looked beautifully sensuous in her disheveled state, her cheeks flushed and hair in a tangle.

Katherine leaned across her horse to whisper to Law. 'The new Regent wishes to see us. What do you make of that, Johnny?'

He glanced down at a magnificent panorama of the Seine Valley and Paris in the distance. 'I think we just rolled that seven, Kate,' he said.

It was evening when they reached the Palais Royal and stood in the antechamber of the Regent's official quarters waiting to be admitted. They had been given no time to change their clothes or wash. The massive doors were opened, and once again, the two adventurers faced Philip Duke of Orleans.

'Welcome back!' he cried, favoring Katherine with a broad smile. 'You look a fright, my dear, but no matter. From now on, you shall have the finest gowns. Whatever your heart desires. Come, we shall celebrate.'

He raised a glass of wine in a toast as his manservant poured for the others.

'To victory! To my dear Katherine! And of course, to John Law, whose financial projections Parliament has approved, which has made this all possible. Welcome back to Paris!'

Behind him, Marie-Louise entered from her father's bedroom, looking as though she has just climbed out of his bed, her red hair a mass of tousled curls. But she smiled brightly at Law. 'Welcome back, Monsieur Law.' Noticing his torn jacket and the scratches on his face, she added: 'It was not a pleasant trip, I see.'

'Count D'Argenson's idea of an escort lacks the finer touches of hospitality, I fear,' Law replied.

'John Law acquitted himself well, Philip,' Katherine exclaimed. 'He fought those brigands bravely. You owe him my life.' Katherine did not mention that it was she who had shot the coachman. She would tell him later when they were alone and thank him for the muff pistol.

'The scoundrels are being taken to the Bastille at this very moment, and there they shall remain until they are as old as the itch,' Orleans said angrily. 'Have no fear, my dear Katherine, I shall repay D'Argenson for his little treachery.'

'But what has happened, Your Grace, that has changed everything since the day you asked us to leave?' It was Law who asked and Marie-Louise who answered.

'Curious, how things turned out, isn't it?' she said laconically. 'You see, John Law, the Parliament didn't in the end, feel that bankruptcy was a total answer for France and Papa was able to convince them to appoint him the new Regent, all because of your fantastic projections. Remarkable, is it not?'

Orleans put his arm around his daughter, nodding agreement. 'Yes, I am pleased to say that my cousin, the Duke du Maine, is out of favor because I have promised the people reforms instead of ruin.' He smiled. 'That is where you come in, Law.'

'Parliament has approved my plans?' Law asked incredulously.

The smile that broadened across Philip's pudgy face made him appear almost cherubic. 'Well, you see, they have little choice now, for I have appointed you my official financial advisor.' Downing his champagne in one gulp, the new Regent got to his feet, a fresh note of authority in his bearing. 'And now it is time to put your theories to the test, Monsieur Law. Even. . . Yes, why not? Even your paper money!'

Law stared at Orleans, then bowed deeply. It seemed to him that the new Regent had grown in stature. 'I am at your service, Sire.'

Marie-Louise came over to Law. 'You spoke to me the other night of power, Law, and what can happen if one loses it.' she said. 'From now on, it is Papa who will have all the power in France. He can do almost anything he pleases.' She smiled wickedly. 'Won't that be nice?

MARIE-LOUISE DUCHESS DE BERRY

THIRTEEN:
THE ONLY NATIONAL BANK!

The year was 1716, and the winter had been particularly hard in Edinburgh. The spring held a chilling frost that seemed to linger in one's bones. Now, with the approach of summer, the skies had finally taken on the bright crystal clarity so characteristic of Scottish days.

In his brother's long absence, William Law had moved into John's room. He gazed down from the window at the trees clad in dancing greenery that glistened in the sharp breeze blowing up from the North Sea. The daffodils, thick along the paths of Lauriston Castle, created a brilliant yellow trail towards The Firth of Forth. Will knew that he would miss the summer and the coming of autumn, which had always been his favorite time. In autumn, he would bag a brace of pheasants for the table and sit around the fire of an evening, with some of his younger brothers and sisters, while Janet played a tune on the harpsichord. His had been a simple, quiet life, and really, he could wish for little more, except perhaps for a wife. Although his mother had been particularly industrious in introducing him to several young ladies of the district, he had not yet met one who could win his heart.

And now he was to leave Scotland, and only the good Lord knew for how long. Will stood at the window looking out and wondered how he would fit in, in the life of Paris. He was not a traveler like his brother. In fact, he had never been abroad. How different he was from Johnny! Two brothers, and so very, very dissimilar. Yet somehow, they had always been close, and he was willing to disrupt his way of life if it would help John.

'Would you be wanting to take these woolen undergarments, sir?' his mother's manservant asked.

McGregor had been there to help John pack when he first went to London on that ruinous trip so many years ago, a trip from which John never returned. John had left with such high hopes, only to be dashed on the rocks of disaster. Now, McGregor was helping the younger Law to leave the only home he had ever known. Home and country. William sighed. He could not be certain when he would return or if he were doing the right thing.

He was relieved of that question of mind when Janet came in. Her cheeks flushed with excitement. She carried a thick, knitted scarf of bright red wool.

'For you, my dear. I have finished it just in time, for I believe the winds in Paris are quite fierce.'

"The weather should be warm now, or so John writes,' Will said, taking the scarf. 'Thank you, Mother. It is beautiful. I shall save it for the winter.' He kissed her cheek. 'But I still do not feel right about leaving you,' he said.

'Nonsense, William,' she told him. 'There are sufficient funds for my needs and McGregor here to look after me; your brothers and sisters are all big enough to take care of themselves if need be, so it is the perfect time for you to leave the nest.'

"But the business…!' Will said.

'The goldsmith trade has served the Laws well, William. But now, John needs you. That is more important.' His mother took another parcel from beneath her arm. It was wrapped in brown paper, and she unfolded it on the bed. 'This is for your brother.' Janet's gift was a pair of heavy silk slippers with the Arms of Lauriston, and the family motto, *Nec Obscura Nec Ima*, worked on them in petit point. She had made them herself.

'They are beautiful, Mother,' Will said. 'John will treasure them, I know.'

He handed them to McGregor, who re-wrapped them and placed them in the trunk. Janet looked towards the manservant.

'Come, let McGregor finish the packing. He will do a better job with you out of the way. Besides, Cousin Archie has arrived.'

'I shall leave nothing out, to be sure, Master William,' the older man said.

'Archie here already?' Will brightened perceptibly, the spirit of the adventure ahead igniting him from his doldrums. He took his mother's arm and started through the hall and down the wide staircase past the line of family portraits. As boys, he and John had indulged in the age-old sport of sliding down the banister, but his descent today was more sedate. Will glanced at the small collection of portraits of illustrious forbears along the staircase wall. There were not that many.

Great grandfather Andrew Law, who in 1595 had been the minister at Neilston. His clergyman son, Will's grandfather, the Reverend John Law, who had been dispossessed of his ministry at Neilston for being on the wrong side of Oliver Cromwell. Dressed in sober black, a reminder of the penury in which he had died, his painted eyes stared out forever unforgiving. But the Reverend had the foresight to place his sons in the business. Because of him, it had become the family business, and for two hundred years, there had been Laws in the gold and silversmith trade in Edinburgh.

There was a portrait of his maternal grandfather, James Campbell, a prosperous Edinburgh merchant. His family had owned lands in Ayrshire, and Janet had brought to her marriage a substantial dowry. There were also several portraits of the Campbell clan who had sat to painters of lesser skills. One simple country painting of Grandmother Law completed what was by no means the portrait gallery of an aristocratic family.

Now, Will would join his brother in a foreign land, leaving all he knew and held dear. But reading John's letter over and over as he had done, anything seemed possible. There was always a tone of confidence in John's words that instilled it in others.

Janet paused on the landing, looking at her son. 'You have missed John, haven't you, Will?'

'Oh, yes. I have missed our tennis games at the watergate near Holyrood Palace,' he said. 'Perhaps we can play again in Paris.'

Janet smiled. 'I knew John would have great success one day. His ideas are sound, although fate has led him down a strange path. But he is a leader. This is what he was born to be.'

Will nodded. Although he was eager to join his brother in this enterprise, he could not, nor ever had seen himself following in John's footsteps.

They found Archie pacing the drawing-room, in a high state of excitement. Since Archie had been elevated in society by the title of 3rd Duke of Argyll and his fortunes had prospered, his face had become more lined, and there was a certain puffiness beneath the eyes. Will attributed it to an over-fondness for the Scottish Whiskie.

'So, Will! It looks as though we shall be traveling companions once more,' he cried, clapping his arms around his younger cousin.

'And this time with more salubrious odds in our favor,' Will said.

Greetings having been exchanged, Archie went on, barely containing his excitement. 'Just think of it! Less than two months since the death of King Louis XIV and on this very May 20th, Letters Patent has been granted to John for his French bank.'

'Is it really, truly possible, Archie?' Janet asked, finding it just a little difficult to believe.

'Well, my dear Janet, the fact that John has asked Will to come to Paris to help him run the new bank should prove it is true,' Archie assured her.

'You can be certain, Mother, that it is a fact,' Will said. 'I should not leave you if I had the very least doubts whatsoever.'

'And Lord Stair, our Ambassador in France, has written to me to confirm it.' Archie added, somehow, viewing this brilliant turn of events as his own victory. 'And I shall take great pleasure in traveling with Will to Paris to pay a personal visit to the new bank's Director-General.'

'Imagine. Director-General. . !' Janet could scarcely contain herself. 'After all this time. And of course, Will must be a part of John's success. But I confess, I do not understand quite how it has all been achieved.'

'It is simple, Mother,' Will explained. 'Since the Regent was not prepared to risk the nation in such a new venture as a *national* bank, he has allowed John to establish a private bank in Paris. To test the banking principle, you might say.›

'But where did John get the money to start it? Surely not from his gambling!' she cried.

'John has written to me in great detail on this point, my dear.' Archie Campbell told Janet. 'You know how meticulous he is in money matters. It is by subscription, has raised this capital. Under the direction of the principal shareholders. It is being super-intended by a committee chosen from amongst the highest mag-istrates in the land.' He patted her arm. 'Do not worry your head about it, Janet. It is a most agreeable plan.'

'And John, the Director-General.' Tears of joy clouded her eyes as she repeated the words in an effort to absorb them.

Archie sat himself down in a high-backed chair by the fire. 'Now then, I think I am entitled to a very large glass of your whis-kie.' He looked up at Will. 'And then we two shall be off, eh? For the channel and to France!'

In the Rue Sainte-Avoie at the Hôtel de Mesmé, an elegant gold-let-tered sign proclaimed that this was indeed the home of the new private Banque Générale, and that John Law was its Director-Gen-eral. Significantly, in large gold script were added the words, "Par Nomination Spéciale Du Régent" (By Special Appointment Of The Regent.)

On this hot July day, a handful of Parisians who looked as though they hadn't two sous to jingle together loitered in the street outside the graceful stone building, waiting to see what sort of peo-ple would enter through those heavy bronze doors. The loiterers came to attention when a carriage drove up, depositing two men in front of the entrance. They were gentlemen, obviously, but their dress was far simpler than that of any French noble's.

'Foreigners,' a man in the crowd whispered. Whispers went around, 'Foreigners. . . foreigners. . .'

William Law and Archibald Campbell descended from the carriage and marched up the steps past dozens of wary eyes. Will paused near the doors to peer through the bank's front window. He could see no sign of life and turned to look back at the people gathered in the street with expressionless faces.

'They don't seem anxious to go inside,' Archie whispered. And certainly, nobody moved to follow Archie and Will as they opened and entered the bronze doors.

'Foreigners,' an old woman in the street told the man with her. 'You saw the way they were dressed? Not Frenchmen, you can bet your last sous on that!'

A tradesman named Troubert, who owned a nearby book shop, climbed up the steps and peered into the window. He hurried back down again. 'What do they do in this bank?' he asked.

'They take your gold and give you back paper. They call it credit!' an old man said.

'Credit *notes*,' another man corrected. 'You can have my word, Monsieur Troubert, it is just another way of stealing from honest citizens,' he assured the tradesman.

'Gold? Where would we get gold in the first place, these days? Business is so bad, who will buy books when they cannot even afford bread?' The bookseller spat on the ground and turned away, hurrying back to his shop.

Indeed, the bank was empty except for a clerk who looked up in surprise at the arrival of Will and Archie. It was clear from his expression that they were the first to enter the premises except for the bank's committee.

Will glanced around. It was a large square room with a beautifully painted ceiling, sparsely furnished, with heavy iron bars at the windows. There was a counting table where a clerk sat in the middle of the room. It was equipped with large brass scales, a series of brass weights, and an abacus for counting. Behind the clerk's table, a caged alcove featured a huge metal strongbox about five feet high, made to John Law's design and had the bank's insignia on it, and a Royal seal.

May I help you, gentlemen?' the clerk asked, eager to serve what appeared to be the bank's first customers.

We have come to see Monsieur Law,' Will told him in his best French, which was none too good. 'I am his brother, and this is the Duke of Argyll.'

The clerk jumped up in excitement at the prospect and greeted them effusively. 'One moment, your Grace. Good Monsieur. He has been expecting you!' He rang his bell. A moment later, the inner door opened, and John Law stepped out.

'John...!' was all Will could say, for he felt a lump rise in his throat at the sight of his brother after so many years.

The Director-General of the Banque Générale wore an elegant dark grey silk coat and breeches and a pale green waistcoat trimmed with discreet gold braiding. His wig was short and brown. His face had aged considerably from the boyish visage that Will remembered. He was harder, leaner, and indeed, Will thought that time and hardship had made his brother more strikingly handsome.

'You look every inch the banker,' Johnny,' Archie cried. 'Not that I have seen many of them.'

'Archie, you old goat!' Law hurried over, shaking Archie's hand, then throwing his arms around his brother. 'And Will. Here at last! I cannot believe it. Come in, come in!'

He led them to the back of the main room and into his adjoining private office. It was tasteful but not lavishly furnished. The desk was of heavy walnut and the curtains of a wine, damask silk. Side chairs and small tables along the walls held large bowls of summer flowers. There were paintings of Italian and French scenes, which Law had chosen from a stored collection at the Palais Royal. A large window faced out to a garden square. Two matching leather chairs faced Law's desk. The new arrivals sat in them, and Law came around his desk, sitting on the edge to face them.

'Welcome to the Banque Générale, gentlemen. Alas, it is not a national bank as I had hoped for, but we are in business none-theless.'

Will nodded. But your bank at last! That is an incredible fact.'

'It is the finest turn of events fortune has ever presented to me, Will. And it has been started with the vast capital sum of six million livres, invested by the shareholders.'

Archie indicated the banking area through the open door. 'A quiet day, I see,' he said. 'No customers.'

'Quiet, yes,' Law admitted. The fact is, to be honest, so far we have not had many customers.'

'How many would that be?' Will asked, a growing concern showing on his face.

'Frankly. . .not any,' Law replied flatly.

Will glanced through the open door towards the Rue Sainte-Avoie. He could see the silhouettes of the gathered watchers, some peering in the window. 'What do they do out there in the street?' he asked.

'God only knows!' Law told him. 'Waiting for something to

happen, I expect.' He rose, coming around his desk to look out towards the street. 'And it will if we don't acquire some custom soon. All of Paris will be able to watch the bank close down.' He looked back at his brother, sadly. 'My mistake in bringing you from Lauriston, Will. I was too hasty.'

'Nonsense, John. I came because I believed in the principles of your bank. And I still do.' He pointed to the street crowd. 'But now you must make the French people believe in it!'

Law nodded thoughtfully. 'I have been thinking about that, Will. We must begin to promote our worth.'

'How do you propose to do that, Johnny?' Archie asked.

'I must get people talking about the bank,' Law said. 'to reach the ears of those who need to hear its praises sung. We must demonstrate the usefulness of our bank in such a manner that the curious may learn its true value.'

'A unique prospect,' Archie exclaimed. 'But how?'

'I've decided to have a proclamation printed and circulated. The printed word carries a conviction of its own, and I warrant, we shall see some results.'

Will and Archie exchanged a look. His words did not totally convey confidence.

Law wasted no time in putting his plan into practice. One week later, in the street outside the bank, the clerk posted Law's proclamation on the wall. Copies were being posted all over Paris. A crowd soon gathered to stare at it. Many who stared were unable to read.

'What does it say? What is it?' hushed voices asked.

'Read it, Jacques. Read it out!'

The bookseller, Troubert stepped forward and began to read it for all to hear. 'This bank has six million livres capital. Divided into 1,200 shares: 5,000 livres each, payable in four installments.' He faced the growing crowd. 'One quarter in gold, and three quarters in banknotes.' The others nodded, unsure of the value.

'What does that mean?' 'Who is this foreigner, Lass?' 'What does he think he is doing in France?' The question was repeated in the crowd.

Law had discovered that many Frenchmen were calling him *Lass*. It seemed that few words in French contained the letter ‹w›.

Law had been watching through the window. Now the bank door opened, and he stepped out, pausing on the steps above the people. They all began shouting at him at once. He raised a hand to get their attention.

'As you can see, friends, this bank is founded on solid capital. I myself offer to hand over five hundred thousand livres of my own money, to be distributed to the poor if the success of my bank is not equal to the promises that I have made!' His declaration brought a buzz of speculation.

'And how are these banknotes of yours payable?' the bookseller, Troubert, asked.

'When you deposit gold, you are given notes showing the exact value by *weight* of your gold. When you bring notes to the bank,› he smiled, ‹along with the many more that you have gained in profit by your investment, you will get back gold on sight if you wish. At face value of the notes,› Law explained.

A buzz went around the crowded street. 'He turns paper into gold?'

'Are you a magician, Monsieur Director-General?' cried a portly man.

'Or an alchemist?' cried another.

Law laughed with good humor. 'A banker, Monsieur.'

'And your loans. To borrow money? What is the cost of your loans?'

'Six percent, only.'

The bookseller Troubert, who had spat on the ground only the week before, now stepped towards Law. 'On terms like those, I will take a chance and come into your bank to speak to you privately, Monsieur Director-General *Lass*! I could use some money for my business!'

'With pleasure, Monsieur,' Law said. Troubert followed Law into the bank, where he arranged a small loan, but no one followed him.

The following day a crowd again gathered to watch what might happen next. And something did. A closed wagon drove up and stopped in front of the bank. A guard hopped down, taking out four large bundles. He wore a bright new uniform with the initials of the bank emblazoned on his jacket. The wagon too, was smartly painted a dark green with the name of the bank in gold.

'What have you got there?' an old man asked.

'The bank's new paper money! Direct from the Mint,' the guard told him and carried the bundles into the bank.

'The mint?'

'Paper money?'

'Not the promissory banknotes?'

'What next?' cried an old woman. 'Paper bread?'

'Paper houses and paper children! Yes, yes! What next?' a ragged woman called out.

Inside, William Law sat at a counting table, an accounts ledger open before him. He began to check through the packages of newly printed currency the guard had brought in. Law came over to inspect the notes.

An old peasant woman pushed her way hesitantly into the bank, a squealing piglet tucked under her arm. 'Where is the Director-General?' she asked.

Law stepped over to her. "I am he, Madame. Can I be of service?'

'I wish to have a loan from your bank.' she said. 'I have brought you my best piglet instead of your six percent.' She held out the animal.

Somewhat taken aback, Law nodded towards the animal. 'It is certainly a handsome pig you have there, but the bank cannot accept livestock as security.'

The woman's eyes filled with tears. 'I was told your bank loaned money. The piglet is all I have, Monsieur. Except for three hungry children at home.'

Law reached into his pocket, pulling out three banknotes. 'A new note for each of them, Madame. With the compliments of the Director-General.'

'Ah!' she cried, handing the notes back. 'It is very generous of you, Monsieur. But they would rather have your gold.'

Law took this in his stride. 'You may exchange these for gold any time you wish, Madame.'

'Like right now?'

'Just see the teller over there,' he said with some disappointment, holding them out again.

She hastily grabbed the notes from his hand, thanking him,

and waddled over to the teller to demand her gold. The teller's glance queried Law, who gave him a nod. The man reached into his box and exchanged the woman's paper money. She hurried out, clutching her gold with her squealing piglet, afraid Law would change his mind.

Will looked at his brother and shook his head. 'Not one depositor. Nineteen requests for loans, and paper money we can't give away.'

Law nodded, then suddenly brightened. 'Will, I think I know just the shepherdess to lead the Parisians into our green pastures.'

It was ten o'clock that same night, and the gaming rooms were reaching the height of play when John Law entered Madame Duclos' casino. He had brought Will and Archie to taste the nocturnal activities of the cream of French society.

'A much livelier group than in London, I'd say,' Archie remarked. Law introduced them to several of the guests, and Archie took place at one of the tables. Will watched Archie win a few times and then lose a few more. His eyes went to his brother, who seemed to know everyone. He watched Law go over to a beautiful young creature slender as a reed with flaming copper hair, playing at one of the tables. She was the center of an attentive coterie and turned from the table to greet Law like an old friend.

'But I am not doing well, Monsieur Law,' he heard her complain. 'I really must learn your rules of this *probability* and *odds*, mustn't I?'

The question didn't really require an answer. Instead, Will saw his brother lead the striking lady aside for a moment, the two speaking quietly with a conspiratorial air. Then with a smile, Marie-Louise rejoined the army captain who was waiting for her at the gaming table, and Law returned to his brother and Archie, who appeared to have won his hand.

As the evening drew on, Vivien Duclos came over to watch Law play with his wooden counters. As usual, he was on a winning streak. 'If it were not for the rest of the players, you would break my bank, John Law!' she said. Will saw her slyly drop something into his brother's palm, whispering. He did not hear her words: 'Fortunately, enough of them lose to keep me in profit.'

That night Archie was among the losers. Will put a few coins on the number six, but mostly, he watched and did not gamble, claiming that dice and cards were no friends of his. It was two o'clock in the morning when Will took a coach back to the apartment his brother had rented for him. Marie-Louise left soon after, with a nod and a wink at Law. 'Tomorrow,' she mouthed as she passed him.

Archie stayed on to play and to lose. He looked around for Vivien, but she was nowhere to be seen. He caught a fleeting glimpse of Law disappearing up the grand staircase.

'What is up there?' he asked the footman. 'More gaming rooms?'

'It leads to Madame Duclos' private apartments,' the footman told him.

John Law used Vivien's key, and the actress greeted him with a waiting bottle of champagne. Her red satin negligée, loosely fastened at the waist, fell open as she raised one black slippered foot to rest it on a damask chair, providing Law full view of shapely red silk stockings tied to her corselet with black ribbons. Law's glance traveled to the tempting voluptuousness of one exposed thigh.

Behind her, he could see that her bed was strewn with pink rose petals scattered across the deep orange velvet coverlet. She poured wine into two tall stemmed crystal goblets, holding one out to Law.

'I am willing to gamble that there will be no losers in my bed tonight,' she said.

He came to her, running a hand across her stocking, fingers pausing at the soft warmth of her skin.

'My dear Vivien, that is a fool's bet. Tonight we shall both be winners.'

FOURTEEN:
MARIE-LOUISE AND POPO

The door was opened by Mouchi, Marie-Louise's lady-in-waiting and confidante. She was a jolly girl of twenty-two with a motherly bosom and a low-cut bodice, which left little to the imagination. Her hair was curled and powdered in the latest fashion; her face, heavily lacquered like the other ladies of the French Court. Law thought it did not suit her round cheeks, and her right eye had a slight squint, which some men found sexually exciting. It was a simple, wholesome country face, and Law thought she would have looked far better with scrubbed cheeks, romping across a field in a plain linen gown with a few sheep trailing after her.

Mouchi had won her place at Court because her father once served old Louis well on the battlefield. His daughter was aide-de-camp to the young Duchess because Mouchi was a willing co-conspirator in her mistress's intrigues. Although Phillip's daughter was capricious and quick to act on a whim, she could count on her lady-in-waiting for her sound counsel—when and if, she felt inclined to take it.

Mouchi greeted Law warmly and ushered him into the salon looking him over and missing nothing. He had put on a full wig, and a green silk coat recently purchased from the tailor in the Rue Quincampoix.

'La...! When first you came to Paris, you were much too foreign,.' she told him. ‹Indeed, you are beginning to dress like a member of the Court, Monsieur! Now you are *à la mode*!' Her eyes traveled down. 'And those stocking clocks do show off your calves.' she said, taking an admiring look at his new silk hose with clocks of gold thread.

'I am trying to lose my simple Scottish ways, Mouchi,' he

said with a touch of sarcasm, which was wasted on her. 'Where is the Duchess? Unless I am mistaken, she has invited me to dine.'

'Indeed, Monsieur, and she will be with you presently. But the Duchess has asked that before supper, you be the first to unveil a new statue of Venus she has bought—from Rome.'

'I am no expert on art, Mouchi,' he protested.

She waved his protestation aside. 'It is to be dedicated in your honor if you approve of the purchase, Monsieur Law.' She gestured him towards the bedroom. 'Madame has had it put in there, away from prying eyes.'

He looked at her questioningly, then nodded. 'Very well, then. If she wishes.'

'La, but she does,' Mouchi assured him.

Law stepped into Marie-Louise's bedroom. A single candelabra supplied the only illumination in the large room. The walls were hung with thick tapestries depicting naked lovers and rampant Cupids, inspiring them to passion. A heady scent of incense filled the air. A canopied bed stood at one end of the room, its heavy satin curtains drawn. Mouchi pointed to a draped figure on a pedestal in the center of the room.

'There it is, Monsieur Law. The Duchess has asked that you examine the statue for any imperfections but assures you, you will find none,' Mouchi announced with a twinkle in her eye. 'You are only to pull the draperies aside, and all will be revealed.'

'Perhaps I should unveil it when the Duchess arrives,' he said.

Mouchi threw him a mysterious smile and shook her head. 'The Duchess insists you must see it alone. I am certain you will find it to your liking.' With that, she left him, closing the door behind her.

Adjusting his eyes to the darkness, Law stepped over to the figure and pulled off the thin muslin cloth. Marie-Louise stood before him completely naked, her skin powdered as white as the marble she was portraying. Holding a garland of flowers aloft in a classic pose, leaves trailing from her hair, she looked like a naiad, a water-nymph slender as a reed except for her breasts, which were small but full and tipped with circlets of rosebuds. There was a deep eroticism in Marie-Louise to which no man could fail to respond. It was not a response Law wished to partake of at this instant.

Marie-Louise tried to maintain the statue-like pose, but a ripple of laughter escaped her lips. 'Surprise, Law! It is I - in the flesh!'

'Good evening, Marie-Louise. I see Dress is to be informal for dinner.' he said dryly, tossing the drapery back at her and proceeding to light a lamp.

She wrapped herself in the muslin and came over to him with a petulant frown. 'And I thought you such a good gamester. Maybe it is *you* who are made of stone, John Law.› She smiled wickedly. 'Although I have heard differently from Madame Duclos.'

'Do you ladies share all your intimate secrets?' He pulled her to him roughly and kissed her—and then as suddenly let her go. 'You are a little temptress, aren't you Marie-Louis

'I did not give you permission to kiss me,' she said with feigned anger.

'Then put on your clothes,' he replied.

It was not going as she had planned. Marie-Louise wasn't prepared for a man who couldn't be brought to heel. Her anger turned into a kittenish pout. 'You do not desire me, Law?'

'I desire not to be one among your lovers, Marie-Louise, including your current playmate, Captain De Riom. Nor do I fancy competing with your husband, whom I have yet to meet. What do you call him? Popo?'

'He is Charles. But Popo quite suits him, really. For he is a bit of a clown. But the darling creature is too much occupied with his brandy and his new stable boy at the moment to worry about me. As for the Captain, I have sent De Riom to the West Indies on official business. He is to return in two years—if he survives the fever.'

'And when would you send me to the West Indies, Marie-Louise?' Law asked. 'When the next charming traveler comes to Paris?'

Marie-Louise stepped away from him angrily, one nipple peeking provocatively over the top of the muslin.

'You are so smug, Law! You have no idea what it is like, this life of the Court. I should go insane if I did not play my little games.' She tossed the garland of flowers onto a chaise. 'Mama spends her days in church, and Papa spends all his time with one new mistress after another. Although I must say, Katherine Knollys seems to have a firm hold at the moment. What substance is there to it all? Power, yes, but where does it lead? With you, for the first time, I felt that life might not be such a hazy dream. That it might have some meaning.'

She reached out to him, and he was about to take her into his arms when a discreet tap on an inner door, paneled in the tapestry so that it was barely visible, was immediately followed by the entrance of a young man no older than Marie-Louise herself. He was not wearing a wig, and his short hair fell about his face in a soft, mousy blond haze.

'Oh! I see you are entertaining, Marie-Louise. Do forgive me for the interruption,' he said, staggering a step closer, staring at Law in the dim light through watery blue eyes. At the moment, they were bloodshot, and his breath suggested brandy. He made a sweeping attempt at a graceful bow, nearly toppling over. 'The famous Monsieur Law, isn't it? Delighted to meet you at last. But perhaps not in my wife's bedroom. Allow me to introduce myself. The Duke de Berry.'

'Enchanted,' Law replied, returning a perfunctory bow.

De Berry's expression was grim. 'I suppose she's told you I don't sleep with her. No matter. I must still defend my honor, d'ya see? So draw your sword, Monsieur!' With that, De Berry drew his rapier and staggered towards Law, raising it in salute.

'Stop it, Popo! You are drunk!' Marie-Louise said.

'Not too drunk to run this blackguard through! Draw, Monsieur, for I will not kill an unarmed man.'

'Your wife's reputation is quite unsullied by me, I assure you, Your Grace,' Law said, hoping to calm de Berry's hot-headed and senseless attack.'

'Draw, I say! Or indeed, I shall finish you here and now!'

Remembrances of the pointless duel fought so long ago and its horrific consequences sent a chill to Law's heart. Forced to draw his rapier, he did not attack but parried a series of de Berry's blows. All he would have to do, he thought, was to kill or even injure this drunken Duke, and he would be finished at the French Court, his bank, no more than a forgotten joke. Marie-Louise tried again to stop them, but Law waved her out of the way. 'Stay back, Marie-Louise!' he cried. 'I shall not hurt him.'

At last, he managed to pin De Berry's sleeve to the door. The young man dropped his rapier, and Law withdrew his blade. De Berry collapsed onto the carpet, feet splayed out in front of him, a sheepish look on his face.

'I thought it was money you were good at, Law. I see you are an able swordsman,' he added with some admiration.

Law helped him to his feet. 'I am sure you are too, Sir. When you have had a bit less brandy.'

De Berry leaned back against the wall, his only injury, to his pride. He turned to his wife. 'Truly, I am sorry if I have made a mess of your evening, Marie-Louise,' he began.

'Just leave, Popo. We shall forget it ever happened. All three of us.'

'Very well then.' De Berry seemed suddenly quite undisturbed by the whole episode. An eager smile touched thin lips. 'Will you ride with me in the morning, Marie-Louise? I have a new horse; my stable boy, Bertil, has been training.'

'No,' she said. 'I have other things. But I will play cards with you in the afternoon.'

'Cards? I think not,' De Berry said with a quick look at Law. 'You play too well since Mister Law has become your teacher.' He pulled himself free of the supporting wall and opened the door once more. 'Do enjoy the rest of the evening.' He gave her a crooked grin. 'I know I shall.' And with a slight nod to Law, he was gone.

Marie-Louise sighed and sat back on the chaise. 'Popo has a way of making scenes and then leaving the stage without a proper exit. He will have forgotten all about this by morning. You see, Law? It is the life I lead at Court."

'Nothing can change your life, he said. 'Certainly not I.'

'Maybe I could change yours,' she suggested. 'That is what power is all about. You have only to ask, Law.'

Law dropped down beside her on the chaise. 'There is one thing,' he said, 'if you really want to help me. It will help your father, too,' he said.

Marie-Louise stood up and went over to her bed. She paused for a moment, then dropped the muslin cloth. Her powdered skin glistening like moonstone in the candlelight.

'First, there is something I want you to do for me...' She

drew back the bed curtains. 'Then you can tell me about it. In here', she said and beckoned to him.

Her body was lean as bone and hard as a young boy's. Her breasts stood firm and high, the nipples two arrogant temptresses. She pulled him to her, her lips urgent against his, her hand seeking the hard pleasure she had awakened. A pleasure she knew could fulfill her.

CUPID BY FRAGONARD

FIFTEEN:
ABSOLUTE POWER

At the Banque Générale, the day had started quietly as usual. The usual crowd milling about in the street, the usual stacks of paper money and banknotes waiting for some customer—any customer—to ask for them. In short, the usual empty bank.

William Law straightened his back and stirred from staring at his accounts book. It was, as usual, painfully bare of entries. His thick Scottish woolen jacket seemed far too warm against the mild first stirring of a Paris autumn. Archie Campbell had returned to Scotland the week before, and without him for company, Will was growing lonely for home. He stared across his counting table and through the window out at the street, wondering what his mother was doing at this very moment in Lauriston.

The weather would already be turning cold and the roadsides, a mass of gold and brown leaves, and if he were there of an early morning, he would be out shooting, and this thickly woven jacket would be none too warm. After breakfasting on some of his mother's oatcakes and a bowl of warm milk with a tot of whiskie in it, he would mount his horse and ride to Edinburgh. He would spend the day at Goldsmith's Hall and, in the late afternoon, ride home again for dinner with Janet. A quiet life, with not too many surprises, which, until now, had agreed with him remarkably well.

Here in Paris, time was slipping away, and although he saw his brother every day at the bank, most evenings John would go off to the gaming houses or the palace, leaving Will to his own devices. In the first instance, Will did not care to go along, and in the second, he was not always included. As much as he loved John, Will could not help but wonder if he had made a wise decision in leaving everything he knew, to join his brother in Paris.

At John's suggestion, Will had been studying French and was able to converse a bit. His teacher, the pretty Mademoiselle Odile Saint Choux, came from an impoverished noble family. She was a good conversationalist and happy addition to his routine. He looked forward to his meetings with her and even dreamed it might lead to something more permanent. Will turned his attention back to the accounts book. Nothing to add or subtract. How long, he wondered, would John be able to carry on the pretense that the bank was a success? When it failed, perhaps they could go back to Scotland together. Archie would intervene once again on John's behalf to try to get the charges dropped against him, at least in Scotland.

Will's attention was drawn to voices in the street. He got up from his table and went over to the window. Outside, the people showed great interest in an elegant closed carriage that was clattering up the Rue Sainte-Avoie towards the bank. Even from a distance, it was clear that the coachman was wearing royal livery. As it came closer, Will could see that the coach bore a royal crest on its side. Behind it, the wheels of an open horse-drawn cart bit heavily into the packed earth and cobbles. Two mounted Dragoons rode beside the cart to guard what appeared to be four heavy sacks piled on it. The coach and cart drew to a halt in front of the bank. Will hurried to John Law's office, flinging open the door without knocking.

'John,' he cried, ‹you must come at once!›

Law rose from his desk and stepped into the banking room. 'What is all the excitement, Will?'

'A royal carriage, John!' Will exclaimed. 'It has stopped here, at the bank!'

Law did not seem at all surprised. The clerk and the teller ran to the window to see for themselves.

The people in the street clambered around the carriage, hoping to get a glimpse of the Royal occupant. Alerted to this mobile spectacle, shop-keepers came out of their shops to watch. It did not take long for a crowd to gather. The Lieutenant of Dragoons seemed satisfied by the commotion he had stirred up. He paused before dismounting and then dramatically pushed people aside to climb the bank's marble steps. He pounded heavily on the bronze doors with the hilt of his saber. William Law stood there, uncertainly.

The Dragoon barged on the door once more. Law turned to his brother, stepping back. 'Aren't you going to open it, Will?'

'Me.? I...? Well, yes, of course,' Will said, hastening to the door.

The Dragoon stood before him and announced in a voice loud enough for all in the street to hear. 'Her Royal Highness Marie-Louise, Duchess de Berry, daughter of the Regent of France, desires to deposit her gold in Monsieur John Law's bank.'

Coming up beside his brother, Law stepped outside to meet the Dragoon and replied in an equally loud tone, 'The Banque Générale is entirely at Her Highness's disposal.'

With that, Law came down the steps into the street, an imposing figure in dark grey velvet with a heavy lace neckband and long brown curled wig. 'Make way!' he called. The people stood back as he walked over to inspect the sacks piled in the cart. Then he turned back towards the bank, calling, 'Bank guard! Come help carry the Duchess's gold, for there is a great deal of it.'

Law stepped over to the carriage and opened the door for all to see Marie-Louise as she stepped out. She was lavishly dressed in an ostrich plumed lavender bonnet crowning her fringe of flame-colored hair. Although the day was not cool, Marie-Louise wore a sumptuous fur-trimmed traveling suit. Diamonds and pearls sparkled at her delicate neck. Upon sight of her, a buzz of excitement hummed through the growing crowd.

'The Duchess herself!'

'Look at her jewels!'

'She has brought gold!'

'Good day, Monsieur Director-General,' Marie-Louise said grandly.

Law bowed low to her and swept a kiss across her gloved hand, whispering too softly for the watchful Parisians to hear: 'Speak up, my dear!'

She smiled and repeated her greeting in a clear, loud voice. 'Good day to you, Monsieur Law. I have come to bring you my gold for safekeeping.'

'Madame, the Banque Générale is honored by your custom,' he almost shouted.

Behind Law, a bank guard emerged to help carry the heavy sacks inside. He hefted the first one down, and Law went over to it, stopping him long enough to open the throat of the sack and reach inside. He drew out a fistful of gold coins and, holding them up for all to see, allowed them to riffle and clink through his fingers back into the sack.

'This large deposit will pay you a handsome interest, your Highness,' he said.

Marie-Louise wore an expression of surprise. 'You say interest, Monsieur Law?'

'Indeed, Duchess, the bank will *pay* you interest.› He stressed the word slightly.

'Ah? So you do not merely keep my money safe for me, but you pay me for the privilege?

Excellent! How much, Monsieur Law?' she asked.

'The sum of three percent,' he said.

A murmur rippled through the crowd, 'Three percent interest! On all that coin!' They filled their eyes with the sight of the gold and tasted the profits Marie-Louise was about to gain.

Law was not unaware of the effect they were having. 'Your Royal Highness, will you do me the honor of stepping into the bank so that we may finalize the arrangements?' he said and offered his arm.

'With pleasure, Monsieur Law,' she said, placing her hand on his arm. With that, the banker ushered Marie-Louise inside. The crowd watched the heavy bronze doors close behind the two and began to speculate in whispers.

Inside the bank, a stunned Will greeted Marie-Louise.

'Count the gold, will you, Will?' Law asked.

Will got out his ledger, and the guard hefted one of the sacks onto the counting table. Will reached a handful of coins off the top of the sack and began to stack and count them. As he reached deeper into the bag, to his shock, he pulled up a handful of sand. He reached into the second bag. It was the same. He looked up at Marie-Louise in astonishment, then turned to his brother. 'John!' he cried, horrified, 'Look at this... Sand! The bags are full of sand...! There is just a thin layer of gold pieces at the top!'

Law began to laugh heartily. 'Don't look in the bags, my dear brother. Look outside!'

Will went back to the barred window and peered into the street once more. By now, the crowd had grown to enormous proportions. 'But I don't understand...?' Will began. 'Where have they all come from so quickly?'

'Word of gold spreads fast. You might almost say, dear brother, that money talks.'

Marie-Louise joined with Law in laughter. 'Now we shall see if your plan has really worked, Monsieur Banker.'

Law turned back to his brother. 'A simple ruse, Will, which I arranged with the Duchess.' He glanced outside, where several merchants were marching up the steps. 'And it looks as though it is beginning to afford us the advantage,' Law said.

There was a banging on the bank's door, this time with a heavy fist. 'The Scotsman gets my money!' called one of the merchants. 'I want a loan,' cried another.

The knocking grew louder as people began pushing in a frenzy to get inside the bank.

'Get those sandbags out of sight,' Law said. The clerks hurried to carry them behind the counter. 'And now, let them in, Will.' He smiled.

'I think at last we are about to have clients. It would seem the bank will not be forced to close its doors after all.'

He turned to Marie-Louise. 'And it is all due to you, Duchess.'

'How amusing,' she said.

He led Marie-Louise into his inner office and closed the door. They could hear the people rushing into the bank to do business. Law kissed Marie-Louise lightly on the lips. Thank you, my dear.'

She turned and sat on one of the leather chairs and smiled at Law possessively. 'And thank you... for last night. We must do it again. Soon.'

In the several weeks that passed after Marie-Louise's visit, the bank started to show a profit. Investors had begun to arrive from outside of Paris. As the weeks drifted into months, it seemed that every man of business wished to have an account at Law's bank. Where first he had found it impossible to sell the idea of banknotes, the demand for paper against specie became so great that Law's banknotes were no longer issued except at a premium.

He had initially declared that the bank would take good commercial securities at 6% per annum. Voluntary deposits swelled his floating capital so much that he lowered the discount to 4%. Soon he could scarcely register in his books all the discountable securities that were flowing in.

Through the following year, whenever Will wrote to his mother or his cousin, the Duke of Argyll, he could not contain his pride in the bank's success and his brother's exalted accomplishments. John Law was exercising a protective influence over commercial affairs in the country, advising and encouraging all. He anticipated small businesses' needs and offered financial support, particularly to establishments whose prosperity was of special benefit to the public. He had revived labor and prevented bankruptcies, including that of France itself. Trade, which everyone had thought dead, began to show signs of life. And the certainty of payment at sight gave an extended currency to the paper notes.

And as the year slipped by, Will Law had been content to stay in France for many reasons, one of them being Mademoiselle Odile Saint Choux.

The following September, Law received a letter from Marie-Louise asking him to come to her apartments. She greeted him with the news. 'This very morning Papa has heard,' she told him. 'Parliament has decided that he be invested with absolute power.'

'I don't understand,' Law questioned. 'I thought as Regent, that he had that anyway.'

She shook her head. 'Absolute, but not *absolutely*, Law. The difference is that now Parliament can no longer challenge him about anything. *Anything!* They are powerless against any decision Papa might make. From this day on, he can say or do whatever he desires! Isn›t that nice?›

Law understood the personal significance this meant. Any new ideas he might have would gain the immediate ear of the one person who could make them a reality. Nothing could stop Law as long as Philip was behind him. Yet he knew there would be a price to pay. Nothing for nothing was ever given in this life.

Marie-Louise came and stood before him. 'And now the Regent has decided to give you what you desire.'

He looked at her questioningly.

'He is going to decree your bank a Royal National Bank! What do you think of that, John Law?'

His surprise was genuine. 'Why. . .I am overwhelmed, Marie-Louise! And I have only you to thank for persuading your father of the wisdom of such a decision.'

She laughed. 'This time you are wrong, Law. I said nothing to him. Father needed none other than you to teach him your brilliance!' She paused. 'Though there are some detractors, your national bank will become a reality. And then you shall be the second most powerful man in France!' She drew him to her and offered her lips. He kissed them lightly. She turned it into a kiss of passion.

'You taste of champagne so early in the day,' he said, drawing away.

She threw him a coquettish smile. 'You shall share a bottle with me tonight, and we shall play at Madame Duclos'. Then, when I have lost enough, and you have won enough, you shall accompany me to my apartments, and in my large bed, we shall play my favorite game, which I think you enjoy as much as I.'

It was an invitation impossible to refuse.

John Law's new private coach was painted a dark green with gold trim to match the bank's colors. Lauriston's Arms were painted on its side, to call attention to the owner's pedigree, slight though it was compared to the French Court's aristocracy. On this particular midday, the coach could be seen standing somewhere it ought not to be—by the side of a country road about an hour's ride from Paris. Law's coachman waited across the road, eating his simple lunch from a basket: bread, sausage, cheese, and wine. He chewed with satisfaction, wiped the perspiration from the inner edge of his collar with the tip of the linen in which his wife had wrapped his bread, and kept his eyes discreetly pointed away from the coach, focused on a field of lethargic heifers who moved only when necessary to flick an angry tail at an irritating fly.

Not far from the coach, and masked by a large clump of trees, Law and a lady were enjoying the last of the September sunshine and sharing a basket lunch of more elegant comestibles: pickled trout, a boiled pigeon in vinegar, cheese from the Navarre, plum tarts, candied apples, and a red Bordeaux from Philip's private cellar. It was spread out in front of them on a linen cloth laid over a blanket.

Perhaps no one would have recognized them today, for Law was dressed in Scottish trews and a loose white shirt, open at the neck. His hair was his own and just grazed his shoulders. She wore a simple homespun dress, no face paint, her blonde hair flying like a flag unfurled on the wind.

'I think I prefer you this way.' He took her fingers and kissing the tips. 'No diamonds. No powder. Just the sun to touch your cheeks and the wind to comb your hair.'

'Stolen moments, Johnny,' she sighed and looped a chain of daisies around his neck to pull him to her. He kissed her with approval.

'Then we must steal more of them.'

Katherine Knollys drew a happy breath, lying back beside him. 'Maybe we were actually meant for a simple life, Johnny. What do you think?'

He laughed deep in his throat. 'I think two weeks of rustic, bucolic glory, and I'd be teaching the cows how to play cards and roll the dice. We're adventurers, Katherine. You and I want the most of everything.'

She reached up and kissed him again, her lips lingering on his. 'I still want the most of you,' she breathed.' But not to own you. No, nobody could. Still, we can – and must arrange other meetings like today.'

He smiled wryly. 'With Philip hovering over you like a watchdog?' He paused. 'I was going to say *vulture*, but that would be ungenerous.'

'Yes, he pays generously for the privilege,' she responded. 'In fact, he's planning a surprise for me. A private chateau at Versailles.' She held a clover between her teeth, the perfect country lass.

'How did you find out?'

She gave him a secretive nod. 'I have my spies, you know.'

'Versailles? Congratulations, Katherine.' There was a hint of anger in his tone. 'Then I suppose we won't see each other at all.'

She looked at him archly. 'You can always pay a call. On your way to visit Marie-Louise.'

He frowned. 'That was beneath you, Kate. Marie-Louise's friendship has been invaluable to me. You know it.'

'Of that, I'm certain, my dear. And Madame Vivien Duclos as well! John Law never wastes time on a friendship that isn't valuable, does he?'

'We both ride ambition, Katherine.'

She nodded. 'A pity it never takes us down the same road '

'How can you say that?' he asked, laughing heartily. 'Here we are together, the whole afternoon ahead of us! And I have arranged for a certain inn not far from here, where we shall find a very private suite awaiting us, with an exceptionally large bed. I am told it's highly popular with travelers. Four people can sleep in it abreast. There's nothing larger except the Great Bed of Ware in England. This afternoon it shall be our playing field, my dearest one.'

He drew her to him, slipping a hand inside the neck of her low-cut bodice to cup the softness of one perfect breast. 'We both know that you belong to me, Katherine,' he murmured.

She sighed, and her lips parted. 'You are a man of a very high order, Johnny. Perhaps you are even a genius. A man who attempts the impossible and somehow makes it happen. I vow, I love you like no other,' she breathed.

His tongue met hers with a surge of passion flowing between them, the more immediate for having been suppressed. 'A pity lovers' vows do not always reach the ears of the Gods,' he said.

'I want you, Johnny. Now.'

'What about that huge bed awaiting us?' he asked.

'We shall get to it. Later. For the moment, this grassy field will serve.'

His hand reached beneath heavy cambric. Her legs parted, and he moved above her to enter the soft, warm haven that was awaiting him.

Unaware of anything but each other, they did not see another figure on the hillside above them. The heavy-set police agent stood beside his horse, with a clear view of the scene below. The man had been following them ever since they left Paris, and now, he was the picture of patience as he made notes for the report that he would give to Count D'Argenson upon his return.

VERSAILLES

SIXTEEN:
BANK NOTES
AND PAPER MONEY

It was in January of 1719, not wishing to miss any of the excitement in an otherwise humdrum day, some local Parisians had paused in the Rue de Richelieu in front of the pale stone Palais Mazarin, wondering aloud in whispers.

Although it was snowing and the biting wind sent white flurries whipping against their bodies, John and William Law stood across the street on the icy ground facing the building, watching workers hoisting a new sign up on this impressive stone edifice. They did not seem to care about the cold as they read the sign:

BANQUE ROYAL DE FRANCE

John Law had submitted a proposal for his BANQUE GÉNÉRALE on October 24, 1715. He'd finally received letters patent from an Extraordinary Meeting of the Council on May 2, 1716. But they had only allowed him a private bank, not a national bank. The BANQUE GÉNÉRALE in the Rue Sainte-Avoie at the Hôtel de Mesmé had flourished for over two and a half years when it was closed by order of the Regent.

Law felt a surge of emotion he had not anticipated as he looked at the words, BANQUE ROYAL DE FRANCE. In his mind, he reviewed the events of the last three years. As he had predicted, the Banque Générale had restored confidence in the country by causing money to circulate. And the Bank's Letters of Exchange suffered no loss, even when the Regent altered the face value of the coin. Law's long-held dream of a national bank was now to be founded only on royal funds. It would be administered under the authority of the child King.

Because the French Parliament had turned down his original plan for a national bank, Law submitted a second plan. This was for a private bank to be administered and funded by himself, with a group of chosen investors. The Duke of Orleans chose to be styled as the private bank's protector; otherwise, that bank had no official connection with the government. John Law had taken all the risks, and in the beginning, he had even augmented the bank's finance at the gaming tables.

From the start, he'd wanted a national bank; but now that it had actually happened, he was suddenly uncertain. He had tried to keep his private bank open, too. But once Orleans had agreed to start a royal bank, he thrust aside any idea of continuing both, and Law's bank was closed.

The worry was that with this new National Bank, only the ten-year-old King would decide what and when notes were to be issued.

'The notes in circulation now are worth nearly sixty million livres. Sixty million livres, Will!' John Law told his brother. 'And now, no new notes are to be printed except by public acts of King and Council.

'But if the specie goes down in value, the existing notes are still to be paid in full, are they not?' Will asked.

Law nodded. 'I insisted on that stipulation, and Orleans agreed, but I must say, with great reluctance.' He frowned. 'And when I told Orleans that I wished to make use of the banknotes and paper money for paying taxes, that worried him slightly.'

'Has he agreed to that?' Will asked, clapping his gloved hands together in the frosty morning air as they watched the workmen leave.

'I insisted that making the bank the cashier of the king would make it stronger and extend its credit. It would make its bills be exactly like our letters of exchange, payable at sight in every city in the kingdom.' Law looked up at a gathering crowd. 'Come! It is time for me to say a few words.'

Hurrying across the street, Law strode up the freshly swept steps to where he could be seen by everyone and raised a hand for attention.

'Citizens of Paris,' he called out. 'In the past two and a half years, The Banque Générale could honestly call itself a prosperous business venture. It has become a part of French life, thanks to all of you.'

A wave of agreement echoed in the thin chill air.

'Friends,' Law continued, seeing familiar faces among the crowd, 'as you can see by our new sign, we have been grant-ed a Royal Charter! Something every Frenchman can be proud of. Thanks to your Regent, the Duke of Orleans, our French bank is the first national bank in the entire world!'

As this sank in, there was a gasp from the crowd. Law smiled and went on. 'Yes, a *national* bank! And we are establishing branches in Lyon, Rochelle, Tour, Orleans, and Amiens!›

Law spotted the bookshop owner from the Rue Sainte-Avoie. 'Monsieur Troubert! Good morning to you! How has your business been this year?'

'Most excellent, 'Sieur Lass...' Troubert said. 'For over two years, I have had credit with your bank, and I have seen a profit of double over last year.' He smiled. 'But do not tell the taxman.'

This brought a ripple of laughter.

'No need, Monsieur Troubert. Today, French banknotes are accepted everywhere, so you can even pay your taxes with them.'

'We are behind you, 'Sieur Lass,' Troubert cried, cross-armed, slapping himself to keep warm.

'John Lass! John Lass!' resounded on steamy breaths.

'And I have more good news for you!' Law informed the people. 'Now that businessmen throughout France have learned how useful a bank can be to their lives, the issue of banknotes has risen from six to sixty million!'

'All paper?' a wary voice shouted.

'Paper, which represents the amount of gold that has passed into the hands of this bank and all its branches.'

Another shout of approval oscillated across the group. Will had come up to the foot of the steps, overjoyed to see how completely his brother had won the people's confidence. Law quieted the crowd with a raised hand.

'And now, I have wonderful news; our bank has been such a success that the Regent has agreed interest rates are four and a half percent!'

Again voices were raised, but it was not Orleans they cheered. 'Long live John Lass and his bank!' echoed down the windy street.

A few weeks later, a Royal coach bearing the Regent's coat of arms rode up, the sound of the horses' hooves muted by the snow. A messenger hopped down and entered the bank. Again people gathered in the street and peered in the windows to see what they might see.

Inside the Bank, the messenger presented John Law with a letter bearing the Royal seal. Law turned to Will with a look of annoyance on his face. 'It is a summons from Orleans,' he said quietly. 'I have been trying to speak to him all week, and although I am living at the Palais Royal, it has been impossible to see him.'

'Do not keep him waiting then,' Will said.

'I have a great deal to say to him,' Law said, annoyed. He came out of the bank, waved to the crowd, and climbed into his waiting carriage. It padded through the snowy streets with muffled tread, down the Rue de Montpensier through white-blanketed gardens to the Rue de Valois in the center of Paris. Law had been staying at the Palais Royal for some time. His rooms were not far from both Katherine and Marie-Louise's private quarters. He could easily manage to see either of them without anyone the wiser, and Law had taken full advantage of it.

The carriage pulled to a stop at the palace entrance. Seeing his approach, the guards threw open the great doors. Law bounded into the building and hurried up the wide staircase and down the corridor to the Regent's official State chambers. As usual, The outer room was crowded with supplicants patiently waiting with the hope that the Regent might hear their petitions for favors.

One of them recognized Law and cried out to him, 'Monsieur Lass! Perhaps you could put in a word for me with the Regent.'

He recognized the man. One who had borrowed two thousand louis' d'or in paper money from the bank. He knew the fellow was there to claim an ancient title attached to some of his lands.

'I shall do what I can,' Law told him and brushed past the other supplicants before he could be approached again.

The footman at the private door to Orleans' chambers greeted him with a small bow. 'He is waiting for you, Director General Law.'

Dressed in flowered silk and wearing the Sash of his office, the Regent was seated on his heavy gilt throne chair in his State chambers. Law noted that he had put on more weight in the preceding months, a man settling into his job and relaxing into worry-free prosperity. There was a new dignity about Orleans, and with it, a new arrogance had crept into the podgy face. The Regent greeted him warmly and offered him a sweetmeat, which Law declined. He did not offer him a chair, and Law stood before him like one of the supplicants, wondering why Orleans had sent for him.

'Well, Law,' Orleans asked finally, 'how does it feel to be the Director-General of a Royal Bank?'

'It is my dream realized, Sir. The new bank has been a great success already. We have at least thirty new customers depositing money each week.'

'Excellent, excellent!' Orleans exclaimed. 'I have seen how people are growing fond of paper money.'

'Sir, I anticipate it will succeed beyond our wildest estimates, once all the branches are opened across the country. The banknotes and paper money are a tremendous advantage to the provinces because it furnishes them with a means of remittance to Paris and avoids the expense and risk of coin transportation.'

'Excellent reasoning, Law. As I have said before, you are an original thinker.' Orleans leaned forward confidentially. 'The thing is, some people have questioned me about you, a foreigner, being given such a high post. But you and I know that you can do nothing without my approval. Is it not so?'

'Indeed, that is so, Sir.'

'And now that you are Director-General of a Royal bank, it is time you stopped living at the Palais Royal. You must own a proper townhouse in Paris. Appearances, Law! We must keep up appearances.'

'A townhouse?' Law asked, not quite following the drift.

'It was Lady Knollys suggestion, really, and I believe a good one. Since you are so occupied with the bank, she has offered to help you locate a proper house.' He helped himself to another sweetmeat. 'The idea has my approval.'

Law could imagine Katherine posing the suggestion to Orleans, perhaps in bed between kisses, arranging to have more time alone with Law. He smothered a smile. 'I am not against buying a townhouse. I am sure Lady Knollys could find me a fitting residence.'

Orleans let his eyes trail the length of Law's body with a hint of disapproval. 'And another thing Law, we must not neglect your appearance, and the effect it has on others. You do not dress like an important man. Change your tailor. Damn it, Monsieur, you must expand yourself to fit your station!"

It was true that the once-London dandy had abandoned thoughts of fine lace and satin coats and embroidered waistcoats in favor of more sober garments when at his bank.

'I shall take care to make a more fitting appearance in future, Sir,' he said.

'So it is settled then? You will find a house of your own. Of course, the bank will pay for it,' so have no concern about the money.'

Law appraised him with some surprise. 'I could not accept that, Sir. I have sufficient money of my own to pay for a house.'

Orleans nodded in agreement. 'I would never stop a man from paying for himself, Law. I hear your winnings have been enormous at Madame Duclos'. She will be anxious to have you play elsewhere, I shouldn't wonder.' He chuckled then added, 'But perhaps not, for I hear she enjoys your company. Vivien knows how to keep a man entertained, I must say. Quite stunningly beautiful legs, do you not agree?'

'Indeed, your Grace as fine as I have seen.' Law did not like the turn of the conversation.

A sober expression visited the Regent's face. 'Now then: To some other business. I have been looking at the bank's figures your brother sent me. As you say, excellent profits. So good, in fact, that I have decided to alter the coinage.'

Law regarded him in disbelief. 'Alter it, Sir? But it is fixed. You cannot change it.'

'Cannot?' Orleans' expression froze. His tone was iced. 'That is a word I do not know, Monsieur Law. The Regent of France can do just as he pleases.'

Law was aware that while making the private bank a Royal Bank did not affect its credit, the Regent had begun to turn it to his own advantage. The government—and the Regent was now the sole voice of government—had borrowed fifty million livres through the issue of new banknotes. Although without pledge or security, these notes were being received with the same confidence as those issued while the bank was under Law's personal direction.

Law felt a rush of heat to his cheeks and chose his words carefully. 'Please recall, sir, that only four months ago, you devalued the notes. Against your financial advisor's advice as to the effect of such an action. Would you now really consider altering the coinage again? It would not be a prudent move, Sir.'

‹The people are getting too much gold for their paper. From now on, my banknotes are to be worth thirty percent less.› Orleans› look said he was not to be brooked. ‹Now you have it, Law!›

Avoiding his financial advisor's eyes, Orleans got up from his chair and strode over to a bowl of flowers, bending to sniff at them. He did not face Law as he spoke. 'The tenor of the notes is to be changed from a real and positive value and in future is to read, "The Bank Promises To Pay The Bearer At Sight So Many Livres In Silver Coin", he said.'

'Silver. . ?' Law asked.

Orleans nodded and moved away from him still further. 'You shall no longer pay in gold.'

Forced to speak to the Regent›s back, Law was fighting to contain his anger. ‹Sir, it is stipulated on the face of each of the notes–*your* notes! that payments are to be made according to the weight and standard of *the day of issue*. Such an action will make money in the notes arbitrary and susceptible to all variations! Surely you are aware of that?'

'Facts and figures - is that all you can think of, Law?' the Regent asked irritably, turning back to him.

Law knew Orleans was in no mood to be crossed these days, always looking for ways to illustrate his absolute power. 'Sir,' he began, 'surely you understand that if the paper money is worth forty livres when a man buys it, then he must get forty livres back when he cashes in the note—or he will have no trust in the system!'

The Regent shrugged laconically. 'We are not bringing in enough money for the Royal purse.'

Law could barely contain himself. 'Sir, the money is pouring in! The bank grows more successful every day. And when the branches are opened...'

Orleans cut him off. 'Too slow, Law. Too slow.' He frowned and waved his arm vaguely in the air. 'I need money now! For other things.'

Law regarded him as though he were speaking to a spoiled child. 'Sir, we are building a tradition in the whole world because people can trust this bank. What is more important than establishing the integrity of the bank?' he demanded, his voice rising in spite of himself.

'The Regent is the integrity of France, Law. Remember that! And there is one traditional rule that rulers forgo at their peril. Each monarch must add to the royal jewel collection.' Orleans nodded as though agreeing with himself. 'So! Now you understand all.' He returned to his throne chair and reseated himself grandly, fussing at the lace on his sleeve.

Law felt his head spinning. 'You speak to me of jewels, Sir? We were speaking of the principles governing the running of the bank and the economy of France! What is it that you say you must buy?'

Orleans fidgeted and drummed a finger on the gilded arm of his throne chair. 'Well, it is really no concern of yours after all, but if you must know, there is a certain diamond I have been after for some time. In fact, your English countryman, Thomas Pitt, has brought it to France, and I am considering buying it. For the Royal Collection, of course.'

Now Law was unable to keep the anger from his voice. 'Sir, you talk to me of diamonds when we are speaking of the currency of this country? Banknotes that must be cashed on first demand! Do you not see that if that principle is violated, then. . . ?'

Orleans cut him off. 'No one is going to criticize you, Law,' he assured him. 'I have seen to that! You may continue to run the bank as Director-General, even though you are a foreigner. Rest assured, I know my enemies. There has been a cabal against me ever since King Louis died, led by the Duke du Maine. He has enlisted Count D'Argenson as his chief cohort.' Orleans' plump fist came down hard on the arm of his chair. For a moment, his face took on an apoplectic flush. Then he continued. 'For the last twenty years, that poxy Count has been mixed up in every strife and intrigue at this Court. Orleans sat back smugly and calmed himself with another sweetmeat. 'But I have fixed his wagon, Law. Count D'Argenson shall trouble me—and you—no more, make no mistake.'

'How have you accomplished that, Sir?' Law asked warily.

Orleans smiled. 'I have appointed him Vice-Chancellor and Chief of the Finance Council.'

Law stared at him, perplexed. 'Perhaps I have missed something? You have given your enemy two titles. . .and positions of such great power?'

'Empty titles, Law,' Orleans replied, chuckling. 'With *no power*! As Minister of Finance, and chief of the Magistracy, D'Argenson must carry into execution and affix his seal to all the measures I devise, without any say in the matter.' Orleans broke into hearty laughter at his own cleverness. 'Don't you see? It is D'Argenson's name and seal that will go on this new devaluation. Not yours or mine!'

'So the public will blame him for whatever changes you make in the currency?' Law asked, incredulous at the Regent's reasoning.

The Regent got to his feet once again. 'Precisely. And now our discussion is at an end, Law.'

But Law was not prepared to end the audience without one last try at rationality. 'Sir, how do you expect your country to conduct business? Above all, with foreign trading markets, if no one can trust the value of our paper money?'

'The matter is closed!' Orleans said angrily.

But Law insisted on having his say. 'Surely you realize that no matter whose name appears on the document, even Louis XIV's, such actions will ruin the bank. Ruin you! And ruin all France!'

'What more do you want of me, Law? Have I not given you your National bank? Made you the Director-General? Now it is up to you to run it smoothly,' Orleans said dismissively.

'The bank, this national bank has departed from the principles of private and mercantile credit on which I had originally fixed it. It is proceeding on the principles of public credit now.' Law paused, trying to control his growing anger. 'Which, in an absolute monarchy, depends on the solidity and the integrity of the sovereign.'

Orleans glared at him angrily. 'Enough, Law! Do not take advantage of our friendship.' He started across the room, a lackey opening the private door to his apartments as he approached. 'Now, I am late in paying a visit to Lady Knollys. I am thinking of building her a chateau at Versailles.' He gave Law a quick look. 'Of course, it shall be a government building.'

'Paid for out of bank funds, you mean?' Law asked angrily.

'That is no concern of yours, Law. Or the banks! Count D'Argenson shall sign the order. Be assured, from now on, nothing happens in France without my express desire. Your paper money is quite safe, whatever price I set on it.' Orleans paused, turning back. 'Oh, by the way, the King is giving a ball at Versailles this coming Saturday. Only five or six hundred people. Nothing extravagant. Marie-Louise would like you to be there.'

'Is the King to be there?'

Law asked, surprised.

'I shouldn't think so,' Orleans said. "Past his bedtime.' He smiled slyly. 'I have invited Count D'Argenson and, of course, my dear cousin, du Maine. It should be amusing.'

Law watched the Regent stride out of the room, wondering what his own title of Director General really meant when he could so easily and so mindlessly be overruled. Only the other day he had said to his brother, 'I have coped with failure, but I wonder how I shall deal with success?' He had been given a license to print money, which was now being made less valuable every day by the Regent's whim.

John Law strode down the corridor and made his way back to his own apartments. Now he could see that this fragile success brought with it a new set of uncertainties—his thoughts drifting to Katherine, wondering if perhaps she could influence Orleans. *But Katherine will always look out for herself, and while I am worried about the bank›s solvency, Katherine Knollys will be living in luxury in a chateau paid for from the bank›s profits!*

It was not only John Law, who was worried. Count D'Argenson was nearly out of his wits because of the new posts he had been given. Fearful that people should suspect his advancement's hollow secret, the Count had invented a role for himself as painful as it was ridiculous. He had chosen to play the part of a Minister bent under the weight of business, sacrificing himself for the public good.

Quite aware of the hypocrisy of the two titles given to Count D'Argenson, the Duke du Maine wondered how the Regent's little game might be of benefit to himself. He decided to pay the new Vice-Chancellor and Chief of the Finance Council an unexpected visit. He found Count D'Argenson in his new offices immersed in an ocean of papers and dictating one letter to four male secretaries at the same time.

'You are a diligent man these days, I see, Count,' du Maine said, resting one dogskin-gloved hand on his sturdy walking stick. 'Tell them to leave,' he ordered, his tone polite but firm, and sat himself down heavily in a delicate gilt chair facing D'Argenson's ornate Bouille desk. He tucked his lame leg behind the stronger one, balancing the weight on one square-toed shoe, its curved heel supporting the other foot.

D'Argenson waved the secretaries out of his presence, with the order: 'See that those dispatches are delivered at once.'

'You are diligent, sir. I commend you.' A sardonic smile somewhat belied du Maine's words. 'But why four secretaries at once?'

'The quickest way to dispatch a letter to four people, and it is essential that I keep the vital flow of urgent letters emanating from my office,' D'Argenson replied with a slightly hysterical look in his eyes.

Du Maine had chosen his wardrobe carefully. But then, he was always careful about his wardrobe, feeling that elegance detracted from his infirmity. His curled black wig softened his sharp features slightly. His angular body strained against the tightly cut grey velvet jacket that flared from his narrow waist across lean hips. Its somber tone was relieved by ornate silver braiding and delicate tracery of silver acanthus leaves. The jacket had taken three months, and four embroiderers to complete and had cost as much as a fine horse., His father, Louis XIV, had made a point of costume as the symbol of power, and du Maine was the picture of authority. 'Diligent, yes,' he repeated.

'H-h-heavily occupied, my dear du Maine,' D'Argenson stammered, a nervous tick troubling his right eye. 'So much to do. So little time.'

'Occupied, yes, indeed you are by all appearances. My observers have been watching you,' du Maine told him. 'You seem to keep yourself busy both day and night.'

D'Argenson looked up at him anxiously. 'You - you are having me watched?'

Merely keeping an eye, as I do on all my friends. For their own welfare,' du Maine replied, laconically. 'I am told our new Vice-Chancellor chooses all hours of the night for his appointments. You have been seen riding through the streets with a lighted torch on your carriage at midnight. Is this, my friend, to show the public that you are not a moment without working?'

'Working? Yes! Always busy, your Grace,' D'Argenson protested, an eye twitching even more. 'How many secretaries I must employ to keep up with all of it.'

Du Maine nodded, smiled, looked at the pile of papers on the desk. 'But what is it you are actually doing, Count D'Argenson?' he questioned. 'Or if I were to put it more precisely, when you *do* it, who listens to a word you say?'

Frightful rancor had accumulated in D'Argenson's heart at what Orleans had done to him, and he felt powerless against it. At the thought, his face became apoplectic. He sputtered but could not reply.

Du Maine frowned. 'Surely you are not standing behind the mad schemes of this foreigner to whom the Regent has given such freedom?'

'Law...? *I*, stand behind *Law*?' D'Argenson bleated. 'The blackguard is nothing more than a crook! A charlatan!' He rose from behind his desk, crossing to the window, staring into space. 'And now that you have made a point of it, your Grace, frankly, I must admit to you that the Regent has put me in a completely detestable position.' He pulled out his snuff-box, taking a soothing pinch. 'I find my appointment, defenseless. Yet even if I wished to do so, I am unable to resign from either post. My resignation would not be accepted!'

'Indeed, the Regent, with his devilish foreign advisor, has

been clever. Perhaps too clever for his own good,' du Maine said, chewing on his cheek.

D'Argenson drew out a large silk handkerchief from his sleeve, sneezed into it, and then turned back to du Maine. He looked as though he'd been shot between the eyes. 'I must place my cards upon the table, your Grace. As you have so rightly suspected, I am neither consulted nor listened to. Yet to my disgust, I am forced to accept full responsibility for every new act concocted by this murderous Scotsman and the Regent!' He waved the handkerchief at du Maine. 'I ask you what am I to do? They intend me, as Minister of Finance, to carry their every whim into execution. And as Chief of the Magistracy, I must—I say *must* affix my seal to all their outrageous measures!'

The color drained from his cheeks. He sat down rather too heavily. The chair made a small noise of protest.

Du Maine nodded, 'And some fascinating measures the foreigner has introduced. He has offered the support of his credit to establishments whose prosperity is of special public interest. He has revived labor and prevented bankruptcies, including France's. Which as you recall, I advocated Parliament! This poxy Scotsman seems to advise and encourage all, and because of him, trade, which was surely dead, has begun to show signs of life.'

D'Argenson looked at his visitor with some surprise. 'But, Your Grace - you make it sound as though his plans are a great success!'

Du Maine fluttered a hand and leaned back in his chair. 'For the moment, perhaps. But that is in itself a problem. The people are beginning to take to Law. He is becoming far too popular.' His voice rose a pitch as he went on. 'And some of this popularity is reflected on the slick façade of that mendacious, equivocating, devious devil, my cousin, Orleans! A man hardened in sin! One who is excluded from salvation, condemned by God!'

Du Maine leaned forward on his cane. 'No, no, it will not do for France! This is a dangerous state of affairs, Count D'Argenson. Dangerous!'

'Dangerous, your Grace?' D'Argenson asked. He had been so consumed with his own rage at Orleans' treatment of him that he had not thought of more far-reaching consequences.

'Don't you see?' du Maine advised. 'The increasing influence of Law over our Parliament foretells some hazardous attempt to throw power into the hands of the foreigner, and perhaps even to a foreign power! The Scots have always been far too comfortable here in France. We have sheltered their Kings and their Queens, their Pretenders, and their nobles. They learn to speak our language too easily, although I must say that I can understand why. It is so obviously superior to their own.'

D'Argenson nodded agreement, taking another pinch of snuff. 'But what is to be done?' he asked. 'How can anyone stop them? I have tried everything I can think of, and one might almost believe that the Regent is bent on destroying himself, for he has raised the price of a silver mark from 40 to 60 livres.'

'So I have been told,' du Maine acknowledged.

'Yes? Well, with the Regent's blessing, I was able to buy gold ingots cheaply in San Mâlo, and I had them coined at 60 livres the mark. Did your spies hear that, too?' D'Argenson asked with a note of annoyance.

Du Maine shook his head. 'Go on.'

'Then I was forced to sign a decree he put in front of me saying you must bring 48 livres in specie weighing 9 ounces, plus 12 livres in State notes to receive 60 livres of the new coinage.'

'Which means if I am correct,' du Maine said, 'that since the new coinage weighs only 8 ounces, the investor loses one-sixth of his money?'

D'Argenson sneezed a nod, turning back at du Maine with a worried expression. 'The Regent thinks to make a quick profit by depreciating the coinage. But I ask you, is it not a pretext for a Civil War, Your Grace?'

'Civil War?' Du Maine nodded. 'It is a miracle that it has not happened so far. But you are not alone in your endeavors, Count. For my part, I have managed to get Parliament to overrule the edict allowing paper money to pay taxes or giving gold in return for them. And best of all, at my instigation, they have brought out an old ordinance forbidding foreigners to interfere in Royal revenue. We shall see how Law responds to that.'

D'Argenson sighed. 'And all to what avail? With Orleans behind him, he will still do what he pleases.'

The visitor removed one soft leather glove revealing a large ruby ring in an ornate gold setting. It had a curious symbol cut into the stone. As he turned his hand in the light, the ring sparkled. D'Argenson could not refrain from eyeing it with interest. Du Maine spoke softly now. 'I must tell you that there are those amongst us loyal to the institutions of France who feel ourselves called upon to guide the country in these perilous times. We have taken the alarm and have formed a private faction. A cabal, you might say. *Men of the Old Finance*, we call ourselves. Men who can see that my cousin Philip, a person who can make a mockery of such a man as yourself, Count D'Argenson, such a person does not belong as Regent of France!'

'A cabal, you say?' D'Argenson considered. He was no stranger to strife and intrigue. It was the breath of life to him. He sneezed into his handkerchief with some relief at the thought.

Du Maine nodded solemnly. 'The Regent has misunderstood your character, Count D'Argenson. As Lieutenant of Police, you have fully enjoyed the reputation of a man of ability. For twenty years, I have seen you terrible in your relations with the multitude, subtle yet sometimes perhaps let it be said, too officious when dealing with the nobility. Nevertheless, you are the very man we seek.'

Du Maine got to his feet, leaning heavily on his good leg. 'I am here to ask you to be a part of our endeavor.'

D'Argenson absentmindedly started to take another pinch of snuff, then stopped himself, weighing the possibilities. 'What is it you propose? And what do the Men of the Old Finance intend to do?'

The Duke's piercing eyes seemed to bore into D'Argenson's very soul. 'There is only one way to stop John Law, and that is to make him overreach himself. We intend to find a way to destroy the Scotsman, and when we do, the Regent will come tumbling down.'

He crossed the room, heading for the door, then paused, turning back. 'Remember, Count, that the Court's greatest appointments have always gone from father to son. I am the eldest son of Louis XIV. He elevated my mother, Madame de Montespan, and he legitimized me. It is I who should be sitting on the throne of France!'

LOUIS XIV, MADAME MONTESPAN
& THEIR CHILDREN

SEVENTEEN:
VERSAILLES
AND MARIE-LOUISE

Though it was not yet dark, the sumptuous Gallerie des Glaces with its seemingly endless expanse of mirrors was already aglow with the lights of thousands of candles glittering from rows of tall marble and ormolu torchiers reflecting into the long gallery. The mirrors were angled just enough to allow a vista of magnificent gardens through the high arched windows, each set back into an ornate marble recess. The finest Italian painters decorated the ceilings, offered images of pomp and ceremony played out under the joyous gaze of cavorting cupids and angels.

It was the first time that Law had been invited to Versailles, and he was not prepared for such grandeur. It outstripped anything he had seen at the English Court or on the continent. Marie-Louise had warned him to dress as befitted the occasion, and after Orleans' admonition, he had ordered a new dark blue silk coat from Orleans' own tailor and allowed the man to add gold and silver braiding. His shoes of velvet stitched to leather had silver buckles and the still fashionable red heels. His waistcoat was of fine Chinese patterned silk. The Regent's wigmaker made his dark, tightly curled wig. He was beginning to look, if not yet to feel as though he belonged in the French Court. But there was still a part of him that was held in reserve.

Marie-Louise gave him a sideways glance from beneath thick blonde lashes as they moved down the long gallery. Certainly, he made a striking appearance, being somewhat taller than most Frenchmen, with broader shoulders and still, a slender waist.

'It is like walking through a fairyland, don't you think, Law?' she said, putting her arm through his, leading him past multiple reflections of themselves. ‹Of all his mistresses, Versailles was grandfather›s greatest love. He took a lifetime to build it, yet he scarcely had time to live here because he hated having workmen about, and he was continually adding more rooms.› She sighed. 'He often said he did not build it for himself, but for posterity.'

'A costly monument to The Sun King's reign,' Law agreed, gesturing towards the intricately painted ceiling. His arm movement was reflected a dozen times in the parade of mirrors. 'And the rooms, how many?' he asked.

'At last reckoning, four hundred,' she said. 'I have not been in all of them myself, nor do I care to go. But as you say: a monument.'

'I prefaced it with *costly*, Marie-Louise. However, I do not think Louis XIV's extravagance will last as long as the pyramids.'

She darted a hint of anger at him. 'You are a strange man, Law. How can you care so much about money and not appreciate splendor? Versailles is an affirmation. A communiqué to the world of France's place in it.'

She caught a reflection of her pale lavender gown, the exact color of her eyes. Stiff silk taffeta bows marched down the front of her dress in an unbroken row. She paused to straighten one and give the lace at her sleeve a tweak with delicate fingers. For the first time since Law had known her, she had powdered her bright red hair. Tiny Lilies of the Valley and pink rosebuds formed a coronet across it. A thin necklace of diamonds and pearls encircled her throat. Two large pearls hung from each ear and brushed gently against her slender neck. The mirrors reflected a delicate, spirited creature, a beautiful nymph admiring herself.

'You are quite perfect, my dear,' he said. 'And I am all admiration. But to answer your question. Yes, Marie-Louise, I do care about money,' Law said, suddenly serious. 'Not just to buy palaces and finery, which have their place, certainly. But money has a deeper purpose. Money can build the commerce of a nation. This nation! Your father has given me the opportunity that nobody else was prepared to give, and with his continued trust, I will raise this nation so high that every kingdom in the world will send their ambassadors to Paris. You see, splendor and money are two quite different things.'

'And beauty?' she asked.

'Oh, yes, I, too, love beautiful things. What man would not? Beautiful women - beautiful objects.' Law paused momentarily to admire a marble statue of a satyr and a faun, then turned back to her. 'But one cannot travel through the world with closed eyes. Just a few days ago, I was in Lyon, seeing our new bank there. I took a carriage back to Paris. When we stopped in a village to change the post-chaise postillions, all the people came out to beg with such miserable, starved faces and such tattered clothes that they needed no other eloquence to persuade one of the wretchedness of their condition.'

Her expression went cold, and her tone became hard. 'There is nothing one can do about the poor, Law. They are a burden for which there is no answer. Always have been and always will be.'

Law shook his head. 'I cannot believe that, Marie-Louise. Your grandfather built this capricious fantasy of stone and glass and filled it with brocade hangings, gold and silver ornaments, and marble statues. To say nothing of his rare and precious orange trees, each in a silver tub. He built all this, Marie-Louise, while France was on the verge of bankruptcy!'

'Nonsense,' she said haughtily. 'The country is not bankrupt now, and Versailles still stands. Maybe not forever like your pyramids, but it will survive long after both you and I are gone and forgotten.'

'It is my bank that has brought France from the brink of the financial pit,' he told her sternly. 'Because of my bank, France has earned the confidence of foreigners. Today, a Frenchman can conduct his business across the whole of Europe by *paper* transfers. The certainty of payment at sight has given an extended currency to paper notes.'

He thought his words might have angered her. Instead, she smiled, then broke into laughter. 'Maybe you *are* a genius, John Law. My father thinks it is so. And at least you know your own worth. Excellent!'

Music drifted from the ballroom in slow and staid cadence. Marie-Louise led him into the sumptuous hall with its painted gallery.

'A bit more splendor, Law; the murals. By the Italian master, Primaticcio. And creating these, he became a wealthy man. But do you think that Grandfather forgot the needy?' She shook her head. 'He built poorhouses for them.' She frowned. 'Horrid places!'

A footman announced them as they entered: 'Marie-Louise d'Orleans, Duchess de Berry. Monsieur John Law of Lauriston!' Many heads turned to see this wonder-man banker who was said to have amassed a personal fortune by his gambling. Ladies whispered behind fans, taking in his graceful figure and well-turned calves in white silk hose. What other strange ideas would he produce? Admiring glances and coquettish smiles were sent his way. Law didn't seem to notice.

There were at least two hundred couples dancing, yet it was not crowded. Others were entering the room now. The footman continued announcing: 'The Duke and Duchess de Guiche! Viscount Gage! The Duke and Duchess D'Antin! The Duke de Saint-Simon! Louis-Auguste de Bourbon, the Duke du Maine !'

Du Maine came down the wide steps with his uneven gait, balancing nimbly on his cane to favor his shorter leg. Spying Marie-Louise across the room with Law, he crossed over to them and kissed his niece on both cheeks. 'Charming, my dear. What a lovely color. Lavender does suit you,' he said. 'And the flowers in the hair. A perfect touch.' His lips grazed the air above her fingertips, his eyes, pinpointing Law all the while. 'I see you are entertaining our great innovator, my dear niece.' He turned to Law. 'What wonders will you surprise us with next, Monsieur Law?'

'I shall be pleased to let you know in due course, your Grace,' Law said forcefully, 'should I have any new ideas to present to Parliament.'

'Parliament. Yes. . .' Du Maine smiled, but there was no warmth in it, his glance trailing past Law to the dance floor. 'I do envy the dancers,' he said. 'My father made the dance a school for chivalry, courtesy, and ceremony in our country, Monsieur Law. All people of culture study it. All but I.' he sighed, then brightened. 'Do you like Versailles, Monsieur? My father took a lifetime to build it, you know. Beautiful, don't you think?'

His conversation was trivial, but Law knew his thoughts were not and wondered what intrigues he was planning. 'After seeing the exact proportions of Italian architecture in Rome, I find the irregularity of its design not quite to my taste,' Law said. 'Perhaps Versailles is too vast to be called beautiful.'

'Vast, you say? Of course, it is vast!' Du Maine bristled, reaching into his pocket and pulling out a carved agate. 'But I assure you, the King was also aware of beauty on a smaller scale.' He handed it to Law. 'Here is perfection in miniature. In fact, it is one of the most delicate pieces of a carving of its kind. The subject is the Apotheoses of Germanicus.'

Law turned the carved agate into the light. 'Ah, yes, Germanicus joining the pantheon of gods. The Romans always liked to deify their generals, did they not? It put the gods on their side even when they were not on the side of the gods. Where did you come by it?'

'I have taken possession of it from among the smaller pieces of the King's collection. None pleased me far as well for a touch-stone.'

He took it back from Law's hand as though Law might be tempted to pocket it himself. 'And now I must find the Duchess du Maine.' So saying, he moved off, skirting the edge of the dance floor with an uneven gait.

Marie-Louis angrily watched his retreating figure. 'My uncle has no right to pluck any treasure he wishes from the Royal collection!' she said.

'The Duke is a clever and powerful man who will pluck more than an agate if he chooses. I would not underestimate him, Marie-Louise,' Law told her.

But across the room, du Maine did not head for his very tiny wife seated in a chair. Instead, he joined Count D'Argenson. talking with a group of men with a distinctly conspiratorial air.

Marie-Louise glared at the Duchess du Maine. 'His pygmy wife thinks that she will get Philip of Spain to overthrow our Regency and set her precious husband on the throne of St Louis.'

'And what is her claim?' Law asked, turning his attention back to the Duchess.

'Her claim? Her father was Louis III de Bourbon. The one they called Monsieur le Duke. That is her claim! But it will never happen, Law.'

'Philip of Spain is a powerful ruler,' Law acknowledged.

'Poo! He is the creature of his wife! And she is my father's sister. I do not think she wishes her brother to be ousted from the Regency unless it would be to put her *own* husband on the throne, and that will never happen.›

Law looked at the girl with some astonishment. 'You surprise me, Marie-Louise. I knew you had a head for intrigue but did not imagine you had one for the intricacies of politics.'

'When it is to preserve my own head, Law,' she said firmly. Her glance went to a Germanic looking woman sitting in a gilt armchair near some other ladies of the Court. 'There is my grandmother! We were speaking of her daughter, the Queen of Spain, yes? Come, I shall introduce you.'

Coming around the dancers, they crossed the room towards an amply cushioned woman with heavy black eyebrows and dimples in her rouged cheeks. Her hair, short in front, was so heavily powdered it stood up like icing sugar, and she, too wore a flowered ornament in it. Curiously, she held a tame duck in her enormous lap. At her side sat her lady-in-waiting, Mme de Brancas.

'Grand Mama's name is Elizabeth Charlotte,' Marie-Louise whispered as they approached. 'But everyone calls her Madame as a sign of respect.'

Madame smiled at Marie-Louise, who curtsied and kissed her grandmother's cheek and introduced Law. The older woman's eyes sparkled as she took in Law's striking figure. 'At last,' she said. 'My son has been hiding you from me. And he knows how I love to keep up with the affairs at Court. I hear you are too quickly becoming one of us, Monsieur. You must come and take tea with Loulou and me.' She indicated the duck. 'Tea. That is the new English affectation, is it not? Or so Lord Stair, your Ambassador tells me.'

'I am Scottish, Madame. Lord Stair is English. But I do enjoy a cup of tea and shall be honored to accept.'

'Next Saturday?' she said. 'Just forty or fifty close friends. At four o'clock. We shall take tea in the English fashion, and you shall tell me how you like our Court, Monsieur.' She did not give him time to reply, speaking at a rapid tempo. 'Have you seen the gardens here at Versailles? All the rocks around have pious sentences inscribed on them to show the devotion that was so fashionable while my brother-in-law was King.' She sighed. 'I believe such devotion died with him; at least I see no exterior marks of this religious fervor. And in Paris, it is no better. At Court, the ladies and gentlemen sit up until three o'clock in the morning at cards, elated with gain or dejected with loss, but neither state puts paid to their foolishness. She patted the duck. 'But then, I hear you, too, are a gambler, Monsieur Law.'

'In a modest way, Madame,' he said.

'Not so modest.' She nodded vigorously, and white powder peppered from her hair onto her ample bosom. 'I myself am forced to be a letter writer, for I must keep in touch with all my relatives in Germany. The Royal family is large there, and I send them reports of Court life at Versailles.' She gave a deep throaty laugh, and the duck stirred with a sharp quack. Her hand smoothed its feathers, and it settled back happily into her well-padded lap.

Since there was no adequate answer to her remarks, Law said, 'An unusual pet, Madame.'

'Loulou? A far better companion than a dog. I much prefer her quack to the yap. She eats less, and occasionally she lays me an egg.' Madame burst into throaty laughter at the thought.

Law was stopped from the further necessity to reply by her son. Orleans came over to present Katherine to his mother. He gave Madame a perfunctory peck on the cheek, patted Loulou, and kissed Marie-Louise with some enthusiasm. 'Ah, Law, you must meet the Duke D'Antin,' he said.

A short, foppish man wearing a wine silk coat heavily embroidered with gold thread and set with pearls and diamonds, D'Antin reached into his cuff for a silk handkerchief, which he waved about as he spoke. 'At last - Monsieur Law! I have been thinking of putting some money with you,' D'Antin said, 'Public opinion seems to be in your favor. I should not wish to miss out on the wonders you offer.' His eyes traveled up Law's figure from his buckled shoes to the dark blue silk of his coat and seemed to come full stop at his eyes.' And I think you must offer many,' he added with a suggestive look.

'I shall be delighted to receive your Grace personally. Whenever you wish to visit the bank,' Law replied quite formally.

'Soon. It shall be soon,' D'Antin replied. 'I shall write to you in advance, and perhaps we can dine together.'

Orleans glanced across the room with a proprietary air. He was wearing pale blue silk tonight, his jacket heavily braided with gold, and his sash of office adorning it. 'D'Antin has erected a magnificent house here at Versailles,' he said, turning back to them. 'I am building one for Lady Knollys quite near it. I have given the Duke the care of preserving the King's pictures until his Majesty is of age. They are not many but they are by the best hands. 'The Archangel' by Raphael is among them.'

Katherine smiled. 'Perhaps I could bring Monsieur Law to see them, your Grace? she asked D'Antin. She turned back to Orleans. 'I have seen them with great pleasure. My favorite is by Michelangelo.' Her eyes met Law's briefly with a hint of other pleasures they might share.

'I should be delighted, Lady Knollys,' D'Antin replied.

'And I too. When I can fit it in with my heavy schedule,' Law added.

D'Antin looked closely at Katherine, his glance resting at her neckline's cleavage flaunting an exuberant curve. 'You speak of Michelangelo, Lady Knollys. He let it be known in word and deed that the male body is the most beautiful.' His eyes had settled on a handsome young man in his early twenties. 'I myself much prefer it to the female form, if you will forgive me saying so.'

It was an opinion John Law did not share. And as much as he might want Katherine at that moment, he knew it would be Marie-Louise's bed he would sleep in that night. Feeling someone's sharp attention behind him, he turned to find himself looking across the room straight into the Duke du Maine's shrewd eyes. The late King's illegitimate son was standing in close tête-à-tête with Count D'Argenson and several other noblemen. An involuntary shiver traveled down John Law's spine.

EIGHTEEN:
THE BED OF JUSTICE

Two weeks after Law met the Duke D'Antin at Versailles, he received a gilded parchment inviting him to dine the following Friday at midday. Law had decided to refuse D'Antin's invitation because he could not spare the time, but that night at one of Orleans' little suppers, Katherine let it drop that she would dine with the Duke that day. D'Antin had offered to lend her some minor paintings from the Royal collection for the new chateau that Orleans was building for her. Perhaps they could ride out together, she suggested? Orleans thought Law seemed reluctant to leave his busy schedule and urged him to go with Katherine. He did not need much urging.

When they arrived at D'Antin's palace, Law was stunned by the richness displayed. It seemed in miniature to be more flamboyant than even the Sun King's extravagance. Gilding and ormolu covered every table, cabinet, and console. The walls were drenched in silk damask in a curious shade of peach shot with gold, with heavily gilded ormolu along the curtain palmettes. There seemed to be more servants than attended a royal feast, and after a sumptuous meal, D'Antin led Katherine and Law into a long gallery hung with paintings.

'The King's collection is so large even with all the palace walls covered, and we must still store some away,' he said. He took them to a large oil depicting a man holding a tablet and a quill looking towards the heavens for inspiration, facing the muse Calliope, Apollo, and several cupids. "This is by Nicholas Poussin,' D'Antin said with a sigh. '*The Inspiration of the Poet*, and was in the collection of Cardinal Mazarin.'

'Truly inspiring,' Katherine told him.

D'Antin turned to the Scotsman. 'If you know your French history, Monsieur Law, you will recall Mazarin was exiled from France for causing a civil war. It forced him to leave behind a fine group of paintings, which came into the King's possession.'

And at no cost to the Royal purse, Law thought.

D'Antin moved on to the end of the room, where some paintings were stacked against the wall and ordered one of the footmen to show them to Katherine. While the footman held each one up for her to see, D'Antin took Law aside. 'I do keep my finger on the pulse, Monsieur Law. And I must warn you, you have made some enemies in the Parliament.' He pulled his silk handkerchief from his cuff and waved it at Law to punctuate his words.

'I am aware of it, Count,' Law replied.

'Count D'Argenson has passed it around that it was you who instigated the devaluation of your very excellent paper money. They are trying to stop using paper money to pay for taxes.' He lowered his voice. 'I warn you, Monsieur, these men want more than to overrule your edict. There is talk of a summons...' He broke off, having said perhaps more than he cared to, as Katherine returned, her cheeks flushed, with the look of one who has fallen into Aladdin's cave. 'I have chosen four, your Grace. With your permission,' she added graciously.

'I shall have them taken to your chateau as soon as it is completed, Lady Knollys.' He saw his guests out to their coach.

Katherine and Law did not talk of paintings on the ride home.

A week later, William Law looked across the desk at his brother in the private offices of the Palais Mazarin, his face showing deep concern. Deeper still, because his brother was taking the matter so calmly. John wore the veteran gambler's unreadable expression, and no one could give away less when he chose to. He had staked his livelihood across too many tables, too many games of chance. Now he was playing the biggest game of all, and he had everything to lose.

'But none of this was your doing, John!' Will cried. "From the start, from the very beginning, you have tried to stop the Regent from taking such actions. And now it has come to this! After you have worked so hard to win the confidence of the public for your paper money.'

'Come, Will,' Law said impassively, glancing out into the street where he could see that the police guard had already arrived and was attracting a few passers-by. He knew what they had come for. To arrest him, as D'Antin had warned. 'Surely you do not think the Duke du Maine would be so foolish as to attack the Regent directly? He is much too clever for that. No, no, my dear brother, it is I who am the key card.'

Will looked at him querulously.

'Have you never built a house of cards, Will? Remove one key card, and the pack comes tumbling down.'

'But how has he managed this?' Will asked, nervously pulling at the band of his neckcloth. He was feeling suddenly hot.

'Du Maine is not alone in trying to destroy the Regent and me,' Law said. 'His dogs-body D'Argenson's lies have made it possible for the Duke with his cabal, to convince Parliament to overrule the edict, which I fought so hard to achieve. To use banknotes to pay taxes; because if paper money can be used for taxes, it is money a citizen can trust.'

'And now this new edict forbids anyone getting gold in exchange for their banknotes!' Will exclaimed, looking nervously outside once more. The stragglers had turned into a crowd, now gathering around the police guard. Voices were being raised in angry protest. 'Those people will not be so easily put off, John. If you do not think of something, I fear this will spell the end of your national bank.'

John Law smiled ruefully. 'There is worse yet, which I have not told you.'

Shocked, Will turned to his brother. 'Do not spare me, John. Have I not traveled all this way and remained here to stand by you and support you?'

'Indeed you have, Will!' Law came and put his arm around his brother. 'Well then, if you must know, Parliament has brought out an old ordinance forbidding foreigners to interfere in Royal revenue.'

'*Interfere*? But what can they be thinking? You *are* the bank!' Will exclaimed.

Law nodded. 'And a Scotsman! Do not forget that. This bank and its founder can only be saved now by a coup d'etat.'

'They could throw you in the Bastille!' Will cried. He moved to the window facing the side street and peered out. That street was empty. He turned back, hopefully. 'Perhaps we still have time to escape. We could get away through the rear of the building, I think.' He was interrupted from further speculation by a sharp knock on the giant doors.

Law shook his head. 'No, Will. But understand, this does not reflect on you. You are safe! And frankly, I've had my share of running. I shall face what comes. And I still have one card to play. You must send word to the Regent. He is the only one who can stop them! Tell him that I shall put myself in his hands.'

He kissed his brother on the cheek and went over to the great door, opening it himself.

Outside, one of the police guards stood at attention. "Monsieur Jean Lass?' he asked.

'*Law*. John Law,' the bank's Governor-General corrected.

The guard looked uneasy. He himself had money on deposit in Law's bank. And his brother-in-law had borrowed from the bank to buy a new heifer for his farm. He cleared his throat. His voice was diffident when he spoke. 'Monsieur Law, I have a personal summons issued by Parliament against you. You are to be escorted by us to the Courts.'

Law nodded. 'You will please note, Officer, that I willingly comply with your orders and am indeed anxious to present my case to the Courts personally.'

'And so it shall be noted on your record, Monsieur,' he said, leading the way somewhat relieved that he had not been asked to use force. He took a closer look at the face of his prisoner. All he had ever heard of Law was good. 'This way, Monsieur. And. . .' he paused. 'I wish you well.'

Law followed him out into the street, where he was greeted with an angry roar. 'We want our gold! Gold for paper! Give us our money!'

Law raised his hands. 'Be calm, friends. Be patient,' he told them. 'I shall speak to the Regent, and you shall see that this mistake will soon be put right, and the bank will be running as usual once again.'

It could not be said that Law's words made much impression. His stomach churning, Will watched Law being led away. Then hastily, he sat down at his brother's desk and wrote a note on the bank's crested paper to the Regent, repeating John's words. He paused to consider if he had done all he could, then an idea struck him.

Picking up the pen once more, he wrote another letter. This one he addressed to the Duchess de Berry. Sealing both with the red wax and the bank's insignia, he called for the bank's messenger and dispatched both letters to the Palais Royal.

Marie-Louise was in her bath when Mouchi brought her the letter. She opened and read it, wide-eyed. 'Parliament has arrested John Law! She exclaimed, standing up in her bathtub, waving at Mouchi for a towel. 'We must hurry…'

'La! How can that be?' Mouchi asked, wrapping her mistress with the large drying sheet as she stepped down from the tub.

Marie-Louise pushed away from her ministrations impatiently. ‹We shall soon find out. Fetch me my blue satin gown, Mouchi. I must see my father at once.'

Mouchi called in two ladies in waiting to help lace the Duchess into a long corset stitched firmly with whalebone rods. They pulled strings at the back tightly over her under-dress, making her waist barely a hand span wide. The corset forced her waist down to a sharp point and pushed her breasts up to peek out of the low cut neckline. The blue silk bodice left white lace sleeves exposed. Marie-Louise fidgeted as they helped her dress. 'Hurry, hurry,' Marie-Louise cried impatiently and waved away a crimped frill of lace that Mouchi offered to be worn across her exposed breasts.

Mouchi clucked her tongue at such daring in daylight and folded back the wings of her mistress's blue silk robe to display the lining. She gathered the cloth into puffs and fastened them with several pearls and diamond clasps on each side. The robe featured a train of the new longer length, and Marie-Louise, her flaming hair unpowdered, again waved away her ladies all except Mouchi and called for her page.

Mouchi went out and returned with a small blackamoor dressed in fanciful breeches and turban; his duty: to carry the Duchess's train. His name was Chuba, and he was ten years old, the exact age of the King, and born on the same day.

She found her father alone in his private quarters. Orleans was playing at toy soldiers with young Louis, now a sturdy lad with a cheerful countenance. She curtsied to the little King and waved her letter at Orleans. 'Terrible news, Papa!' she cried.

Orleans held up his letter. "I have already heard,' he said

'Well then, it does not take a genius, Papa, to see that this move against John Law is merely one step removed from you yourself.'

'I am constantly impressed by your perception, Marie-Louise,' Orleans said, moving a platoon of soldiers behind a hilltop. Chuba came over to watch the miniature battle, staying at a respectful distance from King Louis.

She nodded. 'I too, like my position at Court, Papa. And as long as you are Regent, I enjoy the fruits of your table.'

He chuckled. 'Aptly said, my dear. But I have served my time in the wars under your grandfather, and I am no child in these political battlefields. Trust me to foresee the pitfalls. They shall not catch me napping so easily. I have already embarked upon a course of action; you can be sure.'

'What? What have you done?' she cried impatiently. 'Don't you realize they have put John Law in jail?'

'From what I am told, it would not be for the first time.' But the thought did not seem to disturb him. 'But it is of no matter. I need Law! He is a man of vision. And I assure you, not all the men in Parliament are against me, Marie-Louise or I should not be sitting here at this very moment playing at soldiers with dear little cousin Louis.'

'I am winning, cousin Philip!' cried Louis.

'And so you are, your Highness Louis dear.' Orleans patted him on the head and turned back to his daughter. 'Two men whom I trust, the Duke de Bourbon and the Duke de D'Antin were with me when the missive arrived. With them, I have already devised a plan. Have no fear, my dear.'

He turned back to the child. 'The King himself will be coming to John Law's rescue.'

Little Louis looked up from his soldiers. 'Cousin Philip has promised me a marron glacé when I have done my duty to the Parliament,' he said with a smile.

'And Orleans is a man of his word, dear Louis,' she said, turning back to her father. 'But how do you propose to stop Parliament?'

Orleans rose to come over to her. He kissed her, holding her tightly to him for a long moment, then released her.

' I shall inconvenience them so thoroughly that they will never try such a trick again!' he said with a mysterious smile. 'Remember, my dear. That very body of gentlemen, much against their will, mind you, has already granted me absolute power.'

She looked at her father for a moment and then smiled.

'Inconvenience them' Orleans did. The Regent's first move was to order Parliament to convene an extraordinary session called a Bed of Justice. His further command was sent to every member: *'The Parliament is to proceed to the number of sixty-nine members on foot and in red robes.'* This Bed of Justice was to be held in an old chateau a few hours' walk outside of Paris!

It was a furious group of Parliamentarians who met one early morning and set out on foot from Paris for that special Bed of Justice session. Since nothing had been said about how the men were to travel home on the return trip, carriages followed owners at a discreet distance. One old fellow, a member of the Cabal, had not walked anywhere for years. He started well enough but had the sense to bring three pages; two were to support him, and one to carry the tails of his heavy red robe.

When The Bed of Justice was finely convened in the chateau's large hall, Count D'Argenson, himself quite winded from the walk, began the proceedings with a bitter address against Law. He brought out the facts relating to Law's escape from Newgate Prison and assured the members that Law was still a wanted man.

Two nobles were on Law's side and spoke out in his defense: Francois Louis de Bourbon Prince de Conde and the Duke de D'Antin. They told of the marvelous changes of fortune Law's Bank had brought to the country and were quick to mention that Law's British crime so long ago, killing a man in a duel, was still considered a point of honor in a civilized country like France.

But the most galling sight of all to the Men of the Old Finance was the appearance of the little King himself. The young Monarch, dressed in robes heavily trimmed in gold and lace, the red slippers on his small feet decorated with large bows. He wore a full brown wig fitted to his ten-year-old head and presided over the Parliament seated on a large throne chair next to the Regent. This was the first occasion when the King had honored them with his presence, and little Louis XV played out his role to perfection. At his Uncle's signal, he handed 'Letters Patents' to the Parliament, which he commanded in a small but firm voice. 'These Letters Patent come from my hand, and I wish them to be read aloud.'

The Duke de Bourbon rose and read the King's declaration, his voice loud and clear, so that no member might miss a word: '*By our special favor, full power and Royal authority we have declared, appointed and ordained and by these present, signed by our hand, do declare appoint, ordain, will, and our pleasure is as follows: The Parliament of Paris shall reserve the right of making remonstrances only on the edicts which shall be submitted to it. This Act shall be considered as duly registered.*'

The parliamentarians were so abuzz with excitement that nobody noticed Orleans tuck a wrapped marron glacé into the child's hand or saw little Louis pop it into his mouth.

As the Regent well understood, this declaration, that a child had handed down from the throne to his serving Ministers, was in fact, a political revolution, for by this Act, Parliament lost the right of free intervention in any affairs of general interest.

Parliament could no longer interfere with anything in the land unless asked to do so by the sovereign.

Orleans sat back in his chair and gloated to himself. The country had truly fallen under absolute despotism. His eyes met John Law's. In the place assigned to the accused, Law had not been permitted to speak in his own defense. But he had wisely placed his confidence in Orleans, whose self-interest he knew was now too deeply involved with Law's own welfare to abandon him.

Du Maine and D'Argenson were seated with a row of ministers, all men of their Cabal who were no friends of Parliament—which, after all, had chosen Orleans over du Maine to rule as Regent. That day, it was John Law and the Regent who shared the victory.

Du Maine, who, with his game leg, had managed to arrive at the session well before the others so they would not discover that he had secretly ridden there, took D'Argenson with him in his carriage for the ride back. They would have to find another way to get rid of John Law.

The following day, Law was back in his bank, the street crowd pacified, and word had spread that all was once again back to normal.

But several weeks later inside the Bank, one would not have imme-diately believed that this was the case from the look of worry still etched deeply in William Law's face.

'Do not fret so, Will,' Law told him. 'The time for you to worry was when I was about to be raised high on the gallows in England; not now, when I have been raised to staggering heights by the Regent of France.'

The impossible had happened, and it had been at Ma-rie-Louise's suggestion. Her father has granted Law new powers. He was to replace D'Argenson as Finance Minister. That little joke of the Regent's was over.

'But John,' Will began, 'Finance Minister! And you, a for-eigner. Even with this new post, you have allowed Orleans to. . .'

Law stopped him short. *'Allowed?* I allow nothing, Will. Even the Sun King was unable to achieve turning France into an absolute monarchy. It is like gaming at the tables, Will. It is all chance. You win, or you lose, but no matter what, you must play by the rules.›

'But Orleans has changed the rules, John! The bank has de-parted from the principles on which you yourself fixed it. It is pro-ceeding on public credit! Which is a perilous state of affairs by your own admission.'

Law knew that what Will said was true, but still, he felt he must stay in the game and hope to overcome the obstacles. 'Orle-ans will have to listen when I explain it to him,' he told his brother, wanting to believe it himself. But deep inside him was the worry that somehow, if the wind blew otherwise, he would always be a handy scapegoat for the Regent.

At that moment, the Duke du Maine's carriage was entering

the Rue de Richelieu. Sitting beside the Duke, as they came abreast of the Palais Mazarin, a gloomy-faced Count D'Argenson glowered out at the bank.

'Even though getting rid of me, I cannot believe that the Regent has made a Scotsman Finance Minister of France!' D'Argenson said, his voice slipping badly out of control as he turned towards his host.

'Why are you so angry, my dear?' du Maine replied. '!t is true we have had a small setback, but it is only one battle. The war goes on.'

D'Argenson stared towards the window of the bank, hoping to catch a glimpse of what was inside. He had never set foot in the place. As it was, the carriage moved on too quickly, and all he saw were a handful of people with satisfied expressions coming out of the door.

'And as for you,' Du Maine continued. 'Were you not a mere puppet in that post? I assure you John Law will fare no better. He has been - as you were yourself, elevated to a position of *contre-faire*. A sham! For nothing in France is done without my sainted brother-in-law's express permission. Is that not true?'

D'Argenson nodded reluctantly. 'So it would seem.'

Du Maine chuckled to himself. 'The best swimmers are the most often drowned, my dear D'Argenson. Remember that I told you the way to destroy Orleans is to make John Law overreach himself? By an amazing turn of events, one member of our cabal has found just the person to entice Law into his own destruction.'

'Who or what could stop Law now?' D'Argenson asked glumly.

'Temptation,' du Maine replied. 'The offer of something he cannot resist.'

In his office, John Law rose, coming around his desk and looking out at the street. He saw du Maine's distinctive carriage roll by and had recognized the silhouette of D'Argenson inside. He turned back to his brother. 'What would you have me do, Will? Would you have me quit the bank?' he asked angrily, his voice rising despite himself. 'Why would I do that? To return to Scotland? To be sent back to London in chains?'

'No, John, no…' Will sighed. 'I know you are doing all you can.'

'For the moment, I can only try to keep the bank on an even keel and hope.' The conversation was interrupted by a knock at the door. Will went over to open it.

Vivienne Duclos stood there, radiant in a red traveling suit trimmed in ermine with military frogging across the front. Black ermine tails decorated her matching bonnet, accenting a sweep of dark curls. Her brown eyes flashed above the wide smile of softly painted lips. Will greeted her and excused himself.

Law came over to her, kissing her hand. 'My dear Vivien. What brings you to the bank?'

'What brings half of Paris, John Law? I have decided to keep my savings under the bed no longer and have just made my first deposit.' She waved the receipt at him, frowning slightly. 'It seems it is I who must come to see you these days,' she scolded. 'Why has the new Finance Minister not visited my gaming tables lately?'

'The pressure of work,' he told her, and it was mostly true.

'And the Duchess du Berry, no doubt. I hear she is voracious in bed. But I am not a woman to bear a jealous heart.' She reached her lips up to him.

Law obliged, taking her voluptuous figure into his arms to kiss her. 'A beautiful, uncomplicated and intelligent woman,' he said. 'How I admire you, Vivien.'

She crossed the room; her movement undulating gently. 'Intelligent enough to know what I am missing. You are a man a woman cannot forget easily. Have you lost the key I gave you?' She rested one gloved hand on the edge of his desk, the other raised in a deliberately theatrical pose that showed off the fine curve of her body. Law's eyes traced the line from her full breast to her narrow waist. The wide sweep of her skirt left the rest to the memory of what he had enjoyed in more private circumstances.

He reached into his pocket and extracted a key, holding it up for her inspection. 'I assure you I have not forgotten you, Vivien. The bank will be closed in just a few minutes, and I shall be delighted to escort you home and open your bedroom door for us both.'

Will knocked, then stuck his head in to announce in a whisper, 'John, there is a man outside who insists on seeing you urgently on important business.'

'Tell him to come back tomorrow, Will,' Law said firmly, taking Vivien's hand.

'He insists it is extremely urgent! He has traveled all the way from St. Mâlo, or I would not trouble you,' Will told him, eyeing Vivien apologetically.

Vivien sighed. 'I have spent too many years on the stage, not to know a good exit line.' She crossed the room, turned, and flashed a smile at Law. 'Tonight then, John.' Her departure left a trail of heady perfume behind her.

The man who entered John Law's office introduced himself as Captain Antoine Crozet. Law judged him to be in his fifties. His tanned and rugged features had a certain openness about them. His hair, for he wore no wig, was tied in the back and stuck out in a white shock when he removed his tricorn hat. The hat was decorated with gold braid, and his dark coat of a thick woolen fabric was that of a nautical captain. He looked dusty from traveling and came forward with a swaying gait, extending a hand to Law. Like his face, it was weathered and coarsened by the elements.

'It is a great honor to meet you, Monsieur Law. You have been the first topic of conversation in France ever since I returned to these shores so that I feel I already know you.' The man seemed out of breath, and Law offered him a chair. He sat heavily.

'Your business is so urgent that it could not wait until tomorrow, Captain?'

'There is no time to waste, Monsieur Law,' Crozet said. 'I am not a well man, and I have a proposition to offer the bank. An opportunity so vast that only a man like yourself could encompass it. But first, you must allow me to tell you something about myself.'

Crozet looked exhausted, and Law poured him out a glass of brandy. 'Take your time then, Captain,' he said.

Crozet downed the brandy in one swallow. 'In truth, sir, I have been poorly these past few months, which is what has brought me to you.' He sat back in his chair, and Law refilled his glass. This, too, was downed at a gulp.' A fine brandy, Monsieur!' He leaned forward, eager to talk. 'Well then, Monsieur Law, all my life from the age of nine as a cabin boy, I have been on the high seas. Around the world eight times. Few can make such a claim. For nearly twenty years, I've been a sea Captain and a successful one. Let me say that I was so fortunate in my maritime speculations that by 1712, I was worth forty million livres.'

'A sizeable fortune, Captain,' Law conceded, wondering what the man had in mind.

Refreshed from the brandy, Crozet rose, taking a map from his ample pocket and unrolling the parchment on Law's desk. 'Do you mind, sir?'

'Please,' Law said with a touch of anticipation. It was a map, and it had a familiar look. 'Is this not a map of the Louisiana Territory in the Americas, Captain Crozet?'

Crozet stared up at him, somewhat astonished. 'You are right, Monsieur, but I did not think that you would know of it!' He leaned heavily on the desk. 'Could I perhaps have another tot of that most excellent brandy?'

Law poured the drink, his eyes returning to the map, his finger tracing the length of the river. 'I have been there, Captain, and traveled down that river—the Mississippi.'

Crozet's eyes widened. 'Why then, Monsieur, perhaps you can understand that only a few short years ago when I was still in excellent health and was seduced by the idea of fertilizing a new world. I purchased the Grant of Louisiana from Louis XIV himself, with exclusive trading rights to the entire Territory, which France has had possession of, for thirty years.'

'The Louisiana Territory. . .' Law's hand spread out to cover that section of the map. 'Towards the east and west, its extant is without boundary. To the north, it extends to the French establishments in Acadia.' He looked up with growing excitement. 'And you say that you have the exclusive trading rights to all of this?'

'For sixteen years, Monsieur.' He sat down heavily on the chair once again. 'I did not think to find you so knowledgeable.'

'You want the bank to finance your speculations, Captain? Is that it?'

'No, Monsieur, not at all. I have come to ask if you would be interested in buying my rights entirely. As you can see, I am in no fit state to see my dream come true.'

Now it was John Law's turn to be astonished. He regarded the sea captain with growing inspiration.' The trading rights to the entire Louisiana Territory? What an extraordinary idea, Captain Crozet. Indeed, providence has surely sent you to me!'

Several weeks later, when John Law and Katherine Knollys' carriage drew away from the Palais Royal, she peered out at the beautiful houses as they turned into the Rue St Honoré. 'London may boast that it is nearly twice as large, but Paris certainly has the advantage, Johnny. The streets here are so beautifully proportioned! Not like helter-skelter London, where the streets wind off every which way. Here, they are so neatly paved that a lady can walk down them without fear of a muddy skirt and ravished shoes. And Paris's great houses are beautified by gardens full of flowers.'

'You are such a sybarite, Katherine. Paris also has another face, my dear. 'Sometime, look down the side streets,' Law said grimly. 'Drive through the Faubourg St. Marceau. You will see no fine ladies and gentlemen walking about there. Even the police fear for their lives in those stinking alleyways. There, you will find all the filth and poverty it is possible a civilization can provide, and beggars live in Paris with no hope of escape or a better life.'

Katherine sighed. They were riding past a neat row of magnificent stone houses, heading towards the Rue Castiglione. 'If I am a sybarite, then you are a Samaritan, Johnny. Deliver me, please, from good deeds and do not expect me to feel pity for more than one or two of your beggars at a time.' Her fingers grazed a new diamond necklace Philip had given her only the week before. 'I cannot weep for all the poor in Paris.'

'Perhaps not *all*, Katherine. But I think I have found an answer for some of them. Maybe many,' he mused. 'In fact, an untapped gold mine as big as a continent!'

'Don't tell me you have discovered buried treasure?' Katherine asked, amused at his enthusiasm.

'You could call it that,' Law replied mysteriously. 'Have you ever heard of the Louisiana Territory, Katherine?'

'It is in the New World, is it not? What has all that vast emptiness got to do with you and me?'

His expression grew serious. 'Consider a plot of land. Buy it, build a house on it, and it is worth twice as much. Is that not true?'

'So now you would build a house in the wilderness?' She nodded. 'Marvelous.' 'Not a house, my dear,' he said patiently. 'Houses. Churches. Offices. A city. Build a city, and the land would be worth a fortune.'

Her laughter tinkled lightly. 'Success has gone to your head, Johnny. Now, you're dreaming about empires. Louisiana. . ? There is nobody there to live in your city!'

Law smiled. 'Aye, but there will be when I send out colonists to develop the land. To turn the forests into plantations. They will dig up the buried treasure in the ground and send it back to France!'

'And who will pay for all of this? You will not find it easy to convince Philip of this crazy new scheme.'

He leaned back against the quilted coach seat, looking out at the neat Parisian street where a young couple was strolling, her arm through his. 'When I came to France, the debts of this nation were almost twenty times as high as the annual revenue,' he told her. 'The bank, my bank, has brought new prosperity. People are once again sitting out in the cafés and going to the Comédie Française to watch the plays of Molière.' His expression softened into a smile as he turned back to her. 'As you and I did only last night. Behind our masks, of course.'

She moved a trifle closer, stroking his hand. 'I told you we would find excuses to see each other,' she said. 'You can moan about your beggars if you wish, but do so behind closed doors, Johnny. Even your bank is not rich enough to pay for such a scheme,' she said dismissively. 'But to talk of more practical matters, Philip wishes his new Finance Minister to present sufficient opulence to the world. You are too modest in your tastes for the French Court,' she told him severely. 'To put it another way, you look too much like a Scotsman.'

He reached over and kissed her. 'I am entirely in your hands, my dear.' For the next few minutes, fingers and lips found pleasure in touching. Then abruptly, the carriage entered the Place Vendôme and drew to a halt. Law looked out. 'Why are we stopping here?'

Katherine smiled secretively. 'I did not wish to find you a house too quickly because it would prevent us opportunities like today. 'But unfortunately, I have found the perfect house for you, Johnny.'

He looked out at the smooth stone façade, neatly proportioned in the French Baroque style so favored by the late King.

'What is this place?' he asked.

'The Palais de Nevers. Do you like it?'

'Well, it is ostentatious enough,' he said. 'If this is what Orleans expects of his Finance Minister, you have done well, Katherine.' He helped her down from the carriage, and they proceeded to the great door.

'Knock, Johnny. The servants are still in attendance.'

His knock was quickly answered by a footman, who had obviously been expecting them. He bowed to Law. 'Good afternoon, Monsieur Law,' he said, leading them into a great hall with an ornate marble floor and a wide curved staircase to the upper floors.

'Wait until you see it all, Johnny. You have always told me how much you liked the Dutchman who paints so well.' She led him into a large gallery, indicating the painted ceiling.

'It is by Rubens!' he said with some surprise.

'Do you like it?' she asked expectantly.

He turned to her. 'Truly magnificent, Katherine. And I must admit, for I am no hypocrite, that I could live here quite happily.'

'Everything is for sale. Curtains, furniture, even china. The servants all wish to stay on, Johnny. And since you have no wife to arrange such matters, I have hired a housekeeper who will keep strict order and propriety in your household.' She lowered her voice. 'Yet she can be discreet when necessary. And I have taken care that she is not too attractive,' she added with a wicked smile.

‹I shall move in at once.›

She burst into laughter. 'I can always count on you, Johnny, always ready for the new, and yet you never change your ways. I foolishly thought I might have to convince you that this was the house for you!' She took his hand. 'Now come upstairs. We have just time for some unfinished business in the bedroom.'

He followed her back into the lobby and up the wide sweep of the staircase. The curve of the wall was hung with excellent portraits of French kings and queens. Law recognized the likeness of Henry of Navarre and Katherine de Medici.

'And the paintings?' he asked.

'They stay,' Katherine said emphatically, as they reached the landing. 'Nevers has agreed since they are mostly copies anyway. You are buying an instant *mise en scene,* a setting befitting a Finance Minister of France.' She led him towards a door at the end of the hall. 'Now what was that nonsense you were telling me about the Louisianas?'

'It is no-nonsense, Katherine. I have bought the trading rights to the entire territory from an aging sea captain. I am going to sell paper stocks in the territory to the entire nation.'

She paused, an eyebrow raised. 'What may I ask, is a paper stock?'

'Another invention of mine. The purchaser will buy a piece of the company.'

'What company?' she asked as she opened the bedroom door.

'I am calling it The Mississippi Company.'

'Mississippi?' She wrinkled her nose. 'You should choose a shorter name, Johnny. No one will ever be able to spell it.'

They don't have to. They just have to buy the stock,' he said, closing the door behind them and leading her towards the bed.

It was high and covered with Chinese yellow silk, with heavy damask curtains surrounding it. His lips all the while pressed on hers, he pulled the curtains open and eased her gently onto the coverlet. They needed no conversation and what they shared was like nothing else in either of their separate worlds.

In the carriage returning to the Palais Royal, Katherine once more asked how Law had become interested in the lands of the Mississippi.

He told her all about his visit from Captain Crozet and reminded her, 'I have seen the Louisiana Territories with my own eyes. I was mad enough to hope to start a new life there,' he said. 'But gambling on riverboats and trading beads with savages was not my dream.'

'You never see things in half measures, do you, Johnny?' she said, growing excited by his excitement.

His gaze followed a drifting cloud above the line of poplars edging the road. But his mind was seeing the vast wilderness he had traveled through. 'You may find this hard to believe, Katherine, but floating on a barge down the Mississippi so many years ago, I actually dreamed of such a scheme, never thinking in my lifetime to find any way to make it come true. This will require money—vast amounts of it! Something I never had access to until now. Now, as Finance Minister, I shall have the opportunity to turn this into reality.'

Katherine was dumbfounded. 'Johnny, I know you are a gambler, but such a vast project is even beyond you! Without consulting Philip, you have spent hundreds of thousands of livres of the banks' gold on an impossible investment. Purchased from some old sea Captain, you really know nothing about. How on earth can you hope to gain by it, and what do you think Philip will say when he hears of it?'

Law's face became grim. 'I shall bring Captain Crozet to speak to him personally, and I am certain he will see the wisdom of my project when he understands that it could make France the richest country in the world.'

At that very moment in Count D'Argenson's office, the Count was handing a packet containing ten thousand livres in paper money to the man across the desk from him.

'As we agreed, Captain Crozet.' he said, 'You have done an excellent job, and we thank you. The carriage is waiting outside to take you across the border to Spain, as you have requested.'

Crozet looked into the packet and was about to count the money, then, not wishing to appear untrusting with such highly placed gentlemen, he thought better of it. But he frowned slightly at the packet. 'I would have preferred gold, Count D'Argenson.'

'You can exchange it in Law's bank in Tours, on your way. I would suggest not here in Paris,' D'Argenson added discreetly.

'Of course, of course,' Crozet replied. With swift movements, he stuffed the money into his pocket, looking up. Anyone who might have seen him in John Law's office would have been surprised that the man seemed suddenly less faltering. In fact, he appeared to be a much healthier man altogether. Whatever his ills, his recovery was certainly amazing. 'And my exit papers, Count? You have prepared them, I trust?' he asked, his voice firm and strong.

D'Argenson handed him several signed documents. 'All you need to leave the country.' He looked at the Captain sharply. 'I suggest you do not come back, Captain.'

Crozet got quickly to his feet. 'You have been most gener-ous, Count. I have no wish to return to France, have no fear. My wife and children are now in Spain, as you know.' He bowed slightly to a man sitting in the dark corner of the room and swiftly took his leave.

D'Argenson sat back in his chair, putting his fingertips to-gether and sucking in a deep breath. The man in the corner rose and hobbled over to sit in the same seat vacated by Crozet.

'Excellent, my dear D'Argenson,' the Duke du Maine said. 'Our fish has taken the bait. Bought trading rights to a wilderness in the Americas. Rights that are completely worthless.'

'You are certain they have no value?' D'Argenson asked, suddenly worried.

'Not worth a sou. Captain Crozet tried for years to make back his investment and failed. Even the Spaniards who stripped all the natives of their gold were forced to give it up.'

He allowed himself a vicious smile. 'Now, you shall see how we have caught two fish on one hook.'

No.º 3 6 0 6 7 4 6   *Dix livres Tournois.*

Divifion

L**A** B**ANQUE** promet payer au Porteur à vûe Dix livres Tournois en Efpeces d'Argent, valeur reçeüe. A Paris le premier Juillet mil fept cens vingt.

Vû p.ͬ le S.ͬ Feneſlon.   Signé p.ͬ le S.ͬ Bourgeois.
Giraudeau.   *Delanauze.*

                                  Controllé p.ͬ le S.ͬ Dureveſt.
                                      Granet.

LAW'S PAPER MONEY

NINETEEN:
TRAGEDY AT
FONTAINBLEAU

For several months Orleans had remained in Versailles overseeing the building of Katherine Knollys' chateau, and Law was grateful that his own presence hadn't been requested. He was secretly planning his next revolutionary project, and it had to be perfect before presenting it to the Regent—and then, to Parliament! William Law worked closely with his brother on projected expenditures. The Mississippi System would cost a fortune to earn a fortune.

Initially, a fortune must be raised! There would be ships and tools and equipment, and of course, men and women to be sent there to colonize this new world. The designer of Law's paper money had created stunning paper stocks and spectacular paper shares to catch investors' eyes and purses. Law could not risk being turned down. There would be no second chance.

Marie-Louise had traveled down to Fontainebleau the week before with her husband, Charles de France, the Duke de Berry, whom she called Popo. Law preferred to think of his own relationship with Marie-Louise as far-sighted rather than provident. There was no denying that she had eased his path to success, and he had taken full advantage of it. A man can pretend to love a woman, and she can believe it as long as she doesn't find out with whom he is really in love.

Law still spent an occasional evening at Vivien Duclos's, much to the actress's delight. After a few hours at the tables, they would enjoy a private supper, a bottle of wine, and her bed; adults with mutual respect and separate paths in life. It was less than love, but more than friendship.

One night, lying by his side in her lush bed, Vivien told him, 'I know there is someone who has taken your heart, John Law, but I shall name no names to spare you denying it.' She smiled. 'I do not refer to that little she-lioness Duchess.' She ran her hand along his bare skin. 'You will forgive me saying so, John, but when it comes to the certain lady in your heart, I think that you will never be rich and powerful enough to satisfy her desires outside of bed—where you could satisfy any woman. However, I shall not reveal your secret.'

He did not reply, but it annoyed him that she sensed something between himself and Katherine. While it was true that his relationship with Katherine Knollys had drifted over the years, there would always be something between them that would await the next opportunity. She was Orleans' mistress, but Law was aware that the Regent also had an on-going relationship with his daughter.

'What is keeping you so busy at the bank these days?' Vivien asked, sitting up, bringing his attention back to her. He laughed and drew her into a kiss.

But talking was what she wanted now. 'There is something you are hiding. A secret? Yes, that is it!' She inclined her head to him, looking deeply into his eyes. 'I am good at reading these things, John Law, having watched so many gamblers through the years.'

While Vivien had a good grasp of financial matters, she was a gossip, and he did not wish for all of Paris to know about The Mississippi System before he had finalized approval with Philip, and he was not yet prepared to reveal his plans. He could rely on Katherine not to divulge what little he had told her.

'But there is something, John Law!' Vivien said, not willing to be excluded from his thoughts. 'You must tell me!'

'Be patient, Vivien, and you shall know all,' he said, and partly to stop the conversation, gently pulled her to him, covering her mouth with his. For the next hour, they repeated what they had already practiced that night.

Working at his desk each day and spending most nights gaming at the tables, Law seemed to exist with very little sleep, buoyed up by the excitement of this latest project. When a messenger brought a letter from Marie-Louise asking him to join her for the Court's annual visit to Fontainebleau, Law understood that the invitation was a command.

' *I am bored,*' the letter began. '*Popo is too busy with his newest groom. This boy is sixteen and stupid as he can be, except with horses. He has pale blond hair, bright blue eyes, and a winning smile. I expect that is enough for Popo. You are to come at once, dear Law, to save me from distraction. Wait until you see Fontainebleau for yourself. Its splendid façade is called The Court of the White Horse. I think it will be more to your taste since you did not approve of Versailles' sumptuousness. The famous architect Gilles le Breton built this chateau in 1528, but it is much older and has been a hunting palace since the 12th century. It is not so grand as Louis' palace, although I dare say you would dispute that, as it boasts fifteen hundred rooms.*'

Law set down her letter. Any other time he would have tried to maneuver himself out of such an invitation, but now he was elated. Orleans and Katherine would be there. A perfect time in a relaxed atmosphere, to sell his Mississippi System to Orleans. He would find an opportunity for a quiet moment, somewhere in those fifteen hundred rooms!

Since Louis XIV's time, the Court hunted daily at Versailles, but the much older tradition of an annual hunt at Fontainebleau continued. Law knew that the late King, as did his predecessors, passed some months every year at this seat. The Regent's Court was carrying on the custom.

Marie-Louise had told him that at Fontainebleau, one rode out with curled brass hunting horns blaring, to kill boar and deer. There had been wolves in the old days, but they had become nearly extinct after hundreds of nighttime hunts. Law did not care for hunting, but he knew that anybody who did not partake of Court life's social graces, such as hunting, dancing, witty conversation, and dressing *á la mode*, could not succeed at the French Court. He was prepared to bend his inclinations to French tastes.

He traveled down to Fontainebleau in his carriage bearing the bank's crest. It carried him through a beautiful part of the countryside, but John Law was too engrossed in his papers to observe much of it that day. He spent the time going over plans for his Mississippi System and the finance and preparations it would require to bring it to life. There were projections of the number of ships it would take to carry his colonists and lists of necessary supplies and costs for everything imaginable. He knew that the project would fail without sufficient planning and, most importantly, continued financial support through the tough early years.

Law's carriage passed some of the King's houses, for many of them bordered the palace. When he arrived at Fontainebleau, he was ready to face Orleans with his plans. But he would have to count on Marie-Louise to help him arrange the right moment. As his coach drew to a halt, he found the building impressive enough, Fifteen hundred rooms! Still, certainly not as ostentatious as Versailles. She had told him that Fontainebleau's exact origins were unknown, but every monarch had added something to its splendor.

Pages hurried out to greet his arrival and to lead his coachman and horses away to the stables. A footman came over, checked his name off a list of imminent guests, and signaled over a sedan chair carried by two pages. The footman ordered them to transport Law into the palace.

'I prefer to walk,' Law told the footman.

'But you must ride, Monsieur! It is the custom of the Court', the footman said firmly and waited for him to climb in.

Reluctantly, Law got into the sedan chair and was surprised to be carried right inside the palace and up the spectacular 17th-century horseshoe staircase, all the way to his quarters. Two more pages followed with his heavy trunk. Wishing to impress Orleans, Law had purchased an elaborate wardrobe befitting a man preparing to create an enterprise so vast it would change France forever.

While the apartments could not compare to Versailles in magnificence, the royal suites were equally large and richly ornate. In the first part of the 16th century, Francis I had invited noted Italian artists and architects, including the famous Benvenuto Cellini, to design the frescos and the 'stucco work' inside Fontainebleau. That king had built the vastly opulent ballroom and the many-windowed Long Gallery, which had vistas over all of the outlying king's houses.

The sitting room arranged for John Law was lined in a wine silk damask with a bedroom of black and gold chinoiserie lacquer-work panels. There was a basket of oranges, a bottle of champagne, and a note awaiting him. The latter was on pale yellow paper sealed in wax with the de Berry crest.

He broke it open and read: '*I have a present for you. Marie-Louise.*'

The footman informed him casually that his apartments were next to the Duchess de Berry's, then left him with two young pages to help him dress.

Law wondered what Marie-Louise's present might be. The last time, there had been a statue for him to unveil, and when he did so, she had stood before him laughing, her slender naked body gleaming in the moonlight. Law was no hypocrite. Without her help, he would not have his bank nor be Finance Minister. She had opened doors so wide that this wildest scheme of all might now be possible. Marie-Louise could bare her claws and strike out like a wildcat, and although he had not yet been scratched, he remembered that the Captain de Riom had never returned from the Indies.

The weather had turned warm, and he was hot from the long ride. One of the pages helped him off with his traveling coat while the other brought a washing bowl of fresh warm water. Law removed his lawn shirt and washed carefully. He signaled a page to pour him a glass of wine, sipped it, and feeling more refreshed, waved the page away from his trunk, preferring to choose his garments for himself. The page helped him with a clean linen shirt, a silk waistcoat, and a light grey flowered silk coat with pale cream appliqué borders. He added a heavy white lace neckband, donned a new wig of dark brown curls (he now owned three), and glanced at his reflection in a cheval-glass.

The effect was both elegant and subdued, suitable for the most fastidious courtier, yet not too frivolous— an image to inspire confidence even in those Frenchmen who still resented him because he was a foreigner.

Law dismissed the pages and made his way to Marie-Louise's apartments. His knock brought Mouchi surrounded by a flutter of ladies-in-waiting. She greeted him with a wide smile, then disappeared into the inner chamber to call her mistress. Law entered the room, bowed to the ladies, and crossed to the window. He could see down into the gardens where several fish ponds with brightly colored carp were swimming to and fro. Each fish was at least two feet long and gave off metallic flashes of gold, orange and red in the fading sunlight. Beyond the park, he could see the edge of the forest. Fontainebleau was set in the middle of a spectacular twenty thousand hectares of woodland and had an altogether more rustic feeling than Versailles.

He turned back from the window as Marie-Louise came into the room. Her gown had a distinctly country air about it, pale yellow, embroidered with tiny pink roses and green leaves.

'You have discovered our Japanese fish, I see!' she said, her voice lilting with happiness at seeing him. Her red hair, unpowdered, glistened in the afternoon sunlight as she came to him. 'They are said to have been the gift of an Emperor, and according to the gardeners, some of them are at least eighty years old.' And then with a mischievous smile, she added, 'When I was only a girl, I bribed the chef to catch me one and cook it for my dinner. I pretended a headache and ate it all alone in my room. It was huge, and I must say, delicious. I ate every bite, but afterward, I vomited it all up.' She laughed merrily, then turned to Mouchi. 'Leave us,' she said.

Mouchi and the other ladies made a discreet exit with a curtsy to Law, none taking their eyes off him until out of sight.

'You look like a forest sprite today, Duchess,' he said with a low bow.

'And what has happened to you, Law?' she asked, looking him over. 'You certainly don't look like a foreigner these days.'

'Your father's influence, my dear,' he said, kissing her hand. 'He wishes me to look the part he has assigned to me.'

'You are learning our ways, and we shall make a Frenchman of you yet.' She crossed to her desk and took up a leather portfolio decorated with the Royal crest. 'My surprise!' she said, handing it to him. 'You might say, a small token of affection from my father. You shall have to earn mine.'

He hesitated.

Go ahead. Open it,' she commanded.

Slowly he lifted the flap and removed a document, recognizing Orleans' signature and the Royal seal at the bottom. His eyes traveled up across the neat calligraphy to the heading, which he read with growing amazement. Finally, he looked up. 'The Regent has granted me license to the Royal Mint—and coin issue for the next nine years!'

She smiled. 'I told Papa that it was of no use making you his bank if he did not give you the power to print your own coin as well as all that paper.'

'I am overwhelmed, Marie Louise,' he said, trying to grasp the magnitude of this news.

'And so you should be,' she replied with some satisfaction. Next to Papa, you are finally the most powerful man in France, John Law.'

'It would seem I owe you more than is possible to repay,' he said humbly.

'You can pay with interest, Banker. Love is like a fire. It needs stoking.' She held out her arms. He moved into them and kissed her; desire fed by the aphrodisiac of this new power.

'Will your father dine with us tonight?' he asked, hoping to take Orleans aside with a full glass of brandy in hand long enough to tell him about his plans for developing the Mississippi.

"We dine much later here,' she said. This is the time of day for pleasure, not for business.' She led him into her bedroom and to the large canopied bed in its center. 'Pull back the coverlet,' she commanded.

He obeyed, to find her sheets strewn with rose petals, a heady scent to arouse passions. He threw off the clothes he had so carefully put on and took her, half-dressed, with the fury of exultation. Marie-Louise made love like a tiger, wanting all he could give, fighting for supremacy. And when passion was spent, they lay beside each other for a long while listening to the *click-click* of croquet mallets from somewhere distant in the gardens.

'With you, I feel like a woman,' she told him.

But he was not prepared to give himself totally to Marie-Louise. 'Come,' he said. 'let us dress. You said your father is expecting me.'

When they joined the long table of diners in the great hall, dinner was already being served. Philip scowled at Law, who made an excuse that he had difficulty with his carriage. Philip turned his attention to Katherine, and an opportunity did not arise for Law to broach the subject he wanted most to discuss. They were to hunt early the next day. Perhaps after the hunt, Law thought.

The morning sun had scarcely risen when in a field near the stables, an Arab stallion was being quieted by Popo's newest groom. Albert was a thin lad, no more than fifteen and not very tall, with sad brown eyes and a mole on his right cheek. He wore his hair tied back with a leather thong, and his face never looked quite clean, but De Berry had taken a fancy to him when he saw him in the stables one day and had replaced his then-current groom, Ferdie, with the new boy.

THE HUNT

It was not yet six a.m., but early arrivals for the Royal Hunt were already mounting horses in the courtyard. The Court had previously attended early Mass. Many were arriving via the fleet of sedan chairs, the favorite method of getting about the chateau and the grounds for those who did not take readily to exercise. Naturally, the Royal family each had their special chair and pages.

Several grooms were helping Orleans' mother, Madame's ample frame onto her horse. The over-stout woman loved nothing better than the hunt and rode every day at Versailles or Fontaine-bleau as she had done as a girl in Germany. Some courtiers had brought their own mounts, but most took advantage of the King's stables that Orleans continued to keep for the Court's use. It was a relic of the days of Louis XIV when there were at least two hundred and forty horses and many packs of hounds, greyhounds, and some standard poodles, much favored by the ladies of the Court as hunting dogs, for they were great hunters. Each lady had her dog's thick wooly coat trimmed to an individual design to be easily spotted, for poodles have fur, not hair.

Minutes ticked by while sedan chairs disgorged passengers. Pages were wildly bumping and pushing against each other in a rush to dispose of their charges. One old courtier tripped as he climbed out of his chair and shouted a tirade at his pages. Two pages entering the clearing were jostled in a collision and dropped their sedan chair, tumbling their passenger onto the ground. It was the Duke de D'Antin. 'Lookout, you fool!' he shouted, dusting himself off, swearing.

In the chaos, a lady tore her skirt on a sharp hinge getting out of her chair and erupted into a flood of tears. Two grooms argued over whose duty it was to get which horse, to see their charges safely mounted. One of Marie-Louise's ladies-in-waiting was having trouble mounting her steed. Her groom placed a hand as large as a ham hock not too discreetly beneath her posterior and hoisted her up into the saddle. 'How dare you?' she shouted at him in outrage before settling into her saddle.

The Hunt was turning into a shambles, and it hadn't yet begun. A warning blast from the horn brought some semblance of order. Madame spotted Law and trotted over to him. In her brown riding habit, nearly the color of her horse, she looked like a centaur.

'Ah, Monsieur Law!' she cried in her thick German accent, fluttering heavy lashes at him, a girlish wink lighting her aging face. 'It is naughty of you never to find time to take tea with my duck and me, although I have invited you several times.' She smiled, revealing a tooth missing on the left side. 'But I am of a mind to forgive you if you promise to visit this afternoon at my apartments at three o'clock,' she said. 'We shall have a private tête-à-tête and get to know each other.'

'Law is a very busy man, Mother,' Orleans said, trotting over. 'He has too many affairs of the country to gossip with you and your ladies. You must forgive him, Madame.'

'I am certain there will be time, Madame soon, for us to get better acquainted,' Law said, bowing.

In the stables, Popo came around behind his young groom. He always kept at least six of his own horses at Fontainebleau. 'Where is Vendôme? Why is he not saddled yet?' he asked grumpily.

Albert gave his master a worried look. 'You should not ride Vendôme today, your Grace. I fear he has been skittish all through the night. It could be that one of his eyes is troubling him, for he keeps pulling his head to one side. I've got Marbrue readied for you.'

'Vendôme skittish? I shall teach him skittish. I will ride him, Albert!' Charles de Berry told his groom angrily, coming around to look at the horse. Vendôme was seventeen hands high with a wide strong back and a ton of muscle. de Berry peered at the horse's eyes, which looked normal enough. 'There is nothing amiss with his eyes. Do you think me not capable of gentling Vendôme? Make him ready!'

The groom did not argue. He was used to doing as he was told, and if his master wished to ride the horse, he would not dare to stop him, any more than he had stopped de Berry from riding him the night before. It was the way of the world, and things went well when one knew one's place in it.

The horse gave a whinny and pulled against the steel bit that Albert inserted between his teeth. He slung the fine leather saddle across the horse's back and tightened the straps, then moved the animal into position at the mounting step. Vendôme snorted and rose up on his hind legs, pulling his head as the groom had warned he might, and Albert had great difficulty in calming him.

'He wants exercise, and I shall give it to him!' Popo said, slapping his riding crop lightly across the animal's flank as he had done to the lad only a few short hours before, believing that horses and young boys both needed a taste of the whip at times.

Popo was not, however, feeling at his best. He had been troubled by an abscess of a tooth, and the doctors had been bleeding him. He hated the leeches. That, and the enemas and their other torments in the name of healing. He had tried to forget his ailments in the arms of his new groom. But now the tooth was flaring up again, giving him a searing ache in his head. It made him exceedingly angry. He took a drink from the silver pocket flask of brandy he always carried with him and looked out across the sea of courtiers, horses, and hounds. Popo was assured of an audience to attest to his bravery if the horse was particularly capricious this morning.

He noticed Marie-Louise arriving in her private chair to where Law was standing. Well, he did not care if she had Law as a lover. At least she did not bother him or scold him for his activities, except maybe for his drinking. She used to be fun at cards and a good loser, but now that she was Law's playmate, he was afraid to play against her. Popo was not one for losing.

Grooms were readying the horses. Footmen were pouring stirrup cups. Beyond them, Popo saw Orleans mounted on a large grey, and beside him that English woman, Knollys, his latest whore. Attractive, Popo thought, if one were to like women. But too big in the breasts. He did not mind going to bed with Marie-Louise occasionally when they made a small effort towards having a child. She was at least built like a boy, slender in the hips and her breasts were small. He looked back at her as she mounted her horse. Her cheeks were flushed, and she looked happy. He would have to consider doing his duty by her one night soon and producing that wanted heir. Orleans would like that. But there was still plenty of time. He came around behind Albert, running a hand across the boy's firm young buttocks. The boy winced. 'Hold the horse still,' Popo commanded. 'And yourself, too.'

The boy pulled tightly on the reins holding the horse's head down. Popo climbed on the mounting box and gracefully slid into the saddle. The hunting horns were already calling stragglers to the field. The hounds were barking and straining at their leads, keeping the handlers busy quieting them. There was no doubt his horse was nervy, but Popo shrugged it off. A good run, and he'd soon quiet down. Popo guided Vendôme alongside his wife and Law, who were mounted not far from the Regent.

CHARLES, DUC DU BERRY - POPO

'Good morning, Marie-Louise. Sleep well?' he asked.

'Morning, Popo,' Marie-Louise replied coldly. 'I did if you must know.'

'And you, Monsieur Law? You were comfortable in a new bed?' he asked with some innuendo.

'Quite comfortable, your Grace,' Law said steadily.

'And whose bed were you in, Popo darling?' Marie-Louise asked viciously.

Orleans reined his horse in beside them, saving Popo the need to reply. 'We are hunting *at force* today,› Orleans told his son-in-law. He turned to Law, noting that he sat his horse well. ‹You are a hunter, Law?›

'We hunt at home, Sir. Scotland is known for its mighty stags.'

'So I have heard. But last year, here at Fontainebleau among the game registered and accounted for were at least three thousand stags and hinds and seventy thousand hares.' He laughed. 'And would you believe? One fox, only.' Orleans drank from the stirrup cup offered by a footman. '*At force* today! Running hounds is the noblest and most honorable form of hunting, for it is a thievish form of hunting to shoot with guns and bows, don't you think?'

'I have never thought about it, Sir,' Law replied. This was no moment for a discussion of ethics with the Regent. But Law could not imagine why 'at force', which meant a pack of hounds tearing an animal to ribbons with their teeth, was any nobler than a man killing the prey with a weapon. When he was a lad, he had hunted deer with his father with flintlock rifles, although his father had preferred his old snaphaunce rifle to the more easily managed new Scottish flintlocks with their prettily curled steel stocks. His father had a rule: kill only for meat for the table.

'Good morning, Monsieur Law.' It was Katherine who addressed him. She cut an extremely dashing figure in fine black boots and a pale grey habit trimmed in black military frogging. Orleans had presented her with her own white steed. 'A fine day for the hunt,' she said.

'It is indeed, Lady Knollys.' He inclined his head towards her in a casual way, but a world of communication traveled between their eyes. They were both thinking the same thing. When and where...?

Looking at them, Marie-Louise saw something she did not like. For some reason, it had never occurred to her that there could be anything between Law and her father's favorite whore. But she had no time to dwell on the thought because, at that moment, the Master of the Horse gave the signal, and the hounds were loosed into the forest, and the hunting party galloped off.

'*Bon chance!*' Orleans cried, charging after them. Madame was not far behind, able to keep up with the best of the men.

The forest of Fontainebleau was finely wooded and watered and boasted odd natural rock formations, some looking, Law thought, very like giants or gnomes, and some in the shape of miniature towers. Altogether, the forest had an enchanted look about it. But at the moment, with the chomp and thump of hooves beating on the soft earth and the cries of the hunters and the barking of dogs, John Law thought their entrance into the forest was enough to scare away any sensible stag or send a sagacious hare to ground. Always an excellent horseman, Law enjoyed the beauty of this magical forest and was in no particular hurry to find a quarry.

Katherine dropped back, slowing to a trot beside Law. 'I am across the wing from you,' she said breathlessly, 'in the Royal apartments. Perhaps you can come to me at five o'clock when everyone is resting?' With that, she raced ahead.

He glanced across the swell of riders, seeing that Marie-Louise had caught up with her father. Ahead of her, Popo seemed to be keeping a firmer than usual grasp on his horse's reins as he headed through the trees along the well-worn trail.

The earth was soft and yielding beneath Vendôme's hooves, but Popo's horse was rebellious and kept dragging to the right, wanting to pull off the path. Lack of control of one's horse was not a thing De Berry would readily be prepared to admit, not with his father-in-law breathing down his neck.

Picking up the scent of the quarry, the hounds took a turn off the path and headed deeper into the forest. Then Law noticed that Popo's horse, Vendôme, was cantering out in front of the other riders almost on the hounds' tails and picking up speed.

But the horse seemed not to be following the hounds at all, and it was clear that Popo was having difficulty holding his seat! As the hounds turned to the left, Vendôme veered off to the right, away from the others, and Law heard Popo cry out as his horse pounded through an opening in the trees on a path beaten by bygone riders.

Law urged his own mount forward to give chase. Popo›s horse appeared completely out of control suddenly, running headlong and once more veering to the right. Popo seemed unable to rein him in! Law whipped his own horse to catch up, as Vendôme narrowly missed a tree. Popo whipped and kicked the animal, somehow regaining control as Law approached.

'Are you all right?' Law shouted at him.

'He is frisky, that is all,' Popo called back angrily. 'I do not need your help, Law!'

Law reined in and was about to turn away when he saw Vendôme rear, snort, and once more bolt off. Law gathered in his reins and followed, whipping his horse. Twenty yards ahead of him, Vendôme's feet pounded the ground at a dead run.

Popo bounced up off the saddle and came down hard. 'Damn you!' he shouted, digging his heels into the horse's flesh.

"Give him some rein!' Law shouted. 'Let him have his head!'

But Popo paid no heed, and the creature pounded towards the low branches of a thick tree. To Law's horror, he saw horse and rider part company, as once more Popo catapulted off the saddle! But this time, he did not fall back. There was a single scream from the young noble.

'De Berry. . !' Law shouted. At first, Law thought Popo had grabbed the branch of the tree and pulled himself up. But it was not so.

As Law rode closer, he saw that Popo's body was impaled on a jagged branch. When Law reached him, he heard a soft expiration of breath, then Popo's body went limp and silent. He was hanging from the tree like a broken doll.

Curiously enough, Vendôme, having no rider, came to a halt and stood still for a moment tossing his head to one side. Then he turned and came back to wait beside the tree and his master.

Marie-Louise rode up, her face white with shock. She stopped abruptly, staring at the lifeless body pinned in the tree. Popo's head hung at an odd angle.

'Get him down!' she shouted at Law. Others of the party had by now turned their horses and thundered over.

Law brought his horse under the body, reaching up to Popo. He managed to break the branch, freeing Popo and getting hold of him, bringing his body down across his own horse.

Blood was trickling from Popo's mouth, and his shirt had a dark red stain where the lance-like branch had entered his body. Law turned back to Marie-Louise. 'His neck is broken,' he said. 'He must have died instantly.' She let out a slow moan.

An unearthly silence fell in the forest as though all the birds and animals were listening. The terrible moment was interrupted by the panting of horses and the whispered voices of the hunting party, passing the news of the tragedy down the line of riders. Marie-Louise's eyes filled with tears. 'Poor Popo,' she cried. 'Poor dear Popo. . .'

The Master of Hounds rode up and drew a musket from his saddle holster. He handed it to Marie-Louise, butt towards her, without a word. She knew what she had to do. She took it from him and raised the musket taking careful aim. The others watched silently as she squeezed the trigger. Popo's stallion sagged forward, dropped to the ground, and lay dead.

Law had dismounted and now eased Popo's body to the ground. He was hardly more than a lad.

Tears brimming in her eyes, Marie-Louise stared at Law, her face a picture of mixed emotions. He wondered what she really felt about Popo. Married since they were children, he knew he had been like a brother to her. At Court, marriages were often so arranged. Perhaps Marie-Louise had been lucky that her husband had preferred boys and left her to her own devices. What would become of her now? Now that the fates have decreed that she was a free woman. He saw her looking at him with a curious expression on her face. What, he wondered, could she be thinking?

# TWENTY: MARIE-LOUISE

Several days had passed at Fontainebleau since De Berry›s death, and preparations had been completed for the funeral, which would be a State affair in Paris. The Court was to return there in the morning.

That night, dinner for some sixty people was being served in the Long Hall, whose walls were richly decorated with scenes of the hunt, and images of Diana the Huntress, dating back to the days of Henry IV. At the head of the table, Katherine and Marie-Louise seated at either side of Philip hadn›t spoken since they sat down. Behind them, Law could see into the adjoining room where another fifty of the lesser courtiers were being served in near silence.

Gloom had settled over the courtiers, where silver-handled wooden trenchers were being carried around the table by a small army of footmen. Along the center of the table, serving dishes and platters were already laid out in a traditional style befitting the less formal atmosphere of a royal hunting lodge; all food served at once and everyone helping themselves. Finding conversation reduced to whispers, some diners simply grabbed what they pleased directly from platters on the table and stuffed their mouths.

This was the way it had been in Scotland and England. But in Paris and at Versailles, eating habits at court were normally more elegant, and food was served in the style instigated by Louis XIV, each dish in separate courses. Far too many courses to Law's taste, for though he had a good appetite, he ate modestly. Louis' chef dictated, and the Court greedily gorged on first the fish, then the meats, then vegetables cooked in potages, and last of all, fruits, pastries, and ices.

Philip carried on the late King's tradition in Paris, but when at Fontainebleau, he preferred to play at the simple life, eating whatever was the bounty of the hunt: capon, pigeon, pheasant, deer, wild goose or hare, and salads grown in the kitchen gardens, washed down with good wines from the local vineyards.

Marie-Louise, dressed all in black, had not touched her food, nor had she spoken during the meal. Her face showed the strain of the last few days. Dark circles ringed her eyes. Law had never seen her look so drawn. An unexpected burst of laughter from the end of the long table brought a sharp look from the newly widowed woman. Her scowl produced a hushed silence. She turned to her father with sudden determination, deliberately speaking loud enough for all to hear.

'What the doctor said, Papa, was that the horse had an injury to his left eye. The animal could not see properly! That is why Vendôme went out of control.' Her voice rose even more. 'Popo had traits I disapproved of, but he was an excellent horseman!'

'A fine horseman like his father, it is true,' Orleans said. 'Certainly, nobody could fault Charles in this dreadful accident.'

‹Then I ask you, Papa, what was the matter with Popo›s groom to let him take that horse?›

'You know Charles was headstrong, my dear. Not much on being cautioned by a groom, now was he?' he said, trying to soothe what he could see might become a fit of temper.

She lowered her voice, eyes holding her father's. 'He must be shot.'

'But you have shot him! And quite rightly done, too,' he told his daughter.

'Not the horse, Papa!' Her words cut like flintstone. 'The one Popo was riding the night before.'

Madame, who was sitting beside Marie-Louise, turned to her granddaughter. 'Ach, Louise, if we were to shoot every groom who let a rider with too much brandy in him ride a horse he could not handle, the stables would be soon empty!'

Ignoring his mother, Orleans inclined his head towards the angry girl with a conspiratorial look. 'Trouble yourself no further, Marie-Louise.' He lowered his voice. 'Come to me later, and we shall talk.'

'Yes, Papa,' she breathed, knowing precisely what he was indicating and what he would expect in return. She wore an expression of tremendous satisfaction as she rose from the table, pulling her heavy black skirts around her and swept out. Seeing her mistress leave, Mouchi, further down the table in the pecking order of things, got up from the courtier with whom she had been flirting and followed her out.

When dinner ended, Orleans made a hasty retreat from the table. Katherine rose with a sidelong glance at Law and took Philip's arm. Since the day of his arrival, Law had been unable to broach the subject of his Mississippi project to Orleans. Now, Popo's death had occupied Marie-Louise's and her father's full attention, leaving Law, a man inflated with a great secret, about to burst if he did not reveal it soon. He excused himself from Madame, who had been regaling him with stories about the German Court, and returned to his own suite.

Madame turned to her lady-in-waiting, Mme de Brancas. 'I hear that today one of our Duchesses kissed Monsieur Law's hands. Who knows what other parts of him some ladies might wish to salute?'

Law was preparing himself for bed when there was a knock on his door. A page handed him a cryptic message: 'Take the sedan chair.' It was not signed, but he knew the handwriting as well as he knew his own heart. Hastily he slipped on his jacket and stepped out into the corridor. Two pages attended him. He climbed into the sedan chair.

Her bedroom smelled of lavender. She greeted him in a cloud of white lace and gossamer silk, and he drew her into his arms. His tongue found entrance between parted lips. The touch was enough to send a wave of heat through both their bodies. Never with anyone else, never was it ever like this. He needed Katherine. Had to have her. And she needed him. But like a full-bodied wine, small sips were enough to satisfy—never to glut the appetite, always to leave them both wanting more of that exceptional bouquet.

Leave something for next time. Next time, John Law, his mind kept saying. For he knew as long as they were both alive, there would always be a next time. He rose, eyes lingering for a moment on the curve of one slender shoulder. She stirred as he dressed hastily, having no desire to be found in her room. She reached arms out to him, and he bent to kiss her, then arose with a question.

'Katherine, could you arrange to invite Philip and Marie-Louise to tea tomorrow?'

'Are you missing England so much that you long for a cup of tea, my darling?' she murmured sleepily.

'Actually, I have never much cared for the stuff,' he said. 'But there is something I must tell Orleans, and I have had no opportunity to do so.'

She sat up with a look of vexation. 'It's about this Mississippi foolishness, I'd wager. Do you use me, Johnny, like you do all the rest of them?'

'You know that is not true, Kate.'

'Mmm,' she said. Perhaps it is so natural to you that you do not know you are guilty of it. I have seen how you will do anything to have your way.'

'When I believe in something, I cannot stand aside from it,' he said with a touch of annoyance. 'Would you have me different, Kate?'

'No, no. No different. Although sometimes I think you are truly mad, John Law.' She sighed. 'But perhaps it takes a madman to lead the rest of us to the future.'

He laughed heartily. 'The future, Katherine? I think you only live for today.' He kissed her tenderly. 'Oh, and Kate, be sure that Marie-Louise is present. I am ready to present one of the greatest plans the world had ever known!' 'I honestly do not understand what you are saying, Law,' the Regent of France exclaimed. ‹Have I heard correctly? You have just told me that you bought the trading rights to the entire Louisiana Territory for our bank?'

'Exactly, Sir. The bank now owns all rights to trade with the territory.'

'But Louisiana already belongs to France, does it not?' Orleans asked querulously. He did not like things he could not immediately grasp and comprehend.

'Every mile of it,' Law replied. 'From the territory in the north they are calling Canada, all the way down the Mississippi to the Gulf of Mexico, France holds in its possession an untapped gold mine as big as a continent.'

They were taking tea in Katherine's apartments at Fontainebleau as he had asked. Marie-Louise, thin as a wraith in her black
mourning weeds, was looking at Law incredulously. Since dinner,
she had not seen him having spent the night with her father and
had answered Katherine's invitation with interest. Law, Katherine
told her, was especially anxious that she be there. Now she could
not believe what she was hearing and exclaimed, 'But everyone
knows that wildland is inhabited only by savages.'

'There will be Frenchmen there soon, Marie Louise, I assure
you.' Law announced with confidence. 'You see, the trading rights
are not what I am after. What I have in mind is something much
bigger than trading with trappers for furs. I have formed a company that will raise money to build ships, buy equipment, seed, and
provisions. Money to send out the colonists to...'

'Colonists...?' Philip interrupted him. "You wish to send
Frenchmen to the New World?'

'Indeed I do, Sir. Strong, young men who will take with
them a wife and build homes. Men who will raise children, build
cities, turn the forests into plantations. They shall dig the buried
treasure out of the ground and send it all pouring back into the
coffers of France!' His expression seemed to indicate that it was already accomplished.

'And where do you propose to find these colonists?' Orleans
asked. 'Raid the madhouses?' He took a deep draught of tea from
his bowl as though to wash out of his mind such nonsense coming
from a man whose opinion he valued.

'Perhaps not the madhouses, Sir, but the jails would do
nicely. I have always had a soft spot for prisoners,' he added wryly,
catching Katherine's glance.

'I suppose it is one way to rid ourselves of thieves and murderers,' Orleans said. 'That part of it, I like. But what is this company you speak of? And where will the money come from?' His
forehead furrowed into a frown.' You shall not have a sou from our
treasury for such a lunatic scheme, I promise you.'

Law opened a leather case and drew from it a tidy bundle
of strips of paper slightly larger than the paper money he had so recently invented. He handed them to Orleans. Each sheet was printed with an ornate border, an engraved portrait of the Regent on the

front of it, and on the reverse a representation of lush vegetation and friendly-looking Indians. Orleans felt the paper between his fingers. It was thick and had a rich feel to it. He read the inscription aloud: '*This document is worth ten shares of stock in The Mississippi Company.*'

He looked up in amazement. 'Why on earth should anybody wish to purchase these bits of paper? Surely not just because my picture is upon it, although I will admit, it is a good likeness.'

'Every person who buys this stock will own a share in our new company—and consequently in the New World! And all for the benefit of France.'

'But who would wish to buy a piece of land so far away that they will never see?' Marie-Louise asked.

'One doesn't have to see the Mississippi, to understand its potential, Marie-Louise. The people of France will see the results!' Law said, spilling out a small pouch full of gold nuggets across the table.

Philip's eyes gleamed at the sight of the gold. He picked up one of the lumps, marveling at it. 'This nugget where did you get it? Is there gold in the Mississippi?'

Law cleared his throat. 'You can be certain there is gold, and plenty of it. But frankly, Sir, I must be honest with you. Since I have had no opportunity to take a spade there to dig for myself, these are merely coins from the Mint, which I've melted down.'

'But that is deception...!' Philip said with some surprise.

'Merely a visual projection of what the future holds in store for France,' he replied candidly.

Philip's eyes sparkled, but his tone was stern. 'And I have appointed you my Finance Minister? Explain yourself, Law. What sort of Frenchman would be taken in by fake nuggets?'

Law tossed a fistful of the nuggets into the air, catching them as they fell. 'If you were a young man with little to look forward to, perhaps locked in the Bastille for some crime as small as stealing bread, and you were to see these nuggets, would you not wish for the opportunity to give up your cell and go to the Mississippi, no matter how far away, and start digging?'

'Surely, you do not expect Papa to place himself in such a humble mind as a criminal?' Marie Louis asked.

'Hush, Marie-Louise, I am following Monsieur Law's thinking perfectly,' her father said.

'Well, Sir, to project the matter further. . .' He paused. 'If you were too old or too feeble to go yourself, would you not wish to buy some stocks in a company that could turn you into a richer man overnight, under the gracious and profitable patronage of the Regent of France?'

Orleans' face pursed in thought for a moment, weighing the possibilities. 'Selling shares in a venture nobody has ever seen or heard of before? Speculation in the unknown? Your scheme takes the art of gambling to new heights, Law!' He paused, studying the man he had allowed to manage his country's finances and who had brought them out of the shadow of bankruptcy.

Law felt uneasy under the sharp scrutiny. But then the Regent's face lit up and broke into a wide smile. 'Selling shares in a company, you say? A totally original idea!' he exclaimed.' How did you come upon such a plan?'

Law shrugged. 'To me, it seemed quite obvious. A natural progression from paper money, Sir.'

Marie-Louise's total disbelief softened into smug satisfaction.' Papa was the first one to recognize your genius, John Law! And now you've proved him right.'

'Stocks and shares,' Orleans mused. 'Ingenious. Yes, outstanding, Law. Outstanding!' He paused once more, this time with a querulous expression.' But do you honestly think they will be purchased?'

'By the hundreds. Then by the thousands. If I may remind you, Sir, at his death, the treasury of Louis XIV owed a national debt of 3,111,000,000 livres. Now the treasury is full. Full, your Grace! The Mississippi Company shall make you certainly one of the richest, and the most famous ruler in all of history!' Law was beginning to believe it himself, and his voice rose with the hyperbole when he saw he was playing to a willing audience. 'The name of Philip of Orleans shall live forever in glory!'

Marie-Louise's eyes were dancing with excitement. Her cheeks were flushed. Katherine seemed unusually pale. Orleans looked from one to the other. 'Eh? What do you think, Katherine? You have said nothing.'

'I think...' she paused, her eyes resting on Law, 'I think that Mister Law is the answer to a prayer for France.'

Philip finished his tea off in a swallow. 'Pfha,' he cried. 'How do the English drink this dishwater? Champagne! We must have champagne.'

Two of the footmen made a hasty exit and returned with heavy crystal goblets and a bottle on a tray.

'Pass the wine,' Orleans ordered, and the pale sparkling wine was duly poured. When everyone held a glass, he raised his in salute, a smile once again creasing his features. 'A toast to Finance Minister Law and France's new Mississippi Company! Money to be raised by the people of France.' Then he added stiffly, and his tone became suddenly less jovial. 'Mind you, Law, not a sou from my Treasury.'

I would not dream of it, Sir.' Law's whole body was exploding with excitement, but he maintained a sober expression as he scooped the nuggets into his palm once again and thrust them back into his pocket. But he deliberately left one lying on the table within reach of the Regent.

Orleans' fingers reached out to its knobbled surface. 'Melted down, you say?' He laughed heartily. 'Devilishly clever!'

The one thing that troubled Law slightly was that the sea captain, Crozet, seemed to have disappeared. He had gone personally to the small pension when the man said he was living, but all the concierge was able to tell him was that Crozet had left Paris rather hurriedly with no forwarding address.' Was he taken ill?' Law asked, remembering that the Captain had told him he was ill.

'Not at all,' the concierge assured him.' Hearty and fit as ever a man of that age could be. And paid me every sou with a handsome tip besides.'

Law dismissed his worries about Crozet, although he had thought to present the man himself to Orleans. But in the end, he had been able to sell the Regent on his idea with the aid of the fake gold nuggets. Yes, they had done the trick, and John Law knew just how he would put on a show that would bring out the crowds of Frenchmen ready to invest.

Several months were to pass after Law met with Philip.

Months that saw him busy with preparations for the great day. And now it had arrived. He had taken over the Hôtel Beaufort in the narrow old Rue Quincampoix as the center for his new venture. In it were many ancient dwellings, some dating back to the 15th century. Here, the shopkeepers he had met on his first day in Paris lived above their shops, and there was a busy flow of traffic throughout the daylight hours. The street was well lit at night, having lamps strung across the road on ropes between the houses. Now, with his new authority, Law had ordered the street closed to all but foot traffic.

When the shopkeepers protested that it would bring an end to their business, Law came personally to assure them that they would soon see such crowds as they had never seen before, once his plans were in operation. They had but to wait until the word got about. And John Law was going to be certain that everyone in Paris heard of his latest pursuit.

All that week, his preparations in the narrow street had been hectic. Palace guards cleared away peddlers, while workers unfolded long banners and strung them across the cobbled road at each end, with much shouting and complaints from the residents.

'It is by order of the Regent!' a guard told the people, which did little to shut up complaints.

'What next?' cried a man whose wall had been confiscated. 'It is a banner they are hanging from my house!

An old woman at the bottom of the road pulled her shawl around her and moved hastily towards the banner. 'I cannot read. What does it say?' she asked.

All strained to see what it announced. The tailor stepped forward. 'I can read!' he exclaimed and read it aloud:

'BUY SHARES IN THE MISSISSIPPI.
THE COMPANY OF THE WEST.
JOHN LAW, Director General.'

He read the line beneath it in smaller printing:

'Under the Gracious Patronage of
THE REGENT OF FRANCE.'

Workers had been busy setting up flimsy wooden booths along each side of the pavement. Over each narrow booth was a gaily colored striped canopy with a sign reading:

'BUY YOUR SHARES HERE'

and in smaller print:

'Official Stock Jobber for
THE MISSISSIPPI COMPANY
John Law, Director-General'.

The booths were no more than a stall where the stock jobbers could sit out of the wind and rain with a worktop counter to hold their papers.

'Shares? What does it mean?' a man asked one of the workmen.

'Couldn't tell you that,' the workman replied. 'But I do know this. There is going to be a parade today.'

'A parade? Today?

Why it is not even a holiday.'

'Did you not hear? Monsieur Lass has declared it a holiday,' the tailor told him.

‹What next?› the man whose window had been confiscated cried.

The street was already filling with people who had come to see they knew not what! Excitement buzzed in every doorway as clerks from the bank began taking their places in the booths with sheaves of paper stocks and money boxes.

'What have you got there?' a man called down from his window to the bank clerk-turned-stock jobber, who was laying out his goods on his counter.

'Stocks. Shares in the Mississippi System!' the stock-jobber shouted back. 'You'll all want to buy some before the price rises, and I assure you, it will by the end of the day!'

People from the adjoining streets were crowding in, even though there was nothing to see except the booths and the banners with those mysterious words, **shares**, and **Mississippi**. Then the noise of strange drums and curious yapping yelps turned all attention to the end of the road, where an unexpected sight greeted them.

'It's the parade...! It has started!' someone shouted.

The workman was right; a small parade was coming towards them. But what kind of parade was it? It had begun at the center of Paris, where several Bank clerks led it Behind them was a sight never before seen in Paris. A handful of men, naked save for an odd-looking fox-tailed loin cloth. These were men of a curious dark reddish hue, and they were marching (it must be said) in a somewhat disorganized file, beating on drums made of deerskins and shouting what sounded like a whoop! If it sounded like anything at all. Their hair was long, black, straight, and banded with colorful beads. They had black and white markings on their cheeks.

The crowd was hushed. 'What are they? Where do they come from?'

'Indians!' announced one of the stock-jobbers matter-of-factly.

'From India?'

'No, Red Indians! From Louisiana in the Americas,' the stock-jobber said with some authority.

He did not add that earlier in the morning, he'd seen a rag-tag handful of actors from the *Comédie Française* being made ready for perhaps the most unusual performance of their careers. He had watched the ‹war paint› being applied to men only too glad to brave the elements in nothing but a scrap of fur in exchange for the gold louis d'or each received, though at the moment they had no pockets to jingle it in. Nor did he know the trouble that Law had gone to create those costumes. Three of Marie-Louise's seamstresses had been occupied for several days at the task of sewing the deerskins into the properly scanty garments.

The 'Indians' marched to the end of the road and turned, unsure exactly what was expected of them next. One of them performed a low bow, more suited to a curtain call. On seeing the astonished faces in the crowd, one of the bank clerks in charge hissed an instruction, and the Indians once more began beating the drums with a *Comédie Française* version of a war hoop. Their painted skins were beginning to streak slightly. The greasepaint did not last as well in the heat of the sun as it might on stage with only soft footlight candles to warm it.

Now, more music was coming towards the street. It was a Royal Marching Band with fife and drums. After it came John Law himself riding in an open carriage, resplendent in a dark tan silk jacket, his full wig just grazing his shoulders, his wide pockets were bound with black braid and the whole effect, though one of luxury, had great dignity and style. Here was the image of a man you could trust with ideas, with money, perhaps even with your life.

Law was followed by the royal carriage containing Orleans and Marie-Louise. The carriages came to a stop in the center of the road, and Law signaled to a group of men and women who followed behind them in an open wagon.

This was perhaps a sight even more unusual to the spectator than Red Indians in the center of Paris. Ten roughly dressed men, each one handcuffed to a woman, were standing in the wagon. A priest rode beside them on horseback. There was no doubt that the women were the plainest in all of Paris, perhaps in all of France, but each face was made comelier by a happy grin, although the men to whom they were handcuffed looked none too savory. A banner on their wagon read: BON VOYAGE COLONISTS.

The street was now packed tight with people. It seemed as though half of Paris had followed the parade on foot. Law's strong voice reached the end of the crowd, and for those who had trouble hearing, others passed on his message.

'Citizens of Paris! As you will recall, on the 4th of December in 1718, the Banque Générale was by a declaration of the King, converted into the Banque Royal. We accomplished this by reimbursing the shareholders in coin. Gold and silver, for the *billets d' état* they had paid in. These have now been converted into shares in The Company of the West, a company that includes the Mississippi Company. These shares will remain in the treasury as a fund for the bank and to serve as a guarantee for the public, by order of the Regent himself!›

He indicated the royal carriage, and Philip waved a regal hand at the crowd. Shouts of, 'Long Live the Regent! Long live John Law! 'greeted his words, heavily prompted by the bank clerks. Behind Orleans' carriage bringing up the rear of the procession, was a carriage carrying the Duke du Maine and Count D'Argenson. They had been invited by Philip to attend this event.. 'Commanded' would have been more accurate.

Law raised a hand to silence the people. 'Friends, money furnishes the lifeblood of a nation. Have you not enjoyed the prosperity that paper money has brought you? Have we not opened the doors to trade French goods throughout Europe?'

There were shouts of agreement now. It was true that businesses had flourished, and the new prosperity had stabilized France since Law's bank had come into being. Business People knew it, and everyone had benefited down to the very bottom of society.

'Today, every country wants to sell to the French, and they gladly seek our paper money in exchange for their goods. Now, the bank is offering you shares in the future of France. In *your* future! The shares in the Company Of The West and its Mississippi enterprise that you buy today will be worth ten times what you pay for them in six months. This, I guarantee you!' Such words brought Law the full attention of the people. The silence was tangible. He went on, bewitching his audience with charismatic charm.

'Why?' he asked, though he was not seeking an answer from them. 'Because the money for those shares will be used for developing the lands of the Mississippi. Lands perhaps you will never see. But this money will circulate. The Mississippi investment will bring prosperity to France beyond your wildest dreams!'

Du Maine signaled to a broad-shouldered fellow not far from the carriage. He had planted several hecklers in the throng, hoping to cause some small discord. The man took the signal and began to shout at Law.

'It's a swindle!' Another joined in. 'Who would throw money away on a place we've never seen?'

'Then see it now,' Law exclaimed. 'Let your mind wander down a Mississippi valley, green as the meadows of heaven, stretching from the pearl-tipped Allegheny mountains to the snow-crowned Rockies! Beautiful, virgin Louisiana is waiting for the embrace of France!'

He turned to the handcuffed men and women. 'These Frenchmen you see here have been granted freedom from the Bastille on the condition that they take with them a bride to Louisiana. They will start a new life as free men! And with their wives, they will build a French colony in the Americas. They will dig out the gold, and they will make you all rich! I ask you to support them by digging into your pockets!' He signaled the priest. 'Father, you may now proceed with the marriages.'

While the priest began reading the ceremony, Law went on. 'These colonists will honeymoon on the high seas and build their homes on the banks of the Mississippi.' Law reached into his pocket. 'Since nothing sweetens a marriage like a dowry. . .' He opened a sack full of gold coins and sent a bright golden stream of confetti down on the newlyweds. The bridegrooms fairly danced in the sparkling downpour catching coins, tumbling over each other, dragging their brides willy-nilly. Law pulled out a handful of his melted down nuggets.

'Gold from the Mississippi!' He bellowed. 'People of France, the riches of the Mississippi shall be yours!' He tossed the nuggets into the crowd. Eager hands clutched excitedly, and joyful shouts rose at being the lucky recipient of a nugget. 'Citizens of Paris, the booths are now open to sell shares! I make you this offer. I shall personally buy back your shares in six months for one hundred livres! Those same shares which you can purchase today for fifty livres in paper money!

Cries of 'John Lass - John Law - John Law,' rang out again.

'It is your Regent who deserves your cheers,' Law protested.

'Long live the Regent! Orleans!

Orleans!' came the perfunctory response. But it was Law who was their hero.

In the Duke du Maine's carriage, Count D'Argenson turned to him with a worried look. 'They shout this Scotsman's name louder than the Regent's.'

The stock jobbers, too, began shouting, and the first French citizens moved in to purchase Law's paper promises. Those few who had caught the gold were first at the booths where jobbers traded their gold for paper money to buy the shares. Soon people were fighting each other for a place at one of the booths. One of the tellers cried out as the coins clinked in his moneybox," Don't be afraid that your money should suffer to remain in your hands, gentlemen. I will engage that all shall be taken from you!'

D'Argenson's face held a worried look. 'You know, your Grace, Law's new scheme is shrewd! It might succeed,' he complained. 'Perhaps it was a mistake introducing that sea captain to the scoundrel.'

Du Maine threw him a complacent look. 'Oh, it *will* succeed, my dear Count. And Philip will fly high on Law's coattails. But the highest branch is not always the safest roost.'

Within days and by the hour, the prices of shares began rising. Over the next few months as the news spread, not only Paris but half of Europe poured into the narrow Rue Quincampoix. This ancient street set between the Rue Auxours where the general public entered and the Rue Aubry-le-Boucher where people of quality made their way by carriage or sedan chair— this ancient street had become the center of trade in paper.

In Law's highest expectations, he had not imagined such a quick response. He was forced to set guards at each end of the street and allow only foot traffic, and when people crowded past the guards, Law had gates installed to close the street and ordered them locked each night. Aside from stock jobbers in the booths, some industrious merchants had set up in business for themselves and were buying up all the stock they could lay their hands on, then selling them for a profit in the same street to others who could not get even close to a stockjobber's booth. One industrious fellow who had no booth was perched precariously high on the railing of a householder's balcony for which he paid a handsome rental. He shouted down at the assembly, waving a fistful of stocks. 'Going up! Going up! Sixty livres a share!'

A nobleman pushed forward, shouting back at him, 'It was selling at fifty!'

'That was an hour ago,' the stock-jobber yelled back. The nobleman waved his money, eager to have it taken from him.

The queues lined the streets for several blocks. People waited their turn to enter the gates and take their chances that any stocks might still be available for purchase that day. And when it came to buying the shares, no man stood above another. Nobles hobnobbed with footmen, prelates and princes scowled at each other. Bishops rubbed elbows with shopkeepers, soldiers, workers, magistrates and pickpockets, marquises, and servants. All shouted, cursed, and plotted together or connived against each other to get their hands on John Law's magical shares.

As the news spread across Europe, Frenchmen were soon

joined by foreigners, counting out their money side by side, for shares. The harder it was to obtain, the more people wanted, *must have* shares! Long term friendships were forgotten in the battle for a place. So was sleep, thirst, and hunger. Anyone who already had shares could sell them at a profit. Clergy, laity, peers, and plebeians, even ladies turned unofficial stock jobbers outbid each other in the street. Soon shares were selling at sixty times their original value. Nothing could move anyone from that crowded street until the last share had been sold for the day, and then the people disappeared like a swarm of locust, the gates were locked, and the Rue Quincampoix was once more deserted.

There was no denying that the Company Of The West was a great success from the first day. To celebrate, Philip threw a private party, which was to be followed by a public banquet. Duke Du Maine was among the guests to share in the private festivities. Louis XV sat beside Philip, the little King pale and fragile-looking, under the weight of a velvet crown-cap and ermine-trimmed robes. The Court cartographer brought in a new map of Paris and unrolled it before the child. On it was indicated some proposals for improvements now that the treasury was once more solvent. Louis ran a small finger up the boulevards and down the streets.

'Where is the Rue Quincampoix?' he asked. When it was pointed out to him, he paused, raised his finger, and pointed at the cartographer. 'No, no, this will not do!' he exclaimed. 'Why have you not distinguished the Rue Quincampoix by being gilded?'

'I shall see to it at once,' the cartographer assured him and bowed his way backward out of the room.

'Where is Monsieur Law?' Marie-Louise asked. 'He is not usually late, and to a party in his honor.'

As though on cue, the great doors were drawn open, and in came Law followed by two footmen bearing a gigantic cake on a serving platter.

'What on earth. . .?' Katherine exclaimed.

The footmen set down the platter on a round table in front of the King and Philip. The gigantic construction of sugar icing represented the plan of a city on a river. Streets, buildings, and a cathedral were laid out across the top.

'Why it is a city in miniature!' little Louis cried, climbing down and trotting over to examine the masterpiece of confection more closely. His eyes just cleared the top of the city.

'Indeed, it is, your Majesty,' Law replied. 'The city that will be built on the Mississippi River. It will be France's capital in the Louisianas.'

Louis poked a tentative finger into the frosting and licked it gravely with an appraisal. 'A city of vanilla.'

'Our greatest architect, Monsieur Delatour, has designed the city, your Highness. He will travel with me to lay the foundations.'

The Duke du Maine edged his way among the admirers who had gathered around the cake. 'And what have you named your city, Monsieur Finance Minister?' he asked, staring at it with mild disapproval.

‹The city will be called New Orleans.› Law bowed to Philip, who looked mildly surprised but none-the-less pleased.

'New Orleans. . .' he said, tasting the words.

'An ocean away,' du Maine sniffed. 'Perhaps next, Monsieur Law, you will be building cities on the moon with French money.'

'If I do, I shall be honored to name the first one after you, your Grace,' Law replied coolly.

Orleans dispelled the muffled chuckle that went around. 'Since this city bears my name, I give myself the honor of cutting it.' He proceeded to cut the first slice, handing it to little Louis. Footmen stood by to pass the rest of the slices among the guests.

Marie-Louise took a plate from the footman and carried it over to Du Maine, whose scowl seemed frozen to his face. 'Eat a cathedral, Uncle. You will feel better.'

Du Maine glared at the icing edifice and looked across to a woman in her eighties wearing thick face paint, a former mistress of Louis XIV. "Monsieur Law has taught us the secret of prosperity, Madame de Maintenon,' he said.

MADAME DE MAINTENON

TWENTY-ONE:
THE MISSISSIPPI BUBBLE
BURSTS!

'Colorful, John, though utterly preposterous, I'd say.' William Law said, staring at a large poster decorating one wall inside the Banque Royal.

'People have little imagination, Will,' Law replied. 'They must see what they are being asked to invest in! And they are willing to believe what we show them.' 'They must be willing, indeed!' Will said, staring at an idyllic painted scene below the words, 'BUY SHARES IN THE MISSISSIPPI.' Beneath a cloudless sky, a Garden of Eden was depicted with gold nuggets piled high, and friendly Indians in feathered head-dresses offering baskets of fanciful fruits to eager colonists holding picks and shovels, ready to dig up the treasures in the Mississippi.

A few weeks later, Will rushed into his brother's office in high excitement. 'Did you hear, John? The Rue Quincampoix was so crowded today that even with your new restrictions on entry, now pickpockets are running riot and two women fainted in the street!' Will sank into a chair. 'And the bank is full of people today! But it is not gold they are after, John. It is paper money! Now, they want paper instead of gold.'

John Law smiled and poured his brother a small brandy, hoping it would calm him down. 'That is because the Regent has passed an edict saying that gold and silver are no longer acceptable for shares. Now, a person can only buy shares in the Mississippi Company with paper money!

By the spring of 1719, it seemed that everyone wanted shares in the Mississippi Company, and as the stock prices rose, people who had bought earlier began to sell at a profit. But then, seeing that the prices were still rising, they bought back again, doubling their investment. The Duke de D'Antin, who had already made a profit on his shares, sang Law's praises to Louis Henri, Duke de Bourbon, an influential member of Parliament. Law had heard that Bourbon, too, was becoming a heavy investor.

By the end of 1719, provincials and foreigners swarmed into the capital to speculate on shares. Although for travel to Paris, arrangements had to be made weeks in advance, the estimate of visitors stood between 300,000 and 500,000 people. Anyone with a bed to rent in Paris was getting rich enough to buy more shares.

John Law was forced to issue a decree ordering a guard of archers stationed in the Rue Quincampoix to protect dealers from thieves and rogues and preserve order. But still, the people poured in! All of Europe's attention was concentrated upon this one narrow French street, where all dwellings from basements to attics had been converted into offices. Everybody in Paris neglected work and pleasure to rush off to the stock-jobbers to Buy! Buy! Buy! There was scarcely room in the Rue Quincampoix to write a signature on a certificate.

The situation offering a wealth of opportunities for the quick-witted, and one youth whose wits were never his problem, made his fortune by renting his hunchback as a desk on which self-made brokers could scribble a hasty transaction. One afternoon when Law came into the street, the youth rushed up to him, announcing that his back had earned him enough for ten shares. 'That is if Monsieur Law will grant me the privilege to buy,' he cried, 'because the official booths are all sold out!' Impressed by his enterprise, Law made him a gift of some shares. He did not know that the hunchback resold them within the hour at a profit.

Of the aristocracy, only the Chancellor and the Dukes of Saint Simon and de Rochefoucauld did not invest. De Rochefoucauld would have liked to. 'But why are there never any shares left when I get there?' he complained to Law. As Comptroller of the Mint, John Law could not print shares fast enough to meet the demand.

PARIS IN A FRENZY

Seeing that the narrow Rue Quincampoix had beccme too crowded for practicality, Law's answer was to close down tħe street to further trading. He moved his operation to the Place Vendôme, which was wider and more open. He purchased the Hôtel Soissons, a noble building for one million four hundred thousand livres, from Prince Carignan. In its spacious gardens, Law immediately had one hundred pavilions buiłt for the use of brokers. Not to be cheated of their portion, the bank rented out the booths at a handsome profit:

Five hundred livres a month. Law then issued an ordinance forbidding trading anywhere else.

Katherine Knollys, who had purchased substantial shares herself, asked Saint Simon why he had not invested.' I cannot buy these stocks however much I might like a few, my dear Milady Knollys because, although it is large enough, there is too much noise in the Place Vendôme,' he replied, tucking a lace handkerchief into his sleeve. He glanced wistfully at the shares she displayed and fluttered his rouged eyelids. 'You don't suppose you could sell me a few of those?'

She tucked them away quickly. 'I should not dream of it, Your Grace. They are rising every day. Perhaps you should send your servant.' She smiled. 'If you are not afraid, he will keep them for himself.'

But there was a greater, more serious problem. Trading had unexpectedly moved beyond the bank's control and into the hands of speculators! Law complained to Will that somehow, he must stop the money going into speculators' pockets, and none of it going into financing the Mississippi project.

‹How can you stop them, John?› Will asked. ‹Once they have purchased your shares, the stocks are theirs. They have the right to sell to whomsoever they wish.›

Then suddenly, Law was called to see Orleans. Not sure what to expect, he found Philip ecstatic. He treated Law almost like an equal now and considered him something of a wizard. Philip invited him to sit and offered him a cognac. Though it was early in the day for him, Law could not refuse.

'You are a man who keeps your promises, Law,' Orleans told him. 'I have examined the Company accounts and have seen the profits flowing into the Treasury, and I am ready to admit I did not believe it possible! Yes, gold has poured in! The people have accepted your paper in place of it, and there is no end in sight! All since you secured the management of the Louisiana colony and created these stocks and shares. What new exploit are you planning to accomplish next?'

It was as though Philip expected him to perform like a circus animal with a fresh trick for every show. But if the Regent had imagined catching his Finance Minister unawares, he was wrong because Law had a bag full of tricks ready.

'Your Royal Highness, aside from the four hundred whites and twenty blacks who inhabited the Louisiana Territory when Captain Crozet made over the Vice Royalty of it to the Western Company, in truth, it was a desolate land with red Indians its only occupants. My plan is not to make the Indians into slaves, as the Spanish did in the southern Americas. I am arranging for twelve hundred Indian women of the region to be engaged in making silk in a factory, for which they will receive a fair wage.'

'Will that make a profit?" Orleans asked.

'As long as Frenchmen wear silk coats, Sir, I have no doubt. Also, silver ingots have been found along the banks of the Mississippi River. I am having them assayed at the Mint now.' He smiled mysteriously and sipped his drink. 'But most of all, a rock of solid emerald is said to exist in a territory called Arkansas. I have sent Captain Laharpe there with a detachment of twenty-two men to take possession of it if it truly was there.'

'An emerald, you say?' The Regent's eyes sparkled in anticipation, and he nodded approval to his Finance Minister—a man for whom there was always the next plan, the next scheme, the next strategy.

Knowing he could accomplish nothing without the Regent's blessing, Law had been waiting for the right moment to introduce his latest proposal. Now, having Orleans' attention, he laid out this latest plan for speculators to invest in and concluded with a simple explanation.

Sir, what I propose is to offer *Dealings in Futures*—which I call *Bargains in Primes*. 'Primes are actually quite easy to understand. They are nothing more than agreements to furnish or to receive shares at a certain date in the future. They will be regulated by a decree, which will, of course, be made by you—if you approve the plan.

'Fascinating. . .' Orleans said vaguely. He was never too clear about Law's schemes until he saw the resulting money, and he was willing to support any project that would bring it in at the rate that Law's paper was sopping it up. 'Where did you get such an idea?' the Regent asked.

Having captured Orleans' attention, Law went on with some modesty. 'It is not totally original, Sir. I am patterning the formula after similar dealings that I saw operated by London brokers. Although I intend to make certain simplifying changes.'

That was explanation enough for Orleans. He sat back, sipping his cognac. 'You shall have my consent, Law! Make ready the decree as you wish, and I shall see that Parliament approves it.'

Law hesitated, but it had to be said. 'There is one other matter I must discuss with you, Sir. One that has been troubling me of late.'

'Well, well, go on,' Philip said impatiently, sensing a note of disapproval in Law's face.

'You do understand that our first concern must be the development of the colony! That is what the money has been raised for, and that is where our real fortune will come from! Not from this speculation in the shares, for that can become a spiraling tornado with no good end in sight.'

He paused, seeing Orleans' attention straying. 'This very week, we have sent one hundred and fifty more couples out to the Mississippi! Our colonists have already started a tobacco farm. Fortunately, the vegetation is plentiful, and they have the help of local Indians in planting the crops.'

'Planting?' Orleans exclaimed. 'I do not want the colonists planting. They should be digging for gold.'

Law knew he must be patient. 'Sir, the Company of the West now has a monopoly on all Louisiana's trade, including the beaver trade in the north, called Canada. This will bring in a fortune, perhaps even equal to the gold.'

Nothing is equal to gold!' Philip said testily. 'What else?'

Law knew it was a game to Orleans, which he would continue to play as long as he held the pot at the end of the elusive rainbow that Law was filling for him. He tried once more to make the Regent understand.

'Your Royal Highness will remember that one day at Marly, you did me the honor to say that through the openings which I have made, you began to see beyond the difficulties of the country. I then had the honor to say that the bank was not the most important of my ideas, but that I also had a plan by which I would furnish five hundred million and which should cost the people nothing.'

'Yes, yes, I do recall,' Orleans replied impatiently.

'Sir, with your approval, as you will also recall, I have annulled the grants of those French companies who were trading in competition to our new Company of the West.'

'Which companies?' Orleans asked quizzically.

'The Company of the East Indies and the China Company,' Law said patiently.

'What has happened to them, then?' Philip asked.

'Do not be concerned, Sir. The Bank has absorbed them into The Company of the West, which gives us a monopoly overall. The point is, it places all French trade under your National Bank's control.'

Orleans looked relieved. 'Excellent!' he never understood the discipline that created the financial wonders Law produced, but he was always ready to harvest the profits. 'Persevere, Law! We do not want the sale of your shares to slow down, do we?'

'There is little chance of that, Sir. The market continues to soar. It seems there have been stories circulating of discoveries of mineral wealth and mines along the *upper* Mississippi. It has inspired a new craze of purchasing.›

Philip's eyes brightened. 'Is it true, Law? Is it true?'

'Well, Sir, do you recall those ingots I threw to the crowd on opening day? It seems that someone only now thought to take them to the Mint and have them assayed.'

A wry smile touched the corners of Law's mouth. 'In fact, the nuggets were declared to be even purer than the gold once found in Peru.'

‹Hmm. . .' Philip frowned at his Finance Minister. 'We must make certain that in future the Mint does not use such pure gold in casting our louis d'or. You are the Mint, Law! See to it. Less gold in the coin!'

Law tried to hold back a smile. 'I shall, Sir. But word spreads in situations like this, and once again, the prices of shares have advanced.'

'Good. Good! I have some expenses in mind for the Treasury that could be quite costly.'

What would they be?' Law asked, somewhat alarmed.

Phillip looked slightly nervous and said, 'I shall inform you of that some other time. Now I have an appointment with my architect!' The Regent swallowed his last drop of cognac, rose with a preoccupied look on his face, and was gone. He didn't bother to say goodbye.

Law looked after him for a moment. These days it seemed harder to keep Philip's attention on developing the lands of the Mississippi or to make him understand that it was where the real fortunes were eventually to be made.

As Law stepped into the great hall, he wondered if he might be able to steal an hour for a visit with Katherine. He had not seen her for days. But just then, the great outer doors opened, and Marie-Louise entered the palace, cheeks glowing from her usual morning canter. She signaled to Law in an imperious manner. He came over and joined her, allowing her broad smile to wipe away his doubts about her father.

'I do believe, Monsieur Law, that you must be the most conspicuous person in the kingdom.'

'That I doubt, Marie Louise,' he said, coming to her side.

'Do not be modest, Law. Only yesterday I was speaking to Monsieur Voltaire, who told me he saw you arrive in the Palais Royal, followed by dukes and peers, marshals of France and bishops. And my spies tell me you are besieged in your house by sycophants.'

'Your *spies*, Marie-Louise?' he asked. But he was not surprised.

'Well, at least the Duke de Saint Simon. He says he saw your supplicants force your gate and enter from your garden. And I hear they even fall into your study through the chimney! Whether you are aware of it or no, your servants are doing a thriving business, for there is no getting speech with you without money. The Swiss must be paid at your gate! The lackey, for admittance into your antechamber. And the Valets de Chambre for the privilege of access to your presence!'

'It is true. They give me little rest.' He paused with a sigh, not wishing to pursue this conversation further. 'You really do look ravishing this morning, Marie-Louise.' His lips grazed her slender hand.

'Come along and ravish me then, and we shall rest together.' She said mischievously, leading him towards her apartments, adding with a sly look, 'You know, Law, you are going to have to become a Catholic.'

Was this girl becoming religious? he wondered as he followed her.

John Law did not go home that night. It was not until the small hours that he left Marie-Louise's apartments. But the next morning, he was already at his desk in the bank when his brother came in with a worried expression waving a banknote in front of his brother.

'Look at this, John! Just delivered from the printers. Orleans has changed the tenor of the banknotes yet again!' Will read aloud: *"The Bank Promises to pay the bearer at sight"* He looked up. 'And here is space for the value to be filled in: So many livres in *silver* coin! Silver! How can the Regent expect people to deal in credit at the bank when they receive silver for gold—and the value altered, at that?'

Law stared at the note with surprise. 'But I saw him yesterday! And how many times have I explained to Orleans that the value must be inviolate? With great patience, I might add.' The color rose in his cheeks. 'And only yesterday he told me that *I* am the Mint.'

'When you saw him yesterday, John, did he not tell you what he has done?' Will exclaimed.

'Not a word!'

Will frowned. 'Then, of what use is it that he gave you control of the Treasury, when once again he has walked right over you and declared a depreciation!'

Will collapsed in a chair facing Law. 'It is not good enough, John,' he said firmly. 'The greatest obstacle to the bank and to The Mississippi Company is this continued alteration of the coinage!'

Law rose, pacing the room. The pacing was something he had not done since Newgate Prison so long ago in his cell. And in a sense, once again, he felt himself a prisoner.

Will watched him for a moment, then said, 'When you began your private bank, money was worth the same in paper as in gold. Surely it must remain so with the National Bank if a man is to conduct business by transfers in writing. Above all, the bank must have the confidence of foreigners!'

Law stopped pacing to face his brother. 'In fact, it is worse than you think, Will. The Regent made me Director-General and Finance Minister of France, but actually, I have no power! Orleans has arranged it so that I am responsible for whatever he decides to do. *That* is my real power. The power of a puppet!' He sank back in his chair behind his desk. 'It is the same trick he played on D'Argenson!'

They were silent for a moment. Then Will asked angrily. 'And what do you suppose the Regent is spending this vast sum of money on, if not the Mississippi?' 'Is it for another statue? Another Royal Park? Another Versailles?'

'It's for some spectacular purchase, of that I'm certain, Will. But although I've tried, I've been unable to find out what it is!' An angry John Law moved purposefully towards the door, the banknote in his hand. He closed the door sharply behind him.

The Royal palace garden might have been festooned with roses by a frenzied florist; it was so profuse with flowers. The air was heady with their scent, and the bees in their delirium were far too busy to bother with humans.

'Higher, Philip, higher!' Katherine Knollys cried, 'for France is on top of the world, and so am I!'

To anyone entering Philip's private garden, Katherine seemed to be swept up into the air, only to retreat again. Then up she flew once more, on a swing suspended from a bower of climbing roses. The man pushing her in the swing was the Regent himself.

He stopped petulantly. 'I am tired, Katherine. Now, what was it you were going to tell me?'

The swing slowed, and Katherine traipsed the toe of one satin slipper along the grass, dragging it to a halt. She looked a flower herself in a rose satin gown with delicate pale blue taffeta ruffles that cut a line of scallops across her skirt. Her soft blonde ringlets decorated with a spray of spicy carnations had been tamed into a smooth crown framing her face.

'Tell you, Philip? Only that John Law has invented a new word for you. He calls you a *Millionaire*.'

THE SWING - JEAN-HONORE FRAGONARD

'Does he now?' Philip savored the word. 'Millionaire. Hmm, I like it. And as a millionaire, I am about to show you my first purchase!'

She hopped down, all excited now. The band of diamonds at her throat fought for attention in the sparkling sunlight. 'What is it?'

'I ask you, Katherine,' he asked mysteriously. 'Have you ever looked into the eye of a Hindu idol?'

'I can truly say, Philip, that I have not.' She knew his little games and how he liked to surprise her.

He drew a dark red velvet pouch from the depth of his pocket and loosened the string. 'Hold out your hand, my dear, for you are about to look into the most spectacular eye in the world.'

Gingerly she held her hand towards him, imagining some sort of dried eyeball, some strange religious relic of an ancient Hindu culture. Philip slid the strings of the bag wider and dropped the contents into her palm.

She gasped. This was no fragment of human detritus. This was a diamond the size of a greengage plum. 'Is it real?' she asked skeptically.

'As a diamond, yes. Seventy-five carets without a flaw! As an eye, perhaps it could also be considered real, my dear, for it was one of the eyes of the idol, Juggernaut at Chandergore.'

She rolled it around in her hand: as though holding an incandescent star plucked from the night by some arcane force. 'How did you come by such a thing, Philip?'

His words tumbled out with the excitement of a child who had explored Aladdin's cave and escaped with its richest treasure. 'It was stolen by a slave at Chandergore who hid it in a wound in his leg.' His eyes were bright as he took it from her hand and held it up to the sun.

'But how did it get to France?' she asked.

'Remember that Englishman with the rather too sharp nose we entertained at Court some while back, my dear?'

'Sir Thomas Pitt?' she asked.

'The same. It was brought here by him. Pitt confided in me that the British Court could not afford such treasures at this moment, and I was delighted to announce to him that ours is certainly the richest Court in Europe!"

'What are you going to do with it?' she asked, unable to remove her eyes from its dazzling presence.

His chuckle of delight brought her attention back to him. 'Do with it, my sweet? I shall have it mounted so that it can be worn. And you shall be the first to wear it, Katherine.'

'You... you... are giving this to me?'

'Not *giving* it, my dear. No, no. Thanks to the wealth which is pouring into the Treasury, the State has paid two million livres to your countryman for it, and it shall remain the property of France. But you may wear it. And then one day soon, perhaps, It will be worn by Marie-Louise when she remarries.'

'The property of France. Of course,' she said with some disappointment, the heat receding from her cheeks. 'The Eye of Juggernaut.'

His voice dropped into a more serious tone. 'I think we had best forget that part of the story, Katherine. For although it costs my Treasury two million, the former possessors from whom it was, shall we say, *taken*, might view its ownership somewhat different-ly.' He quickly cleared his mind of such quibbles. 'I am calling it the Regency Diamond.' She had been so excited by the diamond that she only now realized what he had said about Marie-Louise being married one day soon. To whom, Katherine wondered?

THE REGENCY DIAMOND 140.64 carats

TWENTY-TWO: DU MAINE AND D'ARGENSON

'To be honest, John, I cannot follow in detail how you go about creating these projects, as you do, but it is plain to see the effect your theatrics have on the public,' Will told his brother-in-Law's private office at the bank. 'Why, that very first day in the Rue Quincampoix, when you offered to buy back the shares at double the purchase price, I thought you were acting like a wild gambler. But the shares immediately rose to par!' Will shook his head, unsure whether he admired or was apprehensive of his brother's methods. 'You are a sort of magician with a mysterious power—and there is no doubt that your gambling spirit has brought these unbelievable profits.'

'Unbelievable, yes, even to me,' John said. He had not expected such immediate and gargantuan success. 'I have never prided myself on that disinterested curiosity, and that passion for abstract truth which characterizes philosophy, Will,' he replied thoughtfully. 'To me, it is the results that matter.'

'Results, yes. You have achieved those,' Will said. 'You are an original thinker; that is incontestable. Why your treatises on finance are a textbook!'

'No,' Law said. 'My writings have never been anything beyond memoranda in support of the business, which I wished to set afloat. But where the situation demands, I have never made any scruples of acting in contradiction to my principles!' His countenance brightened. 'But Will, despite the Regent's lack of comprehension, there can be no doubt that we have set France back on her feet.'

He rose from his desk and moved across the room to the window, looking out into the street. It was bustling with activity;

then turned back to his brother. 'Remember, in February, the Mint printed one billion nine hundred and six million, four hundred thousand livres worth of new paper shares. Add that to the bank, and it makes a total of two billion six hundred ninety-six million four hundred thousand livres in paper. Paper! Think of it, Will—I have based this country's economy solely on paper! With nothing more than rag, tree pulp, and ink, I have made France the most prosperous kingdom in Europe.' His eyes gleamed with fervor. 'And I have not yet finished! For I will raise this nation so high that every kingdom in the world will send ambassadors to Paris—while the Regent will only dispatch couriers to the other states in return. Nothing can defeat us now!'

And so it would seem to William Law. His brother poured two goblets of whiskie. They clicked goblets and drank a toast to the future.

But there were other forces at work. Forces that intended to see John Law destroyed—and through him, the Regent of France.

On a brisk autumn morning, the Duke du Maine was riding in his closed carriage with Count D'Argenson, accompanied by the Duke's secretary, a consumptive looking young man named Portalis. As they came abreast of the Place Vendôme, du Maine tapped the driver to stop. He handed Portalis a bulky leather satchel. Portalis descended and hurried off into the Place Vendôme, fully aware of his errand.

For a moment, du Maine watched his secretary make his way into the crowded square pushing past eager investors; then, with a tranquil look, he settled back to wait, stretching out his crippled leg as best he could. Only the tapping of his index finger on his gold-headed cane betrayed his tension. Like anger, it was an emotion du Maine rarely exhibited. He had spent a lifetime disguising his true feelings behind a steel blue glance.

Count D'Argenson, not so skilled at masking his moods, fidgeted nervously on the seat beside him. 'I daresay, your Grace, that you have a good and valid reason for sending Portalis out to aid Law's cause by purchasing this iniquitous Mississippi stock!'

A light chuckle oozed up from du Maine's throat. 'Not only purchase it, my dear. But in as large amounts as I can lay hands upon.'

'Am I to assume that you now believe that his wild system—this Mississippi scheme will succeed?'

Mordant confidence lit du Maine's angular features. 'Succeed? Not if I can help it, my dear Count, rest assured. As I see it, Monsieur Law has never had, properly speaking, any scheme at all. Nowhere has he set down a theory that can be considered the exact and complete expression of his conviction.'

'Certainly, he is no man of theory, your Grace. He is a quack! 'D'Argenson spat out.

'Quack?' Du Maine shook his head. 'No, no, I do not think that of Monsieur Law at all. Although this Scotsman has wrapped my cousin around his finger, he is neither quack nor genius.'

Content with his own appraisal, du Maine brought out a hand-painted deck of playing cards with portraits of his father and Madame de Montespan, his mother painted on the backs and dealt them across a tray. 'Come, let us not fret.' He told his sour companion. 'It is bad for the stomach. We shall play a hand whilst we wait for Portalis.'

D'Argenson leaned back into the corner of the brocade coach seat and picking up his cards. 'Well, I, for one, shall have nothing to do with these paper shares!' His voice became more thoughtful. 'Although I have heard that they have become so much in demand and so hard to purchase that people will try any and every which way to gain the confidence of this villain—all in the hope of receiving a special dispensation to buy from the devil conjurer himself. They *beg* this. . .this. . .' he struggled for the word and found it. 'this *corrupter* to take their money, like lambs rushing to the slaughter!'

'An ingenious mind, I must admit. The man is gifted with rare powers of observation and perception,' du Maine said sourly, setting down a card.

It was a full hour later that Portalis placed a bundle of stocks in du Maine's lap. 'I purchased the last fifty shares from Monsieur Law himself!' his secretary told him.

Du Maine raised an eyebrow at the news, then counted them carefully. Satisfied, he laid them beside the money he had won from D'Argenson. 'Well done!' He handed Portalis one share. 'That is for you, sir. We shall repeat our little game tomorrow.'

D'Argenson scowled. He hadn't figured out what exactly was du Maine's game, and it disturbed him that he had been taken only halfway into the confidence of the wily Duke.

'Monsieur Law is much taller than your average Frenchman,' Portalis mused, somewhat in awe.

'So much further to fall,' du Maine said firmly. He tapped for the driver, and they headed away.

John Law tried to make it a daily occurrence to come out of his new home in the Palais de Nevers, which was at one end of the Place Vendôme. He would show himself at the booths and in the park, where enthusiastic customers made way for him, and people shouted, 'Viva Law!' At which he bowed and doffed his hat. One attractive woman in her twenties pushed in front of him in a near state of hysteria. 'Help! Help!' she cried, managing to clutch Law's sleeve, tears streaming down her face. 'Oh, Monsieur Lass, I have just had my pocket picked!'

Her tears seemed genuine enough, and he gave her his attention. 'Please, Madame, ease yourself. How much have you lost?'

'One hundred thousand livres! All my husband's savings,' she cried. 'This morning, I took them out of the pot he kept under our bed! Brought them tied around my waist in my purse! All to buy your wonderful shares! And now some cut-purse has stolen it! My husband does not know I took his money, and I have no doubt he will kill me!" She burst into sobs once more.

'Quiet yourself, Madame, for you shall not be out a penny,' Law assured her, turning to one of the stock jobbers.

From his own pocket, he drew out one hundred thousand livres and purchased the shares for her. A hushed whisper went around from those close enough to hear of Law's generosity.

'Perhaps your husband will consider placing his money in the bank, where it will not only be safe but will earn him interest as well,' he said.

Unable to believe her luck, she took the shares gladly and kissed his hand. 'I shall tell him. You are the savior of France, Monsieur!' she cried and tucked the shares hastily into the ample bodice of her dress. 'Let any thief try to retrieve these!' she cried.

'Truly, Madame.' He eyed her heaving breasts. 'They are hid where only your husband should venture!' Law turned back to the crowd raising his voice. 'Pickpockets and cut-purses are all around! See that your money and shares stay in your hands or in the bank, where they will benefit us all.'

Another rousing cheer greeted his departure. 'Vive Law. Vive Lass!'

Now that Law was a powerful and wealthy man, the Palais de Nevers was the site of constant visitors, and he was perpetually followed day and night. His ante-chamber was filled daily with some of France's finest names; people he could not turn away. He hid in his private apartments and let Jean-Francois Melon, his new secretary, sift through the most important callers. Only a few were admitted each morning. Everyone humbled themselves before him.

One morning Law was surprised by a visit from Katherine, who told him she had brought the Countess of Suffolk who was waiting in his antechamber to meet him. The English Countess was distantly connected to Katherine Knollys through her grandmother, Elisabeth, Countess of Banbury. 'One never knows when one might need friends in high places, Johnny,' Katherine said. 'The Countess is frightfully rich and well connected at the English Court.'

'I expect to be too busy at the French Court to avail myself of her patronage, but please bring the Countess in, Katherine, since she is important to you.'

Dressed in a smart broadcloth traveling suit with velvet trimmings covering her ample frame, the Countess hurried in. She gushed a greeting, telling Law that she had traveled all the way from England just to set eyes on him despite fragile health. And of course, to buy some of his amazing shares that all of England was talking about.

Thinking she looked anything but fragile, he told her, 'The sea air must have done you good, Countess, for you look exceptionally fit.' But he obliged her with several thousand shares and sent Melon to arrange the details, inviting her to dinner with Katherine that night. It was one of the rare occasions lately when he had time for guests. Pleased, the Countess promised to report on his wonders when she returned to London.

A few weeks later, Law was sitting at his desk, writing a letter when his secretary came in and presented a note. Law read it, surprised. 'Here, in Paris, so soon?

Let him in at once, Melon!'

'But, Monsieur Law, how can I? There are several Princes who have been waiting all morning; De Conde and Bourbon are glaring at each other, wondering which will be allowed in first,' the young man said.

'This Duke is my kinsman and stands before princes. You have my special order to admit him and no other,' Law told him with a broad smile of anticipation. Archie had written several months earlier that he was planning another trip to Paris.

Argyll's imposing figure resplendent in a fine silk coat and carrying a leather case, entered, in a high state of excitement. They threw their arms around each other, and there were tears in Archie's eyes as they exchanged greetings.

'Would you believe it, Archie?' Law told him. 'I was at this very moment writing home to Mother telling her to plant cabbages at Lauriston. I am sending her French seeds. They do so very well here, and I have sent sacks of seed to the Mississippi.'

Archie shook his head, but he could not subdue a smile. 'What game is this, John? Your antechamber is filled with people wanting to see my celebrated relative. The Prince de Conde complained that he had been here for an hour and was quite put out when he saw your secretary call for me. And I find you occupied with such momentous business as writing home of cabbages. How can it be that you have time for such trivial pursuits?'

Law sighed. 'Those men can wait, Archie. They don't come out of personal regard, but to solicit me to buy shares when my secretary has told them there are no more to sell. They can well afford to cool their heels for an hour or two.' He led Archie to a small sofa and sat beside him, appraising his cousin.

Archie looked much older and did not move with the ease of earlier days. Still, he was in high spirits after the journey. 'It would seem that all of France is plunged into a delirium of excitement, Johnny! Why the highway leading to Paris was thronged with people from the provinces and many from foreign countries. All hastening to Paris in the hopes that they might still be in time to secure shares,' Archie told him with some awe.

'It is more than I had dreamed, Archie.' Law took up a decanter and poured its amber liquid into two glasses. 'Come, take a glass of Madeira, and you shall tell me the news.'

'I do have news. But first, let me say that I have always had the utmost faith in your talents, John, and now I see that your power here in France is an accomplished fact. You, a Scotsman, are skillfully manipulating the French courtiers, adroitly managing the Regent and. . .'

Law waved his hand in a gesture to say he would hear no more.

'No! Do not stop me!' Archie said. 'I must give you my appraisal of what I have seen and heard.' Archie swallowed a mouthful of Madeira and took a folded paper from his pocket. 'I had a letter before I left, from Lady Mary Wortley Montegu. She is quite a traveler, you know.'

Law nodded. 'I met the lady here when she came to Court half a year ago.'

'Well, she has written to me that you have entirely subdued the French! Let me read you a passage.' His eyes went to the letter, and he searched for the passage. 'Ah, here! She says:

"And now I am speaking of the Court, and I must say I saw nothing in France that delighted me so much as to see an Englishman, at least a Briton, absolute at Paris. I mean Mr. Law, who treats their Dukes and peers extremely 'de haut en bas' (from high to low) and is treated by them with the utmost submission and respect, poor souls. This reflection on their abject slavery puts me in mind of the Place des Victoires..."'

Archie looked back at his cousin. 'She goes on. But the fact is, all of Britain knows you have secured an unparalleled foothold in the French Court, to say nothing of the commercial world. You have conquered and succeeded over difficulties and obstructions, which I must say, could only have been overcome by a man endowed with a sanguine temperament and gifted with extraordinary powers of persuasion!'

Law smiled at his cousin's words, then shrugged resignedly. 'And for it, I am so plagued by suitors for shares that I can get no rest night or day,' he said testily. 'How they stare at me everywhere I go.'

Archie laughed heartily. 'Stare, you say? Let me read you another passage from Lady Mary's letter, for the comments on French manners: *"Everybody here stares. Staring is à la mode. There is a stare of attention and interest, a stare of curiosity, a stare of expectation, a stare of surprise, and it would greatly amuse you to see what trifling objects excite all this staring."'*

Law laughed heartily. 'By God, she has it right, there!'

Archie nodded, returning to the letter. 'She goes on from the staring: *"It would have rather a solemn kind of air were it not alleviated by grinning, for at the end of a stare, comes always a grin. And very commonly, the entrance of a lady or gentleman into a room is accompanied with a grin which is dignified to express complaisance and social pleasure but really, shows nothing more than a certain contortion of muscles that must make a stranger laugh, really."*

Archie composed his face in a grinning grimace. Law laughed. 'That's it exactly, Archie. You've caught the look exactly.'

'Mmm,' Archie said and turned back to the letter. *'" The French grin is equally remote from the cheerful serenity of a smile and the cordial mirth of an honest English horse laugh."* He looked up at Law once again. 'And Lady Mary has not missed the walk. Listen to this!' Archie exclaimed. *"The Frenchman walks merrily, and seems to enjoy the vision and may not be estimated to be happier than any of your solid thinkers whose brows are furrowed by deep reflection and whose wisdom is so often clothed with the misty mantle of spleen and vapours."*

Law chuckled. 'She has certainly taken the measure of the French Court.' He sighed and came over to his cousin. 'But I see enough of them. Come, Archie. Tell me the news of home.' He paused, struck by a look on Archie's face. 'You look like a man who is hiding something.'

With the air of one who has unraveled the secrets of the universe, Archie reached into his leather case and brought out a large parchment document. 'Well then,' Archie said, underplaying his own excitement. 'I do have news that I think will please you.' Archie handed him the parchment, adding dramatically. 'John Law of Lauriston, you have been granted an official pardon from England for the murder of Edmund Wilson!'

Law looked at him questioningly. For a moment, he could not speak. He had not even thought of this possibility. He stared at the parchment.

'And surely all of France must be giving a prayer of thanks for your escape, which I abetted so long ago,' Archie added with a twinkle in his eye.

Law read it, then set down the document thoughtfully. 'I am able to come and go to England as a free man? Now, that it hardly matters anymore.'

'But it does matter, John. And you know it.' Archie reached into the case and brought out a small package. 'I have something else for you.'

Law unwrapped it carefully, taking out an engraved box. He looked at the lid. 'Of gold. From whom?'

'The inscription is inside, John.'

Law opened it and read the words engraved on the inside of the shiny surface: 'The City of Edinburgh grants John Law of Lauriston the Freedom of the City.' He was deeply moved as he looked back at his cousin. 'You were the instigator of this, Archie. Of that, I am certain!'

'I merely brought the matter to their attention,' Archie demurred. 'They needed little encouragement, I must say, for now, all the world has heard of John Law. You are free to return to Lauriston to visit your mother! And to bring your cabbage seeds to Scotland in person.'

There were tears in John Law's eyes. 'Thank you, Archie.' He tucked the parchment safely away in his desk, brightening. 'Now come, let's play a game of piquet as in past times, and I shall tell you what it is like with these Frenchies. The worst are the ladies, who pester me incessantly. I am followed to the point that I have no rest, night or day.'

Archie laughed heartily. 'I have never heard you complain of the ladies before.'

But Law was not to be pacified. 'Even the Regent's mother, the German Princess Palatine they call Madame, is constantly fluttering her eyes at me sending me billet-doux to attend her afternoon salons with her duck.'

'Duck?' asked Archie as they moved over to where a games table was always waiting with cards.

'I'll explain that later..' Law cut and dealt the cards with swift precision as he talked. 'Last week, I was surrounded by ladies at a ball and could not escape. They kept me so long that finally, I said I must excuse myself to piss. «Piss here and listen to us!» one of the ladies cried and offered me a flower pot!.'

Archie chuckled. 'What did you do?'

'I used it, then and there! And another time, an old lady came up to me in the Place Vendôme shouting, "Monsieur Lass!" That is what they call me here. "Monsieur Lass, make me a conception. Make me a conception!" She meant concession, of course. So I called back to her, "I think you are a little too old to achieve that condition, Madame." I swear, Archie, some of them would kiss my bottom for a share of the Mississippi.'

Archie laughed as he set down his cards. But Law was not finished with his tales of woe. 'There is one woman, Archie, who has chased me so much that I have had to give my servants orders not to allow her through my door under any circumstances. But she is not to be stopped. The other night she had her bearers carry her sedan chair to a house where I was dining, where, upon her orders, they gave out a fire alarm. Hearing it, all the guests got up from the table and ran out of the house. When I came out, she had her bearers upset her sedan chair in front of me. The lady tumbled out at my feet, her breasts escaping from her bodice. Shamelessly she did not even bother to tuck them in.'

Archie chuckled. 'The perils of fame,' he said.

'It is no joke, Archie. As I helped her up, I realized that she was the same woman who had been stalking me for weeks. The very same Madame de Simiani. She cried out, "Ah Monsieur Law, I have been trying to see you for so very long. Please, I beg you, allow me to buy one thousand shares of your miraculous stocks before I faint dead away!" She clung to my arm, not letting go of me. In exasperation, I turned to Will, who had been to dinner with me." Please arrange for Madame de Simiani to buy what shares she likes, Will." Only then was I allowed to free myself and get into my carriage.'

Tears of laughter streaming down Archie's cheeks, they continued to reminisce until Law finally gave orders to admit his waiting supplicants.

TWENTY-THREE:
A WEDDING IS PLANNED

Law had managed to convince Orleans that the progress of the State was being hindered by taxation, and he had been allowed to inaugurate certain tax reforms. The taxes on oil, tallow, and playing cards were abandoned. The duty on grain and vegetables moving between the provinces was abolished. The new company offered to develop fisheries without a monopoly. A single duty was imposed on tobacco. The growth of manufactures, the prosperity of the laboring class, and the revival of trade were there for anyone to see. The Bank was now borrowing and lending at only three percent interest. It would seem that Law had truly revolutionized France.

Months rolled by, and at the bank, William Law kept a record of all the Company's transactions, which he went over privately with his brother. His records showed that in June of 1718, the Regent had issued a decree stating that to purchase the latest edition of shares in the Mississippi, one had to possess old shares. The new ones were at four times the value of the old shares, which meant that to obtain ten shares of the new series, a person must own forty of the old series.

'And the Regent himself has become the bank's chief borrower,' John told Will, none too pleased.

'You certainly must stop him.' Will said firmly.

Law scowled. 'You know that I cannot.'

Since there was no solution, Will continued reading out his notes to his brother. 'On the 1st of August, we were awarded tobacco revenue for six years at 4,020,000 livres per annum. On the 4th of September, the period of the grant was extended to nine years. On December 15th, we purchased the privileges and supplies belonging to the Company of Senegal.' He looked up. 'The Treasury is surely swelling, John. But are we moving too fast?'

John Law did not have an answer. He was saved from in-
venting one by the appearance of a visitor being shown in. Seeing
that it was Vivien Duclos, Will excused himself, took up his book,
and left.

'Did you hear what people are calling your shares?'

'Impossible to obtain, I warrant,' Law replied with a wry
smile. 'Word does travel, even to my offices here at the bank, Vivien.
Yes, I've heard that the people call the shares *mothers* and *daughters*,
and each *daughter* must bring along her *mother* as dowry.'

She laughed. She had arrived in a new gilded coach with
two footmen and was dressed like an empress in a richly embroidered riding coat, displaying a cluster of rather gaudy diamonds at
ears and throat.

'Paris is the place to be!' she exclaimed. 'I have heard that
there are nearly five hundred thousand foreigners in the capital
and fortunately for me, a good number of them end up in my gaming house, so it is I who am the winner.'

'You certainly look a winner, Vivien,' he said with genuine
admiration. 'Red always was your color.'

She was too engrossed in her tale to spare time for a compliment. 'Lodgings are so scarce in the city that I have purchased the
building next to mine and turned it into a hotel.' She leaned against
his desk, provocatively. 'The people fall out of my hotel to buy your
shares then gamble their winnings at my tables. These days I accept
shares instead of money.'

'It seems I have made Parisians poor in the morning and
rich by night,' Law said.

You can have your little joke, John Law. But perhaps the
joke is on all of us who are purchasing these paper promises. Who
knows?' She smiled. 'But do not imagine that I am complaining!
I bought five hundred and fifty livres worth of *mothers* this very
morning and immediately doubled my investment right there in
the street. Then I bought again and tripled it! At the moment, I have
forty thousand shares,› she said somewhat grandly.

'I'm delighted to hear you are a rich woman, Vivien,' Law
said. His expression grew serious. 'But it is people like you who
are causing a run on the shares. I am afraid the *daughters* have just
run out. You, of all people, understand gambling, Vivien. And

gamblers. The shares are so sought right now, they are being bought at any price for ready money, or even on credit! Transactions are happening so fast that there is no time to exchange them for coin. Everything is now on paper—my magic paper—whose price rises every hour. Paris had become a madhouse, Vivien. As soon as a new issue of paper is announced, the streets are jammed with eager purchasers.

She threw him a tantalizing smile. 'I am so rich a woman now, John Law, that you might consider marrying me.'

He went to her and took her hand, kissing the tips of her fingers. 'I am not the man for you, my dear. Never was. We both have known that from the beginning.'

She nodded, gave him a lingering look, then moved to the door. 'Never mind. I shall go out and get richer on your marvelous shares. Perhaps I shall pick off a duke for myself.'

'Pick one that prefers women to his stable boy,' he said. 'Because you are an exceptional woman, Vivien.'

'Hmmm,' she said. 'You have not been to the casino in some time.' She reached up to kiss him. He did not offer his lips. Instead, put his hand in his pocket and handed her the key she had given him so long ago.

She took the key, looked up at him and smiled, then turned and left him watching the end of one episode of his life that would be no more.

Madness had truly overtaken not only France, but all of Europe was buying French shares, now selling at one thousand livres with immediate profits of one hundred percent. The next decree from the Regent created new shares, which were quickly called *grand-daughters*. The shares of the Company had reached two hundred percent when Orleans called Law in to see him. Law had heard that the two explorers he'd sent out to the colony, the Monsieurs La Mothe or Cadillac, had returned.

But when he arrived at Orleans' apartments, there was no sign of them. Instead, Law was greeted by an angry-faced Regent.

'How much of what you have told us is true, Law?' Orleans cried. 'Your emerald mountain seems to be invisible! Your gold mines, difficult to find, and even your silver seems of average quality. The only thing you have got right is that the lands are desolate and full of savages!' Orleans' tone had grown shrill with vehemence. 'Is France's explosion of good fortune at an end?'

'Everything takes time, Sir. As we invest our profits from these shares to develop the Mississippi, you will see the profits grow.'

'Grow? In a century, maybe!' Orleans peered angrily at his Finance Minister. 'Is this all another flight of your fantasy, Law? I have had your explorers, La Mothe and Cadillac report directly to me to hear the truth of your tales! They tell me that the wonders attributed to Louisiana by you are fables. Fables...!'

'I should like to speak to them, Sir,' Law said, alarmed. 'There are many things I must ask them.'

'Speak to them? I have sent them to the Bastille!' Orleans said with finality. The Regent was angrier than Law had ever seen him and not finished with his attack. 'Where is the personal fortune you have made from our great land, Law? Have you removed it to Scotland? Or would it be to Amsterdam?'

'Your Royal Highness,' Law said, 'I have given my heart, and all my efforts to France and certainly cannot be accused of draining the kingdom of money. You have only to examine my accounts to ascertain that all my wealth remains here, promoting France's economy, and I have spent my fortune on purchasing French properties. I have bought fourteen estates with titles and have given many Frenchmen employment to maintain them. I chose to buy otherwise derelict estates,' he added.

Orleans pursed his lips. 'Yes, the Duke of Sully has told me that you purchased the Marquisate of Rosny from him for one million seven hundred thousand livres, Law. A sharp price, I would say!'

'Hardly, Sir. The walls were damp and crumbling. The parks had fallen to ruin. With the money I paid him, Sully has invested in the Mississippi and is once again a rich man.'

Orleans nodded. 'Yes, yes, he was wearing a silk coat when I saw him, made by my own tailor. What else? What else?'

'I have bought the county of Tancarville in Normandy from Count D'evreux for eight hundred thousand livres. The lands of Roiffy, Guermand, and De La Marche. The L'Isle Bonne for five hundred thousand from the Marchioness Beaverton. And at your own suggestion, with the aid of Lady Knollys, I bought the Palais de Nevers as my town residence. I have also given vast sums to the poor, to hospitals, and charitable foundations, and have been generous to all.' He paused, softening his tone. 'Sir, I have also made a public abjuration of the Protestant religion and have become Catholic! I hope that now you can truly call me a Frenchman.'

'A Frenchman?' The Regent paused, relenting somewhat. 'Indeed, you are, Law. In heart and soul. Go now, But you can forget about La Mothe & Cadillac. I do not like people who bring me bad news.'

In December, John Law had become a Catholic in the Church of the Récolletes at Melun. He was rich, titled, and of unimpeachable position in the government. Now, nothing, it would seem, could stand in the way of John Law. And in one of their private interludes, Katherine had much to tell her newly 'Frenchified' lover about what was happening in Paris, in case he had not heard.

'Your speculators are calling themselves *Mississippiars*, Johnny. They speak a jargon intelligible only to themselves! It's *the language of the Mississippians! A*nd all of Paris talk of nothing but *primes, polices, cinq cents* and *petites filles, mères* and *filles.* They read pamphlets and pasquinades, cartoons and satires. And in the streets, they sing sonnets about Law and his shares! You must be the most famous man in the world.'

But flattering though it all was, Law was worried by what he saw and heard. He told Katherine, 'I know that you don't totally understand these things, my dear, but these speculators are destabilizing the market. They are turning it upside down. I must do something to stop them, but I am not sure how! Nothing seems to daunt them from speculation!'

Towards the end of 1719, all over France, reckless expenditure, and lavish display were the order of the day. The unwarranted escalating prices of Mississippi Company shares were not to develop the Louisianas but simply, to double the value of the shares. It seemed there was no controlling the situation.

'Several times in the last few days, old coins have been illegally withheld when a re-coinage was ordered,' John told Will.

'And the Regent is in no mood to be lenient on the transgressors. Now, since the public will not follow the Company's regulations and decrees, he has decided on a drastic course of action. Without consulting me, Orleans has arranged to maintain it, he announced, by force.'

'Force? What does that mean?' Will asked.

'I'm not yet certain,' Law said. For weeks, Law had tried but been unable to see the Regent.

They found out what Orleans had meant in January 1720. The Regent commanded his Finance Minister to issue a new decree, arranging another reduction of the coinage value. Now, the Mississippi Company was further authorized to search houses or even palaces, for coin and bullion—which was forbidden to be removed by anyone, from cities in which there was a mint. And all punishments were executed by the Mississippi Company in John Law's name.

When Law was finally called to a meeting, he found Orleans in an angry mood. 'You must do something, Law! This will not do! Your Mississippi Company is out of control! I have had my government agents seize gold and silver coin in the possession of a laborer named Boucher, from the village of Lumigny! At my instruction, they have confiscated his coin in the name of the Mississippi Company—for the benefit of the informer! That should bring the matter to public attention!' he told his Finance Minister.

This meant that Law's name would appear on that order, not the Regent's name. 'Sir, in such a case as Boucher, it may have been the right thing to do,' Law replied. 'But you are aware that offering such a bounty will encourage paid informers? Valets will betray their masters. Citizens will spy on each other. No one will be safe!'

'Precisely!' Orleans said with a smile. 'Certainly, now anyone hiding coin will live in constant fear of treachery now.'

A worried Law left the meeting unsure how to proceed. In the next few weeks, the Regent added to the ban with further restrictions to curb French spending in Court circles. Under a new penalty of confiscation and 10,000 livres fine. The wearing of—or even the possession of pearls, diamonds, and precious stones was forbidden. The ladies of the Court were forced to hide away their jewels for the moment. The Regent was in no mood to be lenient on the transgressors, and it was Law's Mississippi Company whose name brought the charges.'

Although upset by the Regent's tactics, Law could also see that it worked in his favor. When the Finance Minister was asked to appear before the Council chamber, he reported, 'The annual company revenue in the last two years has been 80,500,000 and 131,000,000 livres. This new prohibition will bring more than 60,000,000 livres into the kingdom in less than three months! Money that will be used to develop the Louisianas.'

The British Ambassador, Lord Stair, a man who had no love for Law, said too loudly and too often. *'there could be no doubt of Law's Catholicity, since he established the Inquisition, after having already proved transubstantiation by changing gold to paper.'* His remarks stirred laughter in the English Court.

Men of the Duke du Maine's cabal (who now called themselves the Quadruple Alliance) suggested ways to destroy John Law, and thereby, Orleans. A treasonous letter from du Maine to Lord Stair told him that some European States were concerned about Law's stocks and shares, worried about the new prosperity in France. The letter went on to say that if John Law's System were a success, the increased power and welfare of France would prove prejudicial to foreign interests—especially to England.

Lord Stair wrote immediately to the British Ministry: *"I do not flatter his vanity by putting into* (investing in) *his Mississippi. I do not think it becomes the King's ambassador to give countenance to such a thing. Or give the example for others in England to invest here, which many would have done. I could have made 30,000 or 40,000 Pounds if I'd put myself into Law's hands. But I considered it my duty not to do so. Law says he will raise France so high she will give all Europe the law. He could ruin the trade of England and Holland whenever he pleases. He could break our bank and our East India Company whenever he has a mind. He has said there was but one great kingdom and one great town, France and Paris."*

"Take my word for it, Law's plan is formed to destroy the King of England, and nothing short of Law's failure can save us from a war with France. He will do all mischief in his power, and you can't think that pow-

er too small. He has absolute authority over the Regent - who has absolute authority over France. I have tried every argument I could think of to make Orleans jealous of his power to no avail. Beware how you trust the reins of your chariot to that phaeton Law, for he will certainly overturn it".'

Judging that Lord Stair's machinations would only irritate Law more against England, the British Ministry accused Stair of trying to embroil England with France to gratify a private pique against Law. Earl Stanhope, Secretary of State, came to Paris to see Law for himself. He went away completely won over. Stanhope reported to the British Ministry that he considered John Law greater than Cardinal Richelieu, or Mazarine. The British Ministry was quick to decide which horse to ride. They recalled Lord Stair.

John Law asked for an urgent meeting with the Regent to discuss an incident that had taken place in a Paris tavern on the night of the 22nd of March, 1720. Orleans was already aware of it, and in fact, all of Paris was agog over it.

'We must let the matter drop, Law,' the Regent said flatly.

'With respect, Sir, how can we let it drop?' Law exclaimed with some amazement. 'On the contrary, we must make an example of it! The villain has robbed and murdered a rich stockjobber.'

'Count Horn is no villain. He is a Flemish noble, and he has just turned twenty-two,' Orleans said. 'It was merely a little youthful hijinks that got out of hand.'

Law looked at him, dumbfounded. 'Perhaps, Sir, you do not know all the facts of the case. This noble, Count Horn and two friends of his, invited the unfortunate stock-jobber to a private room in a tavern in the Rue de Venise on the pretext of sharing a bottle. Unfortunately, the stock-jobber got more than his share. These noble youths in their *hijinks* dispatched him with a poniard and divided his sack full of shares!'

'Well, well,' Orleans said, as though he could make the whole thing just go away, 'Count Horn was arrested and taken into custody, was he not? I think that now the best thing we can do is to send him back to Holland. He is allied to several sovereign houses, you know. Including my own.' He sat up stiffly. 'See here, Law, I do not care to let this go any further.'

' Sir, most people are carrying their entire fortunes around in their pockets these days,' Law argued. 'You might consider that if they cannot walk the streets safely, they will not venture out to buy shares. I must insist that it is absolutely necessary to make an example of this murderer. '

'Murderer. . .' Orleans nodded slowly. 'I do see your point, Law. If people are afraid to walk the streets, we would undoubtedly see a sharp decline in the company's profits.' He sighed. 'Very well, then. Corporal punishment, it must be. But not the guillotine. Count Horn shall be broken alive upon the wheel. I shall give the order.'

Law saw to it that Count Horn›s fate was well-publicized. On the 26th, a decree was issued ordering a guard of archers continued in the Rue Quincampoix, where some trading was still being carried on, to protect dealers from thieves and vagabonds and to preserve order in the crowd. That, it was hoped, was the end of the affair.

Later that week, there was a celebration for John Law in Philip's private apartments. John Law had finally been made a citizen of France. Taking his arm with a possessive air, Marie-Louise brought him over to Katherine Knollys. Her eyes rested on the Regency diamond blazing at Katherine's throat. To the annoyance of all the Ladies of the Court, the Regent had announced that he would allow this one jewel to be displayed since it belonged to the Crown.

'I hope you have enjoyed wearing that marvelous diamond, Katherine,' the Duchess told her father's mistress. 'You shall have to return it to my father soon, for I shall be wearing it at my wedding.'

'Then you are to be congratulated, Marie-Louise,' Katherine replied smoothly. 'I shall have it sent to your apartments.' She paused. 'Strange, but I do not seem to know who the lucky man is to be. Have you chosen one?'

'Hasn't Philip told you? How odd.'

Marie-Louise's eyes flashed with something akin to triumph. 'Since the Finance Minister is now Catholic and a citizen of France, he and I are to be married.'

It was quite true that John Law was now eligible to marry into the Royal family. The pieces all fit, and yet, Katherine was stunned. But she was far too good an actress to show it. She barely flicked an eyelash as she congratulated them both. But something in the look she exchanged with Law said she knew he would still visit her bed, and nothing had changed. Nor would it ever change between them.

On a bright sunny morning, a few days later, the Duke du Maine came unannounced to Marie-Louise's apartments. Mouchi let him in with some uncertainty. He and his great-niece had not always been on the best of terms.

'She is still abed, your Grace,' Mouchi informed him.

'No matter.' He waved Mouchi aside. 'We shall talk in her bedroom.' He gracefully manipulated his game leg across the room and opened Marie-Louise's bedroom door before Mouchi could stop him.

Marie-Louise had been day-dreaming about Law and her wedding gown, which was already being made. She sat up in her bed. 'Uncle! What is the matter? Has something happened to Papa?'

'Much has happened to him, my dear. All because of Monsieur Law. But, no, no. He is as right as he shall ever be, I am certain.'

'Then what is it?' she asked with a touch of annoyance. 'You haven't visited me so privately since I was a small child.'

du Maine came over uninvited and sat on the edge of her bed. 'I have something to tell you, Marie-Louise. And although you might prefer not to hear it, I think you will be grateful in the end.'

'What is it about...?' She hesitated, not sure whether to trust anything he might say.

'About Lady Katherine Knollys,' he said solemnly.

She relaxed slightly. For a moment, she'd been afraid it might be about Law. But Katherine and her father - that was a different matter.

'I have had the Knollys woman followed ever since she came to Paris. And I've investigated her doings in England.'

'But why, Uncle?'

'Security risk,' he replied. 'She has a great influence on your father, which affects the State, does it not?'

'Did you find out anything that would interest me?' she asked, already bored. The doings of her father's mistresses never demanded her full attention.

'There are reliable witnesses,' he said. 'There is not a shadow of a doubt about the facts.'

'Yes, yes,' she said. 'What facts, Uncle? You are maddeningly slow in the telling of it.'

'Very well.' He cleared his throat and eased his shorter leg over his other knee. 'Aside from her former husband, Katherine Knollys had liaisons with several men in England. One was no doubt, King William himself. Another was a man named Wilson. Wilson fought a duel over her and was killed. The survivor was sentenced to be hung. His escape from prison is believed to be abetted by Knollys herself.'

'So…?' Marie-Louise said. 'She has had a colorful life. Courtesans like her usually do.'

'That man was her lover. He still is!' He paused for dramatic effect. 'I am speaking of your future husband, my dear.'

She stared at him in disbelief. 'No! You are wrong!' She sat up. 'And even if that were true, whatever the past, he loves me now.'

He reached in his pocket, pulled out a sheaf of papers and handed them to her. 'See for yourself, Marie-Louise. The proof is all here. Count D'Argenson's secret reports on Knollys and John Law. A grassy bed among the sand dunes. Nights at a country Inn. His housekeeper at the Palais de Nevers has supplied details of their secret liaisons. A housekeeper appointed by Katherine herself, I might add. But a few shares in Mister Law's company have oiled her tongue,' he said with some pleasure.

Her eyes scanned the reports, fury growing inside her like a canker. Angry tears wet the corner of her eyes. 'Is my life never to change? Is it not possible that I could find love?"

Du Maine went on hurriedly, seeing he now had her full attention. 'Do you think a man like Law understands love, my dear? Do you think marriage vows made before a priest will make any difference to this newly baptized Catholic who can change his nationality and religion at will?'

Marie-Louise got up, tearing the papers in shreds as she crossed the room. She tossed them into the fire. 'I won't believe it!' she cried.

'Beautiful and desirable as you are, and no one can deny that fact,' du Maine said, 'Law is marrying you for power. Once you are his bride, the Scotsman's position in France is incontestable. And then he will toss you aside as my cousin Philip did your dear mother and he will continue his nights in Katherine›s bed.'

All the blood seemed to have drained from her. Her head felt light, numb, as his words flowed over her.

'He has used you ruthlessly, my sweet child. And you have played right into his plans by helping to make him Finance Minister and a citizen of France.'

A new look of realization came into her eyes. 'Law and Katherine... I have seen looks they exchanged,' she said, 'but I never thought...'

'Now is a good time to start thinking, Marie-Louise. And I for one, have already given the matter a great deal of thought. Why not teach the mighty financier a simple lesson in arithmetic?' du Maine suggested.

When Mouchi opened the door after du Maine left, she found Marie-Louise crying and laughing at the same time.

February 1720 found a worried William Law at the bank poring over figures. All morning, his brother entertained a series of noble visitors who sought his personal intervention in obtaining shares. Seeing the last of them leave, Will hurried into his brother's office with a handful of papers. Law was sitting behind his desk, staring out the window with a worried expression. It was a look he often wore these days. He turned to face Will.

'Every day, more of them arrive begging to buy. More notes will be needed to keep the price from shooting to the moon,' Law said.

'John, that's what I came to talk to you about,' Will began softly, knowing what he was about to say would not be news to Law but had to be said anyway. 'I have been going over last year's figures here.' He set a sheaf of papers on his brother's desk. 'May I remind you of the 120,000,000 new shares issued in September and again in October. . .' He paused as he pointed to the top sheet. 'Here, John. Here is the list of actual issues of notes.'

Law saw the escalation in all its simplicity. On January 5th, 18,000,000 shares were issued. February 11th, 20,000,000. March 1st, 21,000,000. He saw how the April and June totals soared dramatically to 101,000,000. He glanced at July's 240,000,000 more shares as Will pointed to the year's total.

'That's 1,000,000,000 shares we issued last year, John. And all the time the price has been rising. Your detractors, led by the Duke du Maine, say you are doing this to promote speculation.'

'I am as aware of the figures as you are, Will,' Law said wearily. 'And speculation is what I wish to stop. I have offered these primes with a view of checking the rise of the stock. I have done what I could to stop people from rushing to buy futures, hoping that shares will continue to rise,' he said. 'I proposed to deliver shares at 10,000 livres each, thinking it would scare them away. Instead, as we have seen, so many people presented themselves that our clerks could not write enough certificates and we were obliged to have them printed. However, that transaction brought 300,000,000 livres more into the treasury. Now, what exactly is troubling you?'

'Troubling me?' Will asked wildly. 'I'm troubled that the bank is loaning on margins now at two percent interest. That the prices are still soaring out of all proportion! Things are moving too rapidly! That's what's troubling me, John.' Will's brows curled into a frown. 'Where will it all end?'

Law rose and strode around his desk to face his brother. 'I have just written an order for the Company to put 30,000,000 more shares on the market. That should break the price. I want them to fall. But not too rapidly.'

William Law weighed this news before he spoke. His life had altered since coming to France. He had fallen in love with his French teacher, Mademoiselle Odile Saint Choux, and felt that now, his life was in France forever. 'The Company should be able to sustain the price for a fortnight,' he told his brother. 'And what about the necessity to print more and more shares to keep the prices from rising further? Eh, John?

What about that? There is not enough gold in the world to back up this enterprise.'

'Maybe there is, Will,' Law said thoughtfully. 'Since we have amalgamated the Mississippi Company with the Comparie des Indes, Orientales, et de la Chine, I have consolidated all France's rights and monopolies under one roof with the Bank. From now on, all monies and trade will be controlled from one source.' He looked at his brother, questioningly. 'Don't you see? All unnecessary charges of collection and management will be avoided by consolidating into one channel every branch of the public revenue. Taxes will be levied at the cheapest rate.'

Will looked apoplectic. 'Yes, yes, John. It is a wonderful projection. And it will add to the popularity of the company. But can you control that the right investments are made with these funds? Investments to develop the Louisianas, as you have told me so many times. But there is one weak link in the chain of command, is there not?'

John Law looked at his brother with the eyes of a desperate man and nodded. 'How can I control the Regent?' he asked, expecting no answer. 'His mind is on that diamond and chateaux and horses and the like when we are trying to buy ships and supplies.'

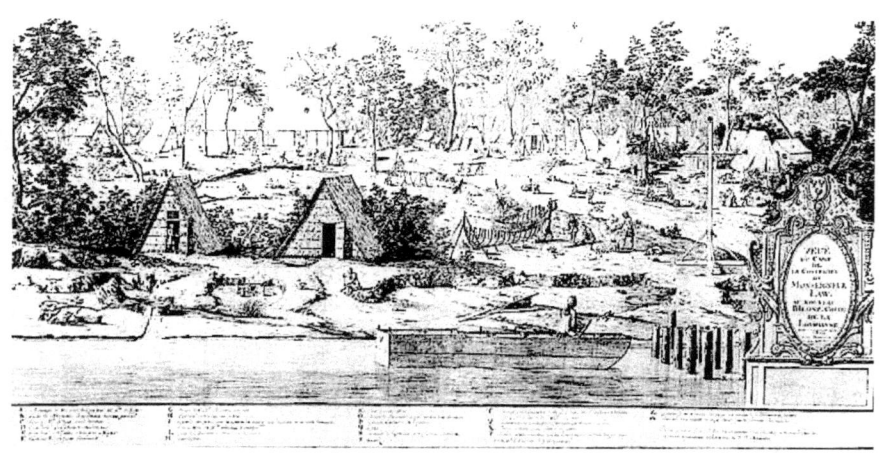

CAMP BILOXI, FIRST SETTLEMENT IN MISSISSIPPI

# TWENTY-FOUR: CHAOS!

Down the center of the Rue de Richelieu came a wagon, It was led by a shiny black coach, bearing the Duke du Maine's royal insignia. It slowed to a stop at the entrance to the National Bank, in the Hôtel de Mazarin, Helped out of his carriage by his footman, the Duke du Maine was flaunting the ban against jewels by wearing pearl-encrusted braiding on his elegant grey silk coat. Leaning lightly on a new ivory-handled stick, he made his way up the steps to the great doors.

People paused in the street to get a closer look at so mighty a personage as du Maine, who came to a halt on the top step. They watched as two of the Duke's footmen began to unload sacks from the wagon and carry them up to the bank's entrance, pausing just behind the Duke. He gestured to his footman, who banged on the heavy doors. A bank guard opened them.

A clutch of Parisians heard the footman's voice as he called loudly to the bank guard, 'I have brought the Duke's fifty thousand paper shares in the Mississippi System, for which the Duke du Maine requests immediate payment to the value, in gold!'

The bank guard opened the door wider and bowed to the duke. 'Will you step inside, Sir?' he asked.

Du Maine glanced around at the gathering crowd waving a lofty hand. 'It is a beautiful day. I shall take the air. What I wish can be done right here, to exchange my paper shares for gold of the realm.' His voice rose louder. 'Will the bank pay? Or are the shares worthless?' People whispered at this question from such a wealthy personage, here to exchange his shares. Word was swiftly passed along.

The bank guard bowed once more and went back inside. A moment later, William Law came to the door, opening it wider. He, too, bowed to the Duke and exchanged formal greetings. Aware of the crowd, Will said loudly, 'Every Mississippi share is backed by gold. You will receive full value, your Grace. May I entreat you to step inside the bank?'

'I do not see why I should be made to enter, Monsieur Law. My shares were bought in the Place Vendôme. I shall exchange them right here and now! Unless you have a problem obliging me!' His voice cut through the clear morning air—in case anyone in the crowd might miss his words. 'I wish to exchange fifty thousand shares in the Mississippi Company for gold!'

Once again, his words were repeated in the crowd. William, at a loss. was about to re-enter the bank when John appeared behind him. 'Good morning, Monsieur le Duke. We were not aware that you were such a big investor,' John said.

Du Maine smiled. 'I do not make a public display of my investments, Law.'

'Only when you dispose of them,' John Law pointed out softly. Then in a loud voice, he added, 'Your Grace may remain outside if you wish, but your shares must enter the bank and be counted. And I assure you that, like any other investor, you shall receive full value.'

He waved at the Duke's footmen, and the bundles of paper were carried into the bank. Law gave the guard an order, and a moment later, a chair was bought outside and placed on the top step. Du Maine sat on it, folding his gloved hands on his cane, sending another of his footmen inside to oversee the counting of the shares.

The Law brothers re-entered the bank and went over to the counting table where two clerks were already laying out the shares. 'Count it carefully, and see that the paper is all true, and no counterfeit,' Law told them.

Will signaled to his brother, and they re-entered John's private office. Behind closed doors, Will faced his brother.

'John, you know we have just made a payment to the Netherlands for ten ships for the Mississippi. We are very short of gold. If du Maine could wait only a week. . .'

Law cut him off. 'That is exactly what he would like, Will!

It would be all over Paris in an hour that the bank had run out of money.'

'In a sense, we have, for the moment,' Will replied, his brows furrowed.

'Immediate payment must be made to du Maine, even if it breaks the bank,' Law insisted angrily.

'But it will. It will, John!' Will whispered.

'That is not going to happen!' John said firmly. 'We will take the gold from my personal account.' Law turned on his heel going back into the bank and over to the teller for a word.

Du Maine's footman watched, eyes bulging as the gold was brought out and counted. The last gold piece was put into a sack, sealed and carried out to the waiting Duke. Law followed it out.

'Paid in full, your Grace. I hope your footmen are armed. That's a great deal of gold to carry through the streets of Paris. Perhaps you would prefer to deposit it in the bank for interest?' It was an idle question, more of a taunt, and he did not expect a reply.

Du Maine merely gave Law an indulgent smile. As his sacks of gold were loaded into his wagon, he turned back to the banker. 'I congratulate you on the soundness of the Mississippi. . .' He paused, his glance searched the far end of the street, and found what he was looking for. He pointed with his cane towards a royal coach, which was just approaching. It came down the street and pulled to a halt behind du Maine's coach '. . .since another shareholder has decided to sell.'

The footman hopped down from the new coach and lowered the step. Murmurs of recognition buzzed through the crowd as a second member of the royal family, the Duchess de Berry, emerged. Her audience was larger because the street had been filling with people. She made a spectacular entrance in a gown of gold cloth with a gilded feather head-dress. Like her uncle, she was followed by a wagon of sacks, much the same as that day she had come to deposit her gold; only these were full of gold, not sand.

Marie-Louise climbed the steps, pausing to kiss her uncle, du Maine. John Law greeted her, trying not to show his surprise. Beneath heavily lacquered cheeks, her face had no expression at all. 'I have come to exchange my paper shares for gold, Monsieur Law,' she fairly shouted. 'All of them for I have grown tired of paper.'

'Certainly, Duchess. Won't you step inside?' he asked.

She walked through the door past her uncle with a swish of skirts. Law took her arm, leading her none too gently into his private office. Once inside, he shut the door and released her.

' Why are you doing this, Marie-Louise?' he asked. 'Du Maine has bled us white just now! It would take weeks to raise the amount you are asking.' He stared at her, trying to see behind her stony façade. 'Are you trying to destroy the bank?"

'What do I care about the bank?' she cried petulantly. 'It is you I would destroy.' She pulled herself up, grandly. 'What a fool you must think me if you imagine that I've helped you build an empire, only to share it with my father's whore!' She waved a hand as he tried to speak. 'Oh, don't try to deny it. I have seen the proof. A record of every night you've visited her bed when my father was too drunk to service her himself. That is the measure of your love for me.'

What a fool he had been. He should have known du Maine would have his spies on him. 'I assure you, Marie-Louise, that relationship is all in the past,' he said with small conviction. 'It is you I have promised to marry.'

'And in whose bed will you spend your honeymoon?' she demanded.

'Marie-Louise, please think of what you are doing,' he said, taking her arm. 'It is not just me you will be destroying. This will be the end of the Mississippi Company—of your father—and all of France!

She did not reply but pulled away from him and marched back through the bank out to her uncle, pausing where he sat waiting for her, leaning on his cane.

Law followed her out. Behind him came the bank guards carrying two more sacks of gold. Law signaled them to carry it to Marie-Louise's wagon. 'The Duchess is receiving gold in full payment for her shares, at a handsome profit!' he said loudly to the crowd. Under his breath, he whispered to the girl, 'Heaven knows what the consequences of this madness will be...'

'There are always consequences, Law,' she said. 'For everything.'

Du Maine's words stopped further talk. 'Love spins like the

wheel of fortune, Monsieur Finance Minister. And when it falls, it lands on hate!'

Marie-Louise turned away from Law. 'I think I shall ride with you, Uncle.'

He rose from the chair engulfing Law with a weary smile of triumph and offered his great-niece his arm as her footmen loaded her sacks of gold into her coach. She turned once more to face her fiancé. 'Goodbye, John Law.' The eyes that met his were cold and empty as a bottomless lake and just as unrelenting. Then, with a swish of skirts, she walked with her kinsman down the steps.

The crowd watched silently as du Maine handed Marie-Louise into the carriage and climbed in after her.

Will and John returned to the bank and closed the heavy doors. The two carriages started away, followed by the two wagons of gold. They had scarcely ridden off when a wave of uneasiness ran through the crowd.

'Law's bank must be broke!' shouted a man who had been planted there by du Maine.

'If the rich and mighty are cashing in, we'd be wise to follow suit!' another shouted. Two youths raced after the last wagon, which was du Maine's. They managed to pull open a sack. Gold spilled over the cobbles. Frantically, men and women dove after the scattered coins, battling like pigs rooting for truffles.

'The shares must be worthless!' another of du Maine's man cried. Hearing him, a rush of people clambered up the bank's steps to cash in whatever shares they had in their pockets.

'Worthless! Worthless! The paper money is worthless!' came the cry that echoed the length of the street.

'I want my gold!'

'Foreign swindler!'

Some of the more aggressive in the crowd surged against the thick doors for entry. John and Will pushed the doors open and came out onto the steps once more. Law called out to them. 'People of Paris, go home and cool your heads! Tomorrow the bank will be open at nine o'clock. Now we are closed for today.'

He had not expected that his words would start a stampede. A flying rock caught Will on the side of the head, and he was knocked to the floor. Law pulled him to his feet and into the bank as cobblestones crashed through the windows before the guards inside could get the thick wooden shutters closed.

'I'll get the muskets,' cried one of the guards.

Are you mad?' Law yelled at him. 'You'll turn this into a bloody massacre!' He ordered them to lock the doors and the vaults, and he sent the bank clerks home through the back entrance. Four guards remained inside the bank with John and William Law.

Within the hour, the riot had swelled into a chaos of senseless destruction, and the street looked like a battlefield. Cries of '*Worthless! Burn the paper money!*' incited the crowd to more violence, and as night fell, bundles of stocks and paper money were being hurled from doors and windows. Torches and braziers illuminated the frenzy of the people. Someone built a bonfire in the middle of the street. And indeed, the flames were being fed with stock certificates and paper money. Several men got hold of a heavy flagpole. Using it as a battering ram. They rushed at the bank doors, crushing underfoot two men in the crowd who had fallen.

While the altercation continued in the street, Law and his brother remained barricaded inside the bank. Will, his head bandaged, was still lying on a bench. Oil lamps illuminated the tellers' cages' bars, throwing strips of shadow across the walls, shadows that reminded Law disturbingly, of Newgate Prison. The guards remained, awaiting orders from Law to fire on the crowd. Orders which Law refused to give.

Senseless violence had, as always, led to more violence. Trampled in the surge of people, dead bodies were hoisted along on the fringe of the human storm. Now the tidal wave of fury thundered back to the front of the bank. 'John Law! We want John Law!' came the chant of the mob. A man's voice called out loudly above the furor of the crowd. 'Look out your windows, foreigner! See what you have done!'

Law went closer to the window and peered out. The two bodies crushed by the mob were carried up and laid at the steps of the bank. Further down the street, he could see a figure hanging from a rope strung across the middle of the street. It dangled hideously in the flickering light of the braziers looking all too real. But it was not.

They had hung John Law in effigy.

JOHN LAW, 1720

TWENTY-FIVE:
ENEMIES AND COHORTS

In the street, people were shouting and pounding on the doors of the bank. John Law turned back from the window to Will, who was lying on the bench.

'I must go out there and face them, Will,' John Law said grimly. 'Make them understand.'

' You're mad, John!' Will cried. 'Those animals will tear you apart.'

'Maybe so. But I cannot stay here.'

'Then I'll go with you!' Will said, trying to get up.

"You can't even stand on your legs,' Law told him, striding to the door.

Outside, those closest to the bank were surprised to see the doors swing open and John Law emerge. The effect was like a jet of oil on a fire. A swelling roar of hate greeted him. He paid it no attention as he started purposefully down the steps and walked directly through the middle of the crowd. Automatically, they made way for him.

At Will's insistence, the bank guards followed Law outside and stood with muskets at the ready. The crowd fell back. uncertain of how to react. A hush fell over them as Law walked straight towards his effigy. Climbing up on an overturned booth, he withdrew a pocket-knife, cutting down the stuffed figure, then turned back to face the crowd.

'Never hang a counterfeit when you can have the real thing!' he called out loudly. Slowly, and with great authority, he pushed his way back to the bank and mounted the steps.

The silence was broken by angry voices shouting: 'Foreign thief! Scottish scum!' and other obscenities—but nobody dared to touch him. A wild-eyed woman, hair streaming in the wind, her gaudy garments torn by the riot, pointed towards one of the corpses. 'Here's the profits of your Mississippi, 'Sieur Lass! Trampled to death trying to sell your worthless stock!'

Now he was facing them from the steps and calling out, 'What is wrong with you French people, eh? Are you unhappy because a foreigner brought prosperity to France? What state was this country in, before I gave you a bank? Where have you seen such riches as your shares in my Mississippi System have given you already? And what have you done with your gains? Bought carriages and houses and fine clothes and jewels. But most of all, you have been buying and selling shares as fast as you could. Speculating! Sending the prices sky-high for a quick profit.' He looked across the crowd. 'Well then, how many here have profited already by your shares, eh?'

There was a grumble of agreement.

'Who among you has lost money— except by burning it up today?' he asked.

There was a hush.

'But have you given any thought to what those shares you bought so eagerly were created for? The reason why the Mississippi Company was formed? Can anyone of you tell me that?' He waited. Pure silence greeted his question.

He went on. 'Was it formed just so you could double your investment within the hour, and double it again in the Rue Quincampoix or the Place Vendôme? Is that what you think all this was about? Eh?' Law's eyes traveled across the crowd of upturned faces. 'And did you also believe that the bank's entire wealth—every golden nugget was kept within these four walls, to be at your immediate disposal? To hand out to you at your every whim?'

His eyes traveled across the faces staring up at him, for now, he had their full attention. 'What are these shares for? What is it you are sharing in? What is it that each of you has bought and owns a piece of, eh?'

They were silent. They were listening to him.

'Your gold has been invested in the lands of the Mississippi!' he shouted. 'That is where your money has gone. Being turned into ships and tools and seed and colonists! Men and women! Who will build the city of New Orleans! Because that is where your real riches will come from!' He paused. His voice had taken on the magical charisma of the man with ideas; the man who can sell them: can bring them to life. Can make them real.

'Look into the future, you French citizens. The future of you and your children! Not today, not tomorrow. Give it some time, and real wealth and security will come pouring back into France. Into your pockets. The wealth that will continue to grow and grow and make this the richest kingdom on Earth!' He recognized a face in the crowd that he had seen many times hanging around the Rue Quincampoix and again in the Place Vendôme. He did not know the fellow's name but suspected him of being an illegal stock-jobber.

'You there! Do you imagine that because this bank has used its gold supply for today that tomorrow, we shall have no more? The National Bank has banks in cities all across this country, do we not? Each of them stores the bank's gold.' His glance traveled down to the dead bodies. 'Look at the damage you people have caused in your foolishness. It was not the bank, not John Law. You. *You* have done this!›

There was a contrite murmured response. For the moment, the anger had been quelled. 'Go home! All of you. Take up your dead and bury them!' he told them.

Several men came forward and picked up the bodies. The street began to clear. Law could afford a confident swagger as he stepped back into the bank. He had won that round. But for how long?

Will had been listening at the window. He regarded his brother with some amazement. 'You have stopped them!'

'For now, Will. It's going to be all right,' John Law told his younger brother. 'It will blow over. Nothing can stop the Mississippi Company.'

But Law was wrong. Du Maine had put the wheels into motion. He'd sent news of the riot to Orleans even as it was happening, hoping to cause Orleans to panic.

And panic Orleans did. The next morning, the Regent sent word to Law to close the bank for the day on the pretext of a Treasury examination of the books. Orleans closed off several streets and ordered the Mazarin Gardens' gates, a popular route to the bank, to be locked and sent soldiers to guard them to prevent people from reaching the bank.

The sight of soldiers only added to the growing unrest in the streets of Paris. A huge crowd had gathered outside the heavy iron gates shouting for their gold. The soldiers were only allowing a small number of people at a time with sufficient identification and cause to be admitted through the gardens to the bank to see Law personally. Those outside the gates grew restless and began to throw cobblestones.

As the crowd's anger mounted and people were pushing on the gates, a nervous soldier fired, killing a coachman and wounding a citizen in the shoulder. But the fury of the crowd was too much for the soldiers, and finally, at a command from the Lieutenant, the gates were flung open. Inside, the soldiers were lined at attention with fixed bayonets. Only a few ventured to force their way in. They paid dearly for their daring. Several were wounded, and one man was run through with a sword.

Twenty people were suffocated in the push, and the Duke du Maine counted the day as his first victory. Convinced that he would be able to pick up the pieces in time to save the country for himself, the Duke began to finesse his plans to destroy Law, and with him, the Regent. But for the moment, Law had managed to transfer enough gold from other branches around the country to quell the unrest in Paris, and the bank was soon back in operation.

February and March rolled by, and the market picked up slightly. Things even looked as though they might return to normal—if normal was what the consequences of John Law's innovations could be called. His operations were constantly undermined by Orleans' complete lack of understanding of, or any real interest in, the project's purpose. The Regent continued to borrow heavily from both the bank and the Mississippi Company to pay the little King's debts. The chateaux, paintings, works of art, carriages, horses, gowns, and jewels for his uncle's mistress, daughter, and wife. In short, debts that the little King scarcely knew anything of, and luxuries Philip could not live without. All were paid for by the State.

'Is there no way to stop his insane spending?' Will asked as he came into his brother's private office with the latest expenditures and income figures.

Law sighed. 'Why are you so surprised, Will? You know the Regent does just as he pleases. When did he ever do otherwise?' He shook his head. 'For the moment, we must put up with it and try to hold things together.'

‹And for how long are we able to do that?› Will asked.

Law sank back in his chair. 'I do not know, Will. I honestly do not know.'

Will thought he had never seen such a worried expression on his brother's face even when he was awaiting the gallows.

Then one morning in April, an angry John Law came storming into the bank in a high state of excitement. He had not even bothered to put on a wig, and his hair hung wildly about his face. He took Will's arm, pulled him from his chair at the accounting table, and nearly dragged him into his private office.

'What is it, John?' Will cried as soon as Law had closed the door. 'What has happened?'

'The worst! I cannot yet believe it. Count D'Argenson has presented to Parliament an edict to devalue the money once again!' Law announced grimly. 'And they are accepting it.'

'But how can he do that?' Will tried to understand the consequences. 'Why, it would be an outright infraction of the Royal agreement, John. Whatever alterations take place in the coin, even D'Argenson, who is now Keeper of the Seals, is aware that old banknotes must still be paid in full.'

'Oh, yes, he knows it as well as you and I!' Law cried angrily. 'Nevertheless, he has done it, Will. And not only he! D'Argenson had the backing of members of du Maine's damned Quadruple Alliance. The Secretary of State, M. Le Blanc, and even the Abbé Dubois are in it.'

'And the Regent has approved it?' Will asked.

'Orleans has approved it, right enough,' Law said bitterly. ‹This time, he has teamed up with his enemy because he sees it as a way to wipe out some of his royal debts. He›s paid all the King›s creditors off with banknotes, hasn›t he? Now, by this—

this foolish, utterly insane edict, at one stroke of his pen, he has canceled 1,500,000, livres of loans to the King from the Mississippi Company!›

Will placed his palms down flat on his brother's desk with an air of finality. 'Then, the bank can say goodbye to credit and confidence. And without that. . .'

He could not finish his sentence.

Law nodded. They stared at each other, silent for a moment. Then Will broke the silence. 'You must go to see him, John. You have persuaded him before, and maybe you can still. . .'

Law cut him off. 'He will not see me, Will! I have tried.'

'I don't suppose Marie-Louise…?'

John frowned. 'Now? She sends my letters back, torn up.'

'And Lady Knollys…?' Will dared ask.

'The less she sees of me for the moment, the better for her.' John turned to his younger brother. 'Will, this time, you cannot aid my escape. And the wall I must surmount is higher than thirty feet.'

'It couldn't be worse,' Will said, crossing to the window as though expecting to see an angry crowd. The street was empty. But it could and did get much worse.

The final folly came on the 21st of May, 1720. Now, a second edict was approved by Orleans, which had been dictated by du Maine. Without a word to Law, Orleans had put it to Parliament. But Law got a copy of the edict and brought it to the bank. In his brother's private office, Will studied the paper his brother had handed him.

John Law sank into his chair. 'This is something I did not foresee, Will. It would seem that by this edict, the Regent›s enemy has become his cohort,' Law told him. 'Since I had no hand in framing this, and since Orleans still won't see me, I've written him once again to tell him how strongly I opposed his issuing it.'

'Yes, yes, 'Will said. 'The blame must not fall on you.'

'I thought to bring prosperity to this country, but today, a Frenchman could starve with 100,000 paper livres in his pocket.'

Will had never seen his brother this defeated.

The following morning when the Law brothers rode to the bank, they found the avenues blocked by the King's soldiers. Recognizing them, the Captain let them through, but there was no possible way for anyone else to get to the bank to exchange money.

As Law's carriage stopped in front of the bank, he turned to Will. 'There is only one thing left to do. Since Orleans will not allow a discussion of the matter, I shall ask to speak directly to the Council when this edict is read out!'

Will stared at him. 'You will be entering the lions' den, John.'

It was an extraordinary step John Law was taking. But a few days later, the Council agreed to allow him to be present when the King's edict was read.

'The King, having judged that the general interest of his subjects requires that the price, or nominal value of the Mississippi Company's shares and banknotes, should be reduced from this date to 8,000 livres, in order to maintain them in just proportion with the coin by 500 livres a month until the following December. Then they are to remain fixed at 5,000 livres. The banknotes are to be reduced equally.'

After the edict was read, Parliament allowed Law to speak. He spoke as strongly as he could against the edict, which he had no part in writing. He explained exactly what it meant in real terms and its effect on public confidence.

Many Parliament members were aware of Law's efforts to keep the Regent in check, and they listened. The discussion went on almost all day. Finally, to Law's relief, Parliament refused to implement the Regent's edict. And they also voted to curtail the Regent's *absolute power,* which they had so foolishly granted. But not all members sided with Law, and they were not yet finished with him.

Now, every day new voices were raised in the street to attack John Law. Many of them were secretly employed by du Maine. A few days later, when Law returned to the Palais de Nevers, he found a sealed note of warning, from Katherine. *'I have heard a secret report that Parliament has ordered you to be sent to the Bastille. You must get out of Paris at once.'*

But Law was still not prepared to run away. He posted a guard at Nevers and wrote to Orleans once more, wording this letter carefully:

'Monsignor, I have committed great faults, I own that. I did so because I am but a man. All men are liable to err. But nothing proceeded from malice or knavery. And you will find nothing of the kind in my con-

duct. I understand at this very moment Parliament is sending a party to seize me and to try and sentence me to death without delay. '

As Orleans read Law's words, it finally dawned on him that his own position could be in jeopardy if they were to arrest Law. And although he, at last, saw his blunder in issuing the fatal edict, he had no idea how to withdraw it. Still, he refused to see Law and sent him instead, a document conferring to him another title: "Counselor of the King."

Will was with his brother at Nevers when the news arrived. 'What does it mean, John? Why is Orleans honoring you with this title now?' Will asked.

Law shook his head. 'It is like all the titles Orleans hands out so readily, Will. Meaningless in themselves,' Law added, grimly. 'But this one has put me directly in the line of fire. Don't you see? Orleans is shifting the blame for his foolishness onto me, as though it is I who advised all his arrogant stupidity.'

'Yes!' Will said. 'Orleans has fallen right into du Maine's trap, and his 'Quadruple Alliance' has succeeded in producing complete chaos in France!'

‹du Maine will not hesitate to bring France to the brink of destruction!' Law said. 'He tried it once and failed, Will. But this time, he may succeed.'

Events were galloping to a head. On March 27th, Law came into the bank in a high state of excitement. He hurried Will into his office to tell him the latest news. 'Parliament has sent a deputy to demand the revocation of the Regent's edict of the 21st of May, Will, and what do you think he did then? Orleans has merely issued another one!'

'But how could he? Parliament has curtailed his power!' Will exclaimed.

'Curtailing him? Orleans has dealt with Parliament! He has removed them to Blois!'

'Blois? Why that's leagues from Paris, John!' Will exclaimed in disbelief. 'How did he force them to go?'

'He sent the Musketeers with four thousand soldiers to conduct them! All members of Parliament are to remain in exile until he allows them to return!' Law sank into his chair behind his desk; his wig was slightly askew.

Will stared at him in silence, hoping as always, that his brother had a plan. Finally, he asked, 'What will you do?'

Law shook his head and shrugged. 'I have done all I can, Will. And now the Regent has gone back to collecting the rents on Paris townhouses. Rents meant to pay off the Mississippi Company's original loan to the little King, which stands at 100,000,000 livres! And Orleans has recklessly canceled 1,500,000 more of the King's debts. Debts the poor child knows nothing of. And also 39,000,000 in interest, which Orleans already owes to the bank.'

Will stared at him in disbelief.

'It's a disaster, Will. I have written to him yet again and begged permission to lay down all my great titles and posts. But my pleas have been of no use. Now he does not even reply.' Law shook his head. 'I honestly see no way out!'

Will stared at his brother for a moment before asking, 'And yet you still think you must stay in Paris, John?'

Law nodded grimly. 'As long as there is one slim chance of putting things right, I must stay.'

Again, they were silent. Finally, Will spoke. 'Surely, this edict will lead to more riots.'

Law nodded. 'Orleans has taken complete control into his own hands, and he has no idea of the consequences. He is destroying the bank. Worse, he's destroying France!'

Law had correctly predicted the outcome. When the news of the rents reached the public, the paper fabric fell, and the banknotes lost all credit. Seeing himself losing control, Orleans took possession of all the leases in the Louisiana Territories belonging to the Mississippi Company and stopped the course of the notes. Then he ordered the bank closed completely. The date was the 29th of May, 1720. The date of the beginning of the end.

It was late by the time Marie-Louise returned to her apartments in the Palais Royal. Mouchi brought her the usual pot of chocolate and the single glass of brandy that she always drank before sleep when she slept alone. And except for the nights he had spent with her, the Duchess de Berry had slept alone since meeting John Law. Marie-Louise picked up the brandy glass and waved the chocolate cup aside with an imperious gesture. She downed the brandy in one swallow and handed Mouchi the glass. 'Undress me.' Her voice grated harshly against the stillness of the room.

Mouchi set down her tray and came over to her mistress. 'La,' she said. 'You must not fret yourself so, Madame! I am sure Monsieur Law will be able to prove himself innocent of any wrong-doing. You shall see, he will very soon be...'

Marie-Louise cut her off angrily. 'Do not speak of matters about which you know nothing!'

Mouchi began unpinning the diamond clasps decorating Marie-Louise's ivory silk skirt and sleeves. It was best to keep her mouth shut with the Duchess when she was in a mood. She did not care to be the subject of verbal abuse, which often enough she had been. It seemed that all of Paris was tumbling down around them, and the Duchess had not been her usual self since the troubles started. Mouchi knew that her mistress had made no effort to see Law. He had sent several messages, and Mouchi had watched Marie-Louise read them and tear them up. Tonight, after being with her father, the girl seemed more upset than ever.

Mouchie unhooked her mistress's gown, and Marie-Louise let it fall to the floor, stepping out of it. Her white skin glistened in the soft glow of candlelight. The faint roundness at her belly was more obvious now. She turned quickly away from Mouchi so the girl would not see it, and pulled on a pale blue silk peignoir, lying across the bed.

'Bring me a bottle of brandy, Mouchi. And take that chocolate away.'

Mouchi curtsied, took up the tray, and backed her way out of her mistress's bedchamber.

But she had seen the curved belly. Her mistress was so thin that even a pea would have stood out on that flat little stomach. This was gossip indeed! Mouchi sighed, wondering to whom she could tell it, as she hurried down the corridor. Now, what would happen to the widowed Duchess and this errant child?

Marie-Louise looked into the mirror, wondering what sort of creature was hidden behind the face she saw. Was she beautiful? Yes, even a modest appraisal must pronounce her beautiful. Many men had wanted her, and Law, too, had wanted her. His child inside her was proof of that. But what else had been inside of her that made her act so rashly?

MARIE-LOUISE

That night she had dined privately with her father and the Duke de Bourbon. For once, Katherine had not been there. The Duke had offered his sympathies about her marriage plans. She had said nothing. Louis Henri Bourbon and her father had talked about John Law. Still, she said nothing. The discussion had swiftly turned into an argument. She was surprised to hear Bourbon speak out in Law's defense.

'Not knowing Mister Law's merit, I went into the faction of the Quadruple Alliance willing to clip the wings of an aspiring foreigner,' Bourbon told Orleans.

Her father had merely nodded. 'Yes, yes. I have made him Counselor of the King.'

Bourbon frowned at the sound of the title. 'Sir, I now know him to be an estimable man. One might even say a blessing to the State.'

'Well, well, but the problems we are having with the bank...' Orleans' voice had trailed off. 'I expect my Counselor to take better care of these important matters.'

Bourbon stared at him. 'But surely John Law is the most wise, exact man ever was calculated for business, Sir. He is a fantastic fellow!'

Marie-Louise was surprised that Bourbon had shielded Law. Her father made no sense at all. And still. . . Still, she had said nothing. What was true anymore? What was right? What should she have said? That she had been the cause? That what had happened to her father and all of France at this very moment was because of her and her uncle? That her uncle, who knew how vain and foolish she could be, had turned it to his own advantage to destroy Law?

And why had she not seen it? Was she so jealously blind that the obvious was obscure? What did it really matter if Law had slept with Katherine? The English woman was a whore, and why should he not bed her if he chose? Men did those things. Her father did them. She did them; she always bedded whomever she pleased. Why had she let it matter so much? Is that what love was all about?

She felt empty, drained of all senses, of everything that she desired. There was nothing to care about anymore. This loss was too great, and it could never be replaced. She threw off her robe and went over to the table by her bed. On it was a large carved ivory box inlaid with turquoise, carnelian, and jade. A gift from some Oriental potentate. She lifted the lid and took out a small lady's pistol with a gold inlaid handle. The flint was in place, and it was always ready to fire. Marie Louise crossed back to the mirror. She wanted to see her face when it happened. Maybe she would feel something if she watched it happen.

She stood before her reflection, wondering why she didn't look any different. Even her belly was only slightly extended. Holding the pistol tightly to grip the trigger, she placed the mouth of the barrel against the swelling. Her hands were small, and the angle she had chosen was difficult. Her index finger tightened on the trigger, and she pulled hard.

The bullet went through her stomach more swiftly than she could have imagined. And the pain. . ! She had not thought about the pain.

A startled, frightened girl stared back at her. It was not the triumph she had expected. Unconsciousness was closing her eyes and mind when she slipped to the floor.

When Mouchi came in with the brandy, she found Marie-Louise crumpled before the dressing table, the gun still in her hand, blood streaming from her belly. With a cry that turned into a moan, she slid down beside her mistress, tears flooding her eyes, and took the girl's head in her hands, rocking the lifeless body back and forth.

John Law made his way from the bank to the Palais de Nevers and barricaded himself inside. Soldiers surrounded the building. He was surprised when his footman announced Lady Knollys. She was ushered into his study, and the footman closed the door discreetly behind them. The household was used to Katherine's sudden appearances. Weeping, she threw herself into his arms.

'I begged you to leave Paris! Why have you stayed?' she cried tearfully.

'I don't think I've ever seen a tear in your eye, my dear,' he said, kissing her cheek. 'Unless perhaps when you missed receiving some jewel, you were expecting.'

She was in no mood for humor. 'Oh, Johnny, you must go immediately! Your Mississippi bubble has burst!' she cried.

He pulled away from her, crossing to his desk. 'This is no bubble, Katherine.' he said. 'I started to build an empire. Cities. Farms! Do you think even du Maine and a few riots can destroy what I have started?' It's there, even if you and I cannot see it.

She looked at him sadly. 'Johnny, I must tell you... I thought you would have heard already, but I see that you cannot possibly have...' She broke off at his questioning look. 'Johnny—Marie-Louise is dead.'

He stared in disbelief. 'Marie-Louise...? But how?'

'She shot herself. Last night.'

Law sank into a chair. 'Why. . .? Why did she do it?'

'When she realized the calamity she had caused, she couldn't face you or her father—or indeed, France.' Katherine paused, seeing his face. 'Were you in love with her, Johnny?' she asked softly.

‹Love?› he asked. ‹You and I have always known we have no place in our lives for such emotions.›

She knew it was true. Love was not what he had felt for Marie-Louise. But Katherine was never in doubt that John Law did know love. Strange and twisted, maybe, but she knew it was the thing he felt for her. Whatever they might name it, that emotion was still shared between them. She stood up, regaining control of herself once more.

‹Philip has finally done as you requested, Johnny. He has stripped you of all your titles. You are no longer Finance Minister. He has canceled all your authority.›

His expression was close to relief. 'Thank God,' he said. 'Thank God...'

'No, Johnny! Don't you understand?' she asked. 'You are nothing now! You are finished in France. and there is no escape! No thirty foot walls to jump from the Bastille. Your fate is sealed. You must leave the country quickly because now they will kill you.' She reached into the satchel she carried and brought out a diamond necklace and a bag of gold. 'I know you too well, Johnny! You have held out nothing for yourself.' She handed him the money and jewels.

He began to protest, 'Kate, you helped me once before to escape death, but I cannot take these.' He rose. 'And I cannot leave Paris! Not while there's still a chance to save the Mississippi.'

She put a finger to his lips. 'There is no Mississippi! It is over, Johnny. Maybe there never was. Maybe it was all your dream and never a reality. But you and I, we have meant too much to each other to be less now. Goodbye, Johnny. At least for a while.' She smiled faintly. 'We do turn up in strange places. Perhaps we shall meet once more.'

She turned away without kissing him, not trusting herself to be in his arms again.

He watched her leave, weighing the odds. In his heart, he knew Katherine was right. About the Mississippi and them... She was in his heart and would always be. He put her jewels and gold into his satchel. It was true he had not taken one louis d'or with him from the bank and had almost cleaned out his personal account in an attempt to pay off creditors and stem the flood.

All for nothing.

But they would not bother Will. Will had no titles, no authority. He would be all right and stay on in Paris with his new wife if he wished. For he had married the girl he'd fallen in love with. Law was certain that Parliament would not actually close the bank permanently. No, that could not happen!

John Law sat at his desk and wrote a farewell note to his brother, assuring him that he would be back as soon as things settled down. Katherine was right. They were both survivors. It was time to retreat and fight again another day.

TWENTY-SIX:
THE GOLD SIGNET RING

When the Mississippi Company was shut down, troops were stationed in various quarters to bridle the fury of the mob. The life of the Regent himself was being threatened, yet he continued to give carefully screened public audiences in the Palais Royal, trying to uphold a façade of normality.

On the 29th of May, 1720, still unable to see Orleans, Law officially resigned. Philip appointed two companies of Swiss Guards to attend his ex-Finance Minister on the pretext of stopping him from leaving France. But with them came a personal note from the Regent, explaining that he had sent them to protect Law from the mob.

John Law was barricaded in Nevers, uncertain what his future might hold when he discovered that he had a few friends in unexpected places, even among the members of the cabal. As Marie-Louise had observed the last night of her life, Louis Henri, Duke de Bourbon, had changed his mind about Law after the second edict. Hearing that the Regent had stripped Law of all his titles, he wrote to Orleans. *The Mississippi Company, had it gone forward, would have exalted France to vast superiority of power and wealth over every other State.* "His words came too late. But still, Law did not leave Paris.

Against both Katherine's and Will's advice, John Law refused to leave until he had seen Orleans because he still hoped that even without him, something could be done to save the Mississippi Company. At last, on July 17th, he received a note from Orleans that he would see him.

He was on his way to the Palais Royal when once more he

was caught in a riot. Du Maine's men attacked Law's carriage with stones and broke it into pieces. The ruffians killed his coachman and maimed one of the horses. With the courage of a Cato, John Law climbed onto the overturned carriage and held up his arms for attention. Someone hurled a stone at him. It grazed his shoulder but did not knock him down. He stood up and attempted once more to vindicate his system.

Somebody shouted, 'Quiet! Let's hear what the blackguard has to say!'

'You have genuine complaints,' he shouted over the crowd, and they began to listen. 'I am on my way to see the Regent right now. As you surely know, nothing can be done without the Regent's approval. If you disperse, I will lay your case before him,' he promised. His voice recorded the genuineness of his position. 'Believe me; I want things returned to the way they were for the Mississippi Company and the bank. I want it more than all of you!'

There was a general murmur of agreement in the mob; nevertheless, a few people had been squeezed to death in the crush. Once more, they brought the bodies before Law like unruly children. He looked at them sadly and shook his head. 'Carry the dead to the Church of Saint Eustache. There is nothing to be gained by any more violence here!'

They let him go to see the Regent. That day he escaped with his life.

Law was determined to make Orleans see the truth of what he had done, no matter what the outcome. When he was ushered into the Regent's presence, he realized that Orleans was at last aware of the dangers to himself. Now, he was willing to listen to the advice of the man who had brought wealth flowing into his kingdom. The wealth that he had drained until it had dried up as swiftly as it had poured down upon them.

Law began with no thought of tactfulness. It was too late for that. ‹Sir, you surely realize that your edicts are so dangerous as to destroy everything. Everything, including your own office! The people were infatuated with the shares, and if we had let things ride, the situation would have settled down.›

He used the plural 'we' to soften the blame he was resting on Orleans.

'You could have paid off the King's creditors. The Company

could have easily paid its dividends. After all,' he reminded Orleans, 'there is an annual revenue of 80 million.'

'Yes, yes, 80 million,' Orleans said, waving it aside as though it were pocket money.

'We could have kept things floating. We still can, until the finances are flourishing once more! The bank could answer all demands made on it of the paper money you issued—without my knowledge. Without the knowledge of your Finance Minister!' It had to be said. 'Sir, if that money were now destroyed!'

Orleans stared at him. 'Destroyed...?'

Law nodded. 'The Bank still controls everything; does it not? All the revenues, all the trade! The government can still earn back the confidence of the people.' Law took the plunge. 'Sir, the Company could still realize its dream. To develop the Louisiana Territory.'

Law had expected anger from the Regent, resentment at being questioned. Maybe even fear at his own position. But Philip looked as though he hadn't understood a word.

'Go home, Law. The Swiss Guards will continue to protect you.' He paused, a worried frown flickering momentarily across his face. 'I shall give the matter some thought.'

Law saw that he was talking to deaf ears. He nodded, bowed, and left. No sooner had he returned to the Palais de Nevers than officers of the police came to arrest him and take him away. The Swiss Guards stood aside. He thought they would take him to the Bastille, but to his surprise, he was brought before the Duke du Maine and Count D'Argenson, who once again had been put in charge of police activities.

Du Maine studied Law with interest, a thin smile lighting his angular features. Finally, he rested both gloved hands on the head of his cane and spoke, his voice triumphant. 'You are a remarkable fellow, John Law. A worthy adversary, I readily admit. A man gifted with rare powers of observation and perception.' Du Maine leaned forward to inspect his enemy's face more closely. 'I give you full credit for your inspiration. And I don't mind saying that if you had brought your schemes to me in the first place, one day, I would have made you King of Louisiana.'

'Perhaps you would have, Your Grace,' Law replied sharply. 'If I had made you King of France.'

'Quick of wit. Yes, you have been a formidable opponent. But the game is up.' Du Maine touched the lace at his throat thoughtfully. 'Though for the moment, unfortunately, you are still too popular a figure with some for me to send you to the executioner. So what to do with you, eh?' He did not expect an answer. 'I am prepared to offer you money from my own account in Holland. The gold in that country, as you are aware, is of quite solid value. I am speaking of a sizeable amount if you will leave this country at once. Count D'Argenson will personally escort you safely across the border.'

He held out a bank draft drawn on the Bank of Amsterdam. It bore his signature. He paused. 'You have a choice. My generous offer, or the Bastille. I have already called Parliament into a special session to order your execution.'

Law took the bank draft and pocketed it. His gesture required no reply. D'Argenson's police guards marched him out to an unmarked carriage. The Count joined him inside the carriage, and they rode in silence until they were outside the city. Once on the highway, D'Argenson stopped the driver and ordered Law out. He climbed down with him.

'I am a man of honor, Monsieur Law. I will not kill an undefended opponent,' D'Argenson said. 'We shall fight a duel.' He signaled to one of his men who brought out a boxed pair of French flintlocks with delicately inlaid butts. 'I hear you are too good with a sword.' He indicated the pistols. 'These are a fine pair by Barthelemi Rousset. I think you will find them to have a true aim.' He paused. 'Your choice, Law.'

'And if I kill you?' asked Law.

'In that unlikely event, my men will take you where you wish,' D'Argenson said.

Law chose a pistol and walked away, the required ten paces. Once more, he faced a man for life or death. The Commander of Police gave the count. Two bullets unleashed themselves at precisely the same moment. Law's bullet hit D'Argenson in the arm and felled him. The Scotsman was shaken but not hit.

The Commander bent over D'Argenson, then looked up at John Law. 'The Count is wounded, Monsieur, but he will survive.

We shall take him back to Paris. He does not wish you to speak of this. Where would you care to go?'

'That is my business. Give me a horse,' he said and shoved the pistol inside his belt. He called back to D'Argenson. 'Tell du Maine he bet on the wrong card.'

John Law rode back to Paris and straight to the Palais Royal. This time he brooked no interference by the guards, and Orleans admitted him to his private apartments at once.

'Were you aware, Sir,' Law told the Regent, trying to restrain his anger, 'that the Duke du Maine had called Parliament into a special session to order my execution?'

Orleans nodded uneasily. 'Parliament is not on my side at the moment, thanks to your bank. What did you expect me to do about it?'

'I shall not moderate my words to you, Sir,' Law said flatly. 'Because the fact is, that one hour after my neck is broken, the Duke du Maine will be Regent of France. And although it was not I who stripped the bank of its resources, I still have a weapon to save your Regency.'

He handed the Regent du Maine's bank draft drawn on his Dutch bank account.

Orleans stared at the note. 'What is this?' he demanded.

'Money du Maine gave me to leave the country.'

'You are giving me this?' Orleans asked with some distrust. 'Why?'

Law's face looked pale in the flickering light of the log fire in Orleans' private reception room. 'Sir, what Frenchman would allow the Duke du Maine to become Regent of this great country when he hides his own gold in Holland? I will stake du Maine's bribe money on keeping you in power!' His tone became more earnest. 'With your kind indulgence, I am now a citizen of France. But I shall leave this country as you request. I will take with me nothing from all my houses and personal bank accounts. All the trappings of wealth and position I have achieved in this country. I shall leave willingly because I believe you can yet regain the confidence of the country. I do not doubt that this storm will blow over. I ask one thing only.' He paused.

'What, Law? What are your conditions?' Orleans asked

with a hint of distrust.

'I want your word that you will bring me back to France. We can yet rebuild the Mississippi Company. That is the only thing that matters to me now.'

Philip looked at him, thoughtfully. He took a long moment before he replied. "Yes, yes. But let it be understood that I have done nothing that was not within my power as Regent.' He paused, reflecting. 'But perhaps you are right about one thing, Law. Perhaps it is better if you leave, for the present.' Orleans studied Law for a moment, then removed his gold signet ring containing the royal seal. 'I shall make you that promise, and when I send for you, my ring will get you safely back across the border.' He handed it to the banker.

'When exactly will that be, Sir?'

'When the time is right,' came the vague answer. Orleans paused, looking closely at the man who had changed his life and this kingdom more than anyone had before, or ever would again.

‹I assure you of my unalterable regard, Law. But now, if you stay, I fear I can no longer protect you. Wherever you should choose to settle, you shall be taken care of.› He nodded thoughtfully to himself. ‹I promise to remit to you the pension of Comptroller General. You shall have an income until you return, Law.› He paused once more. ‹Where do you think you will go?›

Law slipped the ring on his finger. The Regent had chubby hands. It fit the middle finger of his left hand, 'I know every city on the continent. And every gaming house, Sir. I shall go somewhere where the gambling is good. Perhaps Venice.'

'Gambling! Yes,' the Regent smiled. 'You are a genius at that. You shall make another fortune.'

Law left Paris with the sound of voices ringing in his ears. They were singing street songs and pasquinades along the Rue Quincampoix.

The French, he thought, seemed as delighted to revel in their disasters as their triumphs. Cartoons appeared in the streets,

MONSIEUR QUINCAMPOIX
"ALL OR NOTHING"
My shares which on Monday I bought
Were worth millions on Tuesday, I thought.
So on Wednesday, I chose my abode.
In my carriage, on Thursday, I rode
To the ballroom on Friday I went
To the workhouse, next day, I was sent.

Law went directly to the Chateau Guermand, six leagues from Paris, one of the run-down estates he had purchased the year before. After all, he was not certain if Orleans really intended to allow him to leave the country, and he would need more than the

Regent's ring to escape across any border. He did not even have a passport, and he was not certain what to believe. All he could do was wait. His brother had written him from Paris to Guermand that debts were being heaped at his door. Even though the bank was officially closed, the bank clerks who had been ordered to remain at home were demanding to be paid, nevertheless. And there was still the threat of death hanging over Law's head. Finally, in despair, he wrote to the Duke de Bourbon, telling him of his plight.

> *'I have reserved nothing for myself, not even what I brought into the kingdom with me. Consider, my Lord, if being here in the country, removed from my papers and books, it was not in my power to put in order affairs that required not only leisure but also my presence in Paris to arrange properly. And if it is not a piece of great injustice for the Mississippi Company to wish to take advantage of the condition to which I have been reduced and at the dishonest conduct of clerks in requiring from me a payment of sums, I do not in fact owe. No, my Lord, I cannot bring myself to accuse the company of so much as the intention to injure me. That company owes its birth to me. For them, I have sacrificed everything, even my property and my credit, being now bankrupt, not only in France but in all other countries.'*

The Duke had been lucky with his shares and had cashed in long before the bubble burst. He'd purchased vast properties with his profits and had built Chantilly, a palace of regal magnificence. It was better stocked than the King's with one hundred and fifty of England's best racehorses. The nobleman owed a great debt to Law—and Katherine Knollys was not going to let him forget it. She was able to meet with Bourbon privately and ask for his help.

'It is true I have made a little money from your former countryman,' the Duke de Bourbon acknowledged to Katherine. 'Therefore, I shall take immediate steps to come to Law's aid.' He was as good as his word.

At Guermand, Law received Bourbon's letter saying that he had spoken about his plight to the Regent, who had ordered two passports permitting Law to leave the kingdom at Bourbon's request. Bourbon offered to supply Law with *'the sum you require to defray your traveling expenses.'*

Law declined the offer of money, saying that one of his

clerks had brought him eight hundred louis d'or—the balance of his own account. He had only ten *pistoles* in specie left.

But Bourbon came himself to Guermand and brought a post-chaise belonging to his mistress, Madame de Prei. She, too, had profited heavily by investing in Mississippi shares and was more than grateful to Law. The Duke's servants wore dark sour-touts covering their liveries so that the Duke would not be recognized paying a visit to the disgraced ex-Finance Minister. Bourbon told Law that Orleans had promised the passports soon. It was all arranged. 'But my dear sir,' Bourbon entreated, 'you must get ready to leave the moment they arrive!'

To his surprise, later that day, Katherine arrived at Guermand with a catholic priest. She reminded him whatever happened in France, without him there to fight for himself that in times of trouble, men went back to their wives, and Orleans would certainly tell Katherine to leave. But if she and John Law had secretly married, she would be able to leave France and join him gracefully. She had brought the Catholic priest and had arranged all the legal papers, ready for both of them to sign.

If this is what you want, Katherine, we shall be married. Would you like to come with me? he asked.

'Not now', she told him. ‹You will be safer for traveling alone. But you will write to me where you are—and I will do what I can to arrange your affairs with your brother if there is any way to save your Mississippi Company for you to return.

They were secretly married that day, and she returned to Paris with the priest.

Law made immediate preparations for his journey. And as promised, the next day, Messrs de Lassay and Faye arrived at Guermand with two passports and a large sum of gold, which Law grandly declined. Later, he would regret such gestures. The name on his fictitious passport was *M. du Jardin*. It was a name suggested by Law, who had called himself Gardener in his distant travels through the Americas. He sent the last note to Katherine, wording it carefully, fearing it might fall into the wrong hands.

Then, on December 22nd, 1720, John Law left all his estates and possessions—everything in his material world. Left all those closest to him, a new wife and a brother, and once more set forth on a vagabond course.

In Mme de Prie's post chaise, he headed for Brussels on a cold winter's day, attended by four of Bourbon's gentlemen of the horse and six-horse guards. The Duke had arranged for relays set up along the way. When the post chaise was stopped at the large village of Valenciennes, Law was uncertain what to expect. The Governor was called out of his office to question the traveler. Law handed over the fake passport in the name of M. du Jardin.

The Governor took it but did not return it. 'I know who you are, Monsieur Law,' he said. 'You are wanted in Paris, I believe. I shall have to detain you.' Law showed him his correct passport and the Regent's signet ring, then produced a letter from the Regent to the Duke de Bourbon, explaining the different passports and granted Law to leave the kingdom.

The Governor acknowledged the letters, and his attitude changed immediately. He, too, had profited by Law's shares. He handed Law back the passports and invited him into his home. When word leaked out exactly who had arrived in Valenciennes, several people came to pay Law honor and respect.

To his relief, Law was soon on his way again with food packed for him for his journey, and a week later, he arrived safely in Brussels. He sent back the carriage with a polite letter of thanks to Madame de Prie and enclosed a diamond valued at 100,000 louis d'or. It was one that Katherine had given him. Although he knew he might be taken to the Bastille and hanged if he returned to France, John Law would be considered a free man in England and Scotland. It was time to go home. He stopped to rest for a few days in Holland and wrote to Janet to expect him soon. He had not seen his mother for twelve years.

Katherine Knollys had not been idle. She paid a call on William Law, told him of the secret marriage, and offered to help in any way she could. Will was still in Paris settling the bank's accounts, for he firmly believed that the Regent would bring his brother back. He himself was not inclined to leave Paris for he, too, had become Catholic when he married Mademoiselle Odile Saint Choux. Over the next few months, with William Law's help and her own money, Katherine discharged most of John Law's debts, including 10,000 livres owed to a cook at the Palais de Nevers.

DUTCH CARTOON OF LAW

In Scotland, the years had been kind to Janet Law. Although her hair had gone grey and she seemed thinner, her back was as straight as a young woman's, and she had not lost the sparkle in her eye. When John Law finally arrived at Lauriston, mother and son threw their arms around eachother, and held one another without a word. But there were no tears. Too many had been shed in the silence of Janet's room.

That evening before dark, Archie arrived in his fine new carriage. They sat around the large open fireplace, and Law told his mother stories of life in the French Court. Archie assured her every word that Law said was true.

'I am certain that all of this can be put right, Mother. Before the year is out, I shall be called back to Paris,' Law said. 'You shall tire of having me around and be glad to see me go.'

Janet asked about Will a dozen times, and as many times Law satisfied her, his brother would not suffer for any blame thrust upon himself. He described Will's lovely wife and said he was certain that perhaps his mother would travel to Paris as soon things had settled in Paris. She nodded, but neither of them believed his words. He showed her the Regent's ring and told her that he must let Orleans know his whereabouts at all times.

'Of course, he wants you there by his side! Orleans cannot do without you,' Archie told his cousin with more assurance than he felt. 'As soon as Parliament sees how necessary you are to the bank and the Mississippi Company, they will call you back. Meanwhile, I am sure Will can keep things running.'

Law nodded but did not reply.

Janet spoke up. 'Of course, you are right, cousin Archie. John has done so much for their country.'

Several weeks went by, and Archie had been staying with them. Privately, he told Law that he had brought his name up before the Scottish Parliament, but they were firm in refusing to invite him to speak before them. And there were no letters from France. Not even from Will.

'They are probably stopping any post that might be sent to me,' Law told Archie. But he did not pass on his worry to his mother. Finally, Archie, who had his own affairs to attend to, bid his cousin a warm farewell and went home.

After a few more weeks of idleness, Law grew restless. Now, his world was too big for the confines of Lauriston. Janet noticed his restlessness, but she was not certain that the Regent would call for his services again.

'You must find something to do here in Scotland, John. While you wait,' his mother told him. 'Like your father, you were never a man to sit with idle hands.'

He nodded, for it was true. Then his face lit up.

She knew that expression. She had seen it on her son's face when ideas and schemes had been in his mind. 'You have thought of something, I can see, Johnnie. What might it be now?'

He stared out of the long drawing-room window down to the Firth of Forth. A small ship could be seen sailing by. Where was it heading, he wondered? But his mind turned to a new idea. 'Perhaps I can start a little industry here in Scotland, Mother. Something to improve commerce. There is little here that benefits the Scottish economy that I can see.'

He told her that he had seen great bolts of white cloth stretched out in the fields while traveling through Holland. Curious, he had stopped his coach to discover what the people were doing, then sought out the owner and introduced himself. 'The man had heard of me, although he'd not been an investor in the Mississippi, Mother.'

'Well?' asked Janet, 'Whatever were they doing?'

'Bleaching linen by a method unknown in England or here in Scotland. The owner was honored and, I must say, somewhat surprised that a financier might be interested in the simple techniques of his trade. But I tucked the information into the back of my mind, thinking one day I might find a use for it. And I shall put the system into practice here in Scotland. . .' His voice trailed off. '. . .while I wait for word.'

She looked at him in wonder. This brilliant son of hers who'd so recently had the weight of a nation on his shoulders, who was like a magician performing miraculous feats she could admire. However, not fathom, that he could now occupy himself with something so trivial.

Law wasted no time in looking for the right location. A few miles south of Lauriston, he found the ideal spot at Roslin and set up the first bleach field for Scotland's linens. He worked at this business for several months, long enough to establish it. Then once more, the restlessness grew beyond containment. Scotland was no longer his world, and he could wait there no longer.

Janet understood and suggested that the time had come for him to leave Lauriston. He agreed almost too hastily. They said a fond goodbye, and John Law was on the move again.

Traveling aimlessly on the continent under the name of M. de Jardin, he stopped at Lislebonne, where there was a fine casino. The cards and dice still afforded him his best means of survival, and

Law stayed long enough to win some land at the gaming table. But as he won too often at Lislebonne, he was asked to move on.

At each stop, he wrote to the Regent, hoping for a reply. There was none. Finally, he had a letter from Katherine. She wrote, *"I feel the same in myself,"* which meant her feelings had not changed, and *"I shall not let Orleans forget you."* She repeated a conversation she had overheard between the Regent and Louis Henri Duke de Bourbon, of whom she noted: *'His love for his sister-in-law does not prevent his loving his pages as well. He is, I fear, tainted with the prevailing vice of the time. When he and Philip were arguing about how you got out of the country, Johnny, Bourbon said that you acted on orders of the Regent. Philip denied it, saying that the Prince had given you the passports.*

'Bourbon admitted it was true, but he added, not wishing to take the blame on himself, "But Sir, it was you gave me the passports and charged me to carry them to him. It was you who wished him out of France. I merely opposed sending him to the Bastille or delivering him to Parliament. We could have said or done nothing against him that would not have recoiled on us."

The words stung. Law had believed Bourbon to be a true friend. Anger welled in him as he went back to Katherine's letter.

'Of course, as you would expect, Philip grew angry at being challenged, and his face became crimson, and his voice croaked. You have heard him thus, when he is excited, Johnny. "But at least," he shouted at the Prince, "I did not send the carriage or your guards to escort him. You were much more interested in his safety than me. I suffered him to leave the kingdom because I feared his presence would impede the cure of the disorders of the state and obstruct new maxims of government!" You should have heard them, Johnny.'

Law folded the letter. He had been made a scapegoat. Yes, and he had too readily accepted the role because of Philip's promise. He tried to tell himself that Orleans needed him and that he would be sent for. Law had to focus his mind on that, although in his heart, he realized the truth.

There was also a letter from Will. To his shock, his brother told him he had been sent to the Bastille for a short time. But Parliament could bring no charge against him, and so they were forced to release him.

However, all Law's property and holdings had now been confiscated by the Crown.

'*They said that you and I owed eighteen million livres to the bank.*' Will's letter reported, *But I proved to them the charges were false when they inspected our books. The balance, in fact, showed that the bank owed us several million. I fear, dear brother, you shall never see your property again.*'

Property? What did it matter? He had won and lost fortunes many times. When he returned to Paris and had the bank and the Mississippi Company running as before, he would buy a palace bigger than Nevers if he wished. But for now, he must somehow hold his dreams and survive and wait.

When John Law arrived in Italy, he had only £1,000 left of his French fortune. Venice's city of canals was a swirl of aristocrats, rich merchants, bustling with social activities, and the pleasures of the Carnival. Law headed for the famous Ridotto gaming house. Always a man of large gestures, he staked all his money against 100 lira, that double sixes wouldn't be thrown six times running. He had done it before and won.

So many people crowded around the table to watch and place bets that he not only won but this time, he doubled his stake. Lady Luck was on his side! With his winnings, he was able to rent a small palace and, for the moment, to live in some style. Law was quick to make important friends and counted among them, the Imperial and French Ambassadors, Cardinal Alderomi, the Spanish minister, and Chevalier de St George. All had interviews with *M. De Jardin*, and all knew his real identity.

However, Will wrote to him that in France, he was still being plagued by debts. At the advice of Cardinal Alderomi, John Law had his name enrolled on the list of Roman citizens, thereby being exempt from arrest and prosecution for debt, other than by another Roman citizen.

But local government officials had heard of his constant winnings. One of them had even lost money to him. Knowing his reputation, while no one accused him of cheating, he was promptly prohibited from further gambling in Venice. Although his new friends spoke on his behalf to release him from the prohibition,

John Law knew it was time for him to travel on. So on the 15th of March, 1721, John Law left Venice for Ferrara, on his way to Rome. But he had made a few friends, and one of them informed him that some of his French creditors had assigned their debts to a certain Roman citizen. He would be arrested on arrival in Rome! Law hastily returned to Venice, packed his bags, and left Italy altogether.

It was just like the old days. Little money. Miserable carriages. A series of drafty inns with another bed almost every night. *M. De Jardin* traveled to Bohemia, then moved on to Hanover—where, finally, as John Law, he was granted an audience with the parsimonious Frederick William, King of Prussia.

Indeed, the Hanoverian Court was the opposite of the lavish French Court. Law was told that Frederick had sold anything worth money in the palace to wage his wars and had replaced them with the plainest of furnishings. Except for the official translator, few at Court spoke English, but they treated Law with great civility.

Frederick's wife was the daughter of England's now reigning King, George I. Law had heard that King George didn't speak English either and that his Prime Minister, Sir Robert Walpole held great power. He filed this information under *Things to Remember*— should he ever return to England.

And then one day, while in the Prussian Court, he finally received a letter from the Regent. He tore it open with trembling fingers, reading the words. 'You are not forgotten, Law. I assure you that when the time is right, I shall send for you. But the time is not right. Not now. Not yet.'

Orleans had scrawled an effusive signature. There was no money, not even one of Law's old paper bills, which would have had no value anyway. He crushed the letter in his fist. The time...! When would it ever be right again? Law wondered. Once more, following the pattern of his life, Law moved on. This time, to Copenhagen. It was there that he received an invitation from the British Ministry to return to England. At last! Happily, and with lifted spirits, he embarked on the Baltic Squadron, a ship commanded by Admiral Sir John Norris.

John Law set foot once more on British soil on October 20th, 1721. Since 1707, the kingdoms of England, Scotland, and Wales together were known as Great Britain. And although now a French citizen, he was still a subject of Great Britain. He could see no future for himself in Scotland and had ideas of settling in London until he could safely return to France, so he rented a house in Conduit Street, where a good number of prominent people came to pay him homage; people who had profited from his projects in earlier days and wanted to meet him in person—and perhaps have food for gossip about this great financier who had fallen from so high a perch.

Law was welcomed at Court and presented to George I. He met Sir Robert Walpole, who seemed much impressed with the financier and offered 'to see what I can do towards finding a place for you here at Court. Something perhaps in finance.' So Law felt a thin thread of hope.

But he found that he also had his detractors. On the 26th of October, when the British House of Lords met, the Earl of Coringsby stood up to demand on whose orders Admiral Norris had brought Law to England. He maintained it was dangerous to 'countenance such a man as Mister Law who has renounced his allegiance to his native country and, being a friend of the Pretender, and has renounced his God by becoming a Roman Catholic.' With that, he sat down to a minor stir of applause.

When Law heard of this, he shook his head and remarked, 'Coningsby is not entirely accurate since both Protestants and Catholics believe in the same God.'

But he saw that if he had thought to find a place for himself in England, the doors were tightly closed. He wrote a letter to Will:

'Of all the people I've known and helped to amass fortunes within the past few years, I can find only one willing to lend me money. After three months in London, I have made a new friend. Mrs. Howard has offered me financial support. If you recall her name, Will, she became wealthy buying and selling Mississippi shares.'

Suddenly, he was in constant correspondence with Orleans, who wrote to him that he was *'still in need of his instruction'* and requested his opinion on current affairs. Orleans concluded one letter saying that his ‹*only dependence for bringing France to its true value was upon Law›s abilities and knowledge.*›

Law's spirits soared. He felt that any minute he would be called back. He replied to Orleans' letter, *'Sir, I have a project to restore credit and put the kingdom›s affairs into order. I shall explain fully when I return.'* There always had to be a project, and no, he did not have it now. But he would think of one when he returned.

Just to get back, back to Paris…! Have things the way they were. Hold Katherine in his arms once more. Often, he thought of Marie-Louise. It was easy for him to blame du Maine for her death, but surely it was his own fault. What had he really felt for her? The sensuous pleasure, of course. Not love. He had a much stronger motive to marry Marie-Louise. And what if that marriage had been consummated? Then would all this have happened to him?

It was a question without an answer.

If, if, if….

'A project…' In Paris, reading Law's words, Orleans went so far as to approach the Council as to the propriety of recalling Law. The Regent told the Council,' If Law does not return, there can be no doubt but that the power might fall into worse hands.'

But Du Maine had made many new powerful allies in the Council, and too many of them now distrusted Orleans, if they had not done so before.

Law remained in England and waited for the French Parliament to reach a decision. Walpole had promised but done nothing for him, and King George, speaking only German, waved a hand at him, nodded, and turned to one of his mistresses. In desperation, he contacted the Countess of Suffolk in England, distantly connected to Katherine Knollys. She had come to France, and he had entertained her at Nevers while he was still Finance Minister. She had made a great deal of money from the Mississippi Company, and it was she who had arranged to have him presented to King George. A fine gesture that unfortunately led nowhere.

Law wrote to the Countess:

Tuesday: Can you not prevail on the Duke to help me something more than the half-year, or is there nobody who has good nature enough to loan me £1,000? I beg that if nothing of this can be done, that it may only be betwixt us two, as I take you as my great friend and I am very well assured of it by the honor I had done me yesterday at Court by the King. I had another letter yesterday from France with the same thing over again. Excuse this, dear Madam, and only put yourself in my place and know that at the same time you are my only friend I have. Yours, John Law

Teusday

can you not prevaile one the Duke.
to help me some thing more then the
half year. or is there no body that
could have good nature enough to
lend me 1000ᵈˢ. I beg es that if nothing
of this can be done. that it may only
be betwict us two. as I take you as
my real friend. & I am very well assur
of it. by the honour, I had done me
yesterday at Court by the King. I had
another letter yesterday from
france with the same thing over
again. excuse this dear madam.
& only put your self in my place.
& know at the same time. that you
are the only friend I have. yours m Lee

Letter to the Countess of Suffolk
in John Law's hand

But help was not at hand, except at the gaming tables. Law
raised enough money for his passage and left Britain once more for
Venice. He would be careful this time, not to win too often.

BRIDGE OVER RIO SAN MOISÉ, VENICE

The sand trickled down, and time was running out. Four lean years had passed since John Law left France. He had never received the promised pension of Comptroller General, although he mentioned it in every letter to Orleans. Depression was not in Law's nature, and he fought hard to keep his spirits up, still hoping that the Regent would send for him and his world would be right once again.

Then Will wrote to him with news that the King's men had finally confiscated the last of Law's possessions in France. Will's wife had another child on the way, and his life was in France forever now.

John Law had nothing left, but still, he hoped. In Venice again, this time with very little money, he had been reduced to living in a boarding house that did not provide heat. The damp cold of a Venetian winter ate into Law's bones, and he caught a fever. It lingered and settled in his chest. He had developed a cough. But every night, he brushed clean his worn black cloak and tricorn hat, donned the mask to hide his identity, and set out in the uniform of the Venetian carnival and nightlife. Every night *M. De Jardin* would make his way down the narrow cobbled streets, past the church of San Moisé to the famous Ridotto, where the regular players all knew who the tall Scotsman really was.

But these nights, he did not always win. He could not keep track of the numbers like in the old days and was just another player who lost as much as he won. His clothes were wearing thin. He could barely keep himself alive on his winnings to pay his rent or eat regularly.

Then one cold night in August of 1724, he went as usual to the Ridotto. He had only a small stake, and once more, he was gambling with fate. It was nothing like those days when people stood around open-mouthed to watch him play. Now they ignored him, as did the powerful new Venetian friends of a few years ago. Even the local government officials had lost interest in *M. De Jardin*, who lost as much as he won these days.

He had not eaten all day. Perhaps he would win enough to buy himself a good dinner and a bottle of wine to warm the chill from his bones. Law threw his last handful of coins on the number nine. The wheel spun around. It slowed. Stopped. The croupier scooped up his coins. With a sad smile, Law looked up at the circle of masked faces around the table and shrugged. He was about to step away when across the table, one lady raised her mask and looked directly at him.

Katherine Knollys was smiling with the pleasure of seeing him again. He came around the table and drew her aside, raising his mask.

'Katherine - what on earth are you doing here?'

His voice was huskier than she remembered it. He was pale. She had never seen him so. She had been watching him for some time before she allowed him to recognize her.

'I'm your wife, Johnny. Have you forgotten?'

As for Law, delighted as he was at seeing her, he felt certain that no good could have taken her away from Paris and Orleans and, most of all, her new chateau.

She tried to hide the anxiety she was feeling. 'There is news, Johnny. Sad news, I'm afraid.' She paused, unsure of how he would take it. But she had to tell him. To say it out loud. 'Philip is dead. It was quite sudden. A heart attack. Should I say it? Making love to his new mistress.' She gave a wan smile. 'Oh, yes, there is always a younger one.'

The color drained from John Law's face. He stared at her in disbelief. Philip's death was the one thing he had not even imagined. 'And who… who is…?' His voice trailed off.

She sighed. 'There will be no new Regent, Johnny. Louis Henri, Duke de Bourbon, has been appointed Prime Minister of France.'

'Bourbon?' His eyes brightened. 'I considered him a friend. Perhaps he…'

She cut him off. 'As much as Bourbon admires you, Johnny, now there is no place in France for you. For either of us.'

'Then it is over,' he said, trying to make himself believe the possibility he had never anticipated. '. . .finally over.'

She brightened perceptibly. A warm smile stretched across her face. 'Luckily, I got out with most of my jewels.'

'Jewels? Yes,' he said dully. He looked at Orleans' ring, which had never left his finger since the Regent had given it to him with a promise. 'My last stake. . . for one more spin of the wheel.' He looked at her ruefully. 'I cannot take you to dine without a stake, can I, Kate? Maybe you will bring me luck. You always did.'

He lowered his mask and walked back to the table, Katherine at his side. He studied the table and placed the ring on number nine.

The wheel of fortune spun one more time for John Law. The ball clicked against the slot. It bounced into place on number thirteen. The croupier scooped in Philip's signet ring along with a stack of coins.

Law sighed, looking at Katherine. 'Now finally, we are together and I have nothing to offer you.'

'Perhaps I have something for both of us, Johnny.'

She led him out of the casino. They walked silently up the steps of the bridge over the Rio San Moisé. The moon had risen and was throwing a shimmering dance along the narrow canal. A gondolier navigated beneath the bridge dipping his long oar sideways into the dark water. He sang a plaintive love song for his passengers who were huddled together in an embrace. Katherine took Law's hand and looked into his eyes, too moved to speak.

'I have spoiled my life,' he said. 'It is here I should have stayed and developed my talents, dreaming of little pleasures and little scandals, and so heedlessly coming to die as one suddenly comes up against the night on the threshold of a doorway.' He turned to her, his voice low and husky, his still handsome face half-hidden in shadow. 'And yet, I have changed the world more than Columbus's discovery of the Americas. What now, Katherine? What is there for us now?'

'You and me,' she said. 'Always was and always will be.'

He took her in his arms and kissed her, and the old feelings returned, spinning across the years they had spent apart. He held her close to him. The warmth of her body filled him with new life.

Katherine drew back and reached into her sleeve. She took out a rolled parchment. 'It seems I am still hiding things in my clothes for my Jessamy John!' She handed him the parchment, and he opened it, reading by the light of a street lantern. The Regent's proclamation created John Law Governor of Louisiana, *'at such time as he should wish to retire to that place.'* It was dated long before the bubble burst.

'I found it by accident among Philip's papers, and it stuck to my fingers.' She took his arm again. 'Fancy a sea voyage, Johnny?'

John Law looked at her thoughtfully.

'Governor of Louisiana. What an interesting idea,' he said.

LAW LEAD BY HIS COCKRELLS

 EPILOGUE

There can be no doubt that John Law was a genius who understood what effect the principles of Credit could have on a nation's economy. He was anxious to try out his theories on any country that would employ him. France did. His bank was a prototype for today's national banks. His inventions included gambling chips, paper money, stocks, shares, developed dealing in futures, and buying on margin.

His first theories were about trade and commerce. In the 18th century, he was able to apply them and make them work, even under an all-powerful despotic authority. Through the redistribution of wealth, the reduction of taxes, and the promotion of commerce, he hoped to guide France to Utopia and set a standard for the world.

Law made no allowance for the human elements of avarice, selfishness, and greed. He under-rated the power of an absolute monarchy. He over-estimated the difference between confidence and obedience with a population new to such ideas and who were easily panicked. He also underestimated his enemies.

When the bank stopped payment on May 29th, 1720, the treasury had just printed another 1,906,400,000 livres. Adding that to the money in the Banque Générale, it made a total of 2,696,400,000 livres in paper money. Most of it was in circulation.

Several of France's first families profited by the Mississippi, among them the Princes Deux Ponts and de Rohan, the Dukes de La Force, De Guiche, Dantin, and de Lavigne. Although many more were ruined, the India Company (as the Mississippi Company later came to be called) continued to prosper.

To quote one of those who lost everything,' All the paper was not worth a groat.'

At the death of Louis XIV, the national debt of France was 3,111,000,000 livres. At the conclusion of John Law's 'Mississippi System,' the national debt was estimated by some at 1,999,720,540 livres. But it may have been at least another hundred million livres more.

There were 336,000,000 livres in the bank when it was closed. That money went into Philip's pocket and was never heard of afterward. The Regency diamond that Orleans purchased from Sir Thomas Pitt can be seen today in the Louvre Museum in Paris.

'Law's System' was copied in both England and Holland. England's South Sea Bubble was a mendacious scheme designed to enrich a few at the expense of many. It was a far cry from John Law's system, which was founded on a real intention to improve commerce for the good of the only nation who would listen to him, which was France.

It is possible John Law and Katherine Knollys had two children. He never reached his kingdom in Louisiana. Poverty-stricken, he died of a lung infection in Venice in 1729. Katherine returned to England with her daughter, Catherine. Her son William had died.

Law's body was buried in the Church of San Gemigniano. But when the church was pulled down in 1808, his great-nephew, William Law's grandson Jacques, who had become Count de Lauriston and French Military Governor of Venice, had John Law's body moved to the Church of San Moisé.

To this day, there can be seen a white marble memorial stone set into the pink marble flagstones, just inside the main entrance of the church. It holds a special place of honor. The incised inscription is in Latin.

PSL

HONORI - ET- MEMORIAE - / JOANNIS - LAW - EDINBURGENSIS - /
REGII - GALLIARUM - AERARII - / PRAEFECTI - CLARISSIMI /
A - MDCCXXIX - AET - LVII - DEFUNCTI -/ GENTILIS - SUI - CINERES -
EX - AEDE - D - GEMINIANI - DIRUTA - / HUC - TRANSFERRI - CURAVIT - /
ALEXANDER - LAW - LAURISTON - / NEAPOLEONI - MAXIMO - /
ADIUTOR - IN - CASTRIS - / PRAEFECTUS - LEGIONIS - /
GUBERNATOR - VENETIARUM - / A - MDCCCVIII

MEMORIAL STONE CHURCH OF SAN MOISÉ

BIBLIOGRAPHY

1705 - MONEY AND TRADE CONSIDERED by John Law

1720 - BILLS OF ENGLISH PARLIAMENT pub: March 17, 1720

1720 - EDINBURGH EVENING COURANT April 28/29 1720

1720 - MONEY AND TRADE by Law pub: 1720\80 ed. W. Lewis

1720 - LETTERS IN FRENCH AND ENGLISH by John Law

1720 - MISTER LAW'S CHARACTER by Friendly

1720 - FRENCH REVENUES & MISTER LAW, anon.

1720 - STATE OF FRENCH REVENUES (Trade, Finance)

1720 (circa) - LETTERS OF MARY WORTLEY MONTEGUE

1721 - LETTER TO LAW (appendix: Eustace Budgell)

1725 - LETTER TO THE COUNTESS OF SUFFOLK,

1726 -HISTOIRE DES FINANCES PENDANT LA REGÉNCE
       (Law)

1754 - ESSAYS THE DOCTRINE OF CHANCE Edmund Hoyle

1791 - A SKETCH OF LAW

1824 - MEMOIRS OF THE LIFE OF JOHN LAW OF LAURISTON
       J.P. Wood, Edinburgh

1841- EXTRAORDINARY POPULAR DELUSIONS & the
       MADNESS OF CROWD by   Charles Mackay

1847 HISTOIRE DE LA REVOLUTION FRANÇAISE
       Louis Blanc, Vol. 1, Paris

1864 - JOHN LAW THE PROJECTOR W. Harrison Ainsworth,
       London

1887 - AN HISTORICAL STUDY OF LAW'S SYSTEM,
       by Andrew McFarland Davis

Quarterly Journal of Economics April 1887, Boston Press
       George Ellis.

1902 - OLD BAILEY AND NEWGATE by Charles Gordon,
       pub: T. Fisher pub: Unwin

1907 - LIST OF MEDALS OF JOHN LAW (British Museum)

1908 - JOHN LAW OF LAURISTON, A.W. Wiston Glynn, Edinburgh
1925 - LAURISTON CASTLE John A. Fairley
1940 - GAMBLER'S GLORY by M. Harrison
1948 - THE LIFE OF JOHN LAW by H.M. Hyde
1966 - THE SUN KING by Nancy Mitford
1971 - ENGLISH BASTILLE, A HISTORY OF NEWGATE, by Anthony Babbington
1982 - TRIPPLE TREE, NEWGATE TYBURN, OLD BAILEE by D. Rumbelow Harra

Pat Silver-Lasky

Money to Burn marks Pat's incredible 75 years as a professional writer. Born in Seattle, Washington, after four and a half years at the University of Washington, Stanford University and Reed College, she produced and directed their first play. As *Barbara Hayden* in 1949, she co-produced, wrote, directed and acted in 18 episodes of the live TV drama series, *Mabel's Fables* on KTLA She appeared in feature roles in films on television in the 1950s.

An A.S.C.A.P. writer, she wrote lyrics for fourteen published and recorded songs with her first husband Tony Romano, including *While You're Young* for Johnny Mathis. They also wrote songs for two films at Columbia Studios.

Barbara Hayden played the lead in one episode of *Rescue Eight*. In those glass ceilings days, she took the name *Pat Silver* to write three other episodes. Keeping that name, she wrote as a team with her second husband, Hollywood screenwriter/author, Jesse L. Lasky Jr., son of Hollywood film pioneer Jesse L. Lasky. Together, they wrote eight films, 119 TV scripts and four books including the American best-selling historical novel, *The Offer*, and *Love Scene*, the acclaimed biography of Laurence Olivier and Vivien Leigh. Pat directed their play *Vivien,* in its first production at the Melrose Theatre, Los Angeles, and later in London. Their verse play, *Ghost Town* won several awards and their British TV series, *Philip Marlowe* (writers and show runners) won awards in America and Holland.

Pat lectured on script writing at several American Universities and was Script Consultant and Guest Lecturer at the London Film School (1991-1999).

Since Jesse L. Lasky Jr.'s death in 1988, Pat has published 5 more books as Pat Silver-Lasky including *Hollywood Royalty: A Family In Films - with letters from Producer Jesse L. Lasky to Screenwriter Jesse L. Lasky Jr.* She was interviewed by TCM in 2018.

She now lives in Orange County, California, with her husband, cartoonist and painter, Peter Betts.

www.ingramcontent.com/pod-product-compliance
Lightning Source LLC
Chambersburg PA
CBHW070316030726
47505CB00004B/1001